Th

Pr

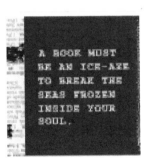

A BOOK MUST
BE AN ICE-AXE
TO BREAK THE
SEAS FROZEN
INSIDE YOUR
SOUL.

READ ME THEN
PASS ME ON!

The Prodigal

Michael Hurley (signature)

MICHAEL HURLEY

RAGBAGGER PRESS
CHARLESTON

MICHAEL HURLEY

The Prodigal
Copyright © 2013 by Michael C. Hurley

www.mchurley.com

Published in the United States by

Ragbagger Press
164 Market Street, Suite D
Charleston, SC 29401
U.S.A.

Cover photo by Guido Mieth/Getty Images

Scripture quotation from
The Holy Bible, American Standard Version
© 1901 Thomas Nelson & Sons

ISBN: 1482694271
ISBN-13: 978-1482694277

Library of Congress Control Number: 2013908298

1 3 5 7 9 10 8 6 4 2

First Edition: June 1, 2013

Manufactured in the United States of America

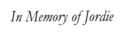
In Memory of Jordie

Also by Michael Hurley

Once Upon a Gypsy Moon

Letters from the Woods

And he arose, and came to his father. But while he was yet afar off, his father saw him, and was moved with compassion, and ran, and fell on his neck, and kissed him. And the son said unto him, Father, I have sinned against heaven, and in thy sight: I am no more worthy to be called thy son. But the father said to his servants, "Bring forth quickly the best robe, and put it on him; and put a ring on his hand, and shoes on his feet: and bring the fatted calf, and kill it, and let us eat, and make merry: for this my son was dead, and is alive again; he was lost, and is found."

—The Gospel According to Luke

The
Prodigal

PROLOGUE

Greece, 1851

The damned are said to wander in a dimension that waits eternally between the sinking and setting of the sun, while the saints of every age abide forever in that moment when the hope of darkness meets the dawn. To those with eyes to see what once lingered in the shadows of twilight, there might appear the long-forgotten image of a boy—a sailor in the sapling of his manhood—running hard through the countryside. Running beside the boy was a girl—an uncommonly beautiful girl—with her hand fixed tightly in his. The day of their flight is lost to legend. More than a century has passed since men lived in whose memories those hours were counted. The place has also fallen out of living knowledge, but when once that black earth was known, it lay upon a hillside in the country of Greece.

The two were pursued on foot by the girl's father. He had seen what happened, and it had lit a fire for vengeance in his heart. There was justice to be done, and he meant to do it.

The father called to his child in the darkness—begging, pleading with her to return to him. Hiding with the boy beneath the orchard vines and running when they could, she dared not answer. The shouting voice gradually faded from their ears. The father was slower than these two. His steps were not given speed by passion and longing. His feet were weary with the spent recklessness of anger, and his sight was dimmed by the grief of loss. Ere long, these children were far from their pursuer. Together yet alone, they were locked firmly in that embrace of fear and hope known only to very young and foolish hearts.

He meant to take her to the ship, this boy, and by means of wind and water secure their final escape. Like the girl, the ship was a sacred vessel—a thing imbued with an unquenchable, indomitable spirit. The boy was only one of the crew, but his shipmates remained in the Gypsy camp, still engaged in the fight that had erupted when the elders found him with her. It was then that he and the girl had fled along a secret path through the orchard to the sea, where she guided him.

O, how hot the elders' anger burned! How red the blood of men they spilled! She was their innocent one. She was their lamb, a gift from God, unlike the other daughters. But that night, that unblemished gift was given freely to this boy.

They were in love—impossibly, hopelessly in love— and filled with a passion fanned in the flames of a hundred campfires before which she had danced, untouched until that night by any man. That night she had danced for her beloved and for him alone. To the darkness of her tent they had stolen, unseen by the others. There, freely and of her own will, she committed the sin that her father had forbidden.

She felt safe with the boy, although she scarcely knew him. In fact, she knew him not at all, according to the laws that prevailed among her people. And yet she trusted him instinctively and completely with her life and with her soul. If it may rightly be said that trust is the leaven of true love, their love was already a feast. In the moment of her decision to stay or go, he had sworn to protect her forever, and she had believed him. She would always believe him.

The grass of the hillside smelled of jasmine and roses. It was a beautiful place—a place no child would choose to leave except to flee an unspeakable guilt. In the hours that followed the lovers' racing footsteps, the verdant perfume of moist leaves and wildflowers gave way to a salted, burning aroma rising from the Mediterranean Sea.

When they arrived in the empty seaside village, crouching unseen beneath the eaves, all was dark and quiet. The boy took the girl by the hand and led her aboard the vessel. He bade her to sit at the bow while he made haste to sail. It was a large ship—too large for most men to handle by themselves—but this boy was a child of the deep and one of the sea's very own. His footsteps were swift and sure along the decks, and his hands were steady upon the helm.

Thieves they were, to take a vessel that did not belong to them and run to sea, yet as if in common purpose with their crime, the ship ran like a thief beneath them. All its sails strained mightily in grave terror of the wind that drove them from the harbor. Thieves they were, yes, and thieves they would remain—through all eternity if it came to that. This was their pact. This was their promise to each other.

Before them loomed the wine-dark sea of Homer's imagination, serene yet fearsome in all its foreboding reality. Beyond and coming steadily closer with each plunge of the ship's stalwart keel lay the Strait of Gibraltar, and there a passage to the waiting world. Leagues back and doomed to fall yet farther behind were many proud and worthy seamen, making ready for the pursuit. Swiftly though they followed, theirs was destined to be a hopeless chase for reasons unknown to them.

On the ocean, under the light of a gypsy moon, the wind was ever in the lovers' favor. Their dowry was the sea and all within it. Their wedding gift was the dream of a life unbound by the ignorance of obedience. Theirs was the world to wander.

Yet unseen, not far away in an orchard, beside a tangled vine that had caught a strand of that lovely hair as it went flowing past, a father sat alone. There, he wept tears unending. There, he gave voice to cries his daughter could no longer hear. He wept for his lost child, and in his mouth was the bitter fruit of knowledge that she was gone forever.

But hope springs eternal for the prodigal's return.

CHAPTER 1

Ocracoke Island, 2010

And so Aidan, the *proud* one, a man who refused above all else to learn from his own mistakes much less the errors of history, came at last to this island. Of course it would be a wild place. A sea place. A dwelling made of memory, sand, and wind. A world that already knew his name. Here he slept, unsuspecting, in the peace of the unborn. But every birth is a time of becoming, and Aidan's time had come.

The first thing he noticed was the ache between his shoulders. It was a familiar, dull pain that came whenever he slept too long on his back. He ignored it as long as he could, but it awakened him slowly with a nagging desire to roll onto his side. He sorely wished for more sleep. Whatever the hour (and he couldn't have cared less about that), he was still far too tired to start the day. But turning, he felt unfamiliar bedding beneath him. It was the grit of coarse, wet sand on bare skin. With eyes still shut, he wondered if he might be dreaming. He wasn't at all sure where he was or why, but it steadily became more obvious that he needed to wake up and find out.

The sound of tumbling surf gradually entered his

conscious mind. In the bright sun, he raised his chin just enough to allow a view beyond his toes through the thin slits of his eyes. There, coming at him from not fifty feet to the east, was a shining ocean. The sheer beauty and excitement of it—a memory of childhood vacations, craning his neck out of backseat windows to catch whiffs of salt air that meant they were getting closer—distracted him momentarily from the question of why he was there at all. It must have been ten o'clock—the rising tide was licking at his feet with every third or fourth wave like a dog impatient for a morning walk.

He had an uncanny sense that he was not alone.

Propping himself up on his elbows, he looked out on a seemingly endless, ruler-straight line of wet, silver-gray sand that shot northward along the water's edge. There was no one. To the south lay the same empty seascape, although in that direction he could detect the slight, gradual curve in the shoreline as it bent westward toward the southern tip of Ocracoke Island. Slowly, some blessed awareness returned. He had come there for a vacation that weekend. But he still could not explain what he was doing alone on an empty beach in the middle of the morning, and—a fact that was only now sinking in—without a stitch of clothing.

He slowly enunciated a meaningless obscenity, as if expecting extra credit for elocution. Clearly this was not going to be, in the usual happy sense of the phrase, *a day at the beach*. This was going to be a problem. Aidan was good at solving other people's problems—and creating them—but there was no remedy for this one. He couldn't say this sort of thing wasn't typical for him. The usual recriminations applied. He just hadn't seen it coming.

Some distance to the north was a bed inside a rented beach cottage where he should have been at that moment. He sat up, thinking that, somehow, he needed to get there.

Sand adhered to every inch of his skin. He must have been rolling in his sleep for hours. As he grabbed his knees, the dull throb in his head supplied the first inklings of memory from the night before.

There had been beer. A lot of beer. He recalled the moon glistening on the foam of breaking waves—and the girl, vaguely—but that was all. Most of the night was still a muddle in his mind, yet he was certain that however he got to where he was, he hadn't gone there wearing no clothes.

As he stood up, sheets of sand fell off his legs, arms, and back, but more of the stuff still clung to him. Standing there in the sun, an earthen vessel, shaking off grains of roughage from the mold in which he had been made, he remained, despite all his shivering, a sand man. He needed to get wet.

The water of the Atlantic was bracingly cold, even in August. Off the Outer Banks, the frigid Labrador Current, heading south, meets her younger and more promiscuous sister, the Gulf Stream—just up from a drunken lark in Mexico—and rudely slaps her in the face. The pitched, never-ending war for supremacy between opposing ocean flows makes for strong rip tides and widely fluctuating water temperatures off Ocracoke. That morning, the North was winning the battle.

The sea rose up and slammed into his shins. He shuddered, hesitating before allowing it to come up to waist level. This was a habit he had acquired as a boy during summers at the Jersey Shore. He had never been the kind just to jump in. He preferred to experience the shock in small increments. This was the way sissies did it, he knew, but because there was no one present whose opinion concerned him, he was content to wade out in fits and starts. In a few minutes he was beneath the waves, glad to linger there awhile as his body grew accustomed to the temperature of the water, and thankful for what nature allowed in the way of a morning bath. The salt water stung his chest and face and legs. He had suffered an impressive sunburn in the hours he had spent sleeping in the morning sun.

The sand gradually sloped away beneath his feet as he waded farther out in the surf, until he lifted off from the Earth entirely and was afloat. He swam in smooth breaststrokes, alternately dipping below and rising above the water, tasting its salty tang around his lips with each breath. He was soon past the breakers where he could relax. Leaning back and allowing his chest and legs to float upward, he felt again the sting of the sun on his belly and quickly sunk back beneath the water. As he did so, a wave lifted him up and turned his shoulders toward the beach like a schoolmarm directing an errant child's attention to the front of the class. He winced again from the prickly pain of the saltwater.

Then he saw her.

He spotted what looked like the figure of a person, seated on the beach, not ten yards directly behind the place where he had been lying when he woke up. Someone *had* been watching him, he thought, regretting then (as he always did) that he ever distrusted his first instincts. Blood raced to his cheeks and a bolt of adrenaline shot down his spine. He felt an impulse to fight—or flee. He could see this was a small person, whoever it was—not half his size—but anyone who had chosen to remain silent and hidden until now likely didn't mean well. His heart began to pound, and he had trouble catching his breath. From a distance he could make out only black hair and olive skin at first, but then he noticed that knees drawn up to the chest accentuated a slender pear shape, below. Neurons deep in his brain instantly identified the female of the species. But confounding any higher order of thinking at the moment was the probability—now becoming more apparent to Aidan—that the woman was just as naked as he was.

He treaded water for several minutes during which they held each other's gaze like two alien species looking out from different worlds of Water and Earth. The woman did not move. When a wave caught him again unexpectedly by the shoulders and pushed him shoreward, his feet found the ocean floor, and he stumbled closer to her like a bashful boy goaded into a dance.

It would of course be necessary to say something. He was a lawyer after all, and not just any lawyer, but one of that special breed of lawyers who try cases before juries. He could always find a way to say *something* even when he meant *nothing*. But a strange feeling—which is to say a feeling beyond the strangeness that was already flying wildly around in his head—began to overtake him. As he walked from the water to the shore he searched for the right words.

"What a lovely day!" came first to mind, but to speak of the weather at that moment was too dissembling even for him.

"Why are you spying on me?" was closer to his true feelings, but it was too plaintive and assumed too much too quickly.

The woman, for her part, said nothing. She continued merely to sit there, legs apart, knees drawn tightly to her chest, making no effort to conceal the part of her womanhood that was now plainly visible to him. Although she took no offense and he intended none, he strove not to gaze anywhere but in her eyes, which gazed inquisitively back at him.

A few moments more passed in silence. From a distance, the woman had appeared serenely calm, but as

Aidan drew nearer, her expression revealed a struggle in her thoughts, as if she were seeking a way to tell him some terrible news. Then she began to move.

His eyes followed her unfolding form. She relaxed her legs. Small, firm breasts, unburdened of any restraint, swayed gently as she rose to her feet. She walked toward him.

The woman stopped at the place in the sand where Aidan had been lying all night and waited for him to come to her. She was athletically toned and perfectly formed. She was not a young girl, but she seemed as comfortable in a state of nature as a newborn baby. If she thought there was anything particularly seductive or remarkable about the fact that she was completely nude in front of a strange, nude man, she wasn't letting on.

Aidan was not athletically toned, nor perfectly formed, nor was he, at forty-five, any longer what most young women would call a *young* man. He was not especially comfortable in a state of nature, but neither did it suit him to go shrieking down the beach in retreat. It was clear the woman had been waiting there for a reason, and he thought he might as well hear it.

But there was something else about her.

As she came closer, he could see that she was *older*, though *how* old he could not confidently guess within a span of thirty years. She could have been thirty-five or sixty-five. Her breasts, still bearing upward with the firmness of youth, were of one even, golden hue that blended into soft, nut-brown, perfectly rounded nipples. Suddenly he felt the impulse—not to flee, but to hide behind something more substantial than his own skin. He needed a uniform to wear—some external armor— to feel at ease.

She had unruly black hair that was woven through with wisps of white and gray, like foam on a wild, moonlit sea. Yet except for fine lines near her eyes and mouth, her smooth skin revealed no more of the secret of her years than did her form. Unmistakable, though, was a long age of sadness in her face, and the burden of many hard days was in her voice when she finally spoke.

"Cover yourself," she said, "and take some wine." She opened the palm of her hand in a gesture toward Aidan's feet. He looked down. Where they were standing, he saw the impression his body had left in the sand and, within it, a neatly folded white cloth next to a half-empty bottle of wine.

And that was it.

He thought he saw her smile at him, but then she turned to the south and walked away. When she had traveled a hundred yards, weaving in and out of the waves and stooping now and then to collect strands of Sargasso in her left hand, the lawyer was still standing where she had left him, still searching for his words, and still finding it hard to look anywhere but in the direction she had gone.

Her voice had sounded unexpectedly hoarse, given the slightness of her frame. There was an accent that he did not recognize. And her words—"cover yourself," and "take some wine"—were spoken more like a liturgy than a conversation. She was most certainly not native to the South or even the queer little corner of the South taken up by this island, where remnants of the King's English could still be heard whenever the hour of "hoi toid" was announced.

He walked back toward the water, staying just out of reach of the waves, and stood there hoping to dry in the sun and breeze. Shading his forehead with his hand and widening his eyes to survey the surroundings, he expected to see his clothes or swim trunks strewn on the beach somewhere. But the rugged expanse of sand was unbroken except for the two small items left where he had slept—placed there neatly as if by a maid tidying

11

up a room.

When he lifted up the carefully folded cloth, it tumbled loose and hung down from his arm. It was a lady's beach cover-up, of simple and plain design, made of white cotton. The bottle of wine was half-empty, with a red-stained cork stuffed well into the neck.

To say that the previous ten minutes had been the strangest of his life would hardly have overstated the matter. But still there remained a sense of something stranger, deeper, and more hidden—something he felt certain he was missing but couldn't put his finger on. It made him again distrust his first impulse, which was to burst out laughing, and his second, which was to run after the woman and demand an explanation. He wondered if there were others hiding nearby who now planned to let him in on the joke or who could perhaps help him make sense of where he was and how he got there. But there was no one, and he heard no sound but the slow rhythm of the sea.

Things being as they were, he was profoundly grateful for the wine and the dress. He wore one and drank the other as he walked north by west through the sea oats, looking, he imagined, like an escapee from rehab who hadn't had time to change out of his hospital gown in the rush to get away. He could not suppress a smile at the absurdity of it. It was the beach, after all, and nobody much gave a damn about anything at the beach.

He started for the top of a high ridge of dunes about fifty yards from the ocean, from where he thought he might spot one of the Jeep trails that crisscrossed the sand flats and follow it back to the main road. He guessed that the cottage he and some friends had rented was about two miles north of where he was. The shortest course was directly across the dunes.

As he walked up a sheer face, the hot sand shifted

beneath his feet, which were soft and tender from too many hours spent in fancy shoes and too few spent on beaches. He moved in long, ungainly strides, hunched over to keep his balance. It was late summer, but the chill in the morning air felt like fall on his wet skin, and the gown—floating up in the back with each step—was only a mocking defense against the draft.

From the top of the highest dune, he could see Pamlico Sound on the west side of the island. He'd spent a few weekend days crewing aboard other people's sailboats in races on those waters. In most places the sound was a tin gray, but it got clearer and closer to blue near Ocracoke, where it escaped the muddy grip of civilization.

Aidan gazed across the sound toward the unseen coast of North Carolina, and his head began to clear. The mainland, "Down East," was thirty-five miles away. The farms and tiny towns in that part of the state were disappearing faster every year. In their place rose up golf courses, mansions, and condominiums for retiring Yankees, whom the delighted local businessmen would joke they were "recapturing one by one," 150 years after the Civil War. The new leisure class that was settling there knew little or nothing of tobacco, cotton, or the work boats and the proud watermen who had once pulled a living out of these sounds. The grande dame of the Old South was dying, and the roots of her memory were increasingly exposed and frayed. Old times there, if not yet forgotten, were by now recalled only in whispers among trusted company.

Aidan was not one of the trusted ones. Born and raised in Philadelphia, he carried no brief for the traditions of the South nor any concern for their passing. To these and all other provincial controversies he preferred the constancy of the ocean. There, the absence of anything created by man meant there was nothing man could destroy. That's why he came to Ocracoke and to every other place along the seashore, as he had done his whole life. The allure of the sea was mystical. Its depths and dangers were never betrayed by its surface, which remained pitiless and unrepentant— the very qualities Aidan had once strived so hard to develop as a lawyer. Cut off by wind and sea, the people who made a living on Ocracoke went about with a keen sense of their own impermanence, from which they acquired the wonderful habit of minding their own business. They had no interest in the struggles or old grudges of the wider world. They usually had all the trouble they could handle, right at home.

The fact was, most everyone who found Ocracoke Island for the first time was looking for someplace or something else. That was true of Aidan. That particular weekend, he had been looking for a place to get away from the office for a few days—to hide, really. He had separated from his wife five years ago. The final divorce, last year, had hit him unexpectedly hard. His work had suffered. Something was greatly out of balance in his life. Whether he was working too much or not enough he didn't know. His trademark confidence was slipping. Beneath the seeming calm he heard a thin, electric buzz that sounded like mania, and it was getting louder. He wondered if others could hear it, too. But whether they did or not, he was in trouble, and he knew it. He just didn't know why, or how much, or how soon trouble would find him.

It was Sunday, and the mini-mart, which stood just outside the village on the other side of the dunes, was usually open but empty at that hour. It was the only place on the island that didn't seem grown in and grown over. It was too new. It didn't fit, and neither did the woman working behind the counter when Aidan walked in, still wearing the dress. She was leaning against a cash register. A wisp of smoke escaped from her mouth and drifted in front of her face.

Unlike the woman Aidan had just met, this one was unmistakably not a young girl anymore, though she dressed like one in a white cotton tee-shirt and running shorts atop skinny legs that were a shade too tanned. She was on the phone, and from her hunched, slouching posture, it looked as if she had been on it for a while. Her lips formed a small, oval pout except when words rolled out of them alongside the smoke, and her gaze was fixed in a distant, expressionless stare toward the sea oats waving at her from the other side of the road, beyond the gas pumps. Aidan's entrance broke her reverie, but only just.

Her eyes drifted over the dress he wore, then to a rack of the exact same outfits hanging on a display stand behind her, then back to Aidan. *Two sizes too small,* she thought. Still, he wore it as well as any of the increasingly enormous New Jersey wives who stopped at the mini-mart with their irritated husbands on fishing trips to the Outer Banks, dreaming of the tropics and settling for buckets full of cold, dead Spanish mackerel instead.

The air conditioning in the mini-mart had suffered its usual bout of distemper the night before. It was as hot inside the store as out, only more humid without the sea breeze. Aidan didn't see the cigarette at first—just the smoke rising behind the counter, then the woman. The adage "where there's smoke, there's fire" never fit a fire as well as it did Bobbi Baker, but Aidan had no way to know that—not yet, anyway. She was not so much an inferno as a smoldering and forgotten flame and therefore all the more dangerous.

She cocked her head to one side to keep the phone

on her shoulder, close to her ear. Her eyes followed Aidan as he walked to the cold lockers in the back. The beach dress wafted up above his naked thighs as he passed a tall, electric fan that had been moved out onto the floor. A broken gear was causing its huge head to move erratically from side to side. Thrumming loudly, it looked and sounded like a dying tyrannosaurus.

Fishing rods and packets of beef jerky hung in neat rows along the aisles, amid little cans of Vienna sausages, bags of charcoal, cylinders of Fix-A-Flat, ant traps, motor oil, and Epsom salts. Aidan observed it all as if for the first time, through the fog banks that still hung just above the surface in his mind. He wondered who chose the items that were sold in gas stations, from which all of Western civilization could be rebuilt, if it came to that.

When Aidan passed the magazine stand, the hem of his dress caught the corner of a display rack and pulled. He noticed a man standing there. He had a rounded belly and was reading a magazine with the guilty urgency of someone who had no intention of buying it. As beer bellies go, his was not yet enormous, but he was young yet. His shirt and shorts still bore the clean, pink stains from the blood of hundreds of long-dead tuna. Aidan quietly unhooked the hem of his dress. He detected a distinctively verdant, salty odor about the man. It was the smell of the Gulf Stream. Aidan guessed that he drove a charter boat or did some other robust, physical labor for a living, so it seemed wise that a man wearing a dress should say nothing.

The juxtaposition of water temperatures in the stream made for wonderful fishing, terrifying waves, well-paid work for charter-boat captains, and shipwrecks. It also made Ocracoke a place between places—a kind of purgatory of the sea.

The bloody man beside the magazine rack, who

smelled of salt and Sargasso, with the rounded but not yet enormous belly, was sipping stale coffee left over from the evening shift. He didn't complain. This was the beach. People who lived here year-round made do by necessity and loved it, and there was no sense in letting a good pot of coffee go to waste.

Bobbi was by now satisfied that the naked man in the ill-fitting cotton dress wandering to the back of her store was likely insane but harmless, which to a greater or lesser degree described most of the people she met every day on the island. She switched the phone to her other shoulder, cocked her head again, and took another drag on her cigarette. She looked past the dress, now, and let her eyes drift down Aidan's lean, six-foot frame.

"He didn't even see it coming," she spoke into the phone, a bit too loudly.

A moment passed.

"Poor bastard," she said, in a stage whisper, and then, softer still, with a tinge of sadness, "What a shame."

Aidan and the bloody man were allowed to hear. They listened, worried now for the bastard.

The cigarette came back to her lips. She shifted her shoulders again to look back at Aidan. He studied her face. The angular cheekbones inherited from her Appalachian forbearers were just high enough to be mistaken for breeding. There was tension in her expression, or perhaps just annoyance. She was blonde haired—newly so—and about his age, he guessed. Her tee-shirt, worn over nothing underneath, tugged at large, *notice-me* breasts. Also new.

"Hold on," she said into the phone, now looking straight at Aidan. "Nice dress."

"It is lovely, isn't it?" Aidan replied. His voice sounded like a truck full of gravel.

"You can't buy that wine on Sunday, Sweetie." She

spoke in a long, slow drawl, pointed to the bottle in his hand, and smiled. He smiled back and placed the wine alongside a bottle of water on the counter.

Aidan captured her stare squarely in his eyes and kept it there. This was the second woman he'd seen today who wasn't from this place.

"You didn't get that accent in Ocracoke," he said.

She paused a moment, with her pouting lips half open, more aware now that she was talking to a man in a dress than of what the man in the dress was saying to her.

"I didn't get these boobs in Ocracoke, either. Who are *you?*" she asked.

The bloody man looked up for the first time and stared past the little cans of Vienna sausages at Aidan.

A stupid expression lingered on Aidan's face. He knew he wasn't fooling anybody that morning and saw no point in trying. Bobbi didn't half expect an answer.

"I'm Aidan Sharpe," he said, extending his hand. "I give up. Where are you from?"

A thin but unmistakable wave of anxiety washed over the woman's face, then receded to the depths as quickly as it came.

"Miami," she said. It was a small lie, casually told. "But I've been on the island for seven years. The name's Bobbi Baker." She waved coyly with one hand but did not take his.

"Well, Bobbi Baker, you're the only person so far this year to call me 'Sweetie,' and for that I am truly thankful."

She told the person on the phone that she would call back later.

"The wine is mine," Aidan said. "It was—a gift. I'm just looking for some water to wash it down. I'm afraid I'll have to pay you for this later." Before she could tell him no, he twisted off the plastic cap of a water bottle, put the bottle to his lips, and took a long swallow right in front of her.

It was a water-bottle robbery. She supposed that she should have called someone or said something, but Bobbi Baker wasn't much for throwing stones. She had left that business back in Atlanta, right about the time when her own glass house came crashing down. Besides, a drink of water was the least of anyone's worries on that island. She just let it go.

"Nice to meet you, Bobbi," Aidan said. "You know, there are a lot of things we're not supposed to do on Sunday." He lifted the bottle of water in one hand and the wine in the other, and walked out.

The bloody man watched him go, then looked at Bobbi, pleadingly.

"Go on, Frank. Get you one. I don't care," she said.

Frank retrieved a bottle of beer from the drink case in the back, then returned to his magazine. There was no rush. The stream would wait.

CHAPTER 2

A man and a woman sat on two towels stretched atop a sand dune about a half-mile from the cottage they had rented for the weekend. They both gazed out to sea, lips pursed and silent, as if they were stoically resolved to reveal nothing in the face of some unseen interrogation. The effects of the night before were waning but not completely gone for either of them.

She was Honor Beckett, a single, twenty-something former debutante, now biding her time as a paralegal and suffering through that interminable weekend with the grasping, over-striving man beside her—her boss or, as she described him to her friends, "the idiot." Boyce Stannard was Aidan's law partner, although he was a lesser light in the heavenly firmament of McFadden Brown, where Aidan was a shining star. Honor was neither a star nor a planet in that galaxy, but rather more of a loose meteorite careening through space who had only lately decided it might be worth her while to kill some time in Boyce's orbit.

"Do you think he's all right?" Honor asked.

"He's all right," Boyce answered. "He's a big boy. He needed to sleep it off, and the beach is as good a place to do that as any."

"We shouldn't have left him there. That was your idea of a joke. I'm getting a little worried, to be honest. I think we need to go back and find him."

"Go back where?" Boyce replied, incredulous. "I could scarcely find my way to the cottage last night, and wherever we were on whatever beach that was, I have no idea now. We'd be searching for hours. Aidan is sleeping on the sand. He'll be fine. How many nights do you suppose Aidan Sharpe has slept on a beach in his lifetime?"

Honor said nothing, annoyed at the irrelevance of the question.

"Well, more than a few I'll wager," Boyce continued, undaunted. "The man has an iron stomach and a head of cement. He'll be just fine. I just wish I could've been there when he woke up. God knows where his clothes are. Poor bastard. He'll get over it, if he doesn't get arrested first. Besides, do you think he'd have fared any better with me carrying him two miles across the dunes? He got to spend a beautiful night under the stars."

"You're supposed to be the man's friend, for God's sake—at least he thinks so. What kind of guy leaves a friend on a beach naked all night after he passes out?"

"A friend who knows him better than you do. Trust me."

Boyce and Aidan had joined the firm together right out of law school. But Aidan had risen farther and faster, propelled by an improbable string of courtroom victories for the firm's most important clients. Boyce came to idolize Aidan as deeply as he resented him. Aidan was an equity partner who received a piece—a big piece—of the pie consisting of the firm's sumptuous annual profits. Boyce was also a partner, but in name only. He received a handsome but fixed annual salary and no pie at all. Still, the title of "partner" allowed him the honor of introductions as a member of an elite club in the oldest law firm in Raleigh, and it separated him from the firm's associates over whom he lorded his seniority.

Honor worked for both of them. A poor little rich kid, she was the daughter of a real estate developer whose chronically bad choices in wives and business partners had kept the firm flush with billable hours going on twenty years. Despite her parents' multifarious pathologies, Honor was a "nice girl," capable of both refined politeness and crudeness, depending on what the situation warranted. For as smart as she was, she seemed very comfortable floating through life, unprovoked by any particular ambition.

In her love life, Honor had drifted from jerk to jerk, and on this trip Boyce had hoped to become the latest candidate in a long line that Aidan was certain would remain unbroken after she had discarded him. They both wanted the same thing—not so much to adore as to be adored—and so they had spent the last three days alternately attracting and repelling each other like the wrong ends of two magnets.

From the top of the dune the ocean breeze smelled salty and sweet. At this latitude, the wind coming off the Atlantic sometimes carried the faint aroma of burning oak from the west coast of Africa, shot through with fine, red dust from the Sahara and flavors of sugar cane, rum, and coriander from the West Indies. It was an intoxicating recipe. Dogs walked around with their noses high in the air to follow the scent. Lovers savored it.

A front had come through three days ago. The wind was now clocking to the southwest, and the surf, which had been nearly calm for a day, was regaining its strength. From far down the beach, the shouts of children drifted in and out of earshot. Their kites skittered and dove on the fluky wind.

By mid-afternoon that day, Aidan had made his way back to the cottage on foot. A note left for him on the kitchen table told him where to find Honor and Boyce. It would be time for all of them to catch the ferry back to the mainland soon.

The kites, rising like semaphore flags above the dunes, guided Aidan along the beach road to the place where Honor and Boyce said they would be. Farther south on that road, closer to the inlet, clusters of trucks with New Jersey license plates took up their daily posts. Beside them, fishermen with Italian and Polish last names would sit in folding chairs in the sand in the bright sun, waiting for the soft, seductive tug of drum and snapper deep in the darkness.

The afternoon was quiet and hot. Even the streams of cars carrying tourists on the main island road from Cape Hatteras had melted away.

Aidan heard the muffled report of the distant, breaking surf, followed by a long pause. "Puff," then again, "puff . . ."

Boyce stretched out on the sand, staring up at the sky through black Wayfarers. His pasty-white skin presented a jarring contrast to his red tartan trunks—Brooks Brothers. Boyce was a bit of a whiner, but he was a well-dressed whiner. As he lay there, he felt a familiar mood of melancholy wash over him. His fortieth birthday, ridiculous as it sounded to him and everyone else, had hit him hard, and he was still nursing his considerable ego over the matter. It struck him for the first time that year that he had become, unquestionably, *old enough*. By this time in a man's life, getting older no longer meant getting better, and a lack of experience was no longer an excuse but an embarrassment. Kennedy was president at forty-three. Forty was plenty *old* enough, he thought. At that age, the question for Boyce was whether he was still *young* enough to finish what he had started, but time would soon tell.

Boyce scrunched his toes up in the sand and felt its

essence beneath his feet. He stood up to stretch and saw Aidan coming. Aidan the Great. Aidan the Trial Dog. Aidan the Unbeatable.

Unlike Boyce, Aidan regarded the law as an art, not a business. He was not naïve about the motivations of his corporate clients, many of whom were bastards of special magnificence, but he had a knack for finding poetic appeal in their causes. It was how he got through each day. The technical machinations of the law had long since ceased to challenge him. The only way he could keep from suffocating under the pointless banality of it all was to conflate every missed cancer diagnosis or botched gallbladder surgery with the pursuit of some loftier ideal or the defeat of some pernicious, social antagonism—to make the defense of his clients about the ideal of justice that Cardozo had once described as "the synonym of an aspiration, a mood of exaltation, a yearning for what is fine and high." Juries loved it because above all else they wanted *to believe*, and clients paid dearly for Aidan's skill in giving people something to believe in.

But of late Aidan had been getting too sloppy even for his own renegade brand of lawyering, and he knew it. It was one thing for a lawyer not to give a damn about himself, but another for a lawyer not to give a damn about his clients. For some time now, he had been going through the motions and phoning it in, even if his unique talents had made that difficult for some to see. Aidan's gnawing fear, in the still hours when he would lie awake at night, was that there was nothing particularly fine or high in himself.

The sun was past the median of its arc in the sky and had begun to accelerate westward toward the final rush of disappearance into twilight. Honor heard Aidan's voice and rolled over on one arm on her towel to look in his direction. She was wearing the same green bikini top that she had worn the night before, and when Aidan realized why he remembered this, he could see something in Honor's eyes that told him she remembered, too.

She was smiling more broadly than usual, to which Aidan could manage no reaction but to grin stupidly back. He sat down quietly beside her and said nothing. The night before on the beach had already begun rushing back to flood the holes in his memory. Boyce laughed hard and loud and asked him something. Aidan ignored him, as he often did.

Honor was quiet. Aidan found a place to lie on his back with his head on a part of her towel. She offered to share the whole thing, but Aidan reminded her peevishly that he was used to sleeping on bare sand. He remembered then what the alcohol had only briefly dimmed of the night before.

It began with an impromptu party for Boyce's birthday. The three of them had eaten a mess of steamed crabs covered in clods of Old Bay at the Black Flag, a pub overlooking the harbor, after which Aidan and Boyce had worn out the band, taking turns dancing with Honor to Marvin Gaye tunes. It was a credit more to the beer than the music that Boyce kept insisting the singer actually *was* Marvin Gaye, secretly returned from the dead.

When they left the bar around eleven, they had a buzz on like a stuck foghorn. To keep the party going, they stopped at the mini-mart for more beer and ice for the cooler. They were sober enough to remember to let some of the air out of the tires so they wouldn't get stuck in Boyce's Suburban, but drunk enough to get lost on the Jeep trails in the dunes. Somehow they drove in circles until they came out onto a stretch of beach that none of them recognized.

No one was there. The surf had settled down for the day, and the water seemed more like a lake. The stars were all out against a pitch-black sky, and the moon was already below the horizon. As they lay on their backs in front of the dunes, looking up into the night, the alcohol swirling through Aidan's head made him feel as though he were flying through space, taking in the whole sweep of the galaxy at the speed of light.

It was here that the movie reel of Aidan's memory flickered and jumped, skipping ahead of some in-between scenes and becoming less coherent. He didn't remember clearly how he got there—only that he was suddenly standing in the gentle surf, holding a beer in one hand and watching Honor. She was egging him on about something, splashing water in his direction. He could see the same green bikini top she had on now—a rather dowdy and firm-fitting thing that said *support* not *sex*, and that looked like it must have come straight from L. L. Bean. It was the kind of swimsuit that matched perfectly the style of clothes she wore to the office—sturdy, classic, a little matronly, and just what Daddy would have ordered.

Honor was on the pretty side of plain, with clear, Nordic skin and chiseled, strong, almost masculine features. She was blonde like her mother and tall and leggy enough to have the kind of confidence that men often mistook for brazenness. Aidan didn't doubt there were a few men in her past who were sorry they made that mistake. She was not what anyone would have imagined as Boyce's type—if Boyce had loved so many women as to acquire a type—but what she lacked in beauty she made up in athleticism and sheer length and strength of limb. And that night she was silly drunk.

The scenes of Aidan's memory flickered and stuttered again, then got clearer. "Come on, you first," she was shouting at him. "You have to go first—the guy always goes first, especially when he's the big boss." She had to be drunk. She worked for both of them, but she'd never called either of them the "boss" before.

By this time Boyce was still sober enough to know that three was a crowd. He walked back up onto the dry sand to lie down. From there he could still see Aidan in the moonlight, with the water around him rising waist-high as he struggled to stand and hold onto his beer.

What happened then Aidan wasn't sure. He knew only that in the next instant the green bikini top disappeared, and he could dimly see two white shapes emerge in the darkness above the water, like twin moons from behind clouds in a night sky.

He came closer. Honor stood facing him, motionless, just long enough that he would know, and know that she knew, that she was satisfying what had been his unspoken, adolescent longing all weekend. As a younger man, in the thrall of just such moments, he had often mistaken what was natural for what was eternal and pledged to love a woman forever. But in an instant, before that delusion could again overwhelm him, Honor kicked and thrust her body underwater.

She darted away in a tactical, halfhearted retreat. Aidan could hear her high-pitched laughter alternately through the breaths she took, drawing him into a chase that he instinctively followed like a hound incapable of any other thought but to dash after a running hare. A competitive swimmer in her school days, Honor could have lapped him around the island and back again had she wanted or needed to, but on this night she yielded when his hand locked onto her ankle and he drew her back beside him. Then the unexpected happened for them both.

She swung around onto Aidan's back, wrapping her long legs around his waist and her arms around his neck.

MICHAEL HURLEY

"There's something on the bottom," she shrieked. "I felt it with my foot. You swim, I'll ride."

Aidan felt nothing beneath his feet but sand and broken shells. He hunched over and reached around his back with both arms to move her farther up onto his shoulders. His hands grasped each cheek of her bottom, which was as naked as the rest of her, and pushed.

As Aidan half-waded and half-swam to deeper water, Honor jutted her chin out and rested it in the nook between his head and right shoulder, the better to see where they were going. She did not speak. She held her arms tightly around his neck—as lovers do. He could feel the skin of her cheek and her breasts pressing into his back. The wonderful smell he could not place was jasmine coming from her hair, which fell across her face onto his with each forward stride.

Together they made their way slowly farther out into a sea that was steadily becoming as calm as a pool, taking care to stay just beneath the surface to avoid the cool night air on bare skin. When the water came up to Aidan's chest, he stopped with both feet resting on the ocean floor. His curiosity could wait no longer. Here, with a deftness even he found surprising, he reached around with his left arm and grasped Honor by the right hip, pulling her off his back and around in front of him. With Aidan supporting her shoulders and legs, she let herself float upward on her back into a cradle he made with his arms. Her eyes were closed, and all but her face, in an expression of quiet meditation, lay just below the surface. Slowly, he lifted her body before him. The water ran down from around her breasts and hips until every inch of her was revealed beneath the stars, like a lost continent rising from the sea. It was then that her eyes opened, and she looked at him.

Aidan stood there, pile-like, holding her aloft as if she were a sacrifice to the gods, her nude form relaxed, her eyes gazing compliantly at his, for a time that lingered far past the point at which the thing that was supposed to happen next should have begun to happen.

He searched for some banality to break the tension, though for him the tension had long passed.

"You—you look good, Honor," he said, stumbling, and immediately wished for the words back. He sounded as if he were scoring a badminton match.

In point of fact, he knew that she didn't look good—she was exquisite. Any fool could see that. Aidan was slain by her form, and he felt the idiot for his need to pretend otherwise.

Still, it was a beautiful evening, and the sea was cool and delicious. Honor seemed quickly to detach from the moment even as Aidan burned with a mixture of regret, self-loathing, and embarrassment.

"Thanks," was all she said in reply.

A second later, as if on cue, Aidan's stomach erupted violently over her body in a fountain of stale beer and crab vomit.

That was his last memory of the evening.

Boyce looked at Honor and Aidan, now lying together on the dune in the bright sun.

"We waited for you to wake up last night," he said. "You were in pretty sorry shape. We figured you could use the sleep."

Honor's mouth curled into a hopeful smile, but Aidan said nothing.

Aidan rolled over and opened his eyes, staring at the setting sun. Boyce seemed barely to be there, except for his swim trunks. The color of the sand was indistinguishable from the color of his arms and legs.

Honor cast a bemused look in Boyce's direction. Her dirty blonde, waist-length hair lay haphazardly around her on the sand like a rumpled beach towel. Boyce had been working up to this weekend with her for months. He was recently divorced, gaining weight, and running out of ways to look thirty. She had been bemused by him all weekend. It was her prevailing attitude—and one that seemed to give her a kind of emotional armor that Boyce had wholly failed to penetrate.

"Do you know Zeno's Paradox?" Aidan blurted out.

The look on Honor's face turned from bemusement to quiet torment. No one answered.

"Zeno's Paradox says that, because every distance is measured by a number that is infinitely divisible, every distance is infinite. So, the distance between where the sun is now and the horizon is infinite. That means the sun can never completely set. This day will never really end."

Boyce had been hanging back, waiting for his opportunity.

"By that logic, that guy's fist in Arnold's place should never have hit your jaw. But it did."

Honor stifled a laugh.

"Besides, the Beach Boys already tried the Endless Summer thing. They're fat and middle-aged—or dead—last I looked," Boyce added.

They remained on that dune for the next three hours—sleeping, talking, and listening to an oldies station that was not quite close enough to come in clearly on the radio. They had a cooler full of ice, bottled water, and ginger ale, and an enormous bag of tortilla chips that Boyce completely devoured, one at a time. As twilight fell, the lighthouse beam swept low near the dunes where the three of them lay, scanning the debris of the last afternoon of the weekend. Out in the distance to the east, from Silver Lake Harbor, came the rumble of the ferry engines turning over for the final passage to the mainland. Aidan kept staring across the sound, fixed upon the setting sun.

Honor turned for a last glance out to sea. The surf had died down. The thin foam crests atop waves rolling in from due east reflected brightly in the waning light. In the distance she could see a gaff-rigged boat, so tiny it seemed it might have been miles offshore, but it was closer. It was already sailing sprightly over the breakers, near the beach. She could faintly make out the figures of two people in the open cockpit. They were on a broad reach before a southwest breeze that had freshened with the warming afternoon air.

Aidan finally turned from the horizon. When he saw the little boat, a smile gathered on his face. He let his mind wander to the past, recalling the absolute freedom of boyhood summers spent on Delaware Bay, sailing boats just like that one—often as not in winds and seas too strong for the size of the vessel and her skipper. He closed his eyes.

A tall, erudite man with a trim white moustache called out to nine-year-old Aidan, skidding along shore in a dory he had borrowed from someone's dock.

"Where are you bound, young fellow?"

"To the islands, sir!"

At that age Aidan had known of no islands in particular, save those that Robert Louis Stevenson had described, nor whether any lay out beyond the bay. But that hardly mattered. The horizon was the thing. He dreamt of it. Because he couldn't see past it, he was free to imagine what glories it might be hiding. Certainly that had not changed in forty years.

The charging sail of the little boat in the surf caught the setting sun, which turned the sailcloth a brilliant orange for just a moment before it dipped behind the next breaker and fell back into shades of gray.

"That's a Beetle Cat, isn't it?" Boyce asked.

Boyce was a sailor. He knew more about boats than just about anyone. He had grown up on the Outer Banks, where his family had a summer place. He knew that a little boat like that, just twelve feet long, could be steered onto the beach and pushed off again with ease. It was just the sort of daysailer one wanted on the banks. Catboats were flat-bottomed and rigged with one wide sail that the helmsman trimmed using a single string. It was simple, pure, and timeless.

"It's a perfect little picnic boat for a beach like this if you can navigate the waves," Aidan remarked.

They all watched now as the two shadows in the cockpit hunkered beneath the gybing boom that whipped back and forth over their heads like a scythe as the little craft traveled up, then down, each breaking wave and drew closer to the beach. The landing was marked by the abrupt shudder of the mast and the unnatural motion of the bow as it dug into the sand.

Out of the cockpit and into ankle-deep water jumped a teenage boy and a girl. They were only silhouettes in the shimmering twilight. A hollow *tock-tock* sound could be heard as crisp, dry pieces of driftwood were dropped on the sand. The light of a small fire emerged. Aidan wished he were beside it. It was a beautiful night for a clambake.

The ferry in the harbor gave a long, slow blast of the whistle. She would leave the dock in half an hour, and the town would again be peaceful on this spit of sand in the Atlantic Ocean. It was a short walk back to their rented house behind the dunes, where their car was waiting. In fifteen minutes, they rolled aboard the ferry and parked, waiting to begin the long ride home.

The giant engines whipped up a swift current in the harbor as the big boat backed away from the dock. It whisked them out between the rock jetties of the inlet and up the shoaling, narrow channel that led to the sound and the mainland beyond. The sun was completely gone.

CHAPTER 3

Father Marcus O'Reilly had long since given up inveighing against flip-flops and shorts at mass. This was the beach after all, people would tell him, and not just any beach. This was Ocracoke—a hippie beach if ever there was one. When they gave it National Seashore status, that disappointed the big hotel developers, delighted the skinny-dippers, and sealed its character permanently. But young families still came here by the droves every summer, and if they were Catholic they came to St. Anne's for six o'clock mass on Sunday, which allowed them just enough time to pack up and catch the last ferry at nine. Marcus counted it a triumph of decorum if he could make it through the day without teenaged breasts spilling completely out of a bikini top at the communion rail.

Marcus was a study in contradiction—a man after the heart of St. Paul. He was Old School when it came to the solemnity and ritual of the mass and the prayers. Many an unwitting penitent who came to confession, full of casual piety, left detesting no sin as heartily as his failure to recite the Act of Contrition to the old priest's satisfaction. But Marcus was more liberal than most when it came to doctrine. In fact, it was often said that no one and nothing could find room to the left of him on the island but the devil and the deep blue sea.

Marcus was also more than a little rough around the edges, having come up in one of the oldest schools around—the Jesuit Academy for Boys in Boston—where turning the other cheek was not part of the catechism. At the age of sixty-eight, he was trim and fit and still had a right cross that could fell an ox, although he had not met any oxen lately who deserved that special attention.

The bishop in Raleigh was among the rising generation of Church leaders nurtured on what Marcus considered the theological "pabulum" of post-Vatican II Catholicism. It was this bishop's singular zeal, Marcus believed, to debase every liturgical tradition once held sacred by millions and reduce the Church in every respect to its lowest common denominator. At a diocesan retreat five years ago, Marcus (well-fueled with gin at the time) had made a few intemperate remarks in mixed company about the bishop "barely starting to shave" and his appointment being pushed through by an uncle in the Vatican whom Marcus described as being "in charge of sharpening the pope's pencils." It got out and did not go over well, as evidenced by the bishop's decision three months later to transfer Marcus to a deserted outpost on Ocracoke Island.

Of all that had left Marcus in this life, and there was much, it was a great irony that his faith doggedly remained. The knowledge of God was as certain to him as the shoes on his feet, and the fear of God was as close as the memory of his sins. They were to Marcus a stain he longed to remove, but for which neither grace nor alcohol had proven an adequate solvent. Atheists and nihilists bewildered and fascinated him. The idea that someone could experience good and evil and, looking out at the world in which those forces were at work, conclude that it all turned on a cosmic roll of the dice, seemed to him an extravagant delusion—like wishing for cotton-candy clouds and chocolate raindrops. It was just too much to hope for. The idea that he might yet descend at the end of his life, forgotten and blameless, into an unthinking, eternal void that wine and whiskey could only briefly glimpse, required a strength of self-deception far beyond any rigor he possessed. To him, those who lived in the confident expectation of eternal oblivion were a marvel of spiritual discipline.

Marcus had been raised in a world very different from the one in which he now found himself. His had been a life of much greater poverty yet far less vulgarity than seemed common to modern America. The fourth son of an alcoholic father in a Boston Irish Catholic family, he had been molded by a Jesuit education, but his soul had been marked more deeply by the kind of blood sport known only to brothers competing for an absent father's attention and approval. The priesthood had beckoned him with the promise of respite from that life of want with a life of being wanted—endlessly—by streams of faithful supplicants. It was a path that had led him through the chaplain corps of the navy and down the dark alleys of men's dying hours, to the memory of which he often returned.

But the peace of this island had been an unexpected gift, and one that he cherished. The bishop mostly left him alone, and here was where he would finish his ministry. Most of the Catholic families on the Banks were vacationers—white and comfortably upper middle class, well ensconced within gleaming, leather-lined SUVs and minivans, with passels of children in the back, sedated in the soft, narcotic glow of Disney movies playing on drop-down DVD screens. Such families were increasingly numerous in the sunny uplands of the suburban South, while their numbers steadily dwindled in the dying mill towns built by their grandparents in the North. Marcus rarely got to know any of them. They would come to the Banks for a week and then be gone forever. But while they were there, the parents came with their bored children on Sunday to mass—indeed as they did each Sunday at home—in the silent hope that when little Eleanor finally went away to college she wouldn't become a Buddhist or have an abortion or marry a liberal Democrat or get a tattoo or listen to public radio. They prayed instead that their children would follow the pilgrim road to heaven or, failing that, to a leafy suburb of Charlotte with good schools. They asked Father Marcus to pray with them in their fear and doubt, which he did faithfully despite his own considerable fears and doubts.

When Marcus had put away the last of the cups from six o'clock mass, he took a moment to sit in the quiet of the sacristy, in a chair he had stolen from the private study of the former rector of St. Anne's for just this purpose. The Sunday evening mass was usually not well attended, and this day had been no exception. Blessedly so, he thought, and without an ounce of repentance. There were only a few of the local faithful who warmed his heart enough to make him want to hold their faith in safekeeping. One of them was now quietly weeping as she prayed on a kneeler far in the back of the nave. Marcus knew it was time to go to her.

Her name was Sarah—or at least that was the name he had given her when she washed up on the island three years ago, stark naked, cold, and hungry. He had been sitting alone on the beach north of the rectory, looking out to sea one evening in early November. Suddenly he saw what seemed at first to be the body of a porpoise struggling in the surf, but as he drew closer he saw it was a woman who had swum ashore from a great distance. She was exhausted and barely conscious from the cold. He wrapped her in his jacket and ran with her in his arms back to the rectory to call the hospital. Three days later, when she had recovered enough to be discharged, no one knew her real name. She would speak only to him. Her accent recalled his memory of Romanian Orthodox boys from tightly knit, working-class neighborhoods in North Boston around Water Street. It was knowledge he had come by dearly. A white scar across the knuckles of his left hand marked the time he had underestimated a boy from that neighborhood, but across some old man's jaw in Boston was also the visible reminder of the last time that man had crossed one of the O'Reilly brothers. Marcus had come away from that experience with the understanding that the Romanian people could—and often did—suffer and survive unimaginable hardship and loss, and yet their loyalty and their faith remained impenetrable. He heard that faith in this woman's voice.

Marcus suspected she was the same woman sought by a search party from the Coast Guard who came by the rectory a week after she showed up. They had heard from locals the story of his rescue of a woman on the beach who fit the description of the woman they had found alone and adrift, seventeen miles out at sea, floating on the burned wreckage of a shrimp trawler that had sailed from Hatteras three days earlier. A Mayday call had gone out over the boat's VHF radio, reporting that fire had broken out in the engine room and that they were taking on water. Four men were reported aboard, but when the Coast Guard arrived to the given coordinates east of Diamond Shoals, no remnant of the boat could be found. Two days into a search-and-recovery sweep of the area, a Coast Guard cutter spotted a charred section of the transom of the trawler floating on the surface with a woman clinging to it. She resisted their rescue like a cornered animal. She carried no identification and would answer no questions. They were beginning the final approach to Fort Macon in Morehead City when they discovered she was missing from the infirmary on board.

When the boatswain's mate came asking questions, Marcus was keeping the woman in a spare bedroom in the rectory. He met the man at the door. Wearing his clerical collar, he told him that the new guest in the rectory was his ailing sister, Sarah Asperati, who had come from Boston to stay with him. The real Sarah had died three years ago. It was obvious that the young man, eager to complete his appointed task, wasn't disappointed by this story. He left as soon as he recorded information from the Social Security card and passport that Marcus had collected from his sister's things. It was a justifiable lie. There was something about the woman and the odd manner in which she had come to him that made Marcus want to tell it.

A social worker at the hospital suggested that Marcus transfer Sarah to a psychiatric hospital in Raleigh for evaluation, but he refused. He decided instead to let her stay in the rectory until she recovered fully and her family could be found. Nurses came from the hospital for the first week to check on her. When she did speak, her words were brief and clipped. She revealed nothing of her past, even to Marcus.

One day, after Sarah had seemingly regained her health, Marcus descended from his study to find that she was gone. The rectory was a rambling, early-twentieth-century clapboard house left to the Church in the will of one of the state's notable Catholic benefactors. It was situated on a raised point of land not far from the old lighthouse, where it overlooked a wide expanse of beach just north of the inlet. The widow's walk on the third story afforded a view for several miles in either direction, and Marcus raced there to look for her.

He saw her soon enough. She was on the beach, surrounded by a crowd of onlookers who stood several yards behind her. At the fore of the crowd was the village sheriff, Ed Classen. Marcus grabbed the binoculars that hung beside the door to the portico and, looking closer, felt his jaw drop. She was, once again, in the buff. Marcus noticed her form then as if for the first time. His rescue on the beach three weeks earlier was such a blur of sudden shock and adrenaline that her physical features had not registered with him. Now that he saw her from afar, he paused to marvel at her. It had been fifty years since Marcus had loved a woman. She was beautifully formed and desirable, he could plainly see, but seeing her like that awoke in him only feelings of pity. He raced down the stairs, grabbed an old raincoat he kept hanging in the net room, and bolted down the path to the beach.

The scene he came upon was as he had expected. Sarah had attracted a crowd of curious onlookers; someone had called the sheriff, and now there was about to be an arrest.

"Ed, let me take care of this. She's not well. She won't hurt anyone."

"The hell you say," Ed replied, lifting an arm marked by a large, red welt where Sarah had landed a blow with the stick in her hand. "I tried talking to her, but she keeps yelling for you."

"I'm so sorry, Ed. It's my fault. I was supposed to be watching her. She's still recovering."

"Sarah, come with me," Marcus pleaded, walking toward her. She lowered her weapon and accepted his offer of his coat. "Folks, go on back now. I'm very sorry. She's pretty shaken up and needs some rest."

Ed Classen looked at Marcus wearily, then turned to the crowd. "You heard him, folks. Show's over. Go on now."

Sarah said little that night other than "thank you" as she accepted some oyster stew that Marcus's housekeeper, Nita, had bubbling on the stove.

Sarah remained in all respects an enigma. She seemed to have three passions. One was for the myopic cleaning and ordering of absolutely everything in her domain. Another was her devotion to the weekly mass, which she seemed to experience on each occasion anew with a heightened, visceral awareness, as if the very breaking of the bread did her mortal injury. And lastly, she longed for something seaward that was unspoken and unseen. For reasons unknown to Marcus, she felt the need to encounter this force unclothed, and two more nude elopements had transpired before he imposed his will on her to wear a white-cotton beach cover-up. He bought her several of them for this very need.

But her naked forays into the sea had not gone unnoticed. Murmurings began that there was something unholy in Father Marcus's compassion for the woman or something other than innocence that belied her immodesty. In the Black Flag, tavern goers came to refer to her as *the Gypsy queen*, and the name stuck. All of this soon reached the reddened ears of the bishop, whose foremost concern was for any possibility of a scandal that might find its way to his door. He pounced on the problem like a cat on a bug.

Marcus was summoned to appear on the tufted carpets of the bishop's palace in Raleigh. The bishop, having satisfied himself that the woman was no longer in need of convalescence or sanctuary, would not abide any answer from Marcus other than his agreement to evict her inside the week.

Marcus feared Sarah might not survive in the world alone, and so he contrived the idea to acquire a boat on which she could remain, anchored in the shoals near the inlet, safely beyond the prying eyes of villagers. He had little income to speak of, but he had incurred no expenses of any significance since he had emerged from the seminary forty-five years ago. In those years and among the fifteen churches he had served, the generosity of grateful widows had amended the usually meager fortunes of a parish priest to a sum now well beyond his needs. He would use a portion of that money, without second thought or regret, to acquire a simple vessel for Sarah. It would be a sailboat or nothing.

He found a sturdy ketch, shoal-keeled and getting on in years but still as seaworthy as the day she slipped her traces, among the dozens of unclaimed maidens nodding sleepily at the brokerage docks of Hutcheson's Marina in the nearby town of Oriental. The owner wanted thirty thousand. The broker thought he would take twenty-eight, but Marcus recognized the owner's name—Simmons—from the roster of diocesan benefactors on a bronze plaque that hung in the narthex of the Cathedral in Raleigh. He insisted on meeting him in person. This the owner happily did, and, upon seeing the Roman collar and hearing Marcus lie about his plans to use the boat to teach sailing to children of migrant farm workers, he dropped the price to what he owed the bank for the vessel, which was ten thousand. Handing him a personal check for that exact amount and taking a bill of sale in return, Marcus stepped aboard and was underway with unexpected swiftness.

Watching the old priest set all three sails with ease and weave his way out of the narrow channel through the shoals beyond the breakwater, it occurred to the broker that he had not given Marcus the engine key, which still hung on a board in the broker's office. Marcus hadn't asked for it. The truth was, Marcus considered the idea of a motor aboard a sailboat to be intrinsically disordered, like galoshes on a duck. From what the broker could tell, Marcus had enough skill in reading the wind that he didn't need an auxiliary. With this thought, a sinking realization came over him that he had just sold far too good a boat for far too little money to a real sailor who wanted and needed it much more urgently than he had let on. He stood and watched, stoically if not a little stupefied, until he could no longer see the name on the transom that was neatly painted in blue and gold letters: *Bel Sogno*.

With more than a little need for persuasion, Sarah was safely ensconced aboard the boat where Marcus anchored her, in an eddy just off to the side of the winding, shifting channel that led from the harbor to the sea. It was a place of some history. Blackbeard was said to have lain in wait there for sailors hoping to challenge him who did not know the surrounding labyrinth of sand bars and tidal channels. They would run aground in their approach, doomed to wait until the pirate and his men looted their vessel and burned it to the waterline. Here at least, Marcus thought, Sarah would be well out of view of inland boat traffic, and ships returning from sea would scarcely notice her as they passed abeam in the channel.

Marcus regularly ferried to Sarah what groceries and supplies he could spare, using a canoe he stored in the dunes beside the lagoon. By the same means he carried her to and from evening mass each Sunday. Sarah fiercely guarded her kingdom anchorage and her little boat, which she spent much of each day polishing to a blazing finish. It proved to be a very satisfactory arrangement for all concerned, and many on the island came to look with affection upon the Gypsy queen, anchored like a sentinel outside their camp.

In the summers Sarah was still given to midnight swims from the deck of *Bel Sogno* across the lagoon, always in the natural state that she preferred. She would sometimes encounter an astonished family who had braved the long walk to the point, but for this purpose she carried with her one of the cover-ups Father Marcus had given her, late though she often was to make use of it. And so did Father Marcus O'Reilly and the unnamed woman he called Sarah, his most faithful parishioner, pass three years uneventfully on Ocracoke Island.

That Sunday night after mass, Marcus returned to the sanctuary where Sarah prayed alone.

"Are you ready to go?" he asked.

He rarely called her by the name Sarah, as they both knew that was a convenient lie, and it seemed pointless to keep up that charade when they were alone. Yet her real name she had not revealed and would, in fact, never reveal to him in all the time he knew her. Without words on this warm Sunday evening, with a gentle breeze coming off of a calm ocean, the two of them began the familiar walk together down the beach.

When they reached the lagoon, Marcus retrieved the canoe from its hiding place, lifted it atop his shoulders, and set it down at the water's edge. Dressed for the occasion—she in her veil and he in his clerical suit—they looked something like a Venetian funeral procession, solemnly streaming toward the *Bel Sogno*.

With the physical ease of a woman many years younger, Sarah slipped from the bow of the canoe up onto and over the rail of the boat and was safely aboard. After a polite thank you and goodbye to Marcus, she disappeared below, through the companionway, into the cabin of her floating home.

Marcus returned to shore, looking back once to see the faint glow of an oil lamp illuminate the cabin of *Bel Sogno*. He had the sense that, for all his many years of labor in the Lord's vineyard, if he could be confident that he had saved only this woman, he would not lose his reward. As the canoe nudged up on the bank of the lagoon with the scraping sound of sand under the bow, a voice called out of the growing twilight.

"Marcus!" Sheriff Classen was a Southern Baptist. He had a theological objection against referring to any man of the cloth by the title *Father*.

"Your little gal was on the beach again today without her clothes on."

Marcus's mood sunk and his shoulders slumped. He remained seated in the canoe. He knew Classen was there, but he could not bring himself to look in his direction. He was growing weary of these complaints.

"Well, I hope you got a good look at her, Ed."

"You know that's not why I'm here. People complain, Marcus, and they expect me to do something about it. A woman called me this morning—a mother with five kids staying in a rental on the point—and said she saw her walk more than a mile back to the inlet not wearing a thing."

"You know, Ed, the mothers of five children who call to complain about Sarah are not upset about her nudity. They just can't stand the fact that they haven't had legs like that in twenty years, if they ever did."

"That's not my concern, Marcus."

"I get it, Ed. I get it. I'll talk to her. I promise."

"I'll have to take her in next time, Marcus, and you know I really don't want that. No one does. She'll listen to you. Just see if you can't make her understand. It's bad enough, having to deal with the hippies skinny-dipping and smoking pot up by the campground. I can't be everywhere at once."

"Understood, Ed."

"You need help with that?" Classen asked, pointing to the canoe. Marcus was tired, but help from Sheriff

Classen wasn't what he needed most. That was waiting for him farther up the beach.

When he arrived back at the rectory, Marcus changed into a favorite pair of khakis and a threadbare cotton sweater. He wore no shoes. Instead, he lightly padded down the stairs in a well-ritualized and never-successful effort to sneak up on Hobo, the twelve-year-old, blind Irish terrier who lay asleep in the den. As he approached, the dog lifted his disheveled face, with wild eyebrows and a beard hanging down in matted, red strands on either side of his jaw, his tail wagging for the approach of his master and the expected invitation to play. He sprung up to his feet and whirled around in one fluid movement that had not changed or slowed, it seemed, in all his long years. The two of them walked side by side, without need of a single word of command, out of the back door of the rectory. Hobo walked by faith, not by sight, and Marcus had faith enough to follow him. He knew exactly what Marcus wanted, and he knew exactly where to get it.

About a mile north of the rectory along the beach, the old dog began to dig furiously in a bank of sand, well back against the dunes. Marcus waited patiently between the dunes and the surf, expecting Hobo to arrive shortly at his side, triumphantly carrying a half-empty bottle of communion wine in his mouth, pleased with himself and seeking his master's approval. When more time passed than was usually needed for these excavations, Marcus walked over to find Hobo digging a hole wider and deeper than usual. The bottle of Sangiovese that was laid in store there two weeks earlier, against the needs of a night like this one, had been pilfered.

Marcus looked all around him, as if someone might

have been watching. He was not aware that anyone on the island knew of his evening expeditions with Hobo to bury wine in various places where it could later be discreetly retrieved. Curious vacationers, he surmised, must have found it.

"It's not there boy. C'mon. Let's go farther up."

Hobo had buried dozens of bottles, each of them opened, corked, and half to three-quarters full, at random locations back in the dunes that only the little dog could remember, from the rectory to the last beach access road—a distance of some five miles. These deposits and withdrawals were the main purpose of their walks together, which had become as regular and routine as bankers' daily business.

It was Marcus's secret vice. He was likely an alcoholic, though he didn't relish putting such a fine point on the matter. It was nonetheless an addiction he dutifully affirmed each week while leading meetings of the local Alcoholics Anonymous chapter in the basement of the church. ("Hello, my name is Marcus . . .") His nighttime walks with Hobo fueled a boyish craving for illicit adventure, but it also spared him the professional and personal calamity of being seen tippling in public. Communion wine was kept locked in the sacristy by Alice Marne, the church secretary. Marcus asked her, in a sleight of hand that passed as a demonstration of his commitment to sobriety, to be the only holder of the key. She discharged her post with a watchful eye, lording over the unopened bottles but leaving it to Marcus to discard the empties. Mass was held each morning at seven, Thursdays at noon, and twice on Sunday. At some masses only four or five souls would be in attendance, which allowed Marcus to divert wine for his own use at a rate of about a half-bottle every second or third mass. Receiving steady orders for more stock, Alice was only too happy to know that the tide of salvation was flowing so freely on Ocracoke Island. For Marcus, it was a private and venial sin—one that he still struggled with, in his quiet hours, but less strenuously so with each passing year.

The answer to the mystery of the stolen Sangiovese was not at hand, but another bottle certainly was. Marcus assuaged Hobo's disappointment with forgiving pats on the head and goaded him on to find the next cache. Watching the little dog streak off down the beach, he thought of his father, Seamus, who had only one foot off the boat to America when Marcus was born. It was not for nothing that Hobo was an *Irish* terrier. Marcus would greatly have preferred Guinness to wine, but until the day the cardinals came to their senses and elected an Irish pope, there was no chance of seeing a bottle of that in the sacristy.

Hobo seemed especially glad to find the second bottle. He would have taken it hard otherwise. Marcus wedged himself into a high bank of the dunes and put the sweet nectar to his lips. Hobo nestled contentedly at his feet and began to desecrate the remains of a horseshoe crab. There, in that holy hour beside the sea, beneath the host of all the stars in heaven, a transubstantiation as real as any ever imagined upon a gilded altar took place for Father Marcus Eugene O'Reilly, as the wine once again became his very Lord, companion, and friend.

Sarah's comings and goings were heavy on Marcus's thoughts that night. He took a sip of the wine and felt his shoulders ease of the tension he carried with him. She had long mystified him. He had done what little research he could, through various social service agencies and friends in police departments who agreed to help investigate her origins and find her family, but he had come up with nothing. He had only guessed from her accent that she might be Romanian.

During a trip home to see family one year, he stopped by the Romanian Orthodox Church on Water Street in North Boston, not far from his old neighborhood. When he handed the parish priest Sarah's picture, Marcus thought he saw some hesitation in the man's eyes. But after looking at it inquisitively, as if he were savoring a memory, he handed it back to Marcus. He was sorry, he said, but he did not know her.

Money was not desperately needed, where Sarah was concerned. She had a remarkable capacity to live lightly upon the Earth. Nita gathered, sewed, and scavenged what was necessary to provide her with a wardrobe and all of her other material needs. Marcus supplied the rest with a small stipend that he held back from the collection. The money he provided for her in this way remained off the parish books, away from the bishop's prying eyes.

With Sarah floating out in the lagoon, separated from the rest of the community, mystery seemed to envelope and hide her like a fog. Marcus could not penetrate it. He felt there was some portent, some foreboding in her coming, though what exactly he could not say. On this question he pondered a while, sitting back in the dunes with Hobo's head resting on his feet, until the wine worked its magic and he felt all wonderings and worries leave him. Soon only the sound of the sea remained, and the slow creeping of the tide. The moon gradually sunk behind him, leaving a faint trail of gray before it disappeared entirely. Then all was darkness on the Earth, while in the heavens a trillion stars shed their everlasting light. It would be morning soon, and time again for mass.

CHAPTER 4

I t was that hour of the night when Bobbi Baker found it most difficult to sleep. When that time came, a cigarette helped, and she smoked them one after another, but these were not nearly as important or as much a comfort to her as the sweet iced tea that she guzzled by the glassful. She sipped one in a steady rhythm now, as she stared out to sea from the balcony of her third-story apartment.

Sea and tea. These were the compulsions she had exchanged for alcohol three years ago. The tea gave her a throbbing caffeine buzz, like an electric power cord to her brain, in place of the high she once got from wine. It kept her always on a fine edge between awareness and nervousness about everything that transpired around her. Rarely was she separated from it. She had to have some cup or glass always close at hand, like a child's pacifier. The sea gave her something entirely different but equally addictive, though if asked, she would be hard pressed to put a name to it. She stared into its emptiness like an oracle.

On this night again, as had occurred each night of this summer and the summer before on Ocracoke, the figure of a man appeared, walking in the dunes with a little dog. Hobo was a beggar and a vagrant of some infamy on the island. Few were the back doors where he had not at some time known the milk of human kindness.

Watching the sea that night as she was wont to do, Bobbi easily recognized Hobo's scruffy form at a distance as he came running frantically up the beach in pursuit of his treasure. She knew what it was he sought, although anyone else would have assumed he was chasing a rabbit or searching for a lost ball. From the vantage point of her apartment, high above the beach, she had observed him recover his treasure from its hiding place and deliver it excitedly to his master many times. It was a curious mission that was given him, but he executed it with a panache that made her smile. Red whiskers, flop ears, and a rueful expression that betrayed his probable guilt for any recent or nearby offense made Hobo irresistible to women and children, and Bobbi was no less susceptible to his charms. She knew equally well the figure of the man who walked beside the dog. There was no one on the island other than Marcus whom Hobo would follow very long or far.

Bobbi and the priest were fellow penitents. The AA meetings he led were a lifeline to her, but no less important was the realization that Marcus, for all his wisdom, regularly stumbled and failed as others did. To see him fail was chiefly why she stayed there, hidden in the darkness. Watching him unawares was a kind of therapy. His benevolent falseness made her own more bearable. Life might have overtaken and defeated her otherwise, though Marcus scarcely suspected that these nightly forays had a therapeutic benefit for anyone but himself.

For Bobbi, the best evidence of the need to amend her own life was sleeping in the next room. His name was John—something. She met him at the Black Flag last night, the latest in a long line of John Somethings. He had been sitting at the bar listening to the music and coolly sipping Coronas when he noticed Bobbi. She had been across the room, keeping Zoot the bartender pinned down with her usual covering fire of nonstop, caffeine-fueled chatter. Then this man walked up and said hello, as men so often did around Bobbi.

It was the same routine from one week to the next. She would try to relax at the Black Flag, sometimes just talking to Zoot, sometimes making small talk with the beach bums and saltwater cowboys who floated by on their way down the banks. She would sometimes pick one and take him home. He would stay for a night or a week or a month or a summer, but never for good. It didn't much matter to Bobbi either, as long as she made it to the mini-mart on time every morning for work.

Bobbi's face showed little of her fifty years, but her heart felt every day of two failed marriages and the downward spiral that had washed her out of Atlanta ten years ago. She came to that city fresh out of high school, looking for work as a secretary. Then just a naïve girl with a big smile, raised in the Kentucky bluegrass and teetering in her first high heels on thin, gangly legs, she looked like a newborn foal from her family's farm. She wanted no one to rescue her, but rescue was repeatedly offered—first by a boy as young and green as she was who couldn't keep her, then by a man thirty years older who kept her far too long. The older man's name was Jody Brent Tucker, but since his boyhood on a South Georgia tobacco farm he had been known simply as "Jo Brent." He was new money from the Old South, and Bobbi's marriage to him was wild fun for a while. But as time went by, the glow of the money and what it could give her began to fade.

Her wounds grew slowly. She salved them at first with alcohol, then—as the years began to take their toll—with plastic surgery to keep her grip on Jo Brent's affection. The more he ignored Bobbi, the more attention his friends paid to her. Their sniveling wives spoke in mocking whispers about "the work" she had done, by which they meant the preternaturally firm, large breasts surgery had given her that were, in fact, more lovely than what nature had given them. When one woman's husband announced he was leaving her, the wife accused Bobbi of an affair, and things went downhill from there for everyone. Six months later, on a sunny day that portended nothing of the storms that lay ahead, Bobbi came home to find Jo Brent sitting on the sofa in the living room with a paper in one hand and a half-empty, tall glass of scotch in the other. The letter politely informed him that Bobbi would be called as a witness in a divorce trial and made it clear that other witnesses would be showing up to testify about Bobbi's "relationship" with the husband. He took a drunken swing at Bobbi and missed. She ran out before he had a chance to take another.

Bobbi heard that the man paid a bundle to avoid a trial. She was more bewildered than angered by it all. She moved to a hotel, then to a tiny apartment. A letter came two weeks later from Jo Brent's lawyer with the divorce papers. A week after that, he froze all her credit cards. She packed her clothes and drove north on I-85 out of Atlanta, with no idea where she was headed. When she had gone as far as she could go, she found herself on Ocracoke Island.

She took the first job offer she saw, posted in the window of the mini-mart. She sold the Mercedes Jo Brent had bought for her and used the money to buy clothes, rent an apartment, and begin again.

That was seven years ago. Life since then had taken on a veneer of normalcy. The AA meetings led by Father Marcus were part of the grain of that veneer. She was not yet happy, she would tell people, but she was no longer desperately unhappy, and that was as close to real progress as Bobbi Baker could hope for.

What Father Marcus hoped for she did not know. She knew his kindness and his concern, and she knew also of the addiction he tried to hide on nights like these, sitting back in the dunes, drinking his communion wine. The poor man could not drink it in the privacy of the rectory, which was kept under Nita's watchful eye. Bobbi would see him sneaking up the beach after dinner at least twice a week, carrying with him one or two half-empty bottles tucked into his coat, with Hobo leading the way. On other nights, he returned and recovered each bottle with Hobo's unfailing assistance—presumably whenever he was in the mood for Sangiovese and solitude. Tonight was such a night.

The truth was, Bobbi was rooting for Marcus, just as she wished and hoped he was rooting for her and for all the lost souls in that island purgatory who were captives to the addictions that enslaved them. If there was hope for Marcus—*and there damn well better be*, she told herself—there was hope for her. She was counting on it. She watched this man, a mortal savior but a savior nonetheless to her and others like her, wrestle with his fears in his private Gethsemane by the sea, only to find that the Lord would not suffer this cup to pass from his lips. It was the holiest hour of her day. And in that nightly vigil, she found something of greater value than all the hours she spent in prayer. It was not the strength to bear her cross she needed most, but the forgiveness to stumble beneath it, as he did.

CHAPTER 5

Day followed night too quickly for Aidan, once again. He only barely resisted the urge to roll over when the alarm went off. From a habit formed of many mornings of lesser willpower, he had long since perfected the art of the six-minute shower and shave. In ten he was dressed and zipping along in a silver BMW on the parkway that led to downtown Raleigh.

Aidan had earned the trust of five large hospitals and a major physician insurer who demanded that he personally handle the cases they needed to keep out of the news, and he was given a corner office and a handsome partnership draw as symbols of that trust. Boyce aspired to run in the same league, but he was content to follow several steps behind Aidan. Boyce knew his limitations and usually managed not to exceed them. He was about to do just that.

Aidan passed Boyce's office on the way to his own. Ducking his head in to say good morning and exchange some pleasant banter about their weekend together on Ocracoke, he saw a look of panic in Boyce's eyes that a lawyer doesn't often see but that is unmistakable in its meaning. It said *malpractice*.

"It's today!" Boyce erupted when Aidan walked in. His voice was trembling. Aidan paused for Boyce to complete his thought. Whatever it was that was *today*, it was not a thing to be welcomed—that much was clear.

"The *Adamson* trial, it starts today, dammit! I have nothing!" Boyce was almost shouting. "I don't have a client. I don't have anything prepared. I don't have *shit!*"

Honor was in the corner of the office, her head bent over a thick file. She was pulling her fingers through a series of folders, anxiously searching for something. Tears streaked her face.

"I swear, Boyce," she said, "there was no notice for a trial starting today. I can't believe it starts today."

It was no small matter. The case in question was a two-million-dollar medical malpractice claim for wrongful death. It was not the sort of case taken to trial casually. Jury selection would last a full week, and the evidence would last at least a month longer. Trying a case of that kind was something like playing in the Superbowl. There was usually a buildup over many weeks ahead of the trial date involving countless strategy meetings with dozens of expert witnesses, nervous clients, and quailing insurance adjusters, and the careful compilation of tens of thousands of pages of exhibits, motions, orders, and outlines. Boyce knew this. In front of Aidan, he began yelling hard at Honor about not giving him the calendar notice of the trial setting that the clerk of court said she sent to him six months ago— the calendar notice that no one could find that morning. Her tears gave way to audible sobs.

Boyce finally calmed down enough to explain things to Aidan. "The clerk called and left a message while we were in Ocracoke about a change in our courtroom assignment for the *Adamson* trial. She said we'll be in the courtroom on the tenth floor instead of the eighth. I called her back this morning and asked, 'What trial?' She said, 'The jury trial that is starting at ten o'clock, with Judge Dawkins.' Somehow I never got the notice. The doctor doesn't know his case is going to trial. He's got patients scheduled all week. None of the witnesses knows what's going on. The adjuster is having a heart attack and can't stop screaming at me. We're not ready. I have never felt so thoroughly screwed."

Honor was now visibly a mess. Obviously Boyce had already decided that she would take the fall. Whatever the mistake, Aidan doubted that she had anything to do with it. In the midst of the paralysis that was seizing everyone around him, Aidan took action.

"Give me the phone," he said, reaching across Boyce's desk, "and close that door." Boyce and Honor responded like a team of surgical nurses. Honor softly shut the door and stood against it with her hands pressed behind her back. Aidan stood at the side of Boyce's desk and looked at Honor as he dialed the number for the main offices of Rampart Insurance. The dried streams of tears on her cheeks, her slumped shoulders, and the puffed bags under her eyes bore no resemblance to the willowy girl who, not thirty-six hours ago, had nothing better to do than to cavort naked in the Atlantic Ocean and dare him to do the same. He realized that the worry in her face wasn't for herself or her job but for Boyce. She seemed genuinely to care about him. He wondered if Boyce had any clue.

"Judy! Hi."

The receptionist at Rampart immediately recognized Aidan's voice. Boyce impatiently listened as Aidan, with a nonchalance and steadiness that seemed superhuman under the circumstances, took the time to chat up the receptionist about her sister's wedding. He was a master of small talk. It was a skill that usually paid off for him.

Aidan asked her to connect him to Steny Dornan, the vice president of claims. That was Aidan's style: go right to the top.

"Steny. Hey, this is Aidan. How are you?" Aidan began.

The conversation continued for several excruciating minutes about Steny's wife and children and their latest vacation until Aidan finally signaled that he had something more serious to discuss.

"Look, Steny. I've got to tell you, I've really screwed something up."

Boyce's posture stiffened. "Here it comes," he whispered.

Honor looked puzzled at Aidan's use of "I."

"You remember the *Adamson* case. I gave that to Boyce Stannard to handle, oh, maybe a year ago."

Steny knew the case well. It had a lot of exposure. Rampart had just increased its reserves to four million dollars—the policy limit—on the basis of Boyce's latest evaluation. It involved a thirty-six-year-old family man and rising business executive who was admitted to the hospital for a routine gallbladder. A few days after the operation, he was diagnosed with an ileus—a relatively common and normally benign complication in which the bowels take longer than usual to start working again after abdominal surgery. The operation was otherwise a success, but the patient was kept in the hospital for monitoring. On the fourth day of a liquid diet, the surgeon decided it was time to introduce solid foods. Six hours later, the man's wife found him stone-cold dead, lying pretty-as-you-please under the covers of his hospital bed, with a pool of vomit dripping from his mouth. The wife sued, claiming that the surgeon moved him to a regular diet too soon. The lost future wages, alone, amounted to six million dollars over the man's forty-year life expectancy. It was the kind of case that Aidan would have considered a challenge to try, but Boyce considered it unwinnable, and he had told Rampart so in no uncertain terms.

Rampart was the largest physician insurer in the Southeast. Its managers knew and trusted Aidan, but they had taken something of a chance in letting Boyce have this case. They had done so on Aidan's recommendation.

"Somehow I forgot to tell the clerk of court to switch my name out for Boyce's as the attorney of record," Aidan told Steny. "I've been getting all the mail, including a notice telling us that the case is set for trial today. I just forgot about it. I feel like such a dope, Steny—I can't tell you. Boyce got a call from the clerk that the trial starts in an hour, and now we've got to go get it done."

Boyce was awestruck by how smoothly and convincingly the lie was told. The realization that Aidan's capacity for deception exceeded even his own considerable skill in those dark arts was something Boyce found especially chilling, under the circumstances. Steny accepted the news with the aplomb of a big-league manager shrugging off the unexpected rout of a Cy Young pitcher in a winning season. When defeat comes to such people of all people, there is no point in recrimination.

Aidan's reputation would suffer, but not fatally. The doctor would scream and rant, but he would come to court. The expert witnesses would complain bitterly about their calendars being disrupted, but they would clear them. The grapevine at McFadden Brown would be alive with gossip about Aidan's "mistake" and eye-rolling over Boyce's bitter accusations against Honor, but none of that mattered. What *did* matter was that, at Aidan's command, a strike team of dozens of junior associates and law clerks who were the cream of the nation's newest crop of brilliant legal minds would now muster for duty. Together with Aidan they would work 'round the clock in a pizza-fueled frenzy—not merely to complete the tasks that were needed, but to complete them flawlessly. Aidan would win, in spite of everything.

That's the way it usually worked.

Suddenly, what had begun that morning as the greatest nightmare of Boyce's life was promising to become the most exhilarating challenge of Aidan's career. They were starting jury selection in an hour, and Steny had only one request: that Aidan take the lead.

When Aidan walked into Judge Dawkins' courtroom alongside Boyce and Honor an hour later, the faces of the opposing counsel revealed obvious surprise and concern. This was Boyce's case. They hadn't counted on facing Aidan Sharpe.

In his younger days, Aidan had built a career on being underestimated by older and more experienced lawyers. Now, no one ever underestimated him. Entire seminars were held for plaintiffs' lawyers around the state to dissect the cases he had won, seemingly against all odds. He had become a major legend in an up-and-coming southern town. He didn't know it, but he was about to throw it all to hell.

CHAPTER 6

"**A**ll rise!"

As the bailiff announced the judge's arrival in a slow drawl, everyone in the courtroom rose to attention.

"Oyez, oyez, oyez. The Superior Court for Wake County, North Carolina, is now in session for the dispatch of its business, the Honorable Shearn Dawkins presiding. God save this State and this Honorable Court. Be seated and come to order."

Judge Dawkins came striding into the courtroom from the door behind the bench. His shock of black hair, barely speckled with gray despite his sixty years, was slicked back with pomade in characteristic fashion. He was a vain man, proud of his good looks and sharp wit. The three crimson stripes specially sewn onto both arms of his black judicial robe distinguished him as a Harvard alumnus in a testament to his vanity. He did not merely take the bench; he made an entrance after the fashion of the justices of the Supreme Court, where he expected one day soon to be.

The *Adamson* case had a preferential setting, which meant there was no other trial on the judge's docket for the next month. Dawkins said nothing for several minutes as he flipped through the papers on his desk. Aidan looked distractedly at the file in front of him. He knew next to nothing about the case, but the client expected him to try it. A glimmer of excitement flickered in his mind. *This will be fun*, he thought. Fun like a game of Russian roulette—for the winner.

The judge finally spoke. "All right, counsel approach."

Once the lawyers were before him, he leaned across the bench and put his hand over the microphone, to keep what he was about to say off the record.

"Any talk of settlement?"

Boyce looked suddenly hopeful and edged forward to speak, but Aidan cut him off.

"No, your honor. We mediated this case back in April. The parties were several million dollars apart back then, and we don't expect that to change."

The judge greeted this news with noticeable disapproval.

"Very well. That's what the jury's here for. We'll tee this one up, then. Margaret, we'll need the jury pool here after one o'clock. About a hundred of them should do. In the meantime, you fellas get me the pretrial order, and I'll hear your motions."

The rest of the morning passed in the tedium of arguments on arcane points of law. It was like batting practice before the big game. Each side curried the judge's favor, hoping to tilt a future evidentiary ruling their way. But all that had nothing to do with what mattered, ultimately, which was the ability to look at twelve total strangers, know what they were thinking and why, and then use that knowledge to convince them to think something else entirely. That was Aidan's rare gift.

Over the lunch break, Boyce brought Aidan up to speed on the facts while their client and his wife waited anxiously in the courtroom for the jury pool to arrive.

Whenever Aidan paused long enough to think about what they were doing, what they were doing seemed surreal to him. Four million bucks and a doctor's career were on the line. The poor man had been paying malpractice premiums in the hundreds of thousands of dollars for years, waiting for the day when his insurance and his lawyer would carry him safely through a crisis like this one. All that time, he probably never imagined that his lead counsel would be learning the facts of his case for the first time over a barbeque plate at lunch, an hour before the jury arrived.

"The dead guy's in the hospital for a simple gallbladder operation," Boyce began, "but he doesn't come out of it too smoothly. He's got several days of fever, and his white blood count's going up."

"Who's the dead guy?" Aidan asked.

"His name was Nate Woolard."

"Infection?" Aidan continued, trying to get the basic facts.

"Nothing comes through on the cultures, so they continue to monitor him. Meanwhile, he's in a hospital bed flat on his back for four days, and he's not keeping any food down. Nothing's moving in his bowels. So they figure out he's got an ileus. You know what that is, right?"

"An ileus, right, right," Aidan responded. He had learned what an ileus was only a week ago, in a deposition in another case, but he didn't see any need for Boyce to know that.

"*Peristalsis*," Boyce continued, "is the word doctors give to the normal, involuntary movement of stool through the large and small intestine. It works on its own—that is, until it doesn't. And when it quits working, that's an ileus. Doctors don't really know what causes it, and they don't really know what fixes it, and that's where the debate comes in."

"Right, I understand," Aidan added.

"The plaintiff's experts say our guy should have fed this man a diet of clear liquids and nothing else until he started to get loose stools. Our guy doesn't do that. It's been four days, his patient is starving, he's starting to hear normal bowel sounds, and his training tells him it's time to try him on soft starches like cereals, banana, toast, and rice."

"Where did our guy train?" Aidan wondered aloud. It seemed like an easy question.

"That's a little harder to sell," Boyce answered, anxiously. "He's an American who trained to be a pediatrician in Guadalajara during the Vietnam War, back when everyone was trying to get into medical school."

"I thought he was an internist?"

"He is," Boyce said. "He didn't do so well with kids. There was an allegation of abuse involving a twelve-year-old girl. Nothing proven, nothing admitted, but in a settlement with the medical board he agreed to go into another field. So, he took a quickie residency in internal medicine and changed specialties."

"Is that coming in?" Aidan asked.

"I'm afraid so—no way to keep it out."

"No problem," Aidan said—lying spectacularly now, even by his own standards. "A hippie draft dodger who went to Guadalajara, smoked a lot of weed, abused a little girl, washed out of pediatrics, and became an internist through correspondence classes. We can sell that."

Then, in a sudden afterthought, Aidan asked with a dismissive but worried laugh, "He's never lost his license, has he?"

"That's another little hard part," Boyce said, apologetically. "He was prescribing a lot of pain meds and not keeping good records of who got how much of what. There were some controlled drugs unaccounted for, some pill counts were off, and some of his patients were taking some pretty heavy stuff for too long. That's a no-no with the DEA, and he got busted for it. The board took away his license for six months, but he was back in good standing when he saw Woolard."

"And that's coming in, too?"

"Like a rocket."

Boyce softened and changed the subject. "Don't you think we can get this case settled? Under the circumstances, I think we should recommend that Rampart pay the policy limit."

"What's that?"

"Four million."

Aidan recoiled at the number. "Like hell! If that snake Moriarity wants seven figures, he's going to have to fight me for it."

Boyce's spirits fell. He couldn't believe they were about to go through with this train wreck.

"Hello, Aidan." The voice was thin and cold and right behind Aidan's shoulders. Two hands slapped down on his back. Jim Moriarity, one of the old dogs of the plaintiff's bar, didn't usually show up for pretrial matters. Boyce wondered what he was doing there.

"Hello, Jim," Aidan said, and turned sideways toward Boyce. "You know my partner, Boyce Stannard."

The men shook hands. Moriarity certainly knew Boyce, but Boyce wasn't his concern. He'd gotten word that morning that Aidan Sharpe had shown up for trial. Moriarity's younger partner was no match for Aidan. Moriarity had come to back him up until the jury came in. He and Judge Dawkins had known each other since law school. That would count for something.

Judge Dawkins had for the most part followed a straight and narrow path on the bench for the past thirty years. Moriarity had burned a twisted path through a small fortune, bankruptcy, three wives and as many mistresses, but somehow he had clawed his way back to the top of the heap. By now he must have been worth twenty, maybe thirty million, Aidan guessed. But he almost never tried a case. His money came mostly from settlements.

After exchanging the usual pleasantries with Moriarity—all of them as sincere and heartfelt as a boxer's handshake before a fight—Boyce and Aidan walked back to the courthouse to get ready for jury selection.

When the jury pool started filing into the courtroom and taking their seats in the gallery, Aidan got that familiar feeling of exhilaration and confidence. When it came to juries, there was no one better at the game. This was his turf. This was where he belonged. Even coming in cold, Aidan Sharpe was the most dangerous man in the room. His every instinct and intuition, honed from a quarter century before the bar, was now loaded in the breach and ready to fire. Not an objection would be missed, not a weakness left unexposed, not an emotion left unexploited to his client's advantage. Aidan was a one-man wrecking crew, and before Moriarity knew what hit him, his case would be a worthless pile of rubble.

From the hundred people in the venire available to be selected as jurors, the clerk called the first twelve names at random. One by one, citizens young and old, black, white, and Latino, some dressed in ties and others in blue jeans, lumbered into the jury box. Aidan knew none of them. Then came the eighth juror.

"Emily Wood," the clerk announced.

Aidan felt a sudden rush of blood to his chest. His heart began to pound. He quickly started to turn in his chair toward the back of the courtroom, where he could hear someone standing up and gathering a purse, but he stopped himself. *Emily Wood.* He knew the name.

When the woman crossed the front of the courtroom and took her seat in the box, Aidan waited until her eyes were past him, then looked at her carefully. She was tall, about five feet eight inches, with thick and straight, shoulder-length brown hair that shimmered in the fluorescent light. She wore a khaki skirt that rose just above the knee, low heels, and a white silk blouse that was open at the neck. The view to the eighth seat in the jury box was not obstructed by the railing. When she sat down, her skirt pulled up tightly around her thighs to reveal the softly tanned skin of her long legs. With a silk scarf below her collar, knotted on one side, she was not too buxom or too beautiful. She looked every inch the respectable, country club housewife. She was pretending hard not to notice Aidan, but in fact he was the only thing she had noticed for the past twenty minutes. She could never forget him.

Emily Wood was a legal secretary. She had once worked for another firm in the office tower where McFadden Brown's offices were located. Six years ago, Aidan walked into the private dinner club on the top floor for a drink and to unwind after work, before heading home. He found Emily sitting at the bar, drinking a martini—her third.

Aidan sat down next to her and broke the ice. She was easy to talk to, and she felt the same about him. She was there for a meeting with her boss, who was late, and though she never quite said so, it became apparent that she was in some sort of trouble with him. As she fumbled for a cigarette and lighter in her purse, Aidan could see her hand shake. He put his hand on hers with all the gentleness he could muster, and for reasons he didn't know or understand, told her things would be all right. She began to cry—just a little, and not for long. Aidan picked up a napkin on the bar and patted her cheek. He called the bartender for her tab and asked the *maître d'* to find them a booth in the corner.

She told him her story, to which he listened with an intense, genuine concern that surprised and revived her. She was thirty-six. Married once, after her first year of college, to a boy back home in a small town in northern California. It lasted only a year—Aidan didn't ask why—but that was sixteen years ago. She'd moved around, in and out of various jobs, mostly as a secretary. She'd been with the law firm of Waller and Aiken for three years then.

"Things aren't working out," she said after the fourth martini.

Emily's boss was Neil Ascyue, an up-and-coming securities lawyer. Aidan knew him by reputation to be a rich smartass. The wunderkind of his Harvard Law School class, he had just devoured his tenth secretary in as many months when he hired Emily. Initially, they worked well together, and she loved the job. He was important and had a lot of energy, and he took her with him to lavish lunches with big clients. That was flattering and exciting to a small-town girl. Neil made partner at twenty-nine and by thirty-two had laid claim to more top-dollar clients than any of the senior partners in his firm. He was billing at one thousand dollars an hour and turning away business. He rode to and from work in a limousine. It was parked in front of their building by seven, every morning, and was still there when Aidan left every night. Aidan heard that he now ruled the roost at Waller and Aiken, and that was no mean roost to rule.

It wasn't her job that Emily was afraid of losing. It

was something else. She was not a woman merely exasperated with her boss, as every lawyer's secretary surely is. There was fear in her eyes. Neil Ascyue had done something to put it there, and it spoke of a threat more urgent and physical than hypothetical and emotional. When he walked up to their table, Aidan could sense it.

"Neil Ascyue," he said, extending his hand.

"Aidan Sharpe."

"I've heard a lot about you."

"Likewise."

Neil never took his eyes off Emily. She tried to look anywhere but at him.

Neil carried on a polite conversation with Aidan while circling behind Emily's chair. Then he bent down and, half-whispering, suggested that Emily join him at another table. She fidgeted. "I . . . I don't know, Neil. I'm awfully tired. Do you think we could talk another time?"

Neil's hand descended to the table. Grasping Emily's arm as if to help her up, he tugged at her to go with him. She resisted with worried laughter, hoping to distract anyone who might be watching from the scene he was about to make.

Aidan quickly reached across the table and put his hand firmly on Ascyue's.

"It's really not time to go yet, is it?"

Ascyue instantly recoiled, snapping his hand backwards and knocking over a glass of red wine into Aidan's lap. There was a collective gasp from the surrounding tables, and a hush fell over the bar.

All eyes were on their table. Aidan stood up, surprised by the cold wetness of the wine in his trousers, and for several seconds the two men stood silently above Emily. Finally, Aidan spoke.

"I have some bad news for you, Neil. Whatever

business you've got with Emily is over. She's just taken a job with McFadden Brown for twice the pay and half the bullshit. It's time for you to leave."

There wasn't any question what Neil would do. He was clearly outmatched and not used to people speaking to him so directly. He wasn't a trial lawyer. Verbal sparring was not his forte. He was a backroom mover, a snake in the tall grass. He dealt in manipulation, not persuasion. And there was no room to maneuver at the moment.

"Very well," Neil began, recovering his composure. "I seem to have forgotten my manners. I'm very sorry to have disturbed your evening. Aidan, please send my secretary the bill for that suit, and—"

"That won't be necessary," Aidan interrupted.

And with that, Ascyue was gone.

Emily spoke. "Aidan, I want to thank you and apologize—"

"There's no need. I know a horse's ass when I see one, and you should too."

She nodded appreciatively. She knew he was right. Neil was a jerk. She had known that a long time. She had let him hurt her, though she could no longer recall the reason why. She felt suddenly safe and free.

Aidan sat down next to her in the booth. "I meant what I said and I said what I meant. Twice whatever he was paying you is what we'll pay you. I have an intuition about you, and my intuition has made me a wealthy man. You call my paralegal Honor at my office on Monday. Here's my card. She'll have everything you need. Welcome aboard, and don't worry about a thing. The sun will rise, Emily."

"I . . . I can't thank you enough. I'm just, just . . ." She started stammering, and tears filled the corners of her eyes. Aidan put his arm around her, and she tucked her face into his chest and began to sob. Her body eased as he drew her in.

"Don't worry. Let me take you home." Aidan raised his hand for the check. A waiter bolted from the place where he had been standing nearby, transfixed by all that had happened.

On the street below the Carolina Bank Tower, Aidan stood awkwardly for a moment, not knowing what to say. Emily was calm and spoke softly. "Come to my place, why don't you. It's just over in Five Points. I can take care of that stain for you—you need to do something before it sets."

Aidan was usually very good at thinking on his feet. This was a moment when that skill might have served him better. He knew the story. He was no idiot. She was an attractive, single, and vulnerable woman, and he had just rescued her from the town bully. He had also just changed her life with a new job and a new beginning. She wasn't just offering him laundry service. He was a married man wearing a wedding ring. He didn't need subtitles to understand what was about to happen. If he were twenty-nine and still single, this sort of thing would have been as easy as breathing. At thirty-nine, he could barely speak.

The elevator brought them to the parking garage— the place where they would choose either to go their separate ways or leave together. Emily was by then quietly in charge. The hint of a smile gathered at the corners of her mouth. Her slim figure was even more attractive now that Aidan could see it in full form, with her standing willingly before him.

"Well, about the pants. I haven't a clue what to do about red wine stains, but if you do, I'll take you up on the offer. Besides, it would be nice to get to know you somewhere outside of a bar, now that we're going to be working together."

As he said these words, Aidan felt a surge of

adrenaline and sexual energy deep in his gut. *So this is what betrayal feels like*, he thought. It was new to him.

He hadn't been with another woman since he had married Jocelyn, ten years ago. As he helped Emily into his car, he felt as if he were watching himself in a movie. It seemed too surreal. Emily sensed this, somehow. She reached across the seat and gently put her hand in his. *Who was this woman*, he wondered, who only moments ago had been sitting terrified and trembling like a cornered quail, and who now was reassuring him like a courtesan guiding a knave.

Emily's small house was surprisingly elegant—a benefit, no doubt, of her former employment. The entrance was almost completely obscured by a lush garden. English ivy encircled the arch above the door. An iron fence was barely visible beneath an entanglement of bougainvillea that bloomed in contrasting white and red flowers. Aidan stopped to notice them as he followed Emily down the walkway.

"The red grow faster than the white," she said, looking back at Aidan. "If I'm not careful, they'll take over, but I try to clip the red ones to give the white ones a chance."

"They're beautiful," Aidan answered, simultaneously transfixed and bewildered by the splendor in the middle of the otherwise ordinary, inner-city neighborhood. "What are these?"

"Day lilies, and these are black-eyed Susans that haven't yet bloomed. They'll grow almost three feet tall when they do. These are petunias, and over here are marigolds, violets, and here, these are pansies."

"How do you keep them all so alive and well?" Aidan asked.

"Love—water and love. That's all any of us needs, don't you think?"

Aidan smiled. "And how about these?" he said,

pointing to a row of brightly pink-colored, small flowers.

"Bachelor's buttons—speaking of which, we need to get you out of yours."

He avoided correcting her reference to him as a bachelor, which he suspected was more of a polite delusion than an error on her part. She took Aidan's hand again. His was white and cold. Hers was blush with color and warm. He felt again the surge of blood race from his head to his gut. *This is it*, he thought. He was entering the home of a strange woman who had made no secret of her attraction to him. He hadn't gotten this excited holding hands since the sixth grade.

Her heels tapped a hollow sound on the hardwood floors of the foyer. The décor was strangely clubby and masculine. She set her keys down and noticed him looking around the room.

"This was *his* place," she said, "before the divorce."

She slipped out of her jacket and laid it neatly across the back of a high stool, and then, in one deft motion, kneeled directly in front him. Her fingers worked calmly to untie and withdraw the end of his belt from the loops of his trousers. She spoke casually as she did this, as if there was nothing even remotely sexual about a woman removing a strange man's pants.

"I've got some soda water. I can blot these down and then steam them. I don't have a steamer, but steam from a hot shower should do the same. It will keep the wine from soaking in and ruining a good pair of pants. I can't thank you enough for what you did for me back there—you know, sticking up for me that way."

She reached up with both hands and took his, hanging at his side.

"It was gallant of you."

Her manner reminded Aidan of a school nurse administering a team physical, and his closely resembled that of a twelve-year-old boy undergoing one for the first time. Before he knew it, his trousers were down at his ankles and she was prompting him to step out of them. He felt like a geek in knee-high black socks, white boxer shorts, and dress shoes.

Once his trousers were off, a great blot of red was revealed on the front of his shorts. Emily paused and looked up at him for the first time, as if sensing that even she needed special permission for what she was about to do.

"Well, what a mess Neil made. Unless you're bashful, I might as well get these while I'm at it. It won't take me long to wash them."

Unless you're *bashful*, she said. Aidan thought about this for a moment. It was as much a challenge as a question. He had been neatly maneuvered into position by a woman with skills clearly superior to his own. His defeat was absolute. His pride would let him express only the utmost, false indifference to whatever she cared to do or not do with his shorts, and she knew it.

What he had clearly assumed she might do next, she didn't do. It seemed she had decided that he would either serve first or forfeit the match. She stood up with his boxer shorts hanging from her hand and, without so much as a curious glance or a knowing smile, began to walk matter of factly toward the laundry room.

Aidan again felt his blood rush. He knew that an opportunity was about to pass him by. A constabulary of teachers, priests, and nuns had taught him the importance of letting girls choose—of being the interested but reluctant gentleman, the giver of corsages, the opener of doors, and the one who waits for the girl to make the first move or clearly announce her willingness to be moved upon. These were the rules of engagement Aidan had honored all his life, and he would now break them.

Before Emily was just out of his reach, he extended his hand and slipped his fingers behind her elbow. Feeling his grasp, she stopped without turning at first, then tilted her head back toward him. Her face bore an expression of annoyance or surprise—he couldn't be sure which. He knew only that if he had just made the wrong move, it would be the last move.

He studied her intently. An hour ago a man had grasped the same arm and made her shudder with revulsion. What Aidan had just done was no less aggressive, and likely more threatening in the long run, but she did not withdraw from him. He felt her arm and her whole body relax, and her momentarily startled expression gave way to a smile of willingness and calm. Turning her shoulders toward him and keeping her eyes fixed on his, she slid her warm fingers slowly and smoothly around his naked waist, sending bolts of nervous energy to his groin. Neither of them spoke. He brought his lips close to hers, noticing for the first time that her eyes were a soft brown. She studied his face carefully for a moment, searching for any hesitation or looming regret. Finding none, she pulled his body tightly against hers, kissing him softly, then deeply. Together they descended as one onto the floor of the house in the shade of the garden. In the silence of that secret place, while night fell softly around them, each took from the other something that was forbidden— and something neither had imagined when the sun rose that morning. It was a sin that would change their worlds forever.

He telephoned her every day afterward for three weeks. She never took his call and didn't take the job at McFadden Brown. Aidan assumed that she'd had a change of heart, and he was resigned to the probability that he'd never see her again. As a result, he knew nothing of Neil Ascyue's arrival at her doorstep in a drunken rage later that night, or her bruised and broken jaw, or the pregnancy, or the death of one twin, Aaron, shortly after birth, and the adoption of the other, Canter, by a wealthy family in New York. He did not know she despised herself for what she began that night, and for how it ended. He would never know these things because she would never tell him. If she did, he might ask questions, demand answers, make plans, and do the things that vain and foolish men do. This she could not abide. She would not let him reopen her wound and lay bare her scars.

Aidan's marriage, which had been slowly bleeding for several years when he met Emily, died soon thereafter of natural causes. After six months, he stopped thinking about the one-night stand with the woman in the garden house, but he never really sorted it out in his mind. It remained a mystery and a beautiful illusion of his past, until his past walked into a courtroom in Raleigh.

Judge Dawkins began to address the jury pool. "Good morning, ladies and gentlemen. I am Judge Shearn Dawkins. You have been called as jurors in a case to be tried in this courtroom. This is a civil matter, not a criminal case. This is a dispute about allegations of medical malpractice. The plaintiff is seeking money damages. If selected as jurors, you will be asked to listen to the evidence and render an impartial verdict as to the facts in dispute."

Aidan had heard the speech a hundred times. It flowed over him inaudibly now, like so much elevator music.

"Now, the first thing I need to know," the judge continued, "is whether any of you know any of the parties in this case or any of the lawyers."

Aidan looked at Emily even as he was screaming at

himself not to. She caught his glance and quickly looked away.

"I will ask the lawyers and the parties to stand as I announce their names."

When the judge called out Aidan's name, he got only halfway out of his chair and stood in a stooped posture. Bobbing his head and smiling sheepishly while glancing left to right and back again, he looked like a vaudeville minstrel hurriedly taking a bow before leaving the stage. His eyes panned across the two aisles full of jurors, making sure to keep his gaze above their faces so that he did not actually look at anyone—especially not at Emily.

"Does anyone here know Aidan Sharpe or his partner Boyce Stannard, with the law firm of McFadden Brown—the attorneys for the defendant?"

There was a long pause. In the corner of his eye, he could see Emily shift in her seat, and he thought he could even feel her palms begin to sweat. Boyce did not know about Emily. No one at McFadden Brown knew. No one knew anything about that night but the two of them. Even to Aidan it seemed like a dream.

As the judge paused for anyone who wanted to speak, Aidan remained half-standing so that the jury could get a good look at him. His eyes at last could not resist coming to rest on Emily. She was looking directly at him, but she uttered not one word. It was Aidan's duty, as an officer of the court, to inform the judge that he knew this juror whether she mentioned it or not. It was sanctionable not to. But if he did that, the judge would ask questions—questions that would lead to answers inconvenient for both of them.

Aidan did not wish to preserve his own dignity by defiling Emily's or betray her trust by revealing an indiscretion that was partly of his making. But there was another reason not to speak. He dared not utter it, but it was there. It was driving him on. He couldn't let it go.

Aidan took his seat but continued to stare at Emily. He was more confident now. He decided he needed to get a good look at her face, and what he was seeing was important. It was the fact, now obvious to him, that she did not *hate* him. Whatever her reasons had been for running from him, hatred at least did not appear to be one of them. As he watched her look back at him, he saw the tension in her face finally give way to a sad and knowing smile. In that moment he saw an opportunity that had nothing to do with love or hate or forgiveness. It had to do with *winning*.

"Very well, then," the judge said, hearing no objections and seeing no hands raised. "We'll hear questions for the panel first from counsel for the plaintiff. Proceed."

The first twelve candidates were seated in the jury box. Emily was the eighth. She took a seat in the front row. The plaintiff's attorneys were allowed to examine these twelve, excuse any candidates who demonstrated good cause why they should not be asked to serve, and peremptorily dismiss up to eight others for whatever reasons, prejudices, or superstitions the attorneys desired. By four o'clock that afternoon, Moriarity had made four peremptory strikes and had announced that he was satisfied with the remaining eight. Emily was among the group that remained. She was certain now to be on the jury unless Aidan excused her—which he knew he still might have to do.

Emily was an ex-lover, Aidan reminded himself. He had been burned by enough berserk ex-lovers to know not to underestimate one. But unseemly as the thought was to him—so much, in fact, that his conscious mind refused to acknowledge he was even thinking it—Aidan knew if she still felt any affection for him, she could be his ace in the hole. On the other hand, if she harbored some lingering resentment or regret—which might be exactly the reason why she had never returned his calls—she could be the nail in his coffin. His instincts (or perhaps his insecurities) told him it was more likely the latter, but it would be impossible to know either without talking to her. The obvious problem was that talking to her was the one thing he was forbidden to do. Jurors were off-limits to the parties and their lawyers, lest any unauthorized contact result in some secret advantage or unchecked influence, which is exactly what Aidan had in mind. Besides, any open conversation in the presence of the judge, and Moriarity would reveal that Aidan and Emily had lied by their silence in failing to acknowledge that they *knew* each other in the biblical as well as the legal sense of the word. And yet, for some reason not entirely clear to him, Aidan was unwilling to let this opportunity pass. He thought that surely it had been placed in front of him, as it were, by fate.

But fate is a fickle master whose will cannot be foretold and obeyed, only feared and awaited. Fear now had Aidan in its icy grip. Aidan was, for the first time in his career, not merely aware that he could lose a case, but truly frightened that he might.

Before discharging the jury pool to go home for the night, the judge gave them the standard warning not to have any contact with any of the parties or their lawyers, not to search for any news about the case on the Internet, in the newspapers, or on TV, and to report to the bailiff any even inadvertent violations of those instructions. They were to return at 9:30 in the morning.

All rose to hear the invocation of recess. The judge left the bench, and everyone in the gallery, and the jury box began shuffling toward the doors in the back of the courtroom.

Aidan looked over his shoulder to watch Emily step down from her seat, gather her coat, and leave.

"Aidan, we need to talk to the client about settlement," Boyce said. Aidan wasn't paying attention. He was looking to see whether Emily took the elevator or the stairs. He bolted from the table and opened the swinging gate at the bar. Moriarity's lawyers still milled around the courtroom. One of them noticed Aidan leave in a rush. He motioned to a somber-looking man in a dark suit in the back of the courtroom, and the man discreetly followed Aidan out.

The wait for the elevators would be a good twenty minutes at this time of day. Emily was heading for the stairwell instead, beneath an exit sign at the other end of the hall. Aidan raced to catch up. The fire door opened and slammed behind her, then opened again fifteen seconds later, as Aidan followed. They were the only ones in the stairwell. She heard someone on the steps above her, looked up at him, and stopped.

He called her name softly and walked down another flight of stairs to stand next to her. Her face showed none of the confidence he had seen in the garden house or the stoicism she had displayed in the courtroom. She stiffened for an instant, then collapsed into his arms and began to weep. He nestled her head in his chest and held her close.

"I couldn't call you, Aidan. It was—it was just awful."

The tears were coming more quickly than her words.

He brushed her hair and comforted her gently until the crying stopped. Then he pulled her face and tilted it up toward him, cupped in his hands. Looking into her eyes, he asked a question that rolled unexpectedly off his lips before he realized he intended to ask it.

"Can you forgive me?"

She seemed startled by the question, as if she had

been expecting him to say something else entirely. After a long pause, she gathered herself and answered.

"You don't need my forgiveness, Aidan. We did something foolish and stupid but completely human. There's no helping it."

Emily's words came to him like an elixir. He hadn't realized until that moment that all he really wanted—the reason he had called her every day for two weeks, and the reason for his sadness when she hadn't called back—was absolution. Now he had it. He breathed deeply, as if for the first time in years, as she lingered in his embrace. That was the affirmation he needed. They were friends, not foes. There was no need to say anything more. He bent down and gently kissed her on the forehead and said goodbye. She watched him ascend the stairs until he was out of view. He could not see the look of bewilderment on her face or recognize his own grievous miscalculation in that moment.

Boyce was packing up boxes of depositions and exhibits to take back to the office that night to review for the next day. Ordinarily that kind of work would have been done months before trial, but this was catch-up time. Aidan took the depositions of the plaintiff's two lead experts and a copy of the pleadings and correspondence files, including all of the evaluations and reports that had been sent to the client.

"I'll be up all night reviewing this stuff, Boyce. Call me if you need anything. It doesn't matter how late."

"Sure," Boyce said. "I'll be doing the same. You're giving the opening statement, right?"

"Absolutely," said Aidan, with trademark confidence.

Aidan would give the opening statement, and it would be a *stem-winder*. It would be the beginning of victory. Aidan would have the jury's rapt attention, and he would draw them into a world through which they would see the evidence in a light that led to forgiveness and acceptance of the defendant doctor. They would hear Aidan and agree with him. He would sound like one of them. He would tell them their thoughts and affirm them, then change them slowly, imperceptibly—the way small changes in the heading of a ship at sea can alter its landfall by hundreds of miles. They would be led in the direction Aidan wanted them to go, although they would believe they were sailing a heading of their own choosing. It was what he lived for. Yet should he fail, Emily would be his guarantee. A verdict is not a verdict unless it is unanimous. Anything less than a unanimous vote would mean a mistrial. In that event, the case wouldn't be reset for trial for months—maybe more than a year—and that would give Aidan more than enough time to prepare. Emily was the one and only vote he needed to hang the jury, and he was certain she'd never betray him. It was a perfect plan.

Aidan opened the door of the refrigerator in his apartment to find a leftover sandwich of uncertain age. Taking it and a diet soda, he trundled into his bedroom office, prepared for the long night ahead. He was disciplined under pressure and wasted no time getting into the files.

He soon became engrossed in the facts of the case. Theories and points for cross-examination of the other side's experts came to him in quick bursts. A theme of the trial took shape in his brain. They could *win this thing*, he thought. They could win it big and shock the world. It was going to be fun.

CHAPTER 7

Aidan met Boyce at the office early the next morning. Neither of them had been to bed, and both were running on coffee and adrenaline.

"You ready?" Boyce said, sticking his head just inside Aidan's door.

"Sure, just give me a minute to get this tie on."

Boyce nodded and slumped down into the red leather sofa that sat in front of the long wall across from the windows of Aidan's office, twenty-one stories above downtown. Aidan stood in the early morning light, fixing his tie in front of a mirror that bore the image of his alma mater.

Boyce stared out the windows into the distance, across the tops of the green-and-gold tree carpet that colored the suburbs surrounding the city. He could see the Earth curve downward toward the coastal plains leading to the sea, 150 miles distant. Aidan's office was larger than most, and the windows let in a glaring morning sun. He kept the blinds drawn most of the time, but the cleaning staff had left them open last night. Boyce's eyes drifted around the walls and to the desk and end table. They held various mementos of Aidan's career: membership plaques for a half-dozen "best lawyer" societies, bar association awards, and letters of commendation. There was a photograph of Aidan standing with Justice Roy Angier, a tall, gray-haired Brahmin who had held a seat on the North

Carolina Supreme Court for nearly thirty years. Aidan had clerked for him after graduating from law school.

When it came time to go, Aidan, Boyce, Honor, and a half-dozen associates strode down the halls of McFadden Brown. They walked through the reception area and over the expansive Persian rug, then out to the elevator landing, which was trimmed in dark mahogany and black marble. The large, brass letters of the firm name, fixed high above the door, were meant to remind all who passed those portals of the firm's invincibility and permanence. It was the most garish of lies.

Boyce and Aidan entered the courtroom with their entourage—a conga line of fresh-faced young lawyers each carrying a stack of boxes full of documents. "It's amazing the motivation that a four-hundred-dollar-an-hour client can inspire," Boyce quipped.

Aidan saw the judge was not yet on the bench. That wasn't unusual—it wasn't yet nine o'clock. The bailiff saw them come in, stiffened noticeably, then left the courtroom in the direction of the judge's chambers.

Aidan glanced quickly sideways as he passed the same tall man in a black suit who had stood beside the courtroom door the day before, at the end of jury selection. He was wearing the same clothes. He looked at Aidan with a fierce intensity that seemed rather out of place. It was just another jury trial, for God's sake, Aidan thought.

As he set his briefcase down on the counsel table, Aidan sensed a peculiar silence in the room. All four of Moriarity's lawyers had their jackets on, though court was not due to begin for another hour. None of them was writing anything. Normally they would be preparing notes for jury selection. No paralegals were milling about and queuing up exhibits. They were all doing and saying nothing.

"Hey, fellas." Aidan offered a tentative greeting in the opposing trial team's direction. Boyce felt uneasy too, and looked at Aidan for some intuition about what was up. The young associates on the plaintiff's team, all of whom looked terrified, offered a mumbled reply that was interrupted by the shrill voice of the bailiff. He had reentered the courtroom just ahead of the judge.

"All rise. Oyez, oyez, oyez. The Superior Court of Wake County is now open and sitting for the dispatch of its business. The Honorable Shearn Dawkins, presiding. God save this state and this honorable court. Be seated and come to order."

"Amen!" came a loud, familiar voice from near the judge's chamber, and Aidan looked in that direction. Standing in the doorway was his old boss Justice Angier, who had come as a spectator. It was unusual to see an appellate judge in the trial division, and especially so since the Supreme Court was in session. Aidan was due there later in the week for oral arguments in another case, although that would now have to be postponed because of the *Adamson* trial. He smiled in Justice Angier's direction but received only a solemn, steady gaze in return.

It was an odd way to start the first day of trial, Aidan thought, but that didn't occupy his thoughts very long. After everyone was seated, Aidan pulled the outline of his jury examination and opening statement out of his briefcase along with various notepads, pens, and markers and sorted them on the table. He noticed that no one else was doing the same.

Judge Dawkins spoke from the bench.

"Before I open court and impanel the jury, do counsel need to be heard?"

James Moriarity rose to his feet. Before he could say more than, "Yes, your honor. We have a motion—" he was interrupted by the judge.

"Sit down, Moriarity! I have your goddamn motion."

Judge Dawkins' voice boomed. Something was not right, but Aidan didn't have a clue what it could be. The judge then leaned forward in his chair. He was staring at Aidan. Aidan had seen Shearn Dawkins plenty mad, over the years, but he had never seen him like this.

Aidan and Boyce looked at each other, searching for some insight. Aidan then turned to look at Honor. Her mouth was hanging slightly open in surprise.

As weird as everything was starting to get, Aidan was still calm. This was his domain. There were rules that applied here, and Aidan knew how to use them to his advantage better than anyone. Whatever was about to make Judge Dawkins explode, Aidan was confident he could defuse it. He stood up.

"Good morning, Your Honor."

"Good morning, Mr. Sharpe."

Score one for the home team, Boyce thought.

"I'm sure you know my co-counsel, Boyce Stannard."

Boyce rocketed to his feet. Aidan continued to change the subject and the tone with which the judge had begun the day. It was going to be another masterful misdirection.

"May I also introduce our lead paralegal for the trial, Ms. Honor Beckett? I'm sure it's just an oversight," Aidan continued, "but I'm afraid we were not given a copy of whatever motion Mr. Moriarity was just referring—"

"And you won't get one, either, Mr. Sharpe—not until you answer my question. I'll ask you again: Is there anything you need to bring to the attention of the Court before we impanel the jury?"

Aidan whitened, noticeably, and looked sideways at Boyce, who slowly sat down. It was clear this was

Aidan's show now. It was also clear that the judge desperately wanted him to reveal something that he could not. He now sensed what that was. He felt his heart race. In the pit of his stomach, a bonfire erupted. There was nothing cool or collected, inside or outside, about him now.

A long minute elapsed with Aidan still standing there, speechless. He could feel a lightheadedness come over him, as he raced through the algorithm of everything that might possibly be about to happen. Whatever it was had something to do with Emily—of this he was nearly certain. It could be something minor, he thought— something trivial—and he would only make it worse— perhaps needlessly much, much worse—by revealing his relationship with her.

Still not answering the judge, Aidan glanced at his client. The doctor looked utterly stricken and was whispering noisily to Boyce. Time seemed to stop. It would be a huge gamble to say nothing, but no less a gamble to admit, in open court, that he had knowingly failed to disclose that he knew a juror. If confronted, he might yet credibly deny that he knew her, and if not, he would still be better off feigning forgetfulness and begging forgiveness than admitting to a willful omission.

By the time he sensed he could wait no longer, he had made his decision. He would let it all ride.

"I beg the Court's pardon, but I have nothing to say on behalf of the defense before we resume jury selection and begin opening statements. I am at the Court's pleasure."

Judge Dawkins looked at Aidan, then looked across the courtroom at Justice Angier, then down at the bench in front of him. His head dropped as though he had taken a blow from behind. After a few minutes, he finally spoke.

"I'll see all counsel in chambers."

Boyce began gathering pads of paper and a pen, but Aidan took nothing with him. Aidan paused briefly at Moriarity's table to let the plaintiff's team go first. Instead, Moriarity dropped his hand, open palmed, in a gesture for Aidan to walk ahead, as if Aidan were preceding him to the gallows. Moriarity was confident—with good reason—that he didn't need to lead on the issue that was about to be addressed.

Walking into the judge's chambers, Aidan was struck by the television in the corner, turned on, its blue screen shimmering. He didn't take Judge Dawkins for a daytime TV man. "Hello, your honor," Aidan said, as he saw Justice Angier again, now standing with his back to the rows of books on the library shelves in Judge Dawkins' office. Justice Angier at first did not speak. He looked down, and in a moment of awkwardness that revealed he was uncertain of what to say—a rarity for the man Aidan knew—murmured his reply.

"Hello, Aidan."

Judge Dawkins got right to the heart of the matter.

"Aidan, I've known you for as long as you've been in practice. You're in trouble, son."

A swarm of tingling nerves flew up Aidan's back and neck. He could feel his hair stand on end.

Judge Dawkins continued.

"Jim's investigator saw you leave the courtroom yesterday, and saw you make contact with a juror. You just stop me when you've heard enough."

Aidan stood, speechless. His eyes drifted toward Boyce, who was sidling to the outer edge of the room. Boyce thought the judge had called them in to start twisting arms for a settlement. Now he just wanted to get out of the line of fire.

"Your honor, I don't know—" Boyce began.

"Save your breath, Mr. Stannard," the judge interrupted. "I'm aware that you have no involvement in this, but I'm afraid it's going to affect your client and probably your firm."

The judge paused a moment as he looked back at Aidan, who was still stone-faced, like a boy in school who knows he is about be expelled but is unwilling to give the principal the satisfaction of knowing he cares.

"Play the security loop, Paul," the judge finally said.

Paul Jameson was Jim Moriarity's investigator, case runner, and general doer-of-dirty-deeds. He emerged from the corner behind the television, where he'd been standing unseen until now. He pressed the button on a remote control, and the shimmering blue screen on the television transformed to a grainy, black-and-white image.

The video showed Aidan embracing Emily in the stairwell for several minutes. Some conversation between them could be heard but not understood. If anyone wasn't sure that Aidan was tampering with the jury, the juror badge clipped to Emily's blouse removed all doubt.

"Mr. Jameson saw you leave the courtroom and follow this juror—I think you know who I'm talking about," Judge Dawkins said. The video then replayed the kiss. It was excruciating to watch.

Looking at Emily on tape, Aidan realized that she was not as engaged in their encounter as he thought she had been. Her eyes were open and staring blankly into the camera as he held her.

"Aidan?" Judge Dawkins called, startling him.

The tape had long since stopped and was frozen on the frame where he told Emily goodbye, as she watched him walk up the stairwell.

Aidan looked at the judge, still unable to speak, and then at Boyce, who glared at him with a seething, unspoken intensity.

Judge Dawkins grew impatient.

"I must tell you, Mr. Sharpe," he began. Aidan knew by the judge's sudden formality that the worst was about to come. "We met with Miss Emily Wood this morning, before you got here. She told us the story of your involvement with each other. Your failure to inform the court of that involvement with her is a serious ethical violation. You know that. That alone would have been grounds for a mistrial and sanctions. But your willful contact with a seated juror during a pending trial is grounds for disbarment. You know that as well. Had you made any effort to reveal those errors to me a moment ago in the courtroom, I might have considered a lesser punishment. You missed that opportunity, son, and I can't tell you how sorry I am—and how sorry Justice Angier is—that you did."

The judge took a deep breath.

Boyce looked at the judge now with a pleading, desperate expression. "I'm declaring a mistrial, and I'm referring your conduct to the state bar for action against your license, Aidan."

The last five minutes had been a blur. For the first time in his legal career, Aidan had absolutely nothing to say. There was no defense. He knew what he had done, and he knew it was wrong. He had made a calculated gamble and lost. There was no honor in it—only abject, total defeat.

"I have nothing to say, nothing to say for myself, Judge," Aidan interjected, even as Judge Dawkins was standing up to leave, "except that I—I made a terrible mistake and I understand . . ."

"Shut up, Aidan! Just shut up!" Boyce erupted, then lunged at Aidan. Leading with both hands outstretched from his smaller, less athletic frame, he shoved Aidan hard, knocking him back over a file cabinet. Boyce followed him to the ground and grabbed the lapel of his suit with one hand, driving a swift punch with the other squarely into Aidan's jaw. Aidan felt the hot sting of his lip splitting open and the warmth of his own blood rolling down his chin. He struggled for only a moment before the bailiff pounced on top of Boyce and had him up against the wall, his hands behind his back.

"Let him go, Sandy," the judge called to the bailiff. "Let him go!"

Boyce whirled around and faced the room. His cheeks were beet-red, and his expression was a mixture of horror and rage. He breathed heavily and leaned back against the wall as the bailiff hovered in front of him.

"All you had to do was help me settle the *fucking* case, you *asshole!*" Boyce screamed at Aidan past the bailiff's face.

"All of you—" the judge interrupted, "all of you get out of here and let me speak with Aidan and Justice Angier privately."

The room quickly emptied. Still glowing on the television set was the image of Emily looking up at Aidan on the stairs, seemingly heavenward, as if she were pleading for mercy. Justice Angier noticed Aidan's preoccupation with the picture, slowly walked toward the set, and turned off the power. The screen imploded into a thin dot of white light that seemed to linger interminably even as it shrank in size. Aidan continued to stare at it, almost certain that he could still detect some persistent pixel of the light in Emily's eyes, in the ethereal darkness.

Judge Dawkins sat on the edge of his desk with one leg pulled up and his hands folded together on his thigh—a posture which revealed the crisp creases in the worsted wool trousers he wore beneath his black robe.

"Aidan," he said, resuming the familiar tone that had marked the many casual conversations between them over the years, "this looks pretty dark, now, and it is, but it's not the end. There will be a penalty to pay," the judge continued, but he stopped when he noticed Aidan was about to speak.

Aidan looked at Justice Angier, then at Judge Dawkins, and reached into his pocket. He pulled out his wallet, withdrew the card that identified him as a licensed member of the state bar, and dropped it on the table.

"I know where this is headed," Aidan began, shaking his head slightly, "and I'm not going there. I'm not going before the bar to say I didn't mean to do what I did or didn't know what I was doing. I just want out. Today. Right now."

The words stunned him as they left his mouth. For fear that his will might fail him, he said them again.

"I need to get out of the practice, I know that now. I'm surrendering my license to you—with my apologies. The state bar can do with it what they wish."

Both judges were dumbfounded. They had expected, as the expressions on their faces clearly showed, another stellar performance from the Golden Boy of the Bar, another *tour de force* leading to some compromise, some stalemate, some strategic redoubt from which he might recover both his reputation and some semblance of victory, but now they realized there was much more troubling this man than what could be seen from the footage of a security tape. They pitied him. Aidan shook their hands and left the room in silence.

CHAPTER 8

Aidan felt someone shaking him awake the next morning on the couch of his office. He'd spent the night staring blankly at the dark horizon far beyond his twenty-first-story window, then at the stars, before falling asleep. Boyce Stannard had come with George Fearrington. George was a senior partner on the firm management committee. That they came together meant they were not there to console him, and he knew that even as the last remnants of a troubled sleep faded from his eyes.

"Time to get up, Aidan," George said.

Aidan pulled himself up on one elbow and dragged a hand through his matted hair. He saw the receptionist close the door to his office behind them. There were tears in her eyes. He kicked away the blanket she had placed over him earlier that morning.

"Rough night?" Boyce seemed to be in a better mood and looking for a way to join the conversation.

"Rough night, rough day, rough—who, what's, uh, what—we need to talk, I know," Aidan said, his mind slowly returning to consciousness. "I turned in my license, and I'm leaving the firm."

"You're leaving the firm?" George responded, sarcastically. He was nodding excitedly, as if he were preparing to throw a punch. "Do you think that's news? We're looking at a whopper of a malpractice suit and the loss of one of our biggest and oldest clients. You're damn right you're leaving the firm."

"My client, George. My client," Aidan responded

Aidan slumped back in the couch, his face buried in his hands. He was not up for this.

"Look, Aidan," Boyce said, in a more conciliatory tone. "Rampart agreed to settle the *Adamson* case for the policy limits last night. Gaylord has already talked to the state bar. You're going to be suspended for a year. After that, if things work out, maybe you can start back. Everyone supports you here, Aidan, and this is your home."

"I have no home."

"We need you to get serious now, Aidan," George replied. He clearly wanted to get matters under control and tucked away. That was what management committees did.

"I *am* serious. My ex-wife went to Roy Barient yesterday, after word got out." Barient was the meanest junkyard dog in the local divorce bar, which was full of lesser and aspiring junkyard dogs of all sizes and breeds.

"When he heard I was out of a job, he ran and got a temporary restraining order to prevent me from taking any money out of my stock and partnership accounts. I can't sell any assets either. He wants it all as security against future alimony payments, and he'll get it. I won't be able to meet them. As of three o'clock yesterday, I've got a credit card I don't have money to pay and thirty dollars in my wallet. Can I buy anyone a cup of coffee?"

"The man is quick, he's quick." George shook his head, incredulously, as he got up to leave. "You've got to hand it to him. He's the worst of the worst in a dirty business. Well, you've made your bed . . ."

And then George excused himself to tend to more important matters. Aidan knew there would be few at the firm who would mourn his loss—certainly not George. In fact, he doubted he'd ever see him again. If anything, Aidan's departure meant that the huge share of the firm's annual profits that used to go to him would now go back in the trough for the drove of greedy backstabbers who called themselves partners. A partnership with a man like Fearrington was a marriage built on money. When the money was gone, the loyalty was gone.

"Aidan—uh, look, you know . . ."

Watching Boyce stumble over his words reminded Aidan that Boyce was no trial lawyer, but he was still a friend. It would take Boyce's own career years to recover, he thought. He owed Boyce more than he could repay.

". . . if you want to stay with me a few days, that's not a problem. You know you're welcome."

"Thanks, Boyce." Aidan smiled, realizing then that the swollen bruise Boyce had left on his lip made smiling painful. "I know you mean it, and it means a lot to me that you do. I need a little time to think, you know? Just a little time. I really . . . I really don't know what I plan to do. These are uncharted waters for me."

With that, Boyce nodded slightly and turned to walk to the door. He paused and looked back, as though he had something else to say, but just smiled and walked out.

Aidan's head fell back against the couch. The leather felt cool from the air conditioning. He looked around his office. Here was where he had made a name and a fortune for himself—both of which were now gone. The place appeared for all the world to exude the status and power of an important, successful lawyer, which Aidan found amusing, given that he was undoubtedly the least important, least successful, and least powerful person in the entire building at that moment.

Closing his eyes, he drifted back into that refuge inside his mind, where sleep had once come easily. He tried hard to quiet every thought. He couldn't say whether hours or minutes passed before he heard the low, familiar voice at the door.

"You look like you could use a drink," the voice said.

"You're damn right I could use a drink. I could use several drinks," Aidan replied.

"Which is exactly why you're not going to take the first one."

Aidan opened his eyes, and a faint smile appeared on his face. It was Gaylord Oliver Dempsey. His six-foot-five-inch frame so filled the doorway that he had to crook his posture to one side to fit in, as though he were peering into the cave of a tiny troll. In his right hand he loosely cradled the leather handles of an ancient, battle-scarred briefcase that faintly bore his initials in gold.

"Hello, Gay," Aidan said.

"Tough jury, I hear."

It was a joke, and a bad one at that. Gay smiled at Aidan from beneath thick, bushy eyebrows and bangs of white hair that were shockingly full for a man of seventy-two. One of twelve founding partners when the firm was formed thirty years ago, he was the last still in practice and as much a part of the place as the paint on the walls. Four presidents, a dozen senators, and untold numbers of judges had sought his counsel through the years. Law clerks and young attorneys idolized him. A patrician who had cut his teeth at Princeton and Yale, he was well known for his sharp and sometimes punishing intellect, but it was a punishment delivered with the soft, melting smoothness of a scoop of butter pecan ice cream. He was as close to a rock star as a lawyer could get. He had noticed Aidan as a promising young associate in the firm and had been a mentor to him throughout his career. That was why Aidan was having so much trouble looking him in the eye now.

"I'm in trouble."

The reality of those words began to sink in as he heard himself speak. Gay offered no banalities in return to soften them.

"Look at me," Gay finally said. "When you talk to a jury about the facts of the case, what do you give them?"

"I dunno, Gay," Aidan said, suddenly feeling impatient. "Lately, I've been more interested in what they can give me. It's been a swell strategy, don't you think?"

Gay sat down on the edge of the table to force Aidan to look at him. This was now Gaylord the teacher talking.

"You argue. The other lawyer argues. The jury's heard the same evidence. They've seen two versions of the same reality. But they'll come away with only one perspective. The lawyer who gives the jury the perspective they can accept, wins the case. Life is not a matter of fact. What is fact or fiction is a matter of perspective."

"Come to the point, Gay. I'm too tired to sing 'Que Será' with you right now."

"Listen to me, Aidan, what happened yesterday in that courtroom can be solved with money. The client can replace you with another lawyer. The firm can replace you with another partner. But what's going on inside of you—the thing in your soul that made you want to take that chance—that can't be fixed with money. And that's good news, by the way, because money right now is exactly what you don't have. What you need is a major overhaul of your perspective—a way to change the reality of your life and whatever the hell it is you think you're living it for."

Aidan couldn't take it anymore. He erupted from the

couch and stood in front of Gay, jabbing his finger at him.

"Godammit, Gay! Don't lecture me. I don't need you to patronize me."

Aidan turned toward the window and pushed his hand across his scalp as if to help himself think. There was no retort from Gay, and there wouldn't be. He was right and Aidan knew it, but Aidan had no capacity at the moment for acting on his advice.

Gay calmly stood up and, without saying a word, reached into the depths of his cavernous briefcase and pulled out a slim piece of white paper with something written on it.

"Here," he said, handing it to Aidan. "I know a man on Ocracoke Island. I served with him in the navy. Father Marcus O'Reilly. He's a Catholic priest, and he enjoys the company of washed-up, self-loathing bastards like yourself. He could also use someone's help around the rectory. He'll give you room and board and help you find some day work around the island until you get back on your feet. The rest of your time will be your own, and I'd use it to clear that head of yours."

Aidan felt a sudden rush of remorse, the way a child feels who has unfairly spurned a loving parent. But he didn't think running off to a summer camp at the beach was the wisest plan at the moment.

"That's ironic. I just came from a long weekend in Ocracoke, right before all this mess began."

"And if you know what's good for you, you'll go right back."

"Thanks, Gay. I don't mean to be such a jerk. I appreciate this—I really do. But I'm not very good with my hands. I'm sure I'll find some work more suited to my skills somewhere in Raleigh." He smiled, sardonically. "I'd make a pretty good paralegal, don't you think?"

"You won't make a pretty good anything where the law or this town is concerned, at the moment. Take my advice, Aidan. I know this isn't what you had in mind, but you need to get far away from here and from this profession for a good while, if not for good. I didn't make these arrangements out of pity. I made them because you need help, and I know the man who can give it to you."

Aidan trusted Gay implicitly, and he scarcely doubted that he was right about everything he'd just said. Deep down in the core of his being, every fiber wanted to resist admitting defeat, but defeat had already found him.

"I'm sorry, Gay, for doubting you. Of course I'll do it. I don't know how I could every repay—"

Gay held up his hand to stop him.

"No need. I know you don't have a dime you can call your own right now. I'll send Gabby along to your house to pick up your things. She'll be there at one o'clock, and she'll drive you to Cedar Island to catch the five o'clock ferry this afternoon."

Gay had it all arranged, which was his special skill. He had a way of moving people and events around him to the success and betterment of everyone.

Aidan could not suppress a widening smile. "You know, all these years I've worried so much about who my enemies were. I should have known that all I needed was one good friend."

Gay gripped Aidan's arm for a moment. Then, with the resolute sadness of a father saying goodbye to a child about to leave home, he walked out of the office.

CHAPTER 9

Gabby Logan's cramped, 1983 Subaru finally rattled into the parking lot of the White Pony Motel, at the end of a one-lane road on Cedar Island that leads to the landing for the Ocracoke ferry. There was only ten minutes to go before boarding time. She had been Gay's secretary for twenty-eight of the last thirty years, and he saw to it that she got a ridiculously generous raise every year. The management committee would erupt in protest every time the issue came up and then begrudgingly go along when Gay refused to budge. She was now making more in salary than some junior partners, none of whom would be caught dead in a rusting Japanese economy car. Why she insisted on driving that firetrap Aidan never understood. On the trip from Raleigh that afternoon, her speed never exceeded forty-eight miles an hour, and by the time they reached Goldsboro—just an hour into the trip—he thought he was going to go right out of his mind. But the old buggy would go no faster, and that was just fine with Gabby.

She never stopped talking to him the whole time. When he thanked her and said goodbye, she leaned over to give him a kiss and a hug with tears in her eyes. He had a sudden déjà vu of saying goodbye to his mother at the start of summer camp. It was so strange to think of all that had happened to change his life in the course of just two days.

Aidan grabbed from the back seat the duffle that contained everything he now owned in the world and stepped out onto the sandy ground. Instinctively, his hand reached back and patted his pocket for the feel of his wallet. Fifty-five dollars—including an extra twenty from Gabby—were still there.

The smell of the water caught Aidan by surprise. He had been standing on this same ferry landing not one week ago, but now the air was cooler and had an even saltier aroma. The boat surged sideways and groaned as the captain brought the engines into full reverse to stop the ferry at the docks.

Once all passengers and cars were aboard the wide, steel-plated decks, the ferry lurched its immense bulk away from the tall pilings that surrounded the landing dock. Steadying himself, Aidan leaned over the rail and watched the water rushing by. Two small children a few feet away, weaving in and out of their mother's legs, were throwing pieces of bread at gulls swirling in the air above them.

It struck Aidan that this was the first time in his life when he really didn't *know* anything. He had no idea of the path ahead. All his life he had been buoyed by an illusion of his ability to control the events around him. Now he controlled nothing, but by the same queer twist of fate, nothing controlled him. There was a freedom in poverty that he was only beginning to discover. Had he been given the chance in that moment to return to the life he had just left, he probably would have taken it, but his sense of what chances in life were most worth taking was getting ready to change. He could feel the change coming even then.

Two hours after leaving Cedar Island, the giant diesel engine of the ferry surged into reverse at the entrance to

Ocracoke, kicking up sand and shells from the shallow water off the stern. A slow approach would take them through the shoaling channel to the narrow rock jetty and into the wide harbor. Twenty minutes later, the metal landing grates landed with a bang on the concrete docks, and the cars began rolling off. Aidan was the only passenger on foot.

Sand lined the main street on which he walked into the heart of the village. The island was less than a mile wide in many places and covered most everywhere by a fine mist of soft, white power carried aloft in the onshore breeze as it moved across the dunes. The stillness of twilight was settling upon the houses and shops.

Up ahead, Aidan could see the Black Flag, where he had been told Father Marcus would meet him. Outside the bar, a portly man in an apron was sweeping water used to hose down the decks. He worked methodically, with more care than comes naturally to most people pushing a broom.

A car from the ferry rumbled past Aidan on the left, full of squealing children. Ahead, an older couple pedaled bikes lazily in the shade of the maritime oaks that spread their gnarled, grasping fingers above the side of the road. Their bicycle wheels made a continuous hiss from contact with the sand on the asphalt. The couple stopped and got off where the road turned and the trees gave way to the open sky. Behind the counter of a snow-cone stand, a teenage boy waited, elbows bent and resting on the counter, his head in his hands. In big letters above him were the words, "Wedding Cake, Flavor of the Month."

Aidan swung his duffle over his shoulder and walked up the wooden stairs to the Black Flag. As he did, the man with the broom looked in his direction and stopped, as though he might have recognized him.

Aidan decided to be friendly. "Aidan Sharpe. How do you do?"

The big man grabbed Aidan's outstretched hand and smiled with unexpected warmth. "Zoot."

Aidan noticed the steely, square-cut jaw of an old athlete and the military bearing. "Father Marcus told me you'd be coming."

The man paused and surveyed Aidan's face for a moment that lingered into awkwardness. Finally, his expression softened. In a quieter voice as he leaned in, he said, "Tough times for you, I understand."

These were tough times—no question. Aidan was glad he hadn't been mistaken for a tourist. Of course, no one on Ocracoke would mistake him for anyone other than the person he was. He did not yet realize that he was now a resident of a very small island.

"Yeah, tough enough," Aidan said, with an unsteady laugh and the beginning of an embarrassed smile.

"You can have a seat there, if you like, while I finish up. Father Marcus will be here to meet you shortly."

And it was as simple as that, Aidan's arrival in his new home. There was no fanfare. Feeling suddenly very tired, he shouldered his duffle and walked to the edge of the deck by the water, where there was an empty booth overlooking the harbor. He sat down, leaned back, and closed his eyes. Five minutes later, a loud thump on the table near his elbow interrupted his reverie. It was a bottle of Newcastle Ale—just one. Aidan stood up to take the hand of the lanky gentleman who stood before him.

"Father Marcus," said the voice, notably more grizzled and hoarse than Aidan expected from a parish priest. "You must be Mr. Sharpe."

"Just Aidan."

"It's a good name at that, young man. Where they make this ale," he said, pointing to the bottle on the table, "it would be Adam, but you look Irish to me." A smile never left the priest's face. "Welcome, Aidan. You're among friends here."

Aidan walked beside Marcus, trying with difficulty to keep up along the road that wound around the harbor and toward the southern tip of the island, near the inlet. It was getting late, and the sun was setting over the sound. The silhouette of a sail ghosting toward shore appeared a bright shade of crimson from the west.

"They moved me here fifteen years ago," Marcus said.

"They?"

"The bishop's boys. Keeps me out of their hair—not that I mind. I love it here. You will too."

The sand-covered asphalt gave way to a narrow and well-traveled Jeep trail. They followed it for another mile and a half until coming to the rectory.

The entrance to the rectory from the road passed through an oddly small wooden gate that led to a lovely garden on the front lawn. Letters engraved on the top bar spelled, "Enter through the narrow gate."

"A little eccentricity of the former occupant," Marcus said, laughing. Turning to close the gate behind him, Aidan saw another phrase—newer—engraved on the other side: "A man passes for that he is worth."

"Who said that?" Aidan asked.

"Emerson—I carved that one."

Marcus was ruddy in the face with deep lines around his eyes and temples. His skin had mellowed to a soft tan. A shock of unruly hair, still more blonde than silver, hung low over his brow. He was a study in incongruity, wearing both a Roman collar and a small, leather scabbard for the rigging knife he kept at his waist. To look at him, one would guess he was just as capable of stabbing a parishioner to death as saving his soul, but when he spoke, his voice was full of peace. His trousers were at least two inches too short at the hem, which was fraying above his sockless feet. He wore a badly scuffed and well-worn pair of Topsiders. His brisk, muscular stride belied his years, and Aidan guessed he would be a poor bet to beat the old priest in a fifty-yard dash.

As they came through the gate, a little girl shot out from the bushes and leaped upon Marcus's chest, blanketing him like a sail before the wind. She must have been no more than six years old.

"Pia!" Marcus called the child's name as though her presence was a great surprise to him, and she squealed with delight.

"Meet our charming new guest, Mr. Aidan. Aidan, this is Piedad, one of the little children of the island. I call her 'Pia' for short, because I call her so often."

"Pia! Pia!" Marcus shouted as he put the child down to run ahead of him. "Go say your prayers!"

The house was old. The same years of sun and wind that had worn lines into Marcus's face had worn lines in the wood framing. It was a handsome edifice—simple, but elegant, in the way some beach houses are. Walking on the stubbly grass around the east side, Aidan could see that the grounds were in need of care. A wide, overhung porch faced the ocean. It was a warming, welcoming place. Aidan was pleased to call it home.

They passed inside to the kitchen, where Nita handed both of them a steaming mug of tea—Earl Grey, dark and sweet. Marcus explained that he had lined up a job for Aidan at Fielding Walker's shipyard, a few miles up the island toward Hatteras. He was expected there first thing in the morning. Aidan's boat-keeping skills were rudimentary, but he did have some experience in carpentry and varnish-and-paint work. Marcus felt certain there would be enough of that needed on the aging shrimp boats around the banks with an occasional sailing yacht thrown in, from time to time.

The priest pointed to a door down the hall. "The first room is yours. The second room is Nita's. Mine is upstairs. Stow your gear and come out when you're ready."

His room was welcomingly austere. There was a twin bed, an end table and a small lamp fitted with an incorrigibly crooked shade, a small wooden desk and chair, and a chest with four drawers. His meager surroundings seemed to him more comedy than tragedy. Just two days ago, he could have picked up the phone and spoken directly to the chief executives of a dozen major corporations around the world. Now he did not own a phone.

The house had an aroma of old wool from the Persian carpets that lay scattered across the wide-planked floors of heart pine. There were books everywhere, from floor to ceiling, and the whole place was in a comfortable state of disarray. After putting away his things, Aidan wandered into the library, where he was reading a crumbling edition of *The Imitation of Christ* by Thomas a Kempis when Marcus came around a corner. He had a dishtowel stuck under his belt. He had already been in the kitchen, helping Nita clean up. A wooden spoon hung from his hand. It was time for dinner.

They ate together, the three of them, at a table in the kitchen that overlooked the garden. Nita asked him questions about his life, being careful to avoid any reference to his legal career or the recent unpleasantness that had brought him there. Marcus talked about boats and the sea, mostly, and his love of both. Aidan saw that Marcus was enjoying vicariously the opportunities that lay ahead for Aidan at the shipyard. His excitement for the challenge of Aidan's new life revealed no hint of empathy or sorrow for the life that Aidan left behind. The loss of the career that Aidan had spent the better part of his life building was of no more significance to Marcus than a castle washed away in the sand. His joy was in the salvation of the fallen and the lost, not the adulation of the faithful and the found.

When Aidan laid his head down to sleep that night, the white coverlet smelled of fresh linen and soap. Lying upon it with his eyes open, he heard again the muffled "puff" of the surf hitting the beach, like distant cannon fire. Drifting rhythmically around the dark ceiling was a thin refracted beam from the lighthouse on the point. It seemed to turn and pirouette to the rhythm of the sea. That was the last thing he remembered before morning.

CHAPTER 10

Marcus was shaking him in the darkness. Aidan slowly gathered his wits to see the priest standing above the bed with the same dishtowel in his belt. There was a chill in the air. Aidan had fallen asleep before thinking to get under the covers, and his entire body was cold despite the blanket that Nita had spread over him.

"Time to get up, now. Something to eat and then off to work."

Breakfast was ready in the kitchen. The hot biscuits with honey and unbelievably strong, black coffee were quite enough. In fifteen minutes they were off for the boatyard. Marcus would walk with him that morning to show him the way.

The beach looked different in the pre-dawn darkness. It must have been about five in morning. The moon was gone, and clouds hid the stars. Aidan looked toward the sound of the surf, but all was black.

"It would take a lot of faith for a boat to find its way out in that soup," Aidan said.

Marcus stopped walking, then turned to Aidan. He knew when an old altar boy was patronizing him, and he wouldn't stand for it.

"Faith? Faith in what?"

Aidan was surprised at the question. He considered himself a Christian—albeit one who was backsliding mightily at the moment, and he assumed the same thing about the priest walking next to him.

"Faith in God, of course."

Marcus, seemingly dissatisfied at the answer, resumed walking. At length, he spoke again.

"Have you ever seen a man who has drowned at sea, Aidan?"

Aidan didn't know what to say. Of course he hadn't.

"Have you ever seen the cold face of a man, knowing that he searched for the God of his faith at the hour of his death and did not find him?"

"What, then—you're telling me you don't believe?" Aidan finally asked.

"I'm afraid you mistake my meaning. What I can tell you is that a man has no greater or lesser need for faith in darkness than in the light. A blind man who knows he is lost is still lost, but he is closer to the truth than the lost man who believes he can see."

Aidan still had no idea what to say, so he didn't try. He was certain that Marcus didn't expect him to. That was the first of only two times when Aidan would presume to engage Marcus in a discussion of faith.

As they reached the road, Marcus stopped.

"Here you are, son. This is the place. Just down this road, then turn right at the highway, and head north another half mile. Fielding's yard is on your left. You'll see it first thing."

Without another word, Marcus turned and headed back down the beach. The sun was now coming up over the Atlantic, and the clouds were starting to clear. In the distance to the north, the masts of the sailboats and outriggers in the shipyard could be seen above the marsh grass.

Aidan walked into the office to find a man bent over a pile of papers on a small desk. He looked up as Aidan came in and immediately sprang to his feet.

"I'm Aidan Sharpe. I'm here for the job. I think Father Marcus—"

"Fielding Walker. Pleased to meet you! I understand you're quite a sailor."

Aidan was surprised at the remark. Not many people knew that about him. He'd won some junior regattas as a boy on Delaware Bay, then a few regional competitions. He'd been recruited for the Olympic team, but his father wouldn't hear of it. The sailing team at the yacht club in Egg Harbor had been his mother's idea. Sailors were "boat bums" in his father's eyes. He feared that Aidan would fall into the go-fast crowd of racing sailors and wind up drifting through life, going from one regatta to the next on the boats of old men with big egos. He insisted that Aidan head to college and give up sailing, but the records Aidan had set, last he heard, still hung on the wall at the club. People used to say that if there were a puff of wind within a mile of the fleet, Aidan Sharpe could find it, squeeze a knot out of it, and beat any boat to the finish line. It was a reputation that didn't follow him to Raleigh, but somehow, it had followed him to Ocracoke. He wondered how, but not enough to ask. He was there to work as a carpenter, not a skipper or a race tactician. And so he grasped the man's hand, said thank you, and waited for what came next.

Walker took a moment to look him over, then asked Aidan to sit. There was some paperwork to complete, but not much. This was a shipyard, not a law office. Aidan's pay would be eight dollars an hour, with a meal provided for lunch brought in by Walker's wife for the workers in the yard. Besides Walker himself, that was six men, including the one Aidan was assigned to work with, Ibrahim Joseph.

Ibrahim was Bahamian. Aidan hadn't seen him sitting

in a corner of the office, but when Walker called his name, he rose up from the corner like a tree. He was taller than Aidan by a good six inches. He was a dark-skinned black man with an imposing presence.

"Joey-mon," as Walker called Ibrahim. "Meet your partner, Aidan Sharpe. Aidan, this is Ibrahim Joseph, 'Joey-mon' for short around here."

Aidan extended his hand, and it was immediately swallowed inside Ibrahim's. There was nothing forceful about him, but as he shook hands with Aidan, his eyes were steely and clear, staring right at him. He turned without speaking and walked through the office door into the yard, ducking his head low as he went. Walker motioned Aidan to follow.

In a corner of the yard stood an elegant, black sloop with beautiful lines. Aidan did not recognize the design, but he had seen similar, old wooden schooners on Long Island Sound as a boy. This one was a sailor's dream—a classic, the stuff of romance, with a price tag to match. She was halfway through an extensive overhaul. On her transom was the name, *Invictus*, and the hailing port, N.Y.Y.C., New York. The letters stood for the New York Yacht Club.

"She's a beauty," Aidan said, as Walker came up behind him.

"Yes," he answered. "But don't let that fool you. She's no lady in a race. This one will run like a thief for the money."

The owner of *Invictus* wanted sixteen new coats of varnish in all. The varnish job alone was costing him $20,000. Aidan learned that the man who had demanded all that work was Reece Ponteau, a New York textile millionaire. His son, who went by the nickname Rowdy, had campaigned *Invictus* all spring and summer in a series of races sponsored by the New York Yacht Club. *Invictus* earned an outright first on uncorrected time in all classes, even though it was technically competing in only the antique classic class created for older boats. Most boats in that category were well-loved laggards with sagging, weather-worn sails that, along with their graying owners, had long since seen the passing of their glory years. They were admitted to big-dollar races to add color and tradition and to keep the money flowing, but nobody ever expected them to win—until *Invictus*.

Winning the Newport-to-Bermuda race at age twenty-two cemented Rowdy's reputation as a wild man of the sea—a risk taker with an extrasensory skill for finding wind and harnessing it to his best advantage. But his propensity to push himself, his crew, and his boats past the limit of their endurance had cost *Invictus* the loss of her rudder in heavy seas. Rowdy fitted a temporary rudder to bring her to Ocracoke on the return leg. He chose Walker's yard for its reputation for restoring wooden boats, which were still common among the fishing fleets of the Outer Banks.

The rest of that first day of work for Aidan and every day for the next five days or six, or twenty—they all seemed to run together like thin coats of varnish, one upon another—passed in quiet concentration. The laughter of sea gulls, the blast of ships' horns, and the distant hum of power tools at work in the yard now and then punctured the silence of Aidan's world, but only briefly, before fading. By day, his universe collapsed into the twelve inches of space that separated his eyes from the woodwork of *Invictus's* frame. The hours he spent at this labor seemed to run, slow down, or stop altogether with the rhythm of his varnish brush as the amber goo thickened, thinned, and congealed in the wavering heat. All the while Ibrahim worked just ahead of him, fixed and speechless within the same dimension of time and space like an orbiting moon, ever present but ever in motion.

At dusk each day Aidan would wander home alone to supper with Nita and Marcus, only to be swallowed by the still-deeper silence of the rectory. There, the volumes in Marcus's cavernous library awaited him eagerly, pressed back against the shelves like wallflowers hoping for a dance. He took his partners each night to his bed, grasping their spines tightly until releasing them in the forgetfulness of sleep. And all the while the beam from the lighthouse traced its ceaseless course above him, in the darkness of heaven.

When Aidan got to the shipyard one day, which was the moment in his life he would remember always thereafter as *the* day—meaning the day when everything that had forever seemed about to begin finally began— Ibrahim was already on his third cup of coffee. He had set out the pots of varnish, mineral spirits, brushes, and towels for their work ahead of time as he always did. Ibrahim was meticulous to a tee. There was no better varnish man on the entire East Coast.

"We continue on the starboard toe rail," Ibrahim said.

Invictus had gorgeous rails of solid teak running the entire length of the deck—port and starboard. Left alone, the "demon teak," as Ibrahim called it, would fade to an unlovely gray. Varnish was an expensive and unnecessary vanity, but it could transform wood to a brilliance and color that was the envy of lesser yachtsmen everywhere. That vanity was what gave them both a job, at least for the moment.

Aidan's and Ibrahim's entire day was devoted to sanding and cleaning in preparation for the ninth coat. It was tedious, muscle-cramping work, and it was close to five o'clock before they were finished. Coming to the last strip of wood, Aidan put his tack cloth in the little paper bucket he'd been carrying all day and stretched his legs outward from where he had been squatting on the boat's forward decks. He let out a moan that bespoke every one of his forty-five years. Ibrahim laughed.

"You're too young, my friend. Too young to be moaning like that."

"You haven't spent the last twenty years sitting behind a desk in a suit."

"Thank God for that. May God save me from lawyers . . . and judges." His voice trailed off.

"Oh yeah, how so?"

Ibrahim said nothing. It was not his way to waste words. There was no falsehood in him, but there were boundaries beyond which he did not wish to go, and he would not be pushed across. The subject of his past was one of them.

Finally, Ibrahim looked up. "You want a drink?"

Aidan had not wanted a drink so badly in a long time. He threw his gear into a corner, and the two men walked down the beach road toward the Black Flag.

CHAPTER 11

Molly McGregor was a *good* girl. But she was also a practical girl, and nobody's fool.

For better or worse—and initially much for the worse she would have to admit—she had defied her father's wish that she study medicine after finishing college with a degree in biotechnology. But what really broke his heart was to see her become a towboat operator on Ocracoke Island. He had brought her to the island for vacations every summer, never realizing and certainly not intending the indelible effect those long, carefree days would have on the bright-eyed, redheaded girl who squealed with excitement when she dangled her feet from the bow of their runabout. Six medical schools offered her admission, and she refused them all. She gave the usual prerogatives: taking time for herself, seeing the world, living life in the moment, and so on. But these were halfhearted explanations that sounded unconvincing, even to her.

Life on Ocracoke was hardly a European Grand Tour—another post-graduate suggestion of her father's that Molly had turned down. The attraction of the island for her was its isolation and unadorned honesty. The simplicity of her solitary life there was all she wanted or ever could want, or at least so she believed.

The waters around Ocracoke were famous for the shoals formed by swift tides that carried millions of gallons of sea and sand into and out of the narrow inlet four times a day. The Coast Guard long ago gave up using buoys to try to mark the channel, which shifted constantly. The ever-changing slope of the sea floor at Ocracoke was the bane of weekend sailors who regularly ran aground on it and a boon to the towboat operators—modern-day pirates, of a sort—who extorted huge fees to pull them off. Molly was one of the pirates.

The idea of tow-boating, like pirating, was to lie in wait until one man's misfortune became the occasion for another man's meal. It was hardly the model of constancy expected by bankers who made boat loans and marinas who expected payment for diesel fuel. The large towboat operators on Ocracoke—there were and ever had been just two—earned their bread aboard sleek, twin-engine race boats capable of great speeds. When a distress call came in from sailors far out at sea—invariably a terrified wife relaying instructions from her screaming, soon-to-be-ex-husband—these operators could span vast distances quickly to reach them. Molly, aboard her seaworthy but relatively slow towboat, the *Sairey Gamp*, could not match the speed of the other towboat captains, who jealously guarded the lucrative business of bringing boats in from miles offshore. There was no place for little redheaded girls in their world. So, Molly created a world of her own.

She knew the waters around the island from long experience, and for that reason she had immediately noticed when Sarah took up residence aboard a well-found ketch in a deepwater lagoon on the north side of the inlet.

At high tide there was only a foot of water above the sandbar that rimmed the lagoon, but the lee of the island kept the surface of the lagoon so calm that an approaching boat could not distinguish the shallows from deep water. Reaching the lagoon in high or low tide required careful navigation through a hidden opening in the bar not more than ten feet wide. Molly had piloted the *Sairey Gamp* through this opening one afternoon to say hello to the new woman in the neighborhood.

Pulling alongside the *Bel Sogno*, Molly tossed over her bumpers to protect the hulls of both boats from damage from the swell, sending out a cheery "ahoy there" as she did so. There was no answer from below, but a woman immediately appeared on deck and walked spritely forward to catch Molly's line. Although they had never met until that moment, Sarah was smiling broadly, as if Molly's arrival was the return of a very old and dear friend. That sunny welcome distracted Molly momentarily from the fact that Sarah was wearing no clothes.

Molly was no prude. She had run bare-assed into the surf ahead of one or two startled boyfriends in her day, and she had spent four years in a sorority house where the lone shower was the subject of daily disputes among dozens of screaming, naked women. Her first reaction was to laugh congenially, expecting to hear an apology for being caught unprepared for company. But no apology came—only a kind smile and a steady calm in Sarah's demeanor that gave no inkling that there was anything unnatural or immodest in her condition.

Molly, though something of a tomboy, was first and foremost a woman, and she had a woman's singular skill to see another woman's flaws with greater powers of observation than even the most voyeuristic of men. Yet what she noticed immediately about Sarah was no different from what Aidan and Marcus had first noticed, which was that Sarah's physical form retained a perfection of shape and suppleness that betrayed nothing of the truth of her age. Her obvious ease made her skin seem the only covering that was natural and necessary for her. Molly felt an unexpected flush of embarrassment at the sense that she, not Sarah, was the one inappropriately dressed.

"Good morning," Sarah said at length, standing on the foredeck of *Bel Sogno* and steadying herself on the forestay. Molly returned the greeting with a smile, but before she could think of something witty or clever to say to break the ice, Sarah warmly asked Molly to lay aside her own clothes on the deck of *Sairey Gamp*, come aboard, and join her.

Molly laughed again, this time with marked nervousness. Father Marcus could have had the courtesy to explain something about this woman to her in advance, she thought. If he had bothered to describe her, Marcus might have said that Sarah was someone who fully realized St. Paul's exhortation to live *in* the world without becoming *of* the world. She expressed that sense of her own separateness most directly in her discomfort with material things. There were many subtle aspects of her character that spoke of this longing in her, but none so conspicuously as her contempt for any pretense of clothing. She guarded her little world aboard *Bel Sogno* like Eden. It was chiefly for that reason that Marcus had, in fact, never been on the boat since the day he installed Sarah aboard her in the lagoon. The only exception she allowed to this habit was for Sunday mass. When Marcus paddled out into the lagoon in his canoe each week to retrieve Sarah, he would find her waiting in full regalia, as if to hide from God the stain of some sin much more grievous than what troubled those praying beside her in flip-flops and tank tops.

Molly's unease that afternoon was short-lived. The whine of an outboard engine behind her broke the silence of the lagoon. A boat full of boys from the local high school, riding someone's father's crabbing skiff, had come to get a closer look at the naked woman on deck and, in doing so, had run hard aground on the sandbar. Molly laughed out loud at this spectacle—first at the fact that Sarah was probably older than the grandmothers of these boys, and secondly at the fact that she probably had a better body than most of their girlfriends.

The lagoon where *Bel Sogno* was anchored was, to be fair to all concerned, the same place where hundreds of English sailors had made the same error—usually their last. The fate of these boys would be kinder: a towing bill that their fathers would begrudgingly pay to the attractive, red-haired skipper of the *Sairey Gamp*, who just happened to be on the scene and able to help far more quickly than any tow operator from the harbor could be summoned.

So it was that Molly McGregor discovered a new business model that saved her fledgling towing venture from bankruptcy and her from the need to run home, tail-tucked, to Daddy, whose *I told you so* was already loaded in the breech. In time, she overcame her skittishness and joined Sarah's revelry aboard *Bel Sogno*, deciding it would be unfair, if entrapment were to be her game, that Sarah should be the only bait. Sarah clearly took great pleasure in Molly's company, and the two of them would talk for hours, lying gloriously naked beneath the golden sun on *Bel Sogno's* capacious foredeck. Sarah, as usual, said very little and nothing at all about herself or her past. But as best she could with her limited grasp of English, she would listen as Molly talked of lost loves or the proper preparation of linguini with clam sauce or local politics or a hundred other topics of the day. As often as not, the two would say nothing at all, enjoying instead hours of silence penetrated only by the cries of gulls. Molly's sole reservation about these interludes came from the wilderness of freckles that began to explode all over the milky white skin of her breasts and hips, where she had always hoped there might one day be a tan.

The two women often shared a delicious, sweetened tea that Sarah brewed from Sargasso seaweed. She gathered it in her daily walks along the beach, dried it in clumps left on the deck of the boat in the sun, and ground the dried leaves to a fine powder. It contained no alcohol, but time seemed to pass unnoticed for Molly whenever she drank it. Its qualities for calming her mind and loosening her tongue were remarkable. Under its intoxicating effects, she filled the hours with a liberality of conversation she did not usually allow herself.

These reveries would continue until they were interrupted, from time to time, by the sound of another sailor caught and struggling in Molly's web. She would then calmly return to her boat, dress, and motor the short distance through the narrow, unmarked inlet of the lagoon to a location where she could throw a towing bridle to the stranded boat and bring it back into deep water. For these ten minutes of easy work she charged the prevailing, confiscatory rate of $675. Terms of payment by cash or credit card were always settled in advance, and the code observed among the island's towboat captains forbade them from undercutting each other.

Molly sometimes encountered hostility from drunken men as they came dimly to the realization that this beguiling redhead, whom they imagined had bidden them to look closer, was now about to collect two weeks' wages for the view. That was never truer than the day she met Rowdy Ponteau.

CHAPTER 12

Rowdy Ponteau was the kind of paradox common among the sons of old money: a vapid young man who had come without strife or suffering into a great deal of wealth but who mightily resisted parting with any fraction of it. He rarely carried a dollar of currency or coin and freely borrowed from those in his company for every necessity, for which invariably they were not repaid. On this day, he and two friends from New York, who had come to spend the week at his father's house in Hatteras, chartered a twenty-nine-foot racing sloop for an offshore jaunt down to Ocracoke. They were coming through the inlet under sail when the image of Molly reading a book on the foredeck of a ketch anchored in the lagoon had its intended effect. Amid hoots of laughter and eager to get a better look, they fell off sharply to starboard into what at the time seemed to be deep water.

Molly had no warning of the sloop's silent approach. She was in her usual place on the port side of the foredeck, looking in Sarah's direction and chattering on about an art show that was coming up in two weeks in Rodanthe, asking Sarah whether she would go with her if Father Marcus gave them both a ride, and attempting to convince her to start selling her Sargasso tea in the village. Then, Sarah suddenly touched Molly's arm. Her eyes were focused on something to the southwest, and her face seemed quickly to darken to a grave seriousness. Molly turned when she heard men's voices. Fifty yards away was the bright red hull of a sloop, nose down where the keel had bit hard into the sand, and the stern riding unnaturally high. The sails luffed sloppily as two men tried to collapse a large, billowing genoa onto the foredeck. They alternately shouted directions and insults to each other. Another man, at the helm, appeared to be laughing so hard he could barely stand.

Sarah was usually indifferent to the men who drove their boats onto the bar for a better look, but not today. She had seen something in the arrival of the red sloop she did not like, though what it was she did not say. She seemed eager to restrain Molly like a wayward child.

"Leave this one," she said.

Molly didn't understand. She let out a nervous laugh as she sometimes did when she wasn't sure she had caught Sarah's meaning.

"I wish I could," Molly replied, "but my boat payment is calling me."

Sarah was serious about not wanting her to go, Molly could tell, and it made her uneasy, but Sarah did not understand enough about her own feelings to explain her sudden apprehension about the red boat. Instead, she simply reached for the cover-up Marcus had given Sarah and hurried below deck.

Molly had a great affection for Sarah but did not know her well enough, even then, to trust Sarah's intuition. All that was on Molly's mind at the moment was the $675 that was waiting for her on the other side of the bar. She called to Sarah, saying "everything will be all right," but got no answer as she boarded the *Sairey Gamp*, which was tied alongside. She found her bra and underpants where she had left them in a heap on the cabin sole and looked out of the port light toward the bar as she hurriedly got dressed. Molly could see the two men on the foredeck clearly now. They had finally managed to corral the headsail and sheets that had been flogging them in the wind. Their boat seemed closer than she had first realized.

The *Sairey Gamp* had a single, inboard diesel engine with a three-bladed propeller and port and starboard bow thrusters. Like a master puppeteer, pushing and pulling the throttle and gears of her little marionette in intricately timed sequences, Molly had complete control over its motion and position in the water. Within two minutes she was underway, and in two minutes more she had passed through the inlet to the lagoon and was standing smartly off the port side of the red boat. She called to the men on the radio, giving the name of the *Sairey Gamp* as her only identification, and offered them a tow to the harbor for the stated fee. Molly was all business in these encounters, not forgetting on this day or any other that the men she was about to rescue had gotten into their predicament for wanting something she had no intention of giving them.

"A woman after my own heart," Rowdy said to himself, smirking.

Molly backed down the engine to bring the *Sairey Gamp* as close to the grounded sloop as she could safely come. She could see Rowdy through the windows in her wheelhouse. He was tall and blonde and, despite the sweltering weather, appeared to be well dressed, without an ounce of sweat or a hair out of place. He looked to be about her age. She knew the type well. *Rich kid. Full of himself.* Her defenses went up. He would be just the latest in a long line of smarmy, good-looking, over-confident assholes she had dealt with in her life. She would be only too happy to take his money.

Rowdy was well defended by a fatalistic sense of humor, and he readily summoned it on occasions such as these when it was most needed—usually when some expensive and unhappy circumstance followed a lapse in his better judgment. For this he was duly famous among the boarding-school chums who kept abreast of his latest shenanigans, whispered through the grapevine of summer socials and dinner parties in the Hamptons. He wore those stories—like the one about the night in Georgetown when he drove his Range Rover down three blocks of sidewalks to cut off a diplomatic motorcade—as badges of honor. They served to regale friends and fellow travelers in his rarefied, cloistered world. He had a steady, cool demeanor and a kind of mental toughness, but these were not traits born of any trial of his character. They merely expressed the confidence of a man who had learned, through frequent experience, to trust in the power of money to insulate him from the consequences of his actions.

Molly tossed a rubberized canister tethered to a line over the port lifelines of the red boat, whose name, *Yo Mamma*, she finally could read as she came around the transom.

Of course, she muttered to herself.

Inside the canister was a standard contract for towage. She called out instructions for them to sign it, place a driver's license and a credit card in the canister, and throw it back. The men stood there in silence. The two on the foredeck looked at Rowdy, who stared at Molly. While preparing the towing bridle to throw onto the foredeck of the sloop, Molly suddenly realized that no one had answered her.

"What's the holdup, fellas?" she asked. "I'm ready to pull."

Rowdy spoke slowly, as if explaining something to someone who understood very little English. "You caught us unprepared, Miss. There's not a single credit card among us." The two men standing on the foredeck, who had said nothing so far, looked at each other and then back at Molly. "I'm very sorry," Rowdy continued, "but we don't have enough cash on hand to pay you. But if you'll get us off this bar and follow us to the harbor, I've got a wallet in my car, and I can pay you there."

It was a lie, and Molly knew it. There was no car in Ocracoke. She hadn't seen that sloop or these men in the harbor before, and they had entered the inlet from offshore. From the looks of them and the dried salt that covered the deck of their boat, they had been at sea for at least a day—probably on passage from Hatteras, although the hailing port on the transom, below the name, was Block Island, R. I.

What she didn't know was that the credit card in Rowdy's $800 handmade eel skin wallet, which he carried in addition to a money clip filled with nearly two thousand dollars of cash, had a two-million-dollar limit with a zero balance. Everything about the man, beginning with his thousand-watt smile, was false.

Molly had every right to leave Rowdy and his boat and crew on the bar. Had they simply refused to pay her, she would have done exactly that, but failing to assist a vessel in distress that makes a bona fide promise to pay was against the law, not to mention bad karma. Throwing the bridle onto the foredeck of *Yo Mamma,* she told the men she would tow them into the harbor and drop them just off of the Admiral's Inn Marina, where they had already made arrangements for a berth for the night. She would meet them at the Black Flag that evening to settle up.

Rowdy shouted his agreement, ran the towing bridle through the fairleads on the bow, then tied the bitter end to the mast. When all three men were safely in the cockpit and Rowdy gave the high sign, the *Sairey Gamp's* powerful engine rumbled into gear, and the pale green sea frothed around her transom like margaritas in a blender. Bending readily to the will of the stronger vessel, *Yo Mamma* yawed slightly to port until it found enough water under its keel to float upright, then came obediently astern of the tug, nodding at the towing bridle like a show pony on the way to the barn.

After entering the harbor and releasing the tow rope, Molly watched the red sloop as Rowdy prepared to maneuver it in a cross-wind into a narrow slip.

This ought to be good, she thought to herself.

As soon as his vessel was free of the bridle, Rowdy gave the order to the two men on the foredeck to unfurl a sliver of sail. The canvas caught enough of a breeze to turn the boat gently to port and afford steerageway into a side channel of the marina. Rowdy, then deftly executing a gybing pirouette, aimed the transom squarely for the dock and glided the boat into place like a Checker Cab parking at the curb. Molly was impressed. She was no less certain that Rowdy Ponteau was an asshole, but clearly he was a talented asshole.

CHAPTER 13

When Aidan and Ibrahim got to the Black Flag, the sun had all but completely disappeared below the horizon. A sunset was a beautiful thing on the island in clear weather, and the Black Flag, with a view that stretched for fourteen miles across Pamlico Sound, was the best place to see it. From that distance, boats seemed to float on sunbeams before disappearing entirely. It was a better show than any movie in town, and—there being no movies in town—locals who could get to the Black Flag in time to enjoy the sunset with a cold beer rarely missed the opportunity.

They walked to a booth in the back. As they passed, Zoot looked up from cleaning his cups behind the bar. He was only half listening to the owner of a local gift shop drone on about the light foot traffic this past summer, the man who was run off the road by a drunk driver, and the resulting campaign to reduce the speed limit in the village from twenty-five miles per hour to fifteen. She would stop to catch her breath every so often, tossing out a question to Zoot to make sure he was still paying attention. Zoot excused himself and followed Ibrahim and Aidan to their table with a menu.

"What are you boys having?"

"Just a Kalik for me," answered Ibrahim. Aidan ordered a Guinness and a cheeseburger—two things in life that offered him genuine comfort. For years he had reassured himself that if he were one day brought so low that all he had to look forward to was a cold pint of Guinness and a warm cheeseburger, he would still say life was sweet. He was then reminded that, at that moment, he was in just such a low place, and that life—if not *sweet*—was certainly not the hardship he had imagined. For one thing, he had made a new friend in Ibrahim.

Ibrahim considered it a sign of God's benevolence to have found a bar that served Kalik this far from the Bahamas. Its slightly bitter taste was a reminder of home for him. He came north from the islands five years ago after hitching a ride on a freighter bound from Nassau. Zoot would never forget that night. A launch manned by two crew from the freighter brought Ibrahim into the harbor at around three in the morning. They were headed for the only lights they could see—the Black Flag—where Zoot was still locking up for the night. Zoot heard the low drone of the motor approaching the dock. The launch tied off, and Ibrahim got out. One of the two crewmen gave Ibrahim a small duffle and came ashore just long enough to embrace him. The boat then left quickly. Ibrahim, carrying only a change of clothes and enough food for a day, turned and began to walk toward the road. He stopped suddenly to stare at Zoot, the man who was staring back at him. To Zoot, Ibrahim looked ready to run.

It didn't take Zoot long to size up what had just happened. He walked up to the young man and, without saying a word, handed him a dog-eared business card from his wallet with Father Marcus's name on it, then pointed in the direction of St. Anne's. That's where most of the strays on this island wound up. It was Zoot who usually saw them first, pouring their sorrows down a bottle at the Black Flag. He would send them on to Father Marcus, who would sort them out and send them on their way with a few dollars in their pockets or find a place for them, as he had done for Ibrahim. Most importantly to them and to Zoot, though, he did it without judgment or criticism—"not like those cold sonsabitches in Morristown," Zoot would say, condemning in one broad stroke every priest he ever knew in the town where he grew up. Zoot admired Father Marcus because he was different. It was not the kind of admiration Zoot would ever express, but if Marcus had said he needed ten men to lift the church off its foundations and carry it into the sea, Zoot would have been the first to show up for the job.

Zoot knew who Aidan was, too, though not like he knew Ibrahim. Ibrahim was a big man, the kind Zoot knew he could count on in a scrape—not that he'd ever had to. Aidan he had not yet altogether sized up, but Aidan had Father Marcus's friendship, and that counted for a great deal where Zoot was concerned. What didn't count for much of anything were the rumors he'd heard about the new man from Raleigh who had washed out of the practice of law and lost everything over a lie. Stories like that never surprised him. Most of the lawyers and judges he'd known over the years were spineless bastards, anyway. He firmly believed that if they lost their money and their titles, in a tight spot a man could expect no more honor from them than from a knife fighter in a dark alley.

Zoot was also unimpressed with the stories being passed around the village about the new man's scandalous history with women. Zoot had learned much from the woeful tales of scores of drunkards in the twenty years he had stood behind a bar. Every man's troubles sooner or later came down to women or money or both—usually both. That was why he had stayed single and poor, and that was why his customers envied and admired him. His life as a bartender had been as celibate and ascetic as that of any priest, and faithful supplicants came as regularly to his altar as they did to St. Anne's.

It was already dark outside when Rowdy Ponteau and his crew walked into the Black Flag. Aidan watched them find a seat close to the bar. He had seen a lot of men like Rowdy over the years—other lawyers mostly— who made a point of dressing well and who carried themselves with the entitled bearing of wealth. The two men with him were clearly not the alphas of the pack. Rowdy called the shots. The three of them sat down, and Zoot brought to their table a bottle of Glenfidditch that Rowdy had spotted behind the bar on the way in. They began to drink shots like they meant it. Zoot already knew enough about Rowdy's father and his money not to worry about telling the men that each of those shots was costing them twenty dollars.

Aidan turned his attention back to Ibrahim, who had settled into a Zen state of satisfaction now that his second Kalik was half-gone. Aidan signaled for Zoot to bring another. He thought that now might be the time to try again to learn something about his co-worker and new friend.

"You ever gonna tell me where you're from and what brought you here?"

Ibrahim looked at Aidan with less apprehension than before, and Aidan saw a sense of resignation in his face.

Of course he would have to tell him, Ibrahim thought. There would be no harm, and even if there were, he could not live entirely underground. Besides, he knew that Aidan had suffered his own fall from grace, and he already felt a kinship with the man who had spent every day with him for the past month, huddled over a pot of varnish.

Ibrahim had thought many times exactly what he would say to someone like Aidan. There was no artful way to put it. So he just told it like it was.

"I am wanted for murder."

The words sounded surreal to Ibrahim. He didn't see himself that way, even if the Royal Bahamian Navy did. He decided to tell Aidan the story that he had shared with no one but Father Marcus since the day he arrived.

Ibrahim and his father had managed a fleet of fishing boats that sold conch to the vendors on Potters Cay in Nassau Harbor. He was walking home from the docks at around one in the morning when a man, who had been sitting in the dark parking lot of a liquor store, spotted him, got up, and crossed the street to approach him. The man had a bottle in his hand. He demanded Ibrahim's wallet.

At first, Ibrahim was not afraid. The man was half his size and appeared to be drunk.

"Go home. I have no money for you," Ibrahim said, dismissively.

The situation escalated quickly. The man broke the bottle across a street sign and kept coming at a brisk, steady pace. Ibrahim, given his size, wasn't used to being challenged. He felt an unexpected wave of fear come over him. He had walked that road late at night all his life, and although panhandlers were common, thieves were rare.

"I don't want any trouble," Ibrahim said, starting to back up.

"They's gon-ta-bey trouble, *mis-tah*, 'less you throw down your wallet."

The man came closer. Ibrahim backed up until he was under a bright streetlight. He saw a cold, blank stare in the man's eyes that meant the rum was probably mixed with cocaine. The man kept coming, waving the jagged end of the bottle. They were in an empty parking lot now, close to the harbor.

"I'll hurt you, man. I'll hurt you! Stand back," Ibrahim warned, now feeling frantic.

He dodged the first swing of the bottle, but the second sliced a long, shallow gash in his gut that burned like fire. Ibrahim's hand was already on the knife before the second swing came. The blade flew like a missile, lodging in the man's throat.

The man stumbled forward, his eyes still fixed in that cold stare. A thin stream of blood spurted from his neck over the front of Ibrahim's jacket before he collapsed on the ground in front of him. His bloody head and neck, with the knife still firmly in place, landed on Ibrahim's feet.

Ibrahim stood motionless for several seconds, then felt the warmth of blood as it ran into his shoe. A second later, a loud "whoop-whoop" from a police siren sounded nearby. Ibrahim looked up. A cruiser started speeding toward the street light where Ibrahim was standing.

Marked with the blood of a man lying dead with Ibrahim's knife stuck in his throat, Ibrahim could think of nothing but to run—hard—for the water. If he could get away, perhaps things might get straightened out later. Perhaps there had been a witness. If he could not escape, he would die a suspected murderer with a police bullet in his back, and all words of explanation would be forever quieted.

Ibrahim ran a course that the police could not easily or quickly follow, but it was clear from the additional sirens he heard behind him that running had only made matters worse. When he reached the banks of the harbor, he removed his bloody jacket and shoes, dove in, and started to swim. The harbor, though long and deep, was narrow. The banks were only a quarter mile apart—maybe less. Ibrahim found himself spinning in circles in the water, not knowing which way to go, and seeing the lights of police vehicles flickering from every corner. His thoughts raced. His belly still burned from the wound, and his arms and legs were weights dragging him down. There would be no escape by land.

Then, something hit him in the head. It was a heavy coil of rope tossed from the deck of a freighter docked at Potters Cay. Ibrahim grabbed it and held on. Three men—one of them a friend of Ibrahim's who had seen him flee into the harbor—pulled the line in, hand over hand, until Ibrahim was up and over the side, out of sight of the police who were now circling the harbor on all sides.

Police aboard a patrol boat came alongside the freighter later that night, asking questions. They had found a blood-stained jacket and shoes, they said. Inside the jacket's vest pocket was a ledger sheet with Ibrahim's name and his father's phone number. The bloody knife removed from the dead man's neck was checked for fingerprints and displayed in a sealed, clear evidence bag.

The men on the freighter heard the police say that the dead man was the royal governor's son—known to everyone as a spoiled playboy and ne'er-do-well whose voracious appetite for cocaine and women sometimes exceeded his father's generous allowance. With the governor's office to deal with, there would be no use in Ibrahim trying to explain anything. Judgment would be swift. The penalty would be death. Political friends of the governor would come to Ibrahim's execution to see justice done.

Ibrahim's friend helped bandage his wound. He also found Ibrahim some dry clothes and gave him a duffle with a few dollars and what food he could gather from the ship. Then he quietly arranged, through a friend on another freighter, bound north and due to weigh anchor before dawn, to get Ibrahim aboard. He left—with no papers, no plans, and no way ever to go home.

Word travelled to Ibrahim's father about what had happened, but it was impossible for Ibrahim to communicate with him for fear of giving away his whereabouts to the police or, worse, entangling his father in a felony to obstruct justice. One week later, as the freighter made its way to New York, Ibrahim chose Ocracoke as a place to come ashore. It was remote, he thought, and not a place where anyone would think to come looking for him. Some intuition told him, too, that it would be safe.

Ibrahim started to tell Father Marcus his story one day, but Marcus stopped him until he had moved inside the confessional at St. Anne's, where they would be guarded against any questions from the police. But no questions ever came. He helped Ibrahim get a job at Fielding's yard. Fielding paid in cash and knew not to ask questions about the men Father Marcus sent to him.

It had been a peaceful—if lonely—life for Ibrahim since then. He didn't look back. He focused all his energy on the task at hand, which was what made him singularly talented for the tedium of varnishing. He could lose himself in his work until there was nothing but the beauty of the wood, and his own world would seem beautiful again for a little while.

Aidan had been listening intently to Ibrahim's story without interruption. He was no one's idea of a priest, but he, too, was receiving Ibrahim's confession. It was a rare gift of trust, and he would honor it above all else.

When Ibrahim finished, Aidan lifted his glass and proposed a toast.

"To justice," he said. "May it ever be blind, and may we ever see clearly enough to stay out of its way."

Ibrahim shook his head and laughed, but before either of them could take another drink, loud voices at the front of the bar caught their attention.

It was seven o'clock, and Molly McGregor had kept her appointment with Rowdy Ponteau to collect the money for the tow. By now Rowdy and his friends were two hundred dollars deep into a bottle of Glenfidditch.

Molly approached with visible caution, seeing the bottle and noticing the obvious difference in the demeanor of all three men compared to earlier that day. Rowdy stood up to greet her. Molly was all of five feet three inches tall. At the helm of the *Sairey Gamp*, she was as capable as any man twice her size, but staring down at these men from the deck of her boat, she hadn't noticed how much larger and more powerful they were. She suddenly had an uneasy feeling about the tank top and short shorts she had chosen, in an uncharacteristically girly mood, to wear out in the hot, dense air that covered the island at night at that time of year.

Rowdy's eyes drifted to Molly's chest as he lumbered forward awkwardly and extended his arms in a hug. She tried to duck out of his way, but she was too late.

"Hell-ooo, beautiful," he said stupidly, his speech noticeably slurred. He wrapped his arms around her and drew her into his body with a sudden force that made it clear he expected resistance and had no intention of yielding to it.

She felt her body compress against his. The scotch on his breath made her dizzy, but only until he forced his right hand down the back of her shorts and inside her underwear. He spread the fingers of his hand across both cheeks and squeezed hard, lifting her feet off the ground in the process.

She screamed wildly. It was not a cry of indignation or anger, but of abject, animal fear. No one had ever held her or touched her against her will. She had never before felt so utterly powerless as she did in that moment.

She kept screaming, but he wasn't letting go. The width of his thick forearm moved farther down into her shorts and popped the button in front, spreading open the zipper. She felt them shift and sag slightly off of her hips. His hand dug deeper, up under her crotch. His fingers were inside her now. He held her feet off the ground in a staggering dance, circling as she rained punches onto his head and shoulders. The stinking breath of his laughter suffocated her. As they spun around the room together, she caught glimpses of smiles on the faces of the two men in Rowdy's crew who were still sitting in the booth. Then their smiles seemed to change as she caught a fleeting image of another face—the angry face of a man coming quickly at Rowdy from behind. His friends shouted a warning that was too late. When Rowdy turned toward them, a punch flew by Molly's face and connected with Rowdy's jaw. He stumbled back and dropped her to the floor. She got up right away and ran toward Zoot for protection behind the bar.

Aidan hated a bully more than almost anything on this Earth. He didn't like them in courtrooms, conference rooms, or barrooms, and he didn't like the man he was looking at now. The fear in Molly's eyes was unmistakable. Aidan felt a primal instinct to defend her, notwithstanding the disadvantage of twenty years and thirty pounds that Aidan faced in the fight. He knew how to make his own chances. He hadn't learned much from his father, but one rule remained indelible: when you can't walk away, hit first, hit hard, and don't stop hitting until the other guy drops.

The first punch had delivered Aidan's message loud and clear. The second one sent Rowdy to the floor.

He didn't stay there long. His only thought, now, was

to attack the skinny bastard who had just cold-cocked him. Aidan stood his ground, ready to use again the right hand that was now throbbing in pain. He never saw the two men who stood up behind him. They grabbed his arms and quickly forced them behind his back to present an easier target for Rowdy.

Aidan struggled like a fly in a web against the two bigger men. Then he noticed the wild expression on Rowdy's face change to something like fear. The men holding Aidan noticed the same and wheeled around to see what was behind them.

Ibrahim had risen from his seat and was now standing rod-straight in the middle of the bar. He seemed more immense in that moment than Aidan had noticed in their work together. At the top of that mountain was a storm not to be trifled with. His arms hung down at his sides, above two clenched fists as big as sledgehammers. One fist held a long stiletto knife. Ibrahim rhythmically waved the tip of the knife in a back-and-forth motion. The muscles of his chest, visible beneath his shirt, were tense and coiled to strike. He said nothing, and the silence seemed to transfix Rowdy and the two men, until they heard the sound of rattling wood.

Zoot had thrown a baseball bat on top of the bar. Molly was shielded beside the cash register, her face streaked with tears. Her eyes were still wide with terror, and her lower lip quivered uncontrollably. Zoot slowly lifted the serving gate to the bar and stepped toward the tables where the two men still had a firm grasp on each of Aidan's arms. Zoot's hand cradled a well-notched Louisville Slugger. He had played the game in the minor leagues forty years ago, dealing no small measure of destruction to countless pitchers with that very weapon, anticipated by deafening chants of "Zoot, Zoot, Zoot" from the crowd. He was prepared to render the same service, now, to Rowdy's head. Zoot was a wide, fat man, but one who, Rowdy could tell, was still big and strong. And Zoot meant business.

The tension was palpable. No one spoke a word. Everything Ibrahim had to say was hanging from his right hand, and what Zoot would add to the conversation was raised above his left shoulder. Every man stood like a chess piece on a board, until Rowdy could no longer resist the impulse toward over-confidence and recklessness that was his nature.

Feigning a punch toward Aidan, Rowdy drew a wide, leveling swing of the bat from Zoot, crouching as it whistled safely over his head. With that threat spent, Rowdy lunged toward Zoot and reached for the bat, but he never made it. A silver flash streaked past Aidan's right eye and came to rest in Rowdy's thigh. Ibrahim's knife drove in all the way to the hilt.

Rowdy let out a high-pitched yelp and clutched his leg as he fell to the ground. The men holding Aidan then released him as if he were a hot iron, and turned to face Ibrahim. These two would have been too much even for him, had it come to that, but another swing of the bat into the back of one of the men's knees evened the score and ended the fight. Aidan, Zoot, and Ibrahim were unhurt and now a united front against the other three, two of whom were on the floor. Rowdy screamed a second time, longer and slower, as he focused intently on the knife still protruding from his thigh like an oil derrick atop a slow gusher of blood.

Ibrahim walked toward Rowdy as the last man standing backed away. Fearing that Ibrahim was coming to finish him off, Rowdy knotted up a left fist and feebly swung it at him while still clutching his bleeding thigh. Ibrahim swatted away the punch as he stooped to the ground and pushed Rowdy's head to the floor. With one knee resting on Rowdy's chest, Ibrahim reached for a napkin on a nearby table, wadded it up at the base of the knife, and pulled the long blade from the wound. A low, guttural moan escaped Rowdy's throat, and his eyes rolled back in his head.

"Here, keep pressure on this," Ibrahim said, pressing the napkin hard into Rowdy's thigh. "Find a hospital. Do not touch this woman ever again. Do not come back to this place."

The one member of Rowdy's crew who was still standing helped the other who had been knocked to the ground up onto a bench. The man's knee was shattered, and he was breathing heavily. Molly was still standing behind the bar. Her eyes were glued to the scene before her, but the tears and the terror were gone.

Rowdy hobbled to his feet, knocking over tables and chairs as he and the two men with him made their way to the door. Zoot had said nothing in all this time. It was then that Aidan noticed the blood rising in Zoot's face.

Before the men reached the door, the bat flew from Zoot's left hand and slammed against the wall, inches from Rowdy's head. Rowdy jumped nervously and spun around on one leg. He looked first at Ibrahim with an expression of dread, then realized it was Zoot who threw the bat. Zoot walked over to him, pushed the other man aside, and grabbed Rowdy with both hands under his shoulders. He forced him back against the wall beside the door. The one unhurt member of Rowdy's crew started to make a move for Zoot, but when Ibrahim raised the knife in his hand as a warning, the man backed off.

A look of astonished terror came over Rowdy's face. He had clearly underestimated this old man, who was as fat as a pumpkin and seemed to move about as fast as one when he was fetching food and drinks for customers.

"The *money*, goddammit!" Zoot shouted.

Leave it to a bartender, Aidan thought, to make sure he didn't get stiffed for a bottle of good scotch by customers who had walked in but were now limping out, fractured, bruised, and bleeding. Aidan looked at the fire in Zoot's eyes and thought he'd probably kill Rowdy if the money didn't soon appear.

With one arm, Rowdy fumbled for the money clip in his side pocket. Zoot snatched it from his hand as soon as it appeared and threw it on the bar in front of Molly.

"Take all of it, sweetheart, and tell me if that's not enough," he said. Molly was too frightened to speak or move. Ibrahim walked over to the bar, gently opened Molly's hand, and put the thick wad of bills into it, saying something too softly to be heard.

Zoot eased his grip, and, with a grimace, Rowdy slid back to the ground on his one good leg.

"Now get the hell out!" Zoot shouted. "If I see any of you in here again, it will be the last time."

Zoot stood in the doorway of the Black Flag for ten minutes, watching in silence—the baseball bat firmly in his left hand, his chest and shoulders heaving with labored breaths. He knew enough about drunks to expect them to come back in with a gun, but they wandered off into the night and never looked back. Their sloop left the harbor unseen under engine power in a hurry. They were headed offshore.

Back in the bar, his hand still throbbing where it had twice crossed Rowdy's jaw, Aidan felt as though he were standing in the aftermath of a tornado. Zoot walked back behind the bar. Molly unburdened herself of all the terror and panic she had endured in the past ten minutes as she dissolved into his arms. She buried her face in the old man's chest and shuddered with long sobs. Aidan saw tears streaming down Zoot's face, too. He turned to Ibrahim, who sat alone at a table with his thoughts, his eyes outwardly fixed in an inward stare. He thought to ask where had he learned to throw a knife so well, then thought better of it. Lots of sailors and watermen whittle with knives and make carvings and such, but not one in a thousand could have hit a moving target the size of a man's leg from that distance so quickly. Where and why Ibrahim learned those skills, and why he still carried a knife, were questions that Aidan was content to leave unanswered.

It must have been half an hour before Molly stopped crying, collected herself, and looked up at Ibrahim, then at Aidan.

"I can't thank you both enough. What you did, and Zoot, well . . . I don't know what I would have done if you hadn't shown up."

She shook hands with Ibrahim, and then with Aidan. She saw blood on the knuckles of Aidan's right hand.

"Let me wash that," she said.

She took Aidan's hand and led him through the gate to the bar and to the sink. With soap and warm running water, she cleaned the wound carefully. Aidan was close enough to smell the perfume in her long, red hair. She had spent some time getting ready to come out that night—her nails and makeup showed it—but her hands weren't soft, as he would expect of a woman. He realized he didn't even know her name.

"I'm Aidan Sharpe, by the way."

"Molly McGregor." She turned to look at him, and he saw a smile for the first time.

"I'm new here—staying with Father Marcus out at St. Anne's. Ibrahim and I work at the yard together."

"Not anymore," Zoot interrupted. "Not on Ponteau's boat. That was the old man's boy."

"What old man?" Aidan asked.

"The owner of *Invictus*—the boat you fellas have been working on."

"The boat will be the least of his worries after I call the police," Molly piped up. Ibrahim suddenly turned his head to look at her, as if she'd said something unexpected. Zoot knew why Ibrahim was concerned about anyone calling the police. The Black Flag would be the first place the police would come, looking for someone like Ibrahim. Zoot and Marcus had agreed to tell anyone who asked about Ibrahim that he had sailed east on a freighter the month before, then pass the word to him to get out of town.

"Molly—" Zoot began, but Ibrahim stopped him.

"Call them," Ibrahim said. "I will tell the police what happened. She should not be afraid of men like that. Call them now."

"What, Zoot—what is it?" Molly demanded to be included in the secret they weren't telling her.

Zoot took a deep breath and held it, looking for a way out of this corner. For all he knew, Aidan, too, was unaware of Ibrahim's past. Aidan decided to speak up.

"Zoot knows that if you call the police, they will interview Ibrahim, and that may cause . . . problems."

Aidan said nothing more, but he didn't have to. For the next hour, sitting with Aidan and Molly and Zoot in the only lighted corner of the dark bar, with the doors locked, Ibrahim told Molly the same story he had told Father Marcus and Aidan of his escape from Nassau. The telling came easily to him—he knew he was among friends. That was something he hadn't dared believe might ever be true again, when he first set foot on the island.

After she heard Ibrahim's story, Molly sat for a long time in silence, then looked squarely at all three men with a grave expression. She wanted them to know she meant business.

"Now you listen to me. It's my decision and no one else's what to do about this, and I'm telling you, there will be no police brought into the matter. I honestly don't know why I would bother after what you men did. Those jerks won't come back into this bar ever again. That's the end of it. Do you understand?"

Zoot was nodding, and so was Aidan, but Ibrahim was silent.

"Do you understand, Ibrahim? No police." Molly demanded an answer, fearing that some chivalry might be observed in secret otherwise.

"You are very kind," Ibrahim said at length. "No police." He lifted Molly's hand from the table and kissed it gently.

"Now *that's* what a gentleman should be," she said, laughing, and the others felt free to laugh with her for the first time since Ponteau and his crew had shown up. Zoot, delighted that matters had been resolved so well, poured them all another round and brought bowls of food to the table. He feigned great offense when Ibrahim offered to pay, and Ibrahim's money was, in fact, never accepted in the Black Flag again.

Molly's expression eventually turned back to business, as she wrinkled her brow.

"About the money," she said. She pulled out the wad of bills taken from Rowdy's clip. Counting up the total—twelve hundred dollars—she shook her head in disgust that she had been so gullible as to believe that the men were broke. She probably should have left Rowdy on the sandbar as she had first intended. But when she thought of Sarah with those men stranded all night within swimming distance of the *Bel Sogno*, she was certain she had done the right thing.

"Zoot," she said, "some of this is yours, for the scotch they drank."

Zoot didn't answer. The bottle of Glenfidditch they had emptied had cost him a hundred dollars wholesale, but he wouldn't take a penny for a drop of what they drank. Molly, unwilling to accept the windfall, offered to split it three ways with Ibrahim and Aidan, but they also refused.

"Well, I can't say this was exactly my lucky day, but I'm taking the lion's share. Zoot, I know your weakness for pie, and since there's no dragging you out of this old bar, that will have to do as payment. You'll be thick in chess pies by the weekend, I promise."

"As for you boys, well, the captain of the *Sairey Gamp* cordially requires your presence aboard for dinner. Dress ship and all. How about tomorrow night?"

CHAPTER 14

It was as still as Christmas Eve when Aidan walked up the sandy path to the rectory that night after the fight at the Black Flag. A bright moon lit up, in neon hues, the nasturtiums that Nita carefully tended each day along the garden path. He bumped his knee again going through the gate, which was almost too narrow even for one person to fit through. On nights like this, the only hint that a vast ocean lay beyond the threshold of the rectory was the flicker of white from the crests of waves that broke softly on the beach. He stopped at the doorstep and strained to see into the blackness that lay beyond. Somewhere out there, he knew, Rowdy Ponteau and his crew of hangers-on were making their way back to Hatteras in light winds and following seas.

Aidan unlocked the door to the rectory quietly, but no matter what the hour of the day, he would never do so quietly enough to escape the notice of Nita. She met him in the hallway with a mixture of concern and opprobrium for the late hour. She was in her robe, carrying a lighted candle in a lantern. The woman simply did not sleep. She always kept her candle and robe close at hand, no matter the hour of the day or the temperature of the air. This simply was her understanding of how life should be lived, which she had brought with her from the hills of Ecuador.

It was precisely because Nita never slept that Hobo

never did, either. Instead, he trailed impassively behind her wherever she went throughout the house. Hobo's love for Nita was both unconditional and unrequited. She held him in thinly veiled contempt, which he bore with heartfelt dejection. But Marcus would not suffer the poor dog, though his sins be as scarlet, to sleep outside or be tied up in the kitchen. And so Hobo and Nita were locked in a never-ending battle against the ingress and egress of hair, mud, and sand.

Aidan tried to hide from Nita the bandage on his hand, but she spotted it just the same. Once she did, there was no avoiding the further inspection, washing, and re-bandaging that was to come, and he dutifully followed her into the kitchen, where this would occur. As she worked her cure, he thought to mention that he had other plans for dinner the following night.

"Her name is Molly McGregor," he said. "She's invited Ibrahim and me to have dinner with her aboard her towboat, the *Sairey Gamp*, tomorrow night in the harbor."

Nita smiled knowingly at this news and, without looking up at him, said, "Ibrahim she wishes to feed. You she wishes to love."

Aidan was startled by this and thought immediately to demur, even though he already knew Nita to be someone who understood more than she revealed. But explaining to her Molly's platonic reasons for inviting both men to dinner would have meant revealing the events at the Black Flag. It occurred to him, then, that Nita had not asked how he injured his hand.

The next morning was Sunday, and Marcus was up early, as usual, putting the finishing touches on his homily. While Aidan was still lying half asleep in his bed, he could hear the priest pacing in his study on the floor above, reciting bits and pieces of the remarks and the readings to guide the faithful. The two met in the hall on their way down to answer Nita's call to breakfast.

"I want to ask a favor of you today, Aidan."

"Whatever you need."

"This isn't something I need, but it is something I want—and that you will want, when you understand me better. There is a woman who needs a ride to church."

"Sure, no problem, I—"

"She's not your average churchgoer, Aidan, and this is not your average ride," Marcus interrupted. He was having trouble finding the words he needed to explain something, but he was too eager to get through breakfast and back to his homily to bother very long with it. He had been putting off asking Aidan to bring Sarah to mass for a week now, and it was hardly Aidan's fault, but he was just going to have to figure things out for himself.

"Look, she's on a boat in the lagoon by the inlet about a half mile south of the church. The *Bel Sogno*. It's the only boat anchored there. If you take the path that leads away from the last park service sign, you will come to a small beach. I have an old canoe stashed back in the dunes there. Use it to head out into the lagoon and pick her up. You'll need to be there at five, sharp, to get her back here in time for six o'clock mass."

Aidan started to fidget.

"The only thing is, I've got a commitment to somewhere at seven tonight."

"A commitment?" Marcus asked, suddenly curious at what Aidan possibly might have added to his social calendar in the short time he'd been on the island.

"A dinner—or really just an invitation to have something to eat together with, uh . . . aboard a boat. There's this girl, Molly—"

Aidan feared that too many details about his planned dinner with Molly and Ibrahim might lead unintentionally to the subject of the fight at the Black

Flag. It didn't appear that Marcus had heard anything about it, and Aidan didn't want him to if he could help it. He valued Marcus's generosity, and the last thing he wanted him to think was that he had some boozing, barroom brawler under his roof. He very much wanted to stay right where he was.

"Molly McGregor?" Marcus interrupted with a smile. "Now there's a lovely girl, Aidan. She invited you to dinner, did she?"

"Yessir. Ibrahim and me."

"Ibrahim, eh? You and he getting along all right?"

"Famously."

"So, what's the occasion?" Marcus asked with a gleam in his eye.

This was the question Aidan had dreaded, but as he took a breath to begin what promised to be a long wind-up to an answer, Marcus changed the subject just as abruptly again.

"Not to worry. I've got to preside at a meeting here at the church at three this afternoon or I'd get Sarah myself. But I'll be able to take her home after mass. You'll make your dinner.

"Now, Aidan . . ." Marcus continued, seeming to come again to a subject of some difficulty. "Sarah is a wonderful lady—a very devout lady and a faithful servant if ever there was one. But she is from a different tribe, of sorts, and you must understand that."

Aidan was at a loss. *A different tribe?*

Marcus didn't have any more time or inclination to explain.

"Just expect the unexpected, and don't let it faze you."

Marcus finished his breakfast far too quickly for Nita's liking and, with the mystery of the tribal woman still hanging in the air, rose and bolted back up the steps to the second floor of the rectory. Aidan remained at the kitchen table for a few moments wondering what possibly could be "unexpected" or would "faze" him about bringing an old woman to mass, but before he came to an answer, Marcus seemed to fly back down the stairs with a sprightliness that belied his years.

"And Aidan," he continued, as if his mind had not left the conversation when his body did, "when you throw a right cross with a bare fist, keep your fingers in a slightly loose grip, like so." Marcus's right arm then shot toward Aidan's jaw like a viper, stopping short but close enough that Aidan could feel the breeze that followed it. Aidan reacted much too late to avoid any blow that might have been intended, but none was. The priest gave him an impish grin and pointed to Aidan's bandaged right hand. "You'll better protect your hands from scrapes like that one."

CHAPTER 15

Sunday mass at St. Anne's was an unexpected pleasure for Aidan. Though raised a Catholic, he had not darkened the door of a church in twenty years—not since serving as godfather at the baptism of a friend's daughter, feeling the fraud and expecting at any moment to be incinerated by a lightning bolt. Since then his experience of the weekly mass came gradually, through the years, to the point where the homilies seemed more to indict than uplift him, and he tired of being in the dock every Sunday. But as was true of Marcus, faith never left Aidan despite his considerable efforts to deny and escape it. It found him each evening at the private altar of his pillow, where his prayers, once unbound by conscious thought and the hindrance of language, rose heavenward. They bore neither praise nor gratitude but only a swift, visceral plea for rescue that rose like a flare, briefly illuminating heaven and Earth before fading. It was the same plea he had made that sleepless night after he strode into a courtroom in Raleigh and traded his career for a lie. Though he doubted as much then as he did now what good it did him, it was the only prayer he knew.

The regular parishioners of St. Anne's, few though they were, came early and stayed late for Sunday morning mass as one might do at a very good restaurant, which Marcus took as a sign that they found some spiritual food there. The din of conversation and laughter rose as high as that in any tavern. Aidan knew none of them save Zoot, who acknowledged Aidan's presence with a nod as he passed on his way to a forward pew. Aidan smiled to see him, his friend in arms. Zoot returned a faltering smile that spoke of their new friendship and their shared secret. Aidan took his seat in the back of the tiny throng until the time came for him to stand and sing "O God Our Help in Ages Past." He did so with uncharacteristic relish and scarcely a glance at the hymnal—a testament to the memory engrained in so many Sunday mornings of his youth.

Father Marcus—the man who had just breezed Aidan's chin with a blistering jab—seemed transfigured by the long, green chasuble he wore as he walked in the processional to the altar for the start of mass. He was fortunate to have this man's kindness, Aidan thought. There was a great depth beneath his informal, often haphazard demeanor. This was most noticeable in the manner of his preaching, which bore no resemblance to the cheery, vacuous, greeting-card theology offered each week in the churches in Raleigh. The pastors there had learned too well not to afflict the comfortable while comforting the afflicted, and their coffers overflowed in approval. No matter how Marcus preached, the offering at St. Anne's never got any more or less meager from week to week, and so he preached as he saw fit.

The tourists on the island had shown up for mass in their usual slovenly attire, while the villagers dressed more neatly but no less formally. Aidan had one suit and one tie that Nita had managed to scavenge, steal, or stitch together for him somehow, of something, from somewhere. He might have called Gabby to ask that she send him a suit from the tiny storage unit she rented for him, but he felt a karmic resistance to the idea. Those clothes were the battle regalia of a lost war and a badge of his dishonor. Putting them on again would only commemorate his defeat. Between the suit Nita had cobbled together and the varnish-stained chinos he had brought to the island, he had the ability to dress either as a guest at a mob wedding or as a clubby vagrant. Knowing Marcus would sooner forgive a lack of taste than a lack of respect, Aidan went with the mob look on Sundays.

Although Nita's suit fit him remarkably well, Aidan felt very much the odd man out in church. No one was so formally dressed, except one fellow. Before Aidan arrived on the island, Charles Choate could usually count on being the only suited worshiper at St. Anne's. But seeing Aidan so garishly dressed on that very first Sunday and believing him to be a fellow traveler, Choate now made a point of greeting Aidan each week with an enthusiastic handshake and a wide grin before Choate took up his usual post at the far end of the front pew.

"This morning's homily," Marcus began, with an air of erudition that commanded the listener's interest and respect, "speaks of the patience and generosity of earthly fathers, of whom all present have been unworthy beneficiaries at some point in their lives. By this comparison I mean to dispel the fear that our Heavenly Father would suffer any of us to perish for eternity any more than a father would abandon his own child to want and despair."

Marcus went on to explain that no one could escape the joy of his heavenly reward any more than an errant child, behaving his utter worst, could escape the gifts of Christmas morning. Our twilight days on Earth were to be lived in the hopeful expectation of morning everlasting in heaven. Aidan felt himself soar, uplifted for only a moment before sinking with this reminder that he would be spending his next Christmas morning alone.

Mr. Choate sat through the mass that day stiffly, as usual, turning sideways during the homily so that the entire parish could not mistake his expression of disapproval. He was clearly having none of what Father Marcus had to say. A retired insurance salesman, Charles Choate had appointed himself Defender of the Faith on Ocracoke, and he considered today's homily yet another example in a long history of Father Marcus's profligacy in rendering Catholic doctrine. He scarcely doubted that Father Marcus meant to pardon the world's Jewry from the pains of hell, where lakes of fire could scarcely have burned any brighter than they did in Choate's fevered imagination.

Choate's doubts about Father Marcus first began when he saw him rend asunder the gates of heaven after being asked, by the child of a remarried, adulterous father, whether Daddy would go to heaven. He protested, as apostasy, the unqualified reassurance given to the child, and he had kept Marcus under close surveillance ever since. Today's homily he would duly chronicle and protest as he did the others in another letter to the bishop, warning gravely of the spiritual calamities to come and requesting again that Father Marcus be replaced by a purer vessel of Catholic orthodoxy. But Marcus had survived the pyres built for him through the years by dozens of men like Choate. To him they stumbled and fell no farther nor any closer to the glory of God than anyone else, and he suffered it all gracefully. He believed Choate's distemper would one day fade to astonished joy in the company of all the Jews, Muslims, pagans, and adulterers he would meet in heaven.

The vicar general in Raleigh, for his part, kept quarter with Choate in his opinion of Father Marcus. But it was an immutable fact that the shortage of priests to minister to the parishes of the diocese grew more dire with each passing year. Besides, the bishop had already banished Father Marcus to the farthest edge of the realm and could not dispatch him farther without throwing him bodily into the sea, though it was his secret dream to do exactly that.

On Sunday afternoons the entire island seemed collectively to exhale the week's woes, and apart from the rush of tourists preparing to return to the mainland on the ferry, the hours of that day passed more quietly than any other. Marcus would retire to his study for a nap after the noon meal, then emerge at around three o'clock to attend the meeting of the Alcoholics Anonymous group that came each week at that time. On this Sunday, Aidan spent the afternoon hours reading in the quiet of his room and sipping a wonderful jasmine tea that Nita had prepared. The aroma of it filled the entire house with delicious incense.

At 2:30, Aidan looked up from his book to check the time. He wanted to make sure he didn't start too late for the inlet to fetch the woman from the lagoon for evening mass, as he'd promised. Outside the window of his room, he noticed a small group of people milling around in the garden. They had gathered for the meeting. One among the group was an attractive blonde. He recognized her from the mini-mart, now seemingly a century ago, when he wandered out of the dunes in a woman's beach cover-up. Bobbi Baker was her name, he was surprised to remember. Also in the group was the bloody man who had been reading a magazine the morning he walked in. Aidan decided to say hello—if only to make the point by his appearance that he did actually have clothes to wear.

The group that met each week at St. Anne's was tightly knit and wildly dysfunctional. There was Bobbi, who had never been nearly so addicted to wine as she was to the attention she received from men in the recovery movement, which was a culture unto itself. Then there were the men who came to troll at these meetings for women like Bobbi. Frank, the bloody man, was addicted to sex, pornography, beer, hot wings, video poker, and just about every other sinful pleasure he had encountered in his life, and he had no intention of giving any of them up. The meetings afforded him an unassailable excuse to be away from his clinging shrew of a wife, and if he had to lie in order to be there, that was a lie worth telling as far as he was concerned.

Everyone who came to these meetings was cheating on *someone* or about *something*. Several were cheating on their wives or husbands or on each other or both. Frank was cheating every chance he got to drink beer and thumb through the girly magazines at the mini-mart without ever buying them. Bobbi was cheating her employer by giving Frank free beer and letting him ruin five magazines a week masturbating in the store bathroom. (She wrote them off as damaged returns.) One summer, when new magazine deliveries didn't come for a month after a big storm shut down ferry service to the island, out of pity she finally lifted her shirt long enough to give Frank a vivid memory to take into the bathroom, instead. But that wasn't cheating as far as Bobbi was concerned. She never understood what all the fuss was about with men and boobs, anyway. That was nothing more than the same simple act of kindness she had shown to the farm boys she knew growing up, on rivers and creeks hidden in the woods near her home in Kentucky. As a result, she was, unwittingly, forever enshrined in the fantasies and bitter regrets of a hundred grown and married men all across the Blue Ridge.

Marcus, whose buried cache of Sangiovese was now

up to seventeen bottles, was the biggest cheater of all. He was cheating heaven, although had he known that his nightly elopements were being observed by anyone other than God, he might well have repented of them. But to be sure, none of them cheated on one thing, which was their unspoken pledge never to tell anyone that they were all cheating on damned near everything. And thus did Father Marcus and his little band of backsliders survive and prosper.

When Aidan appeared in the garden where Bobbi and the others were waiting for that week's meeting to begin, she distinctly remembered him—the man in the dress—and it was clear that he remembered her. He was walking straight toward her.

"Hello, stranger," Bobbi said, holding a lit cigarette cocked away and to the side of her face, one arm cradled by the other at the elbow on her waist. "Fancy seeing you again. This is a meeting for drunks. Are you a drunk?"

"Uh, no," Aidan stuttered, uncertain of his answer, and thinking he might just as sincerely have said *yes*.

"I don't know. Seems like when I last saw you, you were walking around in a dress on Sunday with half a bottle of cheap wine. I think anybody who does that ought to qualify for AA by acclamation. Don't you think so, Frank?"

The bloody man, now dressed in neatly pressed khaki trousers and a collared shirt, extended his hand to Aidan.

"Frank Dawson. Pleased to meet you."

Aidan felt suddenly better known than he wished to be.

"Well, you may be right, but I just wanted to say 'hi.' I'm staying here at the rectory with Father Marcus. I've got to go give someone a ride to mass. Nice seeing you again."

"Likewise," Bobbi said, disappointed she hadn't learned more about this newest resident of their little Peyton Place. But Father Marcus would tell her all she needed to know. She would ask him about the good-looking, young cross-dresser and how it was that he got his hands on a bottle of Father Marcus's communion wine that Sunday in the first place.

CHAPTER 16

Aidan found the canoe behind the dunes where Marcus had said it would be. Lifting it onto his shoulders, he carried it a short distance to a beach at the edge of the lagoon and placed it in the water. After another trip back to the dunes to retrieve two paddles—one to use, one just in case—he was coursing through the lagoon in the ethereal stillness of the late afternoon air.

As he slid down from his seat onto the hull and braced his hips to one side, Indian-style, the canoe dipped slightly off center. He was enthralled to be gliding silently and swiftly under his own power again. The twilight water rushed past him, just inches below the gunwale. His trance was so complete that he never noticed the hull of *Bel Sogno* rising up before his bow like an iceberg.

The stem of the canoe hit the boat with a loud *thunk* that startled him, though not nearly so much as it did the woman who had been sunbathing on the foredeck. He had seen no crew aboard when he started out from shore, but she sprang up as suddenly as if she had been blasted skyward with a fire hose. She landed on the deck in a crouch and faced amidships, braced for a sneak attack. She was a young woman. Aidan watched her open-mouthed from below, as the canoe slowly rebounded from the impact. It was Molly McGregor, and she was completely nude.

He found her to be beautiful in the ordinary yet remarkable way that every young woman is beautiful in the form God gave her. In his eyes, the wild riot of freckles covering her alabaster skin contributed to her allure. There was scarcely a curve on her—a fact that she apparently had kept well hidden beneath her clothes or that Aidan had simply failed to notice. Instead, she shot up in an uninterrupted, straight line from her feet to her chin like a black-eyed Susan.

She looked like none of the women Aidan had ever loved. Observing her startled expression, he was reminded of the occasion in junior high when he went to use the bathroom at a friend's house and surprised the boy's older sister coming out of the shower. The spectacle then—as now—was vanishingly brief.

It took Molly a moment to recognize just who was staring up at her from the green canoe that was now slowly ricocheting shoreward. It should have been Father Marcus, who would have known better than to slam into the *Bel Sogno* and whose arrival likely would have passed unacknowledged by her. But the man who had rammed the boat and who now sat staring at her from the canoe below was someone else entirely. He was someone she already cared for, fatuously, or at least thought she might.

She was indisposed beyond any aid—that was clear. The only avenue of immediate escape without the threat of conversation was to jump. And so to her astonishment, she did. In an almost involuntary spasm of sudden movement, she catapulted away from Aidan and over the opposite rail of *Bel Sogno* in one fluid, well-executed standing backflip, with a red ponytail following behind. It was the very maneuver she had perfected in years of practice at the Tumble Tots School of Gymnastics to the constant cheers of her parents, who could never have imagined this occasion for its use. She landed safely feet-first in the deep water, leaving barely a ripple and making no sound that Aidan could hear from the opposite side of the boat.

Aidan stood up abruptly in the canoe, wondering if his careless error had just become the occasion for a death at sea. But when he looked over the decks, he saw that the *Sairey Gamp* was pulled alongside the port quarter of *Bel Sogno*, where it had been hidden from his view. That was Molly's boat, he knew, and she was climbing up the stern ladder in a rush to get aboard.

Aidan did not try to understand or explain these events. It sufficed for the moment that all was well, and the weirdness of what had just happened, he was certain, could be sorted out later. Then, things became weirder still.

The woman who emerged from the companionway of *Bel Sogno*, unfazed by all the ruckus, was immediately recognizable to him. He knew he had seen her before, and it was only a moment after she had taken her seat in the canoe that he remembered where and when. She watched him as intently, then, as she had that morning on the beach. Then she spoke to him in the same weary voice.

"I know why you came here," she said.

Aidan suddenly realized he had said nothing in his astonishment at seeing this woman again and thought she was probably wondering why Father Marcus had not come for her instead.

"I'm sorry. My name is—"

"I know your name, Aidan," she interrupted. She seemed impatient with his ignorance. "I have always known your name. I have always known that you would come, though I did not know the day or the hour."

She paused a long while, as if expecting him to acknowledge that he understood these things that she "knew" about him and what he was doing there, on the island. He sorely doubted that she knew anything about the events of the trial, or his disbarment, or his ruined marriage, or his ruined life. But these were not the things on her mind.

She finally asked, "Do you know why you are here?"

Aidan was doing his best to suffer this conversation with the deference he felt was due to any woman of her years, and who was quite possibly disturbed, but he had no understanding of her meaning.

"It comes for you, even now. The hour is late," she said, with an air of urgency. "Claim it. Follow where it leads. The life it takes, and the life it gives, is *everlasting.*"

None of Sarah's words made any sense to him. Whatever dementia had left her wandering around a beach naked on a Sunday morning was clearly progressing, he thought.

Sarah said not another word after they came ashore, during the entire walk through the dunes to the church. She looked carefully at her path as they went, maneuvering the hem of her skirts out of the way of thorn bushes. They arrived a few minutes before mass started. Just before she entered the sanctuary to pray, she took Aidan's face in her hands and kissed his forehead, the way a mother kisses a child. He saw tears well up in her eyes, and then she was gone.

Aidan went to find Marcus and tell him that Sarah had arrived safely, but the rectory was empty. He found him in the sacristy, where he seemed to be running behind in getting things ready for mass.

"What's this I hear about you walking around the village in a lady's cover-up with a bottle of wine in your hand?" Marcus asked, fumbling hurriedly with the buttons on his chasuble. "Bobbi Baker had all kinds of questions about you. Watch yourself there, boy."

"I'll keep a lookout," Aidan said facetiously.

"I hate to be late for mass," Marcus said as he rose to

leave. "The Father did not suffer the Son to be late for the cross, you know." He turned crisply and headed for the narthex, his chasuble and stole flowing after him.

Watch myself? Aidan thought. *The mini-mart lady?* He thought she might just be the only normal person he'd met on the island so far. Whatever Bobbi's inner mysteries might be, he was certain there was less cause for watchfulness with her than with catapulting, naked towboat captains, rapacious sailors, knife-throwing Bahamians, and brooding Gypsies.

CHAPTER 17

Ibrahim and Aidan found the *Sairey Gamp* in her slip in Silver Lake Harbor, where they arrived at seven o'clock sharp, as promised. Molly heard their footsteps on the wooden pier and Aidan's "ahoy there," which blessedly signaled either that he had forgotten or was resolved to move on from the spectacle of the *leaper* earlier that day. She was eager to make amends for what—if not her first impression—had surely been her most definitive so far.

"Welcome aboard," Molly called from below deck. An electric current of anxiety ran through her that she was trying hard to convert to cheerfulness. She smiled as she unhooked the gate of the starboard lifeline to allow the two men to step on deck. She accepted a bottle of Chianti from Ibrahim and a bottle of Pellegrino from Aidan. Cradling one in each elbow like a nursemaid holding two newborns, she turned to face Aidan squarely, steadied and braced herself as if she were expecting a pie in the face, and then proceeded to get it over with.

"I don't know what in the world I was thinking out on Sarah's boat. I just freaked out when I saw you. It was so ridiculous. Do you think I'm an idiot?"

Molly let out a burst of nervous laughter before Aidan could answer. Ibrahim looked at Aidan with mild bewilderment. Aidan had not mentioned the naked leaping incident to him, and, realizing this, Molly was immediately grateful for Aidan's discretion.

Molly was now in uncharted waters, and she knew it. She acted as if some manic cheerleader had taken over her body. That person, whoever she was, bore no resemblance to the woman who usually lived there in relative peace and dignity. She kept blushing and cooing and prattling on as she ushered both men below.

A faint aroma of garlic and thyme filled the still air of the cabin. She had prepared a dinner of spaghetti noodles tossed with parmesan, parsley, and slices of roasted tomatoes and squash. There hadn't been time to do anything more elaborate. She had stayed much too late on Sarah's boat that day, but Sarah's brooding had concerned her—so much so that she hadn't felt comfortable leaving her alone.

Standing beside Aidan, Molly felt again the sudden, strange impulse to flee, but another back flip at that moment would have ended things for good. And she wanted the evening to work. In fact, she wanted it too much, and it was throwing her off her game.

She noticed that all of her defenses were down in Aidan's presence. She supposed that the clothing and makeup she wore were not fooling him one bit. Nothing could blur his more vivid, recent memory of her. Just two hours ago, he had seen her in full measure—up close, airborne, and rotated to every possible angle— more plainly than a scoop of vanilla ice cream on a cone. There seemed to be no point in any further pretense or formality, but she knew no other way of courtship.

Courtship? she thought. *My God, is that what we're doing here?*

She felt herself suddenly full of foolish wishes for things she'd never wanted before. The realization that she wanted them was coming on like a flash flood— unexpected and without means of escape. She wanted a real tan, for one thing—not a peace treaty between warring armies of freckles. She had legs—skinny miles of legs—but she wanted hips to go with them. Her whole adult life, she had considered it a blessing not to have an hourglass figure and the pigeon-toed awkwardness that came from trying to run with womanly hips, but now she did not want to run. She wanted to be *caught*. And yes, *dammit*, she wished for bigger boobs—*any* boobs—even though she'd said a thousand times that she couldn't imagine what a stupid bother they must be. She wanted a cuter nose. And, "*God help me*," she thought, she wanted to have this boyish savior named Aidan all to herself.

Molly knew that this was utterly ridiculous and completely juvenile of her. She knew it better than anyone, but no one could have cared less about that than she did at the moment. She had only just met Aidan, but that hardly mattered. As she stole glances at him on the opposite settee, with his tousled hair scattered in disorderly clumps around the faint remnant of a part that hadn't seen a comb since that morning, his cerulean eyes seemed almost to plead for her approval and affection. He had a kind of incandescence—a flame of lost and forlorn innocence that still flickered, deep down, with the possibility of redemption. It was a redemption she would have gladly granted, were it in her power to do so.

There, in the lamp-lit cabin of the *Sairey Gamp*, the six feet, four inches, and 250 pounds that comprised Ibrahim Joseph seemed to fade and all but disappear into the surrounding teak, for Molly. While she felt her breath come and go and her lips continue to form the words of some conversation with both men, her will was straining against her desire to climb into Aidan's lap, run her fingers through his hair, and lose herself in his kiss. Of the many thoughts racing through her head, just then, *"What in hell is wrong with me?"* was leading the pack.

The *Sairey Gamp* had a wonderfully comfortable cabin, with a small dining table to port that was recessed within a U-shaped, cushioned settee. Aidan and Ibrahim took their places by the table while Molly stood up in the galley to finish preparing their dinner. A dim, golden orb of light shone from a brass oil lamp on the bulkhead, swaying back and forth as the ship rose and fell on the wake from a distant boat moving through the harbor. It was now getting dark outside. The world beyond the soft glow of their little home seemed to dissolve into space. The only sounds that could be heard were the tapping of the wooden spoon Molly was using to stir the sauce, the steady *whir* of the blue flame on the burner of the galley stove, and a faint riff from a Bonnie Raitt tune turned down too low on the stereo.

The dinner was uncommonly delicious, and Molly was pleased with herself. But when the conversation turned to Sarah, Molly's expression darkened, and a fog seemed to roll in around her. She spoke more cautiously. Aidan was curious to know just who Sarah was, how she had come to the island, why she wasn't wearing any clothes that day on the beach, and why she was so strangely cryptic today. Ibrahim, who knew Sarah's story and Father Marcus's part in it, caught Aidan's attention and waved him off with a downward glance of disapproval, as if this were a subject it would be impolite to discuss in mixed company. But Molly did not hesitate to answer. She had asked most of the same questions herself at one time or another.

Sarah was a topic of much discussion in the village. Some actually thought she was a witch. Others were convinced she was nothing but a common whore. Marcus privately suspected she might be a prophet who had come to them unawares. He knew enough of the history of prophets to recognize the importance of treating her with kindness and respect—for his own sake if not for hers.

One of the rumors that circulated about Sarah had to do with the story of a passenger on a sailing ship that foundered in a storm on Diamond Shoals, near Cape Hatteras, in 1868. According to survivors, this woman leapt without hesitation into the blackness of the night sea after her infant was torn from her arms by a wave and swept overboard. A photograph of the woman obtained from her family was later printed in the local paper, but neither the woman nor the child was ever found. Some villagers said that Sarah resembled the photograph of that woman and was her specter. Molly, who could plainly see that Sarah was flesh and blood, passed it off as one of the many old ghost stories regularly told in sailing towns.

Molly knew no more about where Sarah came from than did Aidan. She was certain there was a great goodness and a great sadness in her, mixed with a sense of destiny and responsibility. She couldn't describe it any more clearly than that. She just knew that she could trust her, and she felt a compulsion—a moral responsibility—to help her. She never felt so at peace as when she was with Sarah aboard the *Bel Sogno*.

Stirring distractedly the unfinished strands of pasta on the plate in front of her, Molly finally said that she considered Sarah a *seer*. By that she meant that Sarah had a sense of the history of things that had been, and the meaning of things to come. Sarah seemed to live, in a way, between two worlds—suspended between heaven and hell on the waters of the lagoon, not yet belonging entirely to either realm, yet able to see clearly beyond this life into the next. Molly began to tell a story from her past that explained why she believed this.

Molly and her mother had been estranged ever since her mother's affair with a friend of the family had ended her parents' marriage of thirty years. Molly was sixteen when it happened, and her world fell apart—along with her father's life. She rarely spoke to her mother in the years after the divorce and did so less often after leaving for college.

Molly had never mentioned her mother to Sarah, but one day two years ago, Sarah had brought her up unexpectedly in conversation—asking Molly for remembrances of her, then suggesting and finally insisting, despite Molly's perturbed refusals, that she return to see her. By then Molly hadn't seen or spoken to her mother in five years. She arrived home to find her mother in hospice care, her body wracked with breast cancer. Molly's father had known nothing of her mother's illness. He wept openly when Molly gave him the news. They went to see her together. As the three of them cried and laughed, each gave and received forgiveness. Molly and her mother talked about life and love in a way they had never talked before. When the end came, Molly had finally accepted that her mother was a human being like any other—with all of the flaws and potential of the race—and no less worthy of her devotion. Those days changed Molly's life forever.

Molly was not religious, but she knew something of faith, and she believed in things unspoken and unseen. She never asked Sarah to explain how she had known about her mother, or why she had insisted that Molly see her again. To demand an explanation, as if what Sarah had done was a parlor trick that needed only to be revealed to be understood, seemed beneath the dignity of her friend.

That afternoon, before Aidan came for her in the canoe,

Sarah had spent hours staring silently out to sea. It was not her habit to do so. She was usually pleased to sit with Molly on the foredeck as the *Bel Sogno* faced the setting sun and prevailing southwesterly wind, letting the warmth bronze her body as it freckled Molly's. There was a difference in her that Molly could sense. She seemed not to be paying much attention to Molly's usual lamentations. She looked only to the east and said nothing. Molly knew not to pry with questions. She had remained on the *Bel Sogno* much later into the evening than she had intended, for fear that Sarah might be ill.

Aidan did not know what to make of Molly's concern for Sarah or quite how to react, so he merely nodded in sympathy as she related her worries to him. It was not for want of interest, but he found it difficult to concentrate too closely on the enchantment of an elderly Gypsy when the woman in front of him was more enchanting than any he had ever met. In fact, Aidan had watched Molly all evening with growing, quiet wonder. He had long since given up the hope of falling in love again. He didn't really understand what peculiar formula of attraction might make that even possible for him, now. He didn't like the man he became at the end of his first marriage, and his marriage had ended badly. It was not his finest hour, and he did not wish to repeat it. It was during those terrible years that he discovered, contrary to the high opinion he had of himself at the time, that he was quite capable of betrayal, deceit, manipulation, cruelty, self-pity, and cowardice. He never wanted to see that man again, and the surest way to keep him at bay was to stay single. He had kept that pledge to this day. But that night aboard the *Sairey Gamp*, he felt himself wavering for the first time.

Molly was not the kind of woman whom most men would consider "sexy," but she fit perfectly in her own skin. That was something Aidan had not failed to appreciate about her earlier that day, in the lagoon. She had a girlish awkwardness, as if she were still adjusting to the jumble of legs, knees, and elbows that had grown more quickly than the rest of her. But this quality, mixed with genuine kindness, a sophisticated wit, and—not least of all—the fact that she had the courage to live a pirate's life on a pirate's island—proved to be a powerful elixir. By the time Aidan got up to say goodbye, he had drunk quite a bit more of it than he realized.

Molly had a collection of brass bosun's whistles from her father's navy days. They recalled an era when every movement of a ship and her crew was announced by a distinct measure of tones blown from this simple instrument. She kept them aboard the *Sairey Gamp* as curios. Aidan noticed one as he was standing to leave and picked it up. He tried blowing through the mouthpiece several times but could make no sound. Molly took the whistle from him. Pressing it to her lips, she sounded a continuous, low note that blended into a higher note.

"What's that the signal for?" asked Aidan.

"All hands on deck," Molly replied. She then handed him the whistle and said, "Call me sometime."

When she placed the whistle in Aidan's palm, he closed his hand around hers. He then raised her hand to his lips and kissed it softly, just as Ibrahim had done in the Black Flag.

"Now that I know the signal, that shouldn't be hard to do."

That was supposed to be Aidan's exit line, but Molly wouldn't stand for it. Hand kisses were for the Queen of England. Standing on her tiptoes, she grabbed his face in her hands and pulled him down to her level. Gazing intently into his eyes, she planted a wet, wandering kiss that she let linger, just until that moment when she could sense that he wanted more. Then, she let him go with a smile, and sat down.

"I—" Aidan hesitated, once again at a loss for words. Molly cut him off.

"I'll see you soon, Aidan," she said—suddenly a picture of self-control. Aidan looked as if he'd just been swept up into a cyclone and thrown back to Earth.

Ibrahim wasn't expecting or offering any kisses after dinner, but he had been watching Molly and Aidan all night, and he knew enough not to hang around once he'd complimented the cook. When Aidan stepped onto the dock, Ibrahim was already halfway home. Aidan shouted to him and ran to catch up. The house where Ibrahim lived was at the end of Howard Street, in the heart of the village. It was on Aidan's way back to the rectory—a pleasant walk along narrow lanes shrouded in curtains of Spanish moss.

The shake-shingle cottages in the village were gnarled and weathered, and each year their frames bent lower to the mossy earth, like old washerwomen. No matter what, nothing in Ocracoke ever seemed smooth, tidied away, and ready for company. There was a certain neurosis and precariousness to life in this outermost place. It was an aged, thin, and disappearing spit of sand—an underfed stepchild of coastal geology. For Aidan, that was its charm. The island itself seemed slump-shouldered and in need of a haircut and a hot bath.

When Aidan came alongside, Ibrahim asked him about his plans for Molly.

"Plans?" Aidan replied, with feigned confusion. "I stopped making plans where women are concerned a long time ago."

Ibrahim knew a lie when he heard one, and Aidan knew that he knew. The truth was, Aidan had no idea what had just happened on the *Sairey Gamp,* and he was sure he wasn't going to figure it out on the walk back to the rectory. But he did, of course, have a plan.

He wanted to see Molly again. And yes, he also wanted to see her again in the way he had seen her that afternoon for an all-too-brief instant, on the deck of the *Bel Sogno.* The sap was rising in him even with the thought of her, and the idea of turning around and walking right back to the *Sairey Gamp* to tell her so didn't seem as foolish to him as it was. There was an elusive, unattainable quality about Molly. He thought he had learned all there was to know about what women wanted and how to give it to them, but Molly McGregor seemed somehow to be outside the paradigm. The image of the backflip replayed again and again in his mind for the hundredth time. She was no aloof thoroughbred content to run in the traces others had made for her. She was a wild pony who sought the rough ground, made her own path, and invited him to follow at his peril.

CHAPTER 18

Islands have long memories. The things that people are most ashamed of and would wish to hide are apt to be washed up in a storm, for all to see. Once every decade or so, a hurricane would come to Ocracoke that would send the waves surging over the dunes and into the village like a Mongol horde, throwing open stone sepulchers and bidding their occupants, long dead, once more to wander. Bodies yielded up by the sea and those that could not be identified and returned to their proper tombs were placed in old gravesites marked "unknown."

Having said goodnight to Ibrahim, Aidan found his way past the village cemetery on the road to the rectory, thinking long thoughts as he had done most of the night. The moon passed all-but-unnoticed above him. Where two oaks parted to create an opening to the sky, at the edge of a falling picket fence that once protected gravesites now long forgotten, the moon shone brightly on a headstone that Aidan could clearly see, just off his path. He paused to study it.

The marker bore no name and no year of birth or death, but only a verse, barely legible in carved letters now worn with age:

Here lies a woman,
Who perished on the sea.
Here lies an only child,

Her mother's treasury.
The storms of night are over.
Everlasting shines the sun.
May God grant them rest,
In the world that is to come.

It struck him as a touching verse to have been written for someone unknown, and he made a mental note to ask Marcus about its history. But graves and death were far from Aidan's thoughts that night. He was more alive than he had been in years. He felt the return of desires long departed and new resolve to chart a course for his future, though the means to achieve it were still unclear to him.

When he arrived at the rectory, Aidan found the front door ajar. Not seeing Hobo there to greet him and assuming the little dog was late returning from a crime spree somewhere on the island, he decided he had best leave the door open. He could hear the muted verses of a song, and the gentle trilling of a guitar, coming from Nita's room. The record player was a gift to her from Marcus, so that she could play the ancient LPs she brought with her from Ecuador. She fell asleep to the songs sometimes. They were haunting melodies that spoke of heartsickness and longing for home. With a moist, hot breeze blowing in from the sea, Aidan could almost see her in that distant time and place, when she had been a young girl in love. This night, although the hour was late, a dim light still shown beneath Nita's door. There was a slow, rhythmic sound of steps on the wood floor inside. She was dancing. He walked softly down the hall, so as not to disturb her. He felt a warm glow of gratitude for Nita, for Father Marcus, for Ibrahim, and for the sheltered harbor that this place had become to him in a time of storms in his life.

The rectory sat at the end of an unpaved, sandy road that led to the edge of a marsh near the inlet. The man who built it in 1916 as a home for his lonely wife was a Dutch sea captain. When she died, childless, of pneumonia, he gave the house to the diocese. It was the only house on the point, close to the inlet. Because the captain worried that light coming from the windows at night could be mistaken for the nearby lighthouse and lead ships at sea astray, the house was never wired for electricity. What few electric outlets had been installed in the years since were sparingly placed. Marcus could have improved on the situation, but he rather liked it the way it was. It was the reason why Nita went everywhere carrying a candle lantern, but it was not like her to leave one burning on the table beside Aidan's bed when he was not at home. A soft, flickering light leaked from underneath his doorway into the darkness of the hall as he approached his room.

When Aidan closed the door behind him and turned around, he could sense a dark shape in the armchair in the corner, just beyond the edge of the candlelight. He thought at first it was a pile of laundry that Nita had left there for folding. But when he realized it was a person, his heart pounded. Thoughts of the graveyard in the village, and the image of the woman who came from a watery tomb to lie there, suddenly raced through his mind.

He started to shout, but fear snatched his breath. Then she spoke to him. Her voice was cool and calm.

"Don't be afraid. I don't bite."

A woman rose from the chair and stepped into the light. She had been drinking, he could tell, but only just enough to summon the courage she needed to come uninvited to Aidan's room and wait for his return. She looked at Aidan with an unrepentant smile. Her clothes were thrown over the end of his bed. She was wearing a white oxford shirt of his. His shirts were not made for such curves, he thought, as he looked at her. It covered her like a curtain draped over the statue of a goddess. He did not miss it when she pushed it back off of her shoulders and let it fall to the floor.

CHAPTER 19

After cleaning up the galley and quietly congratulating herself for the dinner she had served to Aidan and Ibrahim, Molly sat alone in the cabin of the *Sairey Gamp*. The oil lamp still flickered above her, casting golden shadows on the cabin walls. She was staring straight ahead, yet she perceived nothing of her immediate surroundings. Her mind's eye was focused on the meaning of the day just passed. She was only half listening to the Bonnie Raitt CD—now making its eighth revolution of the evening—that implored her to "give 'em somethin' to talk about . . ."

Her little boat, which she loved, had always been a comfortable refuge. She once thought that the living it afforded her would be all she could ever need or want. But now this shell and her life within it seemed strangely empty, and her heart was restless.

There were two things she could not get out of her mind. One was Sarah and the darkness of her mood that day. There had been a foreboding to her silence. Molly had come to know and love Sarah like an older sister, and she usually grasped the meaning of Sarah's thoughts without need of words, but today Sarah had seemed to wander off without her, away from all that was familiar and comforting between them. Even now, the air was thick with uncertainty and the danger it seemed to portend.

Molly's other newfound obsession was Aidan, but of

him her thoughts were bright and hopeful, not dark and full of fear. She was not sure she dared to believe what she thought she knew—that he was a *good man*. After all, she had spent no more than three hours in his company. *But he had clearly shown his worth, hadn't he, in the Black Flag? Could she ever hope for a better champion?* On all of these points, she was certain only of her uncertainty. This seemed to be just the very kind of silly nonsense that gullible, needy women went through, constantly wondering whether this or that man might be *The One*.

God, how she hated those two words. She had known too many women whose entire lives had been spent dreaming that love and happiness would find them in the arms of some fictional, fabulous man—only to watch that dream slowly fade or, more often, turn into a nightmare. She had always been one of the sensible ones. She didn't believe in fairy tales. She knew her heading and how to keep it. She always had her goal squarely in sight. Now, inside of a single day, all was fog.

Sleep would not come for Molly that night. Whatever was to become of her sudden attraction to Aidan, she knew it would take more than a single day to unfold. But she felt an odd sense of urgency where Sarah was concerned. She sensed that something was afoot, though she knew not what. At last she could no longer resist her compulsion to make sure Sarah was safe. She decided the only way to put her worries aside was to get up and go to her—right away, right then.

The moon was already waning when Molly stepped onto the deck of the *Sairey Gamp*. Although the stars shone all the more brightly in the sky, the water and everything beneath it was dark. There was no possibility in this light of navigating the winding, narrow channel into the lagoon without running aground—even for Molly, who knew the way better than anyone. But Sarah's boat was not anchored so far out that it couldn't be seen by one standing on shore. If she could just see *Bel Sogno's* anchor light, Molly thought, she could rest knowing that Sarah was safe below. After that, all of her questions could wait for the light of day. She grabbed a sweatshirt to ward off the chill of the night wind flying over the dunes, stuffed a flashlight in the pocket, and set out for the inlet with quick, purposeful strides—feeling much better for her decision to go.

After a half hour of walking, Molly passed the rectory. It was about two o'clock in the morning. She could see dim lights coming from two of the rooms on the first floor. She imagined Aidan in his room and wondered whether he too was restless with thoughts of their dinner together. Surely his world had changed as well. It must have. She was certain she had felt his body start to stir when she pressed him close to kiss him. It didn't seem possible to her that she could be alone in these new feelings.

From a distance, on the road where Molly walked, the rectory looked warm and inviting. She imagined within its weathered, clapboard walls the smell of fresh cotton sheets, the feel of firm ground under a table that did not rise and fall with the waves, and the image of steam rising from a claw-foot tub filled to the brim with gallons and gallons of hot, soapy water. These were luxuries unknown to her life for the past three years in the closeted world of a tugboat—even one as lovely and well-appointed as the *Sairey Gamp*. It was a life filled with many wonders, but like any other it demanded compromise. Despite all the joys she had discovered, there were pleasures she had forgotten, some she had lost, and many she had missed.

A quarter mile past the rectory, the beach road reached the edge of the dunes, where it became a foot path that led for another half mile to the landing by the lagoon. The moon was now just a faint, translucent wafer, dissolving slowly into Pamlico Sound. Molly turned on her flashlight, better to see the sandy path through the thornbushes. Her eyes adjusted to the white light that led the way in front of her feet, and darkness enveloped the world all around, until she felt as though she were walking through a long tunnel. When she came out on the other end and extinguished the light, she was standing on the beach looking into the lagoon. A seven-knot wind rippled the surface of the water, and warm cupfuls of it tossed onto her toes. A minute passed before her eyes had adjusted well enough to the darkness that she could trust what she was seeing.

The *Bel Sogno* was gone.

She felt a great wave of anxiety rise within her. The *Bel Sogno* had not moved from that spot since Marcus had anchored her there three years before. Sarah had meticulously maintained every inch of her vessel—all except the engine, which had not been started once in all the years she had lived aboard. Molly had enough experience with diesel engines to know that the one aboard *Bel Sogno* had likely given up the ghost years ago. Even an engine in perfect condition wouldn't run after three years of total neglect. And the hoses and belts on *Bel Sogno's* engine were at least ten years old, badly cracked, and weathered.

But still, the boat was *gone*. She couldn't have sunk—the lagoon was deep but not deeper than the height of *Bel Sogno's* main mast. It would have shown above the surface of the water even if her hull were lying on the bottom. Someone must have *sailed* that boat out of the lagoon, Molly thought, and that would have been no mean feat even in broad daylight.

This turn of events, against the backdrop of the previous day, surely boded something ill. Molly could imagine nothing worse than that her closest friend and confidant—the woman whom she dearly loved as a sister—might be alone on a derelict ship at night off the Outer Banks.

Molly ran in long leaps back up the path, now with no regard for the distraction of thornbushes. She needed to sound the alarm. She needed help, and Father Marcus would know what to do.

The rectory was dark when she rounded the bend in the beach road near the garden gate. It must have been three o'clock in the morning. There was no sign of anyone, but the front door was ajar. She did not wish to wake the entire household. She needed only to find Father Marcus and tell him that the *Bel Sogno* was gone and Sarah with her. Molly would leave immediately aboard the *Sairey Gamp* for the open ocean to try to find her. She wanted Father Marcus to come along. She didn't really need his help to manage the boat. What she truly wanted was a trusted friend and someone to carry a power stronger than her doubts into the deep. Molly believed that Father Marcus had that power, and she trusted in his faith to turn the tide.

As she stepped through the entrance, it occurred to her that she had never been inside the rectory before, though she couldn't say why. She saw a hallway to the left with two closed doors, a dim light spilling out from underneath the first. If this were not Father Marcus's room, she thought, it would be Nita's or Aidan's, and either of them could help her find him. When she pushed the first door gently to knock, it swung partly open—enough for her to see by the light of the candle inside. What she saw then filled her with a strange mixture of revulsion and embarrassment. She felt a sudden burning in her gut and an intense desire to turn and run before they noticed her. Instead, by some involuntary impulse she pushed the door the rest of the way open until it banged softly against the wall inside.

Bobbi Baker shrieked at the noise and jumped up from the bed, her eyes as wide as saucers. Her first thought was not to cover herself. She seemed instead to repent of being anywhere near Aidan and moved quickly away from him as if she believed the intruder were Father Marcus, come to scold her for corrupting an altar boy.

Aidan did not move at first because he was sound asleep. He eventually looked up from the bed at the figure of a woman standing in the doorway, and wearily struggled to focus. It could not possibly be *her,* he thought. Molly watched his face contort and change as he recognized her—as if he were watching the slow-motion approach of a bullet aimed between his eyes.

Molly stood still and straight, held in place as if by an electric charge. But as she recovered from the initial shock, her shoulders gradually slumped forward—her mind far from Sarah. All of her thoughts were bent on the woman standing defiantly naked in front of her who was everything Molly was not, but who apparently was exactly the woman Aidan wanted.

A slow, rolling thunder of violent emotion throbbed through Molly down to her toes. She suddenly spoke in a clear, mocking voice that she scarcely recognized as her own.

"My God, those can't be real."

She immediately regretted, with those words, to have stepped onto that lowest of battlefields reserved for the wars of scorned women, where victory is impossible and every soldier is diminished by the fight.

Bobbi's expression, having come by then from terror to annoyance, came all the way around to disgust and contempt. She surveyed Molly's nondescript form while, with difficulty, she wrangled a bra over two enormous breasts. To Molly, they seemed to defy the very laws of gravity and time.

"I was just going to say the same thing about you, little girly," Bobbi answered.

Molly felt her face flush. She stared resolutely at Bobbi. A glance toward Aidan at that moment would have been a plea for him to defend her—to *choose her*, instead—and she summoned all her will not to do it. She thought to make some biting reply, but no words would come. Anything she might say would smack of envy, and Molly thought it safer to snuff that spark before it became a flame.

But the flame was already spreading. She could make fun of Bobbi's boobs, but the rest of her was obviously original equipment. Bobbi looked like she had stepped right off the pages of those smutty magazines she sold at the mini-mart. Molly could not stop thinking that she looked nothing like the woman Aidan had invited to his bed. He must have been laughing hysterically to himself at her anxious flirting during dinner—she was certain of it. She felt the fool, and suddenly all the forgotten awkwardness of her girlhood seemed as close as yesterday.

That was why she hated him already. She supposed she would go on hating him forever. It would be easier that way. Even his features seemed to distort now, before her eyes. In no more than a day, she knew, the history of their last twelve hours together would be thoroughly marked over, crossed out, and rewritten in her mind. It would bear no resemblance to the reality of what had occurred. It would become a work of fiction in which Aidan's character would be condemned beyond any hope of redemption.

But history and fiction would have to wait. Molly's fear for Sarah flew back to the forefront of her mind, and she remembered the reason why she had come.

"Get up!" she shouted at Aidan. "I need Father Marcus! Where is he?"

Bobbi Baker, now nearly dressed, suddenly felt the third wheel. She tried for a few moments to stand there, folding and unfolding her arms, looking to say something concerned or clever or angry that might appear to make her relevant to whatever *in the hell* was going on—of which she had not the first clue. Aidan had not looked at her since Molly walked through the door. How she became the *other* woman in this one-act play she had no idea, but it was very clear that this was her cue to walk off stage. She gathered her things and left unnoticed, proud afterwards that she kept her composure enough to say nothing more than she did. The *little girly* remark was made in self-defense, after all.

Bobbi spent the rest of that morning in the bedroom of her apartment, trying on a multitude of blouses, bras, and dresses torn angrily from closets and drawers and thrown haphazardly onto her bed. By the end of it, she was again convinced that her breasts looked as real as life itself, and that Molly McGregor was just a jealous, flat-chested, skinny bitch.

CHAPTER 20

Marcus and Aidan ran hard toward the village along the beach road. Despite his age, the distress of being dragged out of bed in the middle of the night, and the shocking news about Sarah that had drained the blood from his face, Marcus matched Aidan stride for stride. They stopped at Ibrahim's house, banging on the door until lights appeared in his and every other window on Howard Street. They wanted another crew member for the rescue, and the *Sairey Gamp* was already making ready in the harbor. Ibrahim threw on a jacket and followed both men to the docks.

Word had spread fast around the harbor that the *Bel Sogno* was in trouble, and even at that hour, the place was busy with fishermen and captains getting ready for the dawn. Several offered to keep a lookout when they made their runs, and others were helping throw extra lines and fenders aboard Molly's boat. Molly's face showed no expression when she saw Aidan among the men on the docks. She welcomed and thanked Ibrahim and Marcus. Over the rumble of *Sairey Gamp's* engine, she crisply gave orders for the handling of lines as the boat got underway. Aidan came aboard uninvited, listening and trying to pitch in where he was needed but clearly not wanted—at least not by Molly. The other men gave her sidelong glances as she spoke only to them in answering questions Aidan asked about this or that piece of equipment and the plan once they got offshore. If there had been any doubt in Aidan's mind that something had passed between Molly and him earlier that evening, he had his answer now.

Bobbi Baker's drunken striptease in his room, and his decision to let her stay, had been an unforced error. As he coiled a bow line on the *Sairey Gamp* and carried it aft on deck, Aidan's hands were going through the motions of his work, but his mind would not leave the subject of the mistake he had made that night and his excuses for making it. *Any man would have done the same*, he told himself. But Molly didn't think he was just *any man*—or at least she hadn't, until she opened that door. He had just lost any chance to prove that her first impression of him had been the right one. He had wanted that chance with her. Now, he wanted it back more than anything. But none of that seemed to matter anymore.

The *Sairey Gamp* entered the breakwater that led from the harbor into the channel. Aidan was standing on deck just outside the pilot house. He could see that a northeast wind was whipping up the seas in the sound. They would be protected for a few moments more in the lee of the rocks of the breakwater that rose high above the harbor, but soon the *Sairey Gamp* would turn her shoulder into the wind and the waves for the long, hard slog offshore. Aidan took a last look back at the sleeping village that only hours earlier had seemed such a bulwark against the storms in his life. Now that world, too, had grown cold and ready to give him his comeuppance. Storms had found him once again, and in this outermost place there was no escape but to flee to the vastness of the open sea.

The chilling wind made its presence felt against the

huddled crew, but the boat's powerful diesel engine and steel hull had no trouble pushing wind and water aside in the channel. The greater danger was below the surface. Molly picked her way cautiously along in the deep middle of the serpentine channel that led offshore. An error in her course of just a few feet to port or starboard could ground the *Sairey Gamp* until morning, and their search for Sarah would come to an abrupt end. Most captains never braved the channel at night. Molly would have to find her way in the moonless, pre-dawn darkness by instinct alone.

Aidan watched her closely. Her face was set in steely concentration as she stood making slight, constant corrections at the helm with both hands on the wheel. Two other captains in the harbor were following her progress on the ship's radio, and she answered their concerned questions on the speaker with the calm, clipped elocution of a seasoned mariner. Molly was right. She was nothing like Bobbi Baker. Aidan could clearly see that now. She was a marvel, and she was *real*. She would have been worth the effort it took to be a better man, if he'd had the ability to become one.

At the rectory, Molly had asked Marcus to come alone—meaning without Aidan—but she hadn't had time to explain why that was important to her, and he was too startled at the news she had just given him about Sarah to ask. Besides, Aidan was already becoming like a son to him. Perhaps Marcus pitied him for all that had happened. He also put a lot of stock in Gaylord Dempsey's opinion, and on that basis alone he would have welcomed Aidan. Molly would have argued the point, but she half expected that, given time, Aidan would do something stupid enough that she wouldn't have to. Yet, the fact that Marcus trusted him at all kept alive the tiniest flame of doubt in her own mind.

When they hit the edge of the channel beyond the

inlet, the *Sairey Gamp* bucked and reared against the full force of the wind. It was not a storm—just a fresh breeze—but any weather that came from the north brought sloppy sailing. The little tug kept her footing in the swells, but to those on board it felt as if she had found her way into a circle of bullies who were each taking turns pushing her around. She was built to take that kind of punishment and much worse. Like all Nordic tugs, she was not fast, but she was exceedingly strong. Through it all, Molly drove her at a steady pace of twelve knots toward the open sea.

The radar scan was set to ten miles. On the outer edge of the circle, a tiny blip could be seen due east of their position, but a larger one was closer, about two miles to the south. Molly threw the helm hard over to starboard and headed for the closer target. It didn't take her long to find it. She soon saw the familiar lighting array of a shrimp trawler, about sixty feet long. She didn't recognize the name. This one was likely out of Hatteras and dragging early—before regulation fishing time started at dawn. The captain was keeping to the south to avoid being noticed. He wasn't answering radio calls, either. He didn't want to announce to any fisheries police, who might be listening in, where he was and what he was doing at that hour. It wasn't until Molly shouted the words *lost boat* that he picked up his mike and answered.

Molly described the *Bel Sogno* to the shrimper.

"Yeah, I seen her," the captain answered. "Damn near ran her over. She was close hauled comin' out of the channel at Ocracoke, all sails flying, rail down and heading due east with no lights. I gave her both barrels on the radio about shining proper lights, but she didn't answer. She just kept goin' like a bat outa hell. Didn't seem to be in no trouble."

What had begun as a rescue was now a race. The *Bel*

Sogno must have been the farther target on the radar scan. Checking it, Molly saw that the blip was now thirteen miles out and moving fast, but under full power the *Sairey Gamp* would be faster. Molly jammed the throttle all the way to the guard, and the engine answered in a loud roar. In the darkness, the white, foamy spray flying over the rails as the boat bucked up and over each wave made it seem as if they were riding a sleigh pulled by wild horses over steep banks of snow.

Ibrahim and Aidan stood by in awkward silence, gripping the rail to steady themselves. Marcus improbably chose this moment to kneel in prayer. Aidan wondered whether he prayed for Sarah's rescue or to aid her in her escape. Aidan didn't know Sarah well enough to understand what could have driven her to sea at night alone, but he wasn't sure they could stop her—or even that they ought to try. Aidan dared not speak these doubts to Molly. She looked only seaward, into the darkness, for some sign.

Within an hour, the radar was showing the target still moving due east but within a range of three miles. It was still dark—too dark to see an unlighted vessel at close quarters, much less across three miles of open ocean. But the first brush strokes of morning were already streaking the eastern horizon.

Just then a thought came to Molly, like the answer to a riddle she had known all along. She didn't know what the answer meant, but she knew somehow in her heart that it was the truth.

"She's racing the dawn." Molly spoke softly to herself, as if to test a thought that was not yet fully formed.

"What?" Aidan asked, not sure he had heard her speak.

Molly answered him, her eyes still fixed on the darkness ahead. "She's racing east—to the sun. She's racing to meet the dawn."

Aidan's mind inexplicably returned to that moment on the dunes at twilight with Boyce and Honor that now seemed an age ago. Barely able to make a sound above a whisper, he mouthed the words he had spoken then— "Zeno's Paradox," as if he felt somehow cruelly indicted by them.

"What?" Marcus asked anxiously, worried he had missed something important. "What's that you said?"

"Nothing, Marcus—just talking to myself." Aidan was embarrassed to be indulging such thoughts at that moment, but still he sensed some connection between the longing he had felt at twilight, sitting on that sand dune with Boyce and Honor, and the hope that now drove Sarah toward the dawn on the open sea.

Molly, for her part, sensed only one thing: that she would lose this race to keep Sarah in their little island home. The thought of never again seeing the one true friend she had in this world seized her with fear, and she fought back.

Molly's right hand jammed the throttle that was already to the hilt. The *Sairey Gamp* kept driving eastward toward the blinking green dot on the radar screen, now only two miles away.

At the first, pale wash of dawn, Molly throttled down the helm and grabbed the binoculars. With the engine running at idle speed, she stepped up to the foredeck and leaned back on the window of the pilot house to steady herself. There was nothing between her and the *Bel Sogno* but a mile of water and air. She settled the glasses onto her eyes and scanned the horizon. They were twenty miles out to sea, smack dab in the middle of the Gulf Stream. Although the wind had subsided, the current rolling north in the stream was still heaping up in big rollers. She saw nothing—which was not altogether unusual. Even the biggest boats can seem tiny on the open ocean. Molly adjusted the glasses to keep them level on the horizon with the rise and fall of the boat. She had searched sometimes for hours to find vessels stranded in the stream that were only a mile or two away. She reassured herself with this knowledge, but she also knew that *Bel Sogno* was not the typical, small powerboat she was called upon to find. *Bel Sogno* had a fifty-foot mast that should have been easily visible at this distance. But nothing was there.

Molly chided herself that she had *just seen* the target blinking on the radar screen only a mile to the east. Sarah could not possibly have gotten away from them. It was still not quite light. The sun was only now barely breaching the horizon. Soon she would see her, Molly thought, but she saw nothing other than the slow rise and fall of miles of blue ocean.

A voice spoke to her from behind. It was Aidan. He was standing behind her, beside the radar display.

"Molly, you'd better come have a look at this. I think there's something wrong."

Molly turned and entered the pilot house.

"What is it?" she asked—aware that those were the first words she had spoken directly to Aidan since the night before, and wishing still that he were not there.

Aidan pointed to the radar screen. "Look, there's nothing. The target's gone." Ibrahim and Marcus had by now crowded behind them and were staring at the screen, too.

"That's not possible," Marcus said, his faith now failing him. He was staring out to sea with an expression of anticipation and worry.

Molly's discipline of deductive thinking took over. She would refuse to accept the conclusion she could see until she had examined and eliminated each conclusion she could not see. First, she threw *Sairey Gamp* back into gear and kicked the throttle hard so as not to lose any more distance on the *Bel Sogno*, wherever she had gone. The boat lurched forward at her command and began making way again, still headed due east, in the direction of the sun that was now rising out of the sea on a clear, cold morning. She adjusted and rechecked every possible parameter of the radar's operation—pulse width, sea clutter control, fast time constant—coming back to the screen after each adjustment to see whether Sarah had returned to her view. There was nothing. Sarah was gone.

Molly left the helm on autopilot and went out onto the bowsprit. She was looking for her friend, staring out to sea like a young widow longing for her captain, hoping against hope, refusing above all else to sink into despair. As the sun at last broke through the mist to reveal a clear dawn on an empty sea, she heard the engine throttle down to a stop, and all was quiet. Molly did not bother to turn around.

Marcus had decided to stop the pursuit. It was fitting he should preside over this ending, like all of the beginnings and endings he had attended throughout his priesthood. He knew that Sarah was gone from this world, though he understood not why or how. He was certain she was finally at peace, and it fell to him, now, to bring peace and comfort to the friends she had left behind. He stepped out of the pilot house and walked forward. Molly was huddled in a ball, the binoculars at her side, rocking slowly back and forth with her arms wrapped tightly around her knees, gently weeping. He sat down behind her, put both his arms around hers, and rested his chin on her shoulder.

"She's all right, Molly. I know it in my heart."

Molly spoke no words. No one did for a long time that morning. There was too much that was not understood and would never be understood—about that day, about Sarah's flight aboard *Bel Sogno*, and about why she had come into their world at all. Now all those questions seemed so small against the overarching reality that she was gone.

No one wanted to tell Molly that it was time to head home. She was the captain, after all. The tiny jurisdiction she commanded, spanning twenty-six feet from stem to stern, was as sovereign as any other on Earth. Within its borders her authority was second only to God's, and even God could not have overruled her without a fight that day. They drifted in silence for an hour at least. Aidan climbed up to the top deck, where he could stretch out and rest awhile. He did not presume to be so familiar as to lie down anyplace where Molly happened to be.

Aidan eventually propped himself up on his elbows, legs outstretched. The sun was climbing higher in the sky, and the warmth of its rays rejuvenated him after the cold and damp of their night ride. He had been staring out at a particular gaseous discoloration of clouds on the horizon for several minutes when he realized that he was seeing something solid and real. He said nothing for a moment, not daring to allow himself to hope or raise false hopes in others, but soon the image on the horizon became unmistakable. There, up ahead, about three miles off of the port bow of the *Sairey Gamp*, was a boat drifting directly toward them. It was not the *Bel Sogno*, they all agreed. After the *Sairey Gamp's* engine rumbled back to life, the gap between the two vessels closed very quickly.

Repeated radio calls brought no answer, and as they came closer, it became apparent why. There was no one on board. It was a wooden, two-masted schooner. No sails. With low, swept decks, she was made for speed. A narrow deckhouse with four bronze port lights on either side opened into a companionway that led below. About forty-two feet long overall, she was almost twice the length of the *Sairey Gamp*. From the looks of her, she had been adrift a very long time. A heavy burden of barnacles and seaweed clung to her hull at the waterline, swirling out from underneath like a woman's petticoat. On the stern, showing faintly under a green patina of algae, was the name, *Cygnet*.

They nearly passed the vessel, all of them standing there in stunned silence, as if watching a funeral procession. But then Molly gave the order.

"Father Marcus, prepare to come alongside, starboard-side-to."

Molly spun the helm around to port in a quick gybe, then came close abeam of the derelict schooner. All three men moved for the starboard rail. Marcus lifted a coiled line from a belaying pin and stood at the ready to make it fast on one of the schooner's enormous deck cleats. Aidan and Ibrahim positioned fenders alongside the hull to separate the two boats from each other. When all was ready, Aidan stepped aboard.

Aidan remembered the feel of the decks of large wooden boats at sea from those he'd been on as a child. They were stiff and solid, like this one. Under the weight of Aidan's frame the boat barely swayed to acknowledge his presence. No one had been aboard her in a long, long time. The wood along her topsides was weathered to a whitish gray and shot through with streaks of blue and green—oxidation from the heavy bronze fittings. The colors mixed and ran in blurred lines along the decks and coamings like a child's sidewalk chalk drawing in the rain. Aidan tested each handhold and foothold warily, expecting he might fall through to the keel without warning, but everywhere he went on deck, the ship was strong and steady underneath him. She had good bones. This was once a regal and proud vessel, he thought. Whatever age and the elements had done to diminish her former glory, she had a heart of solid oak, and he could feel it still beating.

Marcus and Ibrahim followed Aidan aboard the schooner. While they surveyed the rigging, Aidan moved into the cockpit. The louvered, wooden doors to the companionway were swung open, but the cabin below was dark. Aidan could see only the first few steps on the ladder. As he eased his way below, he felt a sudden rush of wind and heard the rapid clamor of wings. Three sea terns erupted in flight over his head, headed for daylight. With his heart in his throat, Aidan stifled a scream. The birds circled high above the ship once, and then flew off to the west. Beads of perspiration streamed down his temples. He felt as if he had just seen a ghost, which was really no surprise given that he was standing aboard what very much appeared to be a ghost ship.

There were no stores, no signs of distress or struggle, no papers, and no evidence of recent habitation. The cabin was ornately carved and gilded. Rainwater entering through the open companionway had badly stained the leather upholstery and weathered the wood in what once was an elegant main cabin. It was clear this had been a rich man's vessel, but now there was no man rich or poor to claim it. So they claimed it for their own.

The *Cygnet* was not the fugitive they had gone to sea to find, but she was the one who followed them home that day. And though none of them knew it then, for her, in time, the fatted calf would be killed, and no expense spared to return her to the royal inheritance for which she had been born.

CHAPTER 21

Aidan and Ibrahim had not shown up for work at the yard the day they went to sea with Molly, and Fielding was uncharacteristically glad for their absence. He had news he didn't relish giving them. But when he looked out from his office and saw the *Sairey Gamp* steaming into the slipway with a derelict schooner in tow, he forgot about everything else.

After *Cygnet* was handed over to the yard boss, Molly stood on the pier, recounting for Fielding their search for Sarah. All the details would later be reported to the Coast Guard station in Elizabeth City that was responsible for patrolling this section of the Atlantic.

Fielding looked at his feet and shook his head. He had long admired Sarah's gumption. Over the years he had given Marcus whatever Sarah needed in the way of supplies and parts at no charge for the maintenance of *Bel Sogno*. The news was no small sadness to him. He had mourned the loss of more ships and sailors in his forty years on the Outer Banks than he cared to remember, and it never got easier.

Molly came to terms with Fielding for the storage of *Cygnet*. Yard fees would accrue and be applied to the proceeds from her eventual sale. She needed a lot of work, but finding a buyer would not be hard. Fielding was a connoisseur of wooden boats and seemed particularly fascinated by this one. The elegance of her design and the strength of her construction were uncommon. She was like nothing he had seen from any yard on either side of the Atlantic. She was rather more like one of the ships from the great age of sail on display in the museum in Mystic, Connecticut. But she was sea-worn and tired. She would need someone's love and devotion if she were to be brought back to life.

The men helped the yard crew maneuver the schooner into the slings of the travel-lift, to be hoisted from the launch bay and moved to a location "on the hard" until plans could be sorted out for the salvage. By law she was Molly's boat, as the captain of the vessel who salvaged her, but by agreement she belonged equally to all four who were aboard when she was found.   Fielding saw Aidan and Ibrahim standing in the back of the yard, where *Cygnet* was being braced by jack stands placed along the underbody of her hull. He wasn't proud of what he had to tell them.

"Fellas, I need to speak to you."

Aidan and Ibrahim looked at each other, mentally rehearsing what they considered to be the fully adequate excuse for their late arrival to work that morning.

"I heard you all had some trouble with Rowdy Ponteau at the Black Flag the other night."

Zoot's prophecy rushed to mind. *Here it comes*, Aidan thought.

"I got a call from his father. His dad's the one paying to refurbish *Invictus*. He was mighty pissed about what you all done to his son—"

"You should have seen what the bastard did to Molly," Aidan interrupted.

"I know. I know. I heard all about it from Zoot. But it can't be helped. Mr. Ponteau told me to take you guys off work on the boat, and I don't have another job to give you right now."

Ibrahim took the news like a gunshot to the chest. Boat work was the only work he knew how to do, and working at the yard was the only job he could get without papers. He would be unable to support himself. He would have to leave this place.

"There are plenty of other jobs. You mean you *won't* give us work," Ibrahim barked back. He was ready for a fight.

Fielding's face immediately flushed. Ibrahim had seen in Fielding's eyes something Aidan had not, but now it was obvious to Aidan, too. Reece Ponteau hadn't told him just to take them off the *Invictus*. Fielding had no intention of letting Aidan and Ibrahim work ever again, anywhere in the yard. A few rumors passed along by Ponteau to the right people could sink Fielding's business. Fielding had backed down, and he was embarrassed and angry that he'd been called on it.

"Now look here, there's no cause for getting ugly about it. You boys picked your poison when you started throwing knives and punches in a bar, and it shouldn't surprise you that it's come to this. Besides, he was going to be sending down his own crew of men anyway to get the boat ready, now that there's going to be a race."

"What race?" Aidan asked.

"Mr. Ponteau's race. He's the head of the New York Yacht Club. I suppose he can hold a race anywhere he damn well pleases. With *Invictus* laid up here in Ocracoke for repairs, he's relocated the Blue Million. It will begin off of Ocracoke in four months' time. There's a lot of work to be done between now and then."

"The blue *what?*" Aidan asked.

It had been a long time since he had paid any attention to the ocean sailboat racing circuit. Weekends off from the practice of law hadn't permitted him to enter more than the occasional club race for the past twenty years.

"The Blue Million," Fielding explained, "is the long-distance ocean race sponsored by the New York Yacht

Club every year. It comes with a million-dollar purse for the winner. They usually run it nonstop from Bermuda to the Caribbean, but this year they're starting from Ocracoke, and as sorry as I am for you fellas, I'm damn glad of the work."

On their way out of the yard, Aidan and Ibrahim passed the marina office. On the bulletin board was a brightly colored poster printed with the words "Blue Million" and a picture of a Bermuda yawl stretching her legs on the open sea, rail down and headed for weather. The poster was emblazoned with the names of various banks, breweries, brokerage houses, and other sponsors. A pad of entry forms was glued to the bottom. Aidan tore one off as they walked by.

"What for?" Ibrahim asked.

"Something to wipe my ass with."

CHAPTER 22

It was late October. The days were getting shorter, and so was Aidan's patience. In the months that followed, he and Ibrahim found odd jobs around the island: leaky faucets, broken windows, doors that wouldn't close, painting and hauling and cleaning. But the work was spotty, amounting to only one or two days a week. The rest of the time, which was most of the time, Ibrahim was drinking up twice his wages at the Black Flag—or he would have, if Zoot had bothered to charge him. It was sorrowful for Zoot to see, but he had nothing else to offer him, and he knew Ibrahim couldn't go home.

When he wasn't hustling for work, Aidan spent his time wandering down the beach, gazing out to sea, as if he expected some answer to walk out of the waves. Gradually he got over the acute phase of regret about ruining his chances with Molly, but it remained a sore spot for him. He hadn't understood at the time what the kiss meant to her—how much hope and anticipation and desire had been wrapped up in it, and how much of herself she had given to him in letting him see, even briefly, that side of her. He understood, now, what finding him and Bobbi together in bed only hours later had done to her. It said something to her about him that he had long feared was true: that for all of his pretensions to the contrary, he *wasn't* a good man. Not by a long shot.

Aidan worked on amending that error in himself in various ways—by trying to ease Nita's work around the rectory, in small kindnesses he tried to show the people he met, and in grudgingly accepting his own failings. But the friendship with Molly that he hoped might be repaired only withered. He saw her occasionally in passing, but no more than that. In the two months after they brought *Cygnet* ashore, she hadn't said more than "hello" to him.

Aidan and Ibrahim may have been unwelcome at the shipyard, but nothing could keep Marcus out. *Cygnet* held great interest for him—eventually supplanting his love of the Sangiovese that lay buried in the dunes. He came in his coveralls to the shipyard in the late afternoon each weekday and stayed until late at night, gently coaxing *Cygnet's* exquisite form out of the barnacles and rot and rust. One night, after Fielding and most of the yard crew had gone home, Aidan saw Marcus pressing his face close up against the hull of *Cygnet,* as if he were whispering words of comfort to a frightened child. Aidan wandered in to see what in the world he was doing. He stood there for a minute just watching him, before Marcus acknowledged his presence.

"There is something in this ship that I cannot see," Marcus finally said. "I did not understand Sarah, or where she had come from or why she was here, yet I sensed there was something holy in the answers to those questions. It is the same with this ship, and as with Sarah, all the answers remain hidden. This ship has a story to tell."

Aidan knew what Marcus meant about Sarah. He had felt the same thing the day he first met her and when he saw her again in the lagoon. There was something deep beneath the surface, something beyond his powers of perception, something that his heart could sense but his eyes could not comprehend. But what that had to do with this ship was beyond him.

Marcus called him closer.

"Feel the wood of this keel on your face, Aidan."

The underbody of the *Cygnet* had been washed free of the barnacles and seaweed that enveloped her when she was found—a rare gratuity from Fielding. But she had not been sanded at all. Despite this, the old keel was surprisingly smooth and fair.

"I'll wager this ship is more than a hundred years old, Aidan, but I'll be damned if I can find a shred of evidence that she ever existed. I have called the registry of ships at Mystic and the Coast Guard—twice. There is no record of a wooden yawl named *Cygnet* of this vessel's size and age. Nothing."

Aidan ran his fingers over the framing of the keel, marveling still at the smoothness of it. He didn't know much about wooden boats, but he'd raced a few Herreschoff Twelves on Cape Cod, and he knew what a single season could do to the hull of a wooden boat. The keel of the *Cygnet,* while as well aged as the rest of her, was rock-solid and slick as glass. It was remarkable.

"What kind of wood do you suppose this is?" Aidan asked.

"African mahogany. You can tell by the shape and fineness of the grain. Whoever built this boat spared no expense. Look at these timbers. There's not a butt joint in all forty feet of her. You couldn't find standing mahogany that large anywhere in the world today. It's amazing."

Aidan aimed his eye down the length of *Cygnet*'s frame to better appreciate what Marcus was trying to show him.

"The grain is perfect. There doesn't seem to be a

mark on it, except for that down there."

"What?" Marcus asked.

Aidan moved his eye forward along the hull.

"There, look, it's some sort of impression in the wood at the bow. You can barely see it—no telling how long it's been there. It looks like tunneling from wood weevils."

Marcus pressed his cheek against the hull and looked down the planks leading forward in the direction where Aidan was pointing. There, in the space below the bowsprit where the name of a vessel might ordinarily be painted, was the faint remnant of an etched design— scrollwork of some kind. He stood back from the boat and tried to view the scrolling square on, but from that vantage point he couldn't make it out. There was definitely something there—or had been—but it was too weather-worn to be seen except when viewed from the side, down the plane of the wood.

It was not unusual for elegant wooden vessels to use elaborate filigree, often inlaid with gold leaf, to decorate the bowsprit. But this design was different in that it was broken up—it was not a single, continuous flourish but a series of asymmetrical, disconnected lines.

Without a word, Marcus left Aidan and went trotting down the yard toward the paint shed. He returned in five minutes with a carpenter's blue pencil and a long sheet of white paper trailing behind him like a bridal veil. Placing the paper on the bow he rubbed the pencil frenetically until an impression of the scrollwork was transferred to the sheet. Then he stepped back, laid the colored paper on the ground, and stared at the image.

Several minutes passed as Aidan waited expectantly, not willing to ask the obvious question. Marcus tended to go off into these trances of hyper-concentration, and it was best not to disturb him until he'd emerged from them of his own accord. Then, all of sudden, he did.

"I see it now." Marcus spoke without lifting his eyes from the image on the page.

"*What?*" Aidan demanded.

Without answering, Marcus took another section of paper and repeated the transfer from the same scrollwork on the opposite side of the bow.

"Identical!" he shouted. That didn't seem terribly unusual to Aidan. *Why wouldn't a filigree design on the bow be the same on both sides?* he wondered.

But it wasn't a design.

"They say the same thing!" Marcus exclaimed.

"*Say?* Say what?" Aidan was growing impatient, now, to be let in on the discovery.

Marcus took a breath, as if he were about to recite something from memory with too little practice to be sure he would get it right.

"'*If-ti-qad sha-abb.*' It's Arabic—an older, more formal dialect that I haven't seen since the seminary. If my memory serves me correctly, the literal translation is 'lost young son,' but the common expression is 'prodigal.'"

CHAPTER 23

Marcus's official purpose in going to Boston, as far as his bishop was aware, had been to deliver the news of Sarah's passing to the pastor of the Romanian Orthodox Church in person. Marcus wasn't at all sure the pastor even knew Sarah—in fact, the man had earlier denied it—but Marcus harbored a suspicion that he knew more than he revealed. It was that suspicion that allowed Marcus to travel from Ocracoke to Boston with a clear conscience for the more pressing errand he had in mind.

He found the same priest at the rectory, there, whose eyes had seemed to glimmer in recognition of Sarah's photograph three years earlier. Now, those same eyes betrayed neither sadness nor surprise at word of her disappearance at sea. Sensing that Marcus regarded this as callous and uncaring, the other priest seemed to offer an explanation by asking a question.

"Do you know anything of the history of the *Roma*, the Gypsy people of Europe, Father Marcus?"

Marcus knew more than he cared to let on, but most of it was filled with old prejudices and stereotypes that would have been impolitic to relate to the pastor of a Romanian church.

"If you did, you would not mourn this woman, nor expect me to."

Marcus did not divine what the priest meant to imply by this remark. Instead, Marcus moved the discussion to

205

other topics and, once certain he had done the kindness he intended, thanked the priest for his generosity, begged his forgiveness that he could not stay longer, and quickly took his leave. Marcus wasn't the least bit sentimental about so neatly tidying away the life of his friend. The important business he was hurrying to attend to seemed more connected now to the memory of Sarah than stuffy cathedrals and darkened, scented altars.

Upon leaving the church he took a bus directly to the wharf district in Boston. He carried a folder with photographs of *Cygnet* and the paper images he had made of the ship's scrollwork under his arm. He was still hoping to satisfy his nagging curiosity about the origins of this vessel, not the least of which was the suggestion of some aberration in the time and manner of its appearance, roughly at the moment of Sarah's disappearance. But rather in spite of his years as a priest than because of them, Marcus had a preferential bias against the supernatural explanation for the comings and goings of everyday life. Perhaps, he thought, the woman at the New England Registry of Historic and Classic Ships, who knew nothing of an old wooden schooner named *Cygnet,* would know something more of a boat named *Prodigal.*

The New England Registry was a venerated institution dating back to the early 1800s, and judging by the price of the artwork on the walls, someone had been venerating it quite a lot over the years. Marcus sat impatiently, his back hunched forward and his hands folded and hanging between his knees, in a darkly paneled room with tufted, leather sofas and black toile chairs. It looked like it could be the reception area of an overpriced law firm. A neatly dressed woman with a perfectly clipped Boston accent opened the door to greet him. A Radcliffe girl—or perhaps, Wellesley—he thought. It had been several years since he had been home to New England.

"Welcome, Father Marcus," she said, "I'm Mary Margaret." She ushered him into a room filled from floor to ceiling with the cracked and peeling, leather-bound volumes of ships' registries, log books, plans, drawings, and charts of every size and description. Particles of dust hung in the beams of sunlight streaming through tall, narrow windowpanes caked with peeling paint. In the center of this mess sat an ancient wooden desk and two creaking, Windsor chairs. Atop the desk rose two incongruous emblems of modernity: the glowing white screen of a computer monitor and a can of Diet Coke. They were the only things in the room other than the woman that didn't appear to be at least two hundred years old.

"I apologize for the mess. We're digitizing our East Indies library for the Internet. My job is to put it all together and start uploading it online. We are due to go live in another six months." As she spoke, Marcus recognized that she was indeed very young—a fact that was hidden over the telephone by her refined manner and intelligent voice. She was some wealthy Boston yachtsman's daughter and a good Catholic girl, he would have wagered.

She looked over his notes on the dimensions and deck plans of the *Cygnet,* coming at last to the images he had traced on the paper.

"I'm sorry. I did a little more research after you called, and I'm still coming up with nothing on a small schooner or any ship of this size built before 1930 named *Cygnet.*"

Marcus wilted with disappointment, but Mary Margaret wasn't finished.

"I did, however, find something on a 42-foot schooner named *Prodigal.*"

Finally, he thought: a turn in the tide.

"It's a little crazy—a mystery of sorts. *Prodigal* is the name of a lost vessel described nowhere but in the log book of the yacht *America*, in 1851. There was a Moroccan-flagged yacht of that type and design that registered, along with several other vessels, to compete in an exhibition regatta against *America* in the year it won the first running of what later became known as the America's Cup, off the coast of England."

The woman went on to explain that word had spread throughout Europe of *America's* embarrassment of British yacht designers, who were regarded at the time as the best in the world. Before returning to the States, the owners of *America* decided to capitalize on her fame and make some money touring the ports of Europe, offering match races to challengers for substantial entrance fees. "Every boatwright in the Mediterranean was building a vessel to compete against the fastest ship on Earth. We have records of several new designs from that era," she added.

Apparently the last exhibition match *America* sailed was off the coast of Greece. The winner of the race was never officially determined. There was a protest of the result underway when the vessel that was the subject of the protest—*Prodigal*—went missing. "The boat is listed as a wooden schooner owned by the Moroccan royal family. And I'm afraid that's all I have. There's no record of *Prodigal* after that, but of course there wouldn't be if the vessel went down," she said.

Yet this vessel lived. Marcus knew it. He had been aboard her, touched her. Why and when someone had renamed her the *Cygnet* he could only guess, but it was already clear that there was a good deal more to this ship than met the eye. As he pondered the librarian's story, she added one more, completely unexpected detail.

"Here, I prepared this little synopsis of our records on *Prodigal* for your colleague. I didn't have it ready when his office called earlier. Would you mind taking it to Monsignor McIver when you head back to the college?"

Marcus knew Jimmy McIver well. They had gone to seminary together forty years ago—that is, when they weren't swimming in pints of free Guinness at a pub just off campus. The owner would sooner have charged his mother for salt than taken money for beer from two boys studying for the priesthood. Marcus had talked Jimmy out of quitting the Franciscans and getting married when he got an undergraduate theology student pregnant. He also helped quietly arrange for the child's adoption and payment of the girl's expenses without drawing the attention of the head of Jimmy's order. Now, McIver was a monsignor, a respected professor of antiquities at Boston College and—rumor had it—a favorite of the Holy Father to become the next archbishop of New York. He broke with many of the leaders of his order in supporting the Vatican's crackdown on the feminist movement among American nuns. He had endeared himself to Rome by being one of the few American clergy of standing who toed the Church line on bedroom issues. He frequently appeared on cable talk shows to defend whatever was coming out of the Vatican. He and Marcus had kept up an occasional correspondence over the years, but Marcus's political views could not have been farther from his— though no different than what they had both believed when they were younger.

Mary Margaret had unknowingly revealed that Monsignor McIver was making inquiries about a ship named *Prodigal*. She had made the mistake of assuming that the two of them were working together. Marcus decided not to correct her.

"I certainly will tell Monsignor McIver. It's not a problem at all." Marcus's answer was completely truthful. His next stop would be Boston College. His old friend had some explaining to do.

It had been a long time, and Marcus O'Reilly was a sight for Jimmy McIver's sore eyes. After arriving in the richly appointed rooms of McIver's office, Marcus all but forgot about *Prodigal* for a moment. The two men resumed an effervescent and long-interrupted conversation about old neighborhoods and old friends. On the wall, staring down from a color photograph as Marcus sunk into the folds of a ponderous chair, was His Holiness, Pope Benedict XVI, Bishop of Rome, Vicar of Jesus Christ, Successor of the Prince of the Apostles, Supreme Pontiff of the Universal Church, Primate of Italy, Archbishop and Metropolitan of the Roman Province, Sovereign of the State of the Vatican City, and Servant of the Servants of God.

The years had been generous to Jimmy. His waist size must have fully doubled, Marcus thought, and all around him were the emblems of a distinguished, prosperous, and well-respected academic career. Marcus was a study in sharp contrast to his old friend. His ruddy skin showed the effects of the sun and constant wind of the Outer Banks. His thin, muscular frame had so far escaped Nita's persistent efforts to widen him to a more respectable girth for a sixty-eight-year-old man. And his bank balance, unlike Jimmy's, gave a pitiful accounting of his many years of labor in the Lord's vineyard.

"So you've got it, have you?" Jimmy cut right to the chase.

"Got what?"

"Come on, now, Marcus. The woman at the registry called to tell me you had left your hat—here it is, by the way—and it was only natural for me to inquire what my old friend was doing in Boston. You've found the *Prodigal*. Where is she? Tell me all about her!"

"Whoa! Hold on!" Marcus began, hoping that laughter would hide his surprise. "I didn't say I had anything but some questions about an old boat." Marcus clutched more tightly the envelope containing his photos and notes. "Why don't you start by telling me what you're looking for?"

McIver paused a long while, saying nothing as he and the Holy Father both stared intently at Marcus. He had arm-wrestled the man seated in front of him often enough, years ago, to know that when Marcus O'Reilly held the upper hand he never yielded his advantage. Eventually, McIver opened a side drawer underneath his desk, pulled out a small, leather-bound volume, and tossed it on the table in front of them without saying a word, as if that object alone were the answer to Marcus's question.

"The Vatican received this last month and sent it to me for further investigation. It's a journal, written in Arabic in the year 1868. The story it tells is quite remarkable and should be of great interest to you. If I remember correctly, you once had a fascination with artifacts and archaeology. Well, this one goes almost all the way back."

Monsignor McIver settled in, as if he were beginning a history lecture to a class full of attentive graduate students eager to absorb his considerable knowledge.

"In the third century, as Christianity was spreading throughout the Mediterranean, a Moroccan king sent royal emissaries to the Holy Land on a mission to bring back artifacts of the life of Christ. They didn't find the

True Cross—that had long since been spirited off by Emperor Constantine. But what *was* for sale to the highest bidders in the bazaars of Jerusalem when they arrived were relics of the crosses of the two thieves who died at Calvary. Constantine had uncovered them alongside the cross of Jesus, but he had left the thieves' crosses behind. Some believed that the cross of the penitent thief—the one whom Jesus said would be with him that day in paradise—had some special power to save the souls of the damned. There was only one problem."

"What was that?" Marcus asked eagerly, suddenly absorbed by McIver's words like a tender acolyte.

McIver burst out laughing, as if he could no longer abide the rapt seriousness of his audience. "They didn't know which thief went with which cross."

After another minute of coughing laughter McIver recovered himself, and continued.

"So they took a relic of each cross home with them to the king. They carefully placed them in the cargo of the caravan so that no man who might be tempted would be able to escape with both pieces. Then—and this is the part of the story that reminds me why I first loved antiquities, because it seems this sort of thing *always* happens to cover the tracks of history: the caravan was set upon by thieves in the desert. Only one man in the party lived to make it back to the king, and he carried with him only one of the two relics."

"So they still didn't know which thief's cross they had," Marcus chimed in.

"Exactly—which means that they also didn't know whether it was a relic of damnation or salvation, of good or evil—if, in fact, it were real at all. So, the king hid this one relic away in the palace, where it remained in a place of dubious honor, until 1851."

"What happened then?"

"The king on the throne in that year had two sons. The younger son was known as a playboy and a gambler. He loved to spend the kingdom's money on fast women and fast ships. He spent much of his time on the royal yacht, a forty-two-foot schooner that he had aptly named *Prodigal* in a kind of self-fulfilling prophecy. He was also fascinated by mysticism and superstition and religious relics of all kinds, including the royal family's claim to the thief's cross."

"Was he a Christian?"

"No, hardly, but then neither were the thieves who stole the relic in the desert, almost two thousand years before him. As it is written, Marcus, 'Even the demons believe, and tremble.' It appears that the king's younger son was hedging his bets, which is nothing different than what some in the Church still do today."

Marcus felt the barb but chose to ignore it. "Go on," he said.

"When news of the challenge match against the yacht *America* reached Morocco, the king's younger son delivered *Prodigal* to Casablanca to be completely refurbished for the race. Then, without his father's knowledge, he removed the wooden relic of the cross from the palace and had it interred in the keel of the ship—a kind of rabbit's foot to help him in the race, if you will. The prince didn't truly believe that any power resided in the cross, nor did he have any way to know whether it was the cross of the penitent thief rumored to have such power, but he figured it was worth a shot."

Marcus felt his head swim. Images of Calvary and the salvation of mankind, once clear in his mind, were now mixed with the image of an old boat stored in Fielding Walker's yard beside a NASCAR poster, a Coke machine, and a sign that said "Cold Beer."

McIver studied Marcus closely. He knew that Marcus hadn't heard the most important part of the story yet, but from his reaction so far he sensed that Marcus had some intimate knowledge or connection to the ship. And the ship was the one thing that McIver—and the Vatican—wanted very badly.

"So, he's got a magic boat. He wouldn't have been the first to think so," Marcus added, skeptically.

"No, actually, he doesn't think anything of the kind. Stealing the relic from the palace and putting it in the keel was more of a prank against his father than anything else. This boy was drunk and always looking for women. By the time of the race, he'd forgotten all about the relic. He was more concerned about what his advisers were telling him, which was that *Prodigal*, at half the size of *America*, was mathematically incapable of winning. He almost dropped out to save face. What happened next changed his life forever."

"And that was . . . ?"

"The *Prodigal* sailed against *America* and won."

"I thought there was no record of that."

"There isn't, except in here," McIver answered, pointing to the leather diary on the table, "and in the log of the *America*."

Marcus stared at the tiny leather volume for a long time in silence, trying to normalize his breathing and his pulse before speaking.

"So, that's what the Vatican has you working on, McIver?" Marcus finally asked. "*That* is what you're chasing—an old man's bedtime story about a magic yacht? Why not a magic carpet?"

Marcus was bluffing, and it was working. McIver seemed to grow impatient.

"Let me be sure you understand what I'm telling you, Marcus. *Prodigal* won on real time, not corrected time." McIver had crewed on enough sailboats in his younger days to know exactly what that meant and to be impressed by it. "She beat the fastest ship in history—a vessel more than twice her size—by seven lengths. That's like a Dodge Dart winning the Daytona 500."

"So says the prodigal son," Marcus demurred, now trying harder than ever to hide his excitement.

"And so says the log book of the *America*. The result was not official, but it was still recorded."

"There must have been some reason why the result of the race was never verified—some mistake," Marcus wondered.

"The diary gives us the reason—and I for one believe it," McIver replied.

Marcus was excruciatingly eager to hear the rest of the story, but he couldn't let on. It would be imprudent to reveal anything now, he thought. He didn't understand why McIver, much less the Vatican, would be so fascinated—or worried—by the possibility that someone might have found the *Prodigal*, but knowing that he didn't know was ample reason to be cautious.

Marcus sat quietly for awhile. An old racing sailor himself, he knew quite a bit about boats and speed and what it took to make one seaworthy. *Prodigal* was a beautiful, heavily built boat. She had the pedigree of a classic, but he never would have picked her to win a race against a much larger vessel.

"Seven lengths, you say?" Marcus asked. "That must have caused quite a stir among the New York boys."

"*America* was the flagship of the newly formed New York Yacht Club, of which John Cox Stevens was the first commodore. He was also head of the syndicate that owned the boat. It would have been a huge embarrassment, which certainly explains the protest."

"Protest of what?"

"The owners of *America* were convinced there was something irregular in the design of *Prodigal*. Some even thought she was hiding an engine of some kind for the added propulsion they thought was necessary to give a boat of that size so much speed. They lodged a protest with the race committee. *Prodigal* was quarantined in the harbor at Athens until race officials arrived to crawl over her hull, inside and out. Meanwhile, the prince had come to believe that his new boat really did bear the cross of the penitent thief, and that it had been blessed with unnatural speed by the angels."

"Or it was just another bat out of hell," Marcus added, trying to throw cold water everywhere he could. "So where did she wind up?"

"I was hoping you could tell me, Marcus."

"Really, you don't know? Why would I be able to tell you anything?"

"For the same reason you made inquiries at the registry about the *Prodigal*. What are you looking for, Marcus? What do you know?"

Now it had come right down to it. There are mortal sins and venial sins, but some lies are neither, and the lie that Marcus was about to tell was one of these.

"Well, I could have saved you the suspense. I've just got an interest in a little schooner named *Cygnet* that some friends of mine salvaged off the Carolina coast. They heard I was going to be up this way paying respects to the family of a parishioner. The young woman at the registry, Mary Margaret—charming girl, very helpful—thought that the design of the *Cygnet* sounded similar to the *Prodigal*, but it turns out it is two feet shorter. See—I've got some photographs."

Marcus took two photographs out of the envelope, being careful not to reveal the rest of its contents. The photos showed the transom with the weathered but clearly legible name *Cygnet*. Monsignor McIver examined them closely, seeming alternately deflated and relieved that he wasn't facing a standoff with an old friend over a ghost ship mixed up in Vatican politics.

"But you've got my curiosity up, Jimmy. How on

Earth could you or anyone know so much about this old boat?"

"Courtesy of his royal highness, the prince of Morocco. It's all in that journal in front of you. You'll understand why when I tell you what happened next: While *Prodigal* was laid over in Athens during the protest, all the crew was moved off the yacht to allow the inspectors to do their work. So, these lads were staying at various inns around Athens. For a week or so, they had nothing to do. Every night, they headed out together to drink and gamble at a Gypsy camp up in the hills. The women all danced for the customers, but there was one young woman in particular, the virgin daughter of the clan patriarch. She would dance completely unclothed and unashamed before the men. The Gypsies believed her innocence was insufferable to the damned. One young boy from the crew of *Prodigal* became infatuated with her. He came to see her every night. He brought her gifts and planned to ask for her hand in marriage. She had the same feelings for him in return. When she danced, she looked only at him. Jealous tempers flared among the other crew. One of them decided he would take her for himself, but no sooner had he extended his hand toward her than the father relieved him of it with a sword. A riot erupted in the encampment. Many men died in the fight. In the confusion, the boy and the girl escaped into the town together. He boarded the *Prodigal* with her and took her to sea, alone.

"A rescue party went after them aboard the *America*, but Stevens' prize schooner was no more of a match for *Prodigal* in the pursuit than it had been in the race. *America* finally gave up and headed back to Athens. Later that night, a violent storm swept in from the west, through Gibraltar. Several ships at sea foundered in that gale. *Prodigal* was widely assumed to be among them.

She was never seen nor heard from again."

"So she is sunk, then?" Marcus asked.

"Widely assumed by everyone but the prince. He never accepted the idea that *Prodigal* could be destroyed. He didn't think the angels would allow it. He never returned to Morocco. He lost his mind and his fortune wandering all over the ports of Europe searching for his ship. He finally wound up a sick old man, living out his last days among the Jesuits in the monastery on the island of Syros. He believed that God had punished him for his licentiousness as a young man. It was in Syros that he wrote in this journal the entire story I have just told you, as a kind of confession."

"And it's only now coming to light, two centuries later?"

"The Jesuits on Syros were scholars in many subjects, but Arabic was not among them. Aside from the fact that no one in the monastery could read it, the journal was assumed to be the private reminiscence of a dying old man and not of great scholarly interest to the order. It occupied a place on a shelf in their library from whence I doubt it scarcely moved until three years ago, when the monastery was closed, the property was sold, and the library was relocated to the Vatican.

"As with everything that enters the Vatican library, the journal was translated and transcribed. When the translator read the story, he brought it to the attention of the chief curator, who brought it to the attention of the vicar general, who sent it to me, to get to the bottom of the matter."

"And you should publish it, Jimmy," Marcus said. "It would make an excellent novel that would bring a handsome royalty for the Holy Father. But it's beneath your scholarship as an archaeologist, don't you think? Surely you don't believe this ship has been afloat somewhere for 150 years?"

McIver paused awhile, then staring keenly at Marcus, replied, "Don't you?"

McIver didn't trust Marcus, for reasons more theological than personal, and he wasn't at all sure that Marcus hadn't finessed something with the *Cygnet*. He could swear from the way the woman at the registry described her conversation with Marcus that it was Marcus who had first uttered the name *Prodigal*, but on second thought, he wasn't sure.

Marcus stood to say his goodbyes, and the conversation between the two men turned again to younger days, before all that politics and pretense had done to separate them. Then, just as Marcus was leaving, McIver upped the ante.

"You know, I've heard that, years ago, boats with names written in the Arabic alphabet were required to exhibit English translations before they would be allowed to compete in Western regattas."

"Is that so?" Marcus answered, trying to appear unconcerned with where the conversation was headed.

"Yes. Sometimes the names were hilariously mistranslated. A famous Yemeni ketch whose name was *Desert Wind*, in Arabic, is listed in the registry of boats competing in the 1956 Mediterranean Invitational as *Hot Farts*."

Marcus and McIver both erupted into deep belly laughs. It was the best feeling Marcus had had all day, but it was short-lived. He looked at his watch, as if to suggest he had reason to be in a hurry, which he did not. His flight didn't leave for another six hours. "Well, I really must be off. I have a plane to catch."

"Absolutely, my friend. I won't delay you any longer with old stories. Have a pleasant trip, and enjoy your work with your friends on the boat in Ocracoke—the *Cygnet*, I think you said. By the way, what is the meaning of that word?"

Monsignor McIver knew full well what a cygnet was. He had asked the question only to make Marcus answer it and in that way silently acknowledge what they both knew: McIver wasn't buying his story.

"It is the term for a young swan," Marcus answered.

Monsignor McIver let the answer hang suspended in the air a while, along with any conclusions to be drawn. The two then said their goodbyes.

When Marcus was halfway down the teetering and ancient, wooden stairs of Brooks Hall—too far to hear the phone ringing—a call came into Monsignor McIver's office. He had told his secretary that afternoon that he was not to be disturbed, but she knew to send this caller through without asking. She was certain the monsignor would want to share with so close an ally, benefactor, and friend the news of the meeting he had just concluded. It was Reece Ponteau.

CHAPTER 24

Marcus didn't trust Jimmy McIver any more than he imagined McIver trusted him. Something just didn't add up about the intensity of the Church's interest in the legend of an old boat. The Vatican heard from thousands of crackpots and deranged believers every year, all claiming to have discovered some relic imbued with mystical power. The Church didn't send someone of Jimmy McIver's stature to chase after all of them. Granted, he thought, the diary of the prince and the log of what happened in the race against *America* were reliable historical records, but only of some unexplained phenomenon—not the work of angels; unless, of course, McIver already knew the phenomenon to be genuine.

Gradually, what seemed at once to be the most fantastic and the most plausible explanation began to gather at the corners of Marcus's mind, as he stared out of an airplane window into a sea of clouds. The quest for the Holy Grail in the Middle Ages had traveled on the faith that *only one* cup was passed at the Last Supper. Had the imagined power of the grail been discovered in another vessel of lesser birth, the authority of Christendom would have been rent asunder. By the same logic, Marcus began to wonder whether McIver wasn't so much eager to find *Prodigal* as he was worried that Marcus already had. If that were true, there could be only one reason: McIver already had the cross of the other thief.

Finally, the pieces of an invisible puzzle were coming together. Marcus had done enough work in antiquities to know that molecular architecture obeys the same rules in plants as it does in humans. Two trees of the same species each have a unique DNA signature. If brought side by side, the wood of one cross could be distinguished from the wood of another. The cross of one thief at Calvary—the good thief, one would naturally assume—found to be imbued with some supernatural quality, would be a theological marvel. The crosses of both thieves—one who died full of penitence and the other who died full of contempt—each marked with the same imprimatur of salvation, would be a theological earthquake.

The Gospel is clear. At the foot of the crucifixion, paradise was promised only to the "good" thief, not his vitriolic partner in crime. Two thousand years of moral theology had been based on the notion that only by confession, repentance, and virtuous amendment—all assisted by the kindly offices of an earthly Church—can mankind reach that glory achieved by the good thief. If those who have spurned forgiveness even at the hour of their death can know the same redemption and grace, there is great hope for mankind but arguably less need for priests and popes and cathedrals.

Marcus had no way to know any of this, but in his own reckless way, he was now nearly certain of all of it—and just as worried as ever. He didn't trust that his own performance at the college was enough to convince McIver of his story about *Cygnet*. At the airport, he switched his connecting flight from Washington to Raleigh and planned to spend the night. It was seven o'clock the next morning when he walked into Gaylord Dempsey's office.

Of course Gay was at the office early that morning as

he was every morning. He still ran circles around most of the other lawyers at McFadden Brown. He was already at his desk when they arrived in the morning, and he was usually still in his office—the only light burning in the building—when they tucked themselves into bed at night. It was a favorite joke at the firm's parties each year that when young associates prayed "now I lay me down to sleep," God gave Gay a right of first refusal on whether their souls to keep. He had the kind of gravitas that most lawyers never achieved, regardless of their technical proficiency or knowledge of the law. He could change the course of a case or motion merely by his presence. Wherever Gay was on board, there was a feeling of calm reassurance that all would be well—and it usually was. Reassurance was exactly what Marcus was seeking in Gay's office that morning—along with a good deal of money.

"Father Marcus!" Gay rose to his feet and extended his hand with a broad smile, his height reminding Marcus that this was a man of stature in every sense of the word. "I got your call last night. To what do I owe this special honor, and how is our boy Aidan doing?"

"All is well, Gay—thanks to your generosity, as usual. And Aidan is a wonderful young man. I have very much enjoyed getting to know him. I believe he has benefitted greatly from his time on the island. He has a good heart."

"I know, Marcus. I know. I wouldn't have sent him to you if I didn't feel strongly about it. What happened to him here in Raleigh, well—"

"You don't have to explain it to me, Gay. I haven't spent the last forty years on the other side of a confessional without learning a thing or two about human nature."

"Indeed," Gay nodded, smiling.

"There's not a mark on that young man's soul that has been written in indelible ink, and that's not something I can say of everyone."

For the next two hours, Marcus related the story of Sarah, of Molly, of the fight at the Black Flag, of Sarah's flight to the sea, the discovery of *Prodigal*, of the Blue Million, and all that he had since learned from Jimmy McIver. Central to the story was Marcus's faith that something precious resided in the heart of his phantom ship—that same rare quality he had sensed in Sarah. He feared that it, too, was in danger of being lost. Through it all, Gay listened carefully, not saying a word. When Marcus was done, Gay opened a desk drawer, pulled out a sheet of paper, and began writing. It was a personal check for $50,000.

"It sounds like you've got a race to win, and you'll need money to get ready."

It was much, much more than Marcus had expected or would have had the courage to request, if Gay had allowed him to get to that part of his speech in which he had prepared to ask for money. But as he thanked Gay warmly, Marcus privately worried that it would not be enough—that no amount of money spent on rigging, paint, and sails could restore the sense of balance and calm that had shrouded his life, Sarah's, and their little island before the events of the last two weeks. He realized then that, like the father who defended his young daughter in the Gypsy camp, he had come to love Sarah with a fierceness and urgency he had not felt before. What connection her life and that of the old wooden ship now sleeping in a yard in Ocracoke could possibly have to the events that occurred two centuries ago in the hills of Greece, he could not yet permit himself to imagine. He knew only that he, too, must help *Prodigal* escape and let her prove her worth again—

to run before the wind, as she once had in the days of her youth, to run like a thief from everyone and everything that pursued her.

Marcus arrived back on the island late that afternoon after a tedious, two-hour ferry ride. He walked straight to the shipyard, bypassing the rectory. Opening the wide gate, he looked eagerly down the row of boats to the very end. There stood *Cygnet*, a redheaded stepchild among dozens of well-loved, gleaming yachts. Beside her, to his great surprise and alarm, stood a man preparing for an assault with an electric rotary sander. Judging from the awful whine echoing through the yard, the power setting was on *high*.

Marcus started to run toward the man, but he was not close enough to reach him before the electric sander had nearly reached the keel, roaring for the attack. He shouted for him to stop, but the noise of the machine drowned out every other sound. There was only one way to stop him. Marcus hurled himself through the air in a sidelong tackle.

The big man landed on his stomach. The sander flipped over in his hands and, still hard at work, began fairing out the surface of his coveralls on the way to his skin. He yelled more out of fear than pain, then rolled over and threw Marcus off of his back like a fly on a horse. When he rose to his feet with both fists at the ready and saw the man who had assaulted him, he could not have been more surprised than if a legion of angels had just lifted him up and thrown him into the sea.

Fielding had seen from his office what had happened. He ran shouting into the yard, fearing now that his mechanic was reaching for Marcus to exact a revenge that might send the entire row of boats in the yard tumbling over like dominos.

"Hold on, there! What the devil is going on?"

Marcus accepted the man's hand and pulled himself up. Catching his breath, he began a profuse apology. Fielding stood there, waiting for some explanation.

"No machines, Fielding," Marcus said, still puffing hard. "There can be no machine sanding of this vessel. She's to be handled gently, and under my supervision. I didn't have time to do anything but stop you, young man. I couldn't be more sorry."

"There's no harm done, Father," the mechanic replied, patting the old man on the back.

"Hand sanding?" Fielding was incredulous, now. "You and the others barely have the money among you to pay for yard fees to keep this old wreck here, much less for hand work. We've got to clean her up just enough to get her sold for salvage and hauled out of here—I've got other boats waiting for this spot."

Marcus reached into his pocket, pulled out the check from Gay, and handed it to Fielding.

"There'll be no selling this boat, and there'll be no machine work. Is that clear?"

Fielding studied the check closely. He vaguely recognized the name, but he didn't doubt that it was real. "Well, it's your money, Marcus, and if you want to throw it away on this old boat, I won't be the one to stop you."

Fielding told the mechanic to put away his gear and check out for the day.

"And another thing . . ." Marcus was now dead serious and staring straight at Fielding. "I expect you to let Ibrahim and Aidan back in here to work on this boat. You know damn well what happened down at the Black Flag—everyone on the island knows—and it's a pitiful shame that you're making those two bear the brunt of it. They won't go near the *Invictus*, but as long as I'm paying your rates, I expect the same courtesies and privileges as Ponteau. Is that understood?"

Fielding could see that Marcus meant business. He was a tough old priest, and his love of the Lord had done nothing to soften him.

"All right, that's fair enough, but if I hear of those men tangling with Mr. Ponteau's crew or any knife fights around here, I'll throw the lot of you out, boat and crew."

After Fielding left, Marcus stood for a moment by the ship that had been fixed in his thoughts for the past two days. He placed his cheek against the shoulder of her keel and breathed deeply. He closed his eyes and tried to imagine scenes of the story Jimmy McIver had told him, but all he could see was darkness. Yet there was life and hope within her, he was certain.

Later that evening, with Nita excitedly whirling in the kitchen of the rectory and coming in and out of the parlor to fill cups of tea and plates of shortbread, the three other salvors of *Prodigal*—Aidan, Ibrahim, and Molly—answered Marcus's call for a meeting. The air was tense with a mixture of excitement and dread. He explained to each of them the turn of events of the past forty-eight hours. His purpose was to inform their decision.

"I can't tell you that the boat we brought back from our search for Sarah is the *Prodigal* of Monsignor McIver's journal, and, in fact, the odds are decidedly against it. And in case anybody is wondering, I'm not going to stand here and suggest to you that Sarah was a 150-year-old Gypsy princess, but—"

"Then I will," Aidan interrupted.

"I will too," Molly followed.

And with these words, Marcus felt a ponderous burden settle over the room and directly onto his shoulders. He knew that faith—whether in ancient relics, ghost ships, or Gypsy princesses—was a very hard thing to deny once it had been sincerely declared. Now it was clear what they had to do, for he believed the very same thing, though he had dared not utter it aloud until now.

Ibrahim looked at both of them intently, but said nothing. Something else was on his mind.

"Well, my friends," Marcus continued, "you'll have to forgive an old cynic. I have spent so many years trying to convince superstitious widows that their dead husbands were not speaking to them from a pot of petunias in the church garden, that—"

"Wait a minute—somebody else has heard that?" Molly interrupted him.

She relished Marcus's look of hesitation for as long as she could bear it before breaking into a wide smile and deep laughter. They all joined her in the joke, and the sound of their teasing rose to the rafters. Nita peeked in quickly, wondering if perhaps they had gone from tea to wine.

"It is a malady unique to priests," Marcus said, "that they are called to search and pray and yearn for God in faith for so long that they scarcely recognize Him when he shows up.

"You must race, then. You must run like thieves for Nassau and leave them all in your wake! What will become of *Prodigal* then I cannot say, but thankfully that decision is not yet upon us. 'Sufficient to the day is the evil thereof.' Besides, if you win this race, you'll have a million reasons to spit in the eye of any man who would lock her away in mothballs along with Sarah's memory. You *must* run the Blue Million!"

All of them were cheered at this decision, except Ibrahim, who continued to sit in silence.

"What say you, Ibrahim?" Marcus asked.

"Don't forget that I come from the Bahamas. It's a place full of ghosts and the ships they sailed. You don't have to convince me that *Prodigal* is such a ship, or that Sarah was such a woman. But no matter what I believe, I cannot return to Nassau. I cannot race with you."

Ibrahim's words quieted the mood among them. This unlikely crew, who had been drawn together unwillingly by the loss of one mystery and the discovery of another, sat for a long time in silence. Nassau meant capture, prosecution, jail, and death for Ibrahim.

In his mind, Aidan ticked off the possibilities. Marcus would be a crewman as able-bodied as any man half his age, but he could not abandon his parish. Molly had her own vessel to worry about and a business to run. Besides, he doubted that a week at sea with him would be her idea of a good time. There had to be another way, and he had an idea what it might be.

"I can get Boyce Stannard to crew," Aidan said. "Boyce is my old law partner and a racing sailor. He knows his way around boats. The Blue Million is still months away. I'll call him tomorrow. McFadden Brown is full of sailing bums. If he can pull together six other guys, we'll have a crew of eight. Nassau is 760 nautical miles of course-made-good from here, staying west of the Gulf Stream. Allowing for angles of tack and leeway, I figure we'll put a thousand miles under the keel before we get there. At an average hull speed of, say, eight knots, that's 125 hours or a little over five days of sailing."

"*Invictus* will cover it in three," Ibrahim said, shaking his head.

"What?" Aidan chuckled, thinking that his friend was joking, but he saw that Ibrahim wasn't laughing. "Thanks for the vote of confidence, but—"

"I have sailed aboard that boat, Aidan—last summer," Ibrahim persisted. "We took her out for a sea trial to gauge the stress points on her rudder. She posted twelve knots on a beam reach in as much wind without breaking a sweat."

"That's not possible," Aidan replied.

"I'm afraid it is, Aidan." Marcus shared Ibrahim's worry. "I've not sailed aboard her, but I've heard the same story Ibrahim just told us. She's won the Newport to Bermuda race in each of the last five runs. The Blue Million will be just another notch in her timbers. You'll have to do a lot better than eight knots to beat that boat."

"She sails like a demon . . ." Ibrahim's eyes were distant now as he followed his memory to sea. "And the bastard who drives her, he's—"

"And the bastard who drives her is a coward named Rowdy Ponteau who bullies women to make himself seem tough," Aidan said. "The last I heard, he and his crew got their asses handed to them in the Black Flag."

Aidan wouldn't stand for any fawning testimonials where Rowdy was concerned. And he wasn't about to show fear in front of Molly.

Molly looked directly at Aidan for the first time all night. She smiled sadly and then looked down. What Aidan and Ibrahim had done for Molly that night in the Black Flag had forged a bond of friendship and loyalty among them that remained unbroken, but that's as far as it went for her with Aidan. She knew that he probably meant well. His eyes still held a strange fascination for her, but she admired them now only from afar. She couldn't let him get close again—and he had no idea just how close he'd gotten. She might have climbed right into his bed that night, if Bobbi hadn't been there. In fact, she wasn't altogether sure that wasn't her chief reason for going to check on Sarah in the first place. But whenever she thought of that night now, all she saw in her mind's eye was another woman with a figure that made hers seem ridiculous in comparison. The thought of it made her sick to her stomach.

Taking risks in love wasn't easy for Molly—it never was, for all the reasons it usually isn't for girls who learn early that they're not one of the "pretty ones." She had been carrying around a list of her flaws for a long time, compiled from a lifetime of awkward third dates: she was too thin, her hair was too red, her chest was too small, her legs were too skinny, and so on. It was the kind of criticism that had toughened her up and made her take chances in every other area of life in which her looks didn't matter. She read that list to herself every time a new guy came along who promised to add to it. But she hadn't thought of it at all that night she had dinner with Aidan. That night, for the first night in a long time, a man had made her feel like the only woman on Earth—that is, until she stepped into Aidan's room and saw the list made flesh in the form of Bobbi Baker.

Not that it mattered now, anyway. She was certain that Aidan, after all that happened that night, believed she was out of her mind. No doubt he was only too glad to have dodged whatever bullet he must imagine she had in store for him. Her reaction to walking into that room had been over the top, she knew. It wouldn't make sense to anyone who didn't understand all of the hopes and fears that walked in with her. She had hated Aidan for weeks, but now those fires were dying down, and she wanted nothing more than to find shelter and warmth in his arms. Yet she was so, so far away from him.

It came down to the fact that she just didn't trust him—not the way a woman needs to trust a man. It was too dangerous. "Fool me once . . ." she recited to herself. With any other man, she could have—and would have—let bygones be bygones. But she knew that bygones with Aidan wouldn't *stay gone*. He might take her in, and he might even fall in love, but someday, somewhere, another Bobbi Baker was bound to walk into his life and remind her of all that she was not. That was a risk she just couldn't take.

Love, hate, and regrets aside, Molly believed in what they were all doing now. She believed that Aidan, for all his faults, had the character, courage, and mental toughness to win this race, if it could be won.

"Don't let this race psych you out," Molly finally said. "If one-tenth of the story Marcus heard about *Prodigal* is true, *Invictus* will never see her coming."

CHAPTER 25

The next two months seemed to fly by. During that time, Aidan and Ibrahim worked side by side every day, sun up to sun down—chipping, sanding, caulking, painting, and varnishing—with a vigor far beyond the endurance of any paid laborer. Each task was performed by human hands, unaided by motorized machinery of any kind, according to Marcus's directive. Aidan had only rudimentary skills for this work, but Ibrahim showed the quiet competence and efficiency of a master carpenter. Aidan followed his example closely. Their work was eased by the fact that *Prodigal* suffered from none of the complexities of modern boats. There was neither electrical wiring nor any auxiliary means of mechanical propulsion. As a consequence of these blessings, there were no batteries, no corroded switches, no oily bilges, and no rusting fuel tanks. The absence of an engine spared them from a thousand woes usually owing to the petulance of valves, filters, pumps, and sensors.

The simplicity of *Prodigal's* design was a thing of beauty. There was a tiller instead of a ship's wheel; therefore, her steerage was not a thing contrived by the indirect operation of pulleys, lines, and gears, nor a hostage to the delicate temperament of such things. The helmsman's slightest touch was communicated directly from tiller to rudder, and every nuance of the ship's movement was spoken directly to him in reply, such that hull and helmsman were kept in constant conversation. All of the running and interior lights were oil-fueled and therefore easy to restore to service with no more than wicks and lamp oil. The glow of the ship's lamps made a quiet sanctuary of the interior spaces, bathing in a soft light all of their hours spent replacing worn upholstery, refitting cabinet latches, reseating leaky port lights and hatches, repairing wood joinery, and removing and re-bedding the heavy iron chain plates. Marcus escaped at every chance he could to join them, alternately working by their side and fluttering above them like a nervous bird. Each section of the deck and hull planking was tested, and several boards were removed and replaced with strong white oak, but Marcus would not suffer any section of the keel to be disturbed in any way.

Day by day, *Prodigal* emerged and reawakened as if from a long sleep. It was decided among her salvors that she would remain *Cygnet* for a little while longer, for all public intents and purposes. That name afforded her the continued privacy and protection of the ruse laid by Marcus in Boston. But concealed beneath a tarp that was secured carefully against outside inspection, the proper name—to be unveiled when the time came—was applied in careful brush strokes of black and gold.

The matter of sails for the ship needed to be addressed and quickly. They would not be easy to construct to custom specifications. On this subject Marcus also had some very particular requirements. He traveled all day by ferry and automobile to Oriental to meet with a sailmaker of no small reputation. His name was Carl Johansson, a fastidious Swede with a penchant for intricate stitching and a sturdiness of construction that produced sails renowned the world over for their toughness. Canvas from his loft had survived intact and continued to serve its owners through strong gales in dozens of major ocean races when sails of lesser art had been reduced to tatters. It was said that a ship could founder and plummet to the bottom of the sea with all her rigging, but any jib made by Johansson would sail on without her. Marcus feared for that reason that he would arrive at the back of a long line waiting to see his old friend, and that there would be too little time for Johansson to start—much less finish—a whole complement of sails necessary for a schooner the size of *Prodigal*.

Johansson was uncharacteristically idle when Marcus arrived. He obviously had been waiting for him all day. There was no one else in the loft. He looked much older than Marcus remembered him, and there was a weariness of care and worry about his face. He grasped Marcus's hand and held it warmly.

"It is good of you to come, Father."

"Well, I don't suppose you know why I'm here, I—"

"I know very well. I have been waiting for you. I had feared you might not come, but now you are here. Let us talk of *Prodigal*."

Marcus's surprise was unmistakable.

"Do not worry, your secret is safe. I have lived and worked on these waters for many years. There are not many of us left. But there is still nothing that happens on these sounds that passes unnoticed. I will build your sails for you. I will build them strong and fast. You have my word."

The rest of the afternoon was spent going over the details of the weight and construction of sail cloth needed to achieve the right combination of durability and responsiveness. Reef points, chafing gear, bails, and grommets were all reviewed carefully until Johansson had a detailed set of instructions for two mainsails, a genoa, a jib, a staysail, a spritsail, and two storm sails. It would be an impossible task for any other sailmaker to complete in four months, and Johansson had less than two. He vowed to work night and day.

"I have the money to pay you in full, Carl, and certainly more than the usual price is called for because of the time." Marcus took out a checkbook.

"There will be no charge," Johansson said, staring at him sternly.

"Carl, that's really not—we have the money."

"There will be no charge," Johansson insisted. He held Marcus's hands again, and his eyes began to fill with tears. "I have seen this ship in my dreams. I will make these sails for Sarah. Promise me that you will pray for her, Father, and for your old friend Carl?"

"Of course, Carl. I will pray for you both regardless, you needn't worry of that, but—"

"Pray for her and for me, Father. And do not ask me to take your money. I beg you. This is my gift to the Church."

Johansson looked toward the door of the shanty, recalling some unpleasant memory.

"Those men from New York were here last week. *Big shots.* They offered me more money than I have been paid in a year to make only one sail for their boat. They spoke of you, and of this race, and they laughed. They laughed at your boat and the men working on her for thinking that she could sail in this race."

A defiant smile spread across Johansson's face.

"I told those bastards that I would not make them anything—not a sail, not a towel for them to wipe their asses with. I asked them to leave. They cursed me, and they cursed you and your boat as they walked out. I felt filthy after speaking to them."

Johansson shook his head, recoiling as if from a bad dream.

"I will make sails for *Prodigal,* and they will stand the

test. You have my word."

It was ten o'clock that night before Marcus was back on the island with good news about the coming delivery of sails. Aidan was waiting anxiously for his return. He was waiting, too, for a call from Raleigh. He sprang up from the chair in his room when Nita knocked on the door to tell him that Boyce Stannard was on the phone.

"Aidan, it's good to hear your voice. How are you holding up out there?" Boyce spoke with a confidence and ease Aidan had not remembered about him.

"Just another day in paradise, Boyce. How are things in the big city?"

Aidan fully explained all the details of the race—the logistics of the start, the watch schedule, the expected time of arrival, and a return flight by air from Nassau for Boyce and the other crew members. Boyce didn't hesitate or waste any time in answering.

"I'm in."

"Really, just like that?"

"You bet. The only thing I had on the calendar for the first two weeks of March was a conference in Las Vegas I've been looking for a reason to get out of."

"What about the others?"

"Have you forgotten, Aidan, that associates at McFadden Brown are lower than *whale shit*? I already know which ones to ask, and they'll say yes if they know what's good for them."

"Or they'll face the wrath of Boyce Stannard?" Aidan remembered a time when that would have been a good joke.

"You're damn right. This isn't the summer camp it was when you were running things."

"I can just imagine," Aidan laughed, but he knew that what Boyce said likely was true.

"They'll either crew this race or they'll be reviewing

documents for the next six months in Poughkeepsie. Count seven of us in. We'll meet you on the island at the pre-race party at the yacht club, the night before."

CHAPTER 26

The final days of planning, logistics, hard work, and preparation seemed to pass even more quickly than Marcus had feared. Before anyone had a chance to get nervous about what lay ahead, it was March, and the race was upon them. Aidan would never forget the day. The pre-race registration party was due to begin that evening at five o'clock. Yachts of all sizes crammed onto every dock, finger pier, breakwater, and piling in the shipyard's small turning basin. More overflowed to various places around the island. Ocracoke was not used to such high-class company. Crabbers, menhaden fishermen, and shrimpers in the village were stowing million-dollar boats wherever they could find some extra room. Among the visiting dignitaries were two Swann 60s from Denmark, a Moody 51 from Lisbon, a Morris 53 from Long Island, and at least a dozen sleek, missile-shaped J-boats of lengths varying from 36 to 43 feet. Above them all—a black-hulled ship brooding like a dark lord—was *Invictus*.

There was barely an open patch of water for *Cygnet*, as she still was known, to splash down in Fielding's turning basin early that morning as Marcus, Ibrahim, and Aidan stood by like expectant fathers. She was finally ready to be launched, and not an hour too soon. The tarp across her transom, hiding her true identity, remained firmly in place. She slid confidently into the water. Marcus felt a swell of pride and a rush of anxiety

239

like a parent watching a child about to wander off into a dangerous world. But *Prodigal* floated high and true. She sat well above her waterline, dry as toast and bobbing as gingerly as a cork.

Marcus caught the lines to bring *Prodigal* into the slip they had prepared while Ibrahim and Aidan stood on deck, poling her into position. When all lines were made fast and she was snug in her berth, they returned to the rectory to make final preparations for the registration party, where Aidan planned to meet Boyce with the rest of their crew.

Aidan was in his room, sorting a few clothes for the race, when an elderly gentleman arrived. He was at the doorstep holding a huge, brown box. Two more were at his feet. The man seemed excited to see Aidan, as if he had seen him before.

"Hello, can I help you?"

"You are Aidan!"

"Yes, that's me."

"You are younger than I expected, but otherwise as Father Marcus described you. I am Carl Johansson, the sail maker."

Aidan breathed a sigh of relief. Ever the lawyer, he had feared for a moment that the man was a process server sent by his ex-wife's divorce lawyer to entangle him in some pointless controversy on the eve of the race.

"Come right in! Father Marcus is expecting you— and here, let me help you with those."

When Marcus looked out of his second-story window and saw Carl Johansson standing at the doorstep, the priest went bolting out of his room and bounding down the stairs like a child on Christmas morning. Ibrahim was summoned from the garden to join them. With Johansson beaming, the three men went through the boxes, unfolding, caressing, and commenting on the finer points of each sail as if they were newly tailored suits from Saville Row. Marcus insisted that Johansson accompany them to the party, but Johansson still had not gotten over his encounter with Rowdy Ponteau and the men from New York. He wanted nothing to do with any party Ponteau would be attending.

Aidan used the phone in the rectory to make a rare long-distance call directly to Boyce's cell, to check his progress on the ferry, but the call went straight to voice mail. He would have to wait to speak to him at the club.

The Ocracoke Yacht Club was something of an oxymoron. For one thing, there generally weren't any yachts—mostly just broken-down crabbers and rotting shrimp trawlers. The men who made a living aboard them would deck them out once a year in colored blinking lights, take their wives, and go tooting drunk around the harbor in a Christmas flotilla until they ran up on a sand bar, where they would sleep it off until the tide came and floated their boats again in the morning. That was usually the highlight of the yacht club social season. Dues were fifty dollars a year to cover beer, electricity, and pest control. The clubhouse had been erected when it was still possible to get an environmental permit to build near a marsh. The picnic tables on the deck were almost always swarming with mosquitoes, noseeums, and sand fleas. There had not been a blue blazer or a pair of Weejuns in the place since 1984, when the governor's motorcade made a wrong turn on a campaign stop and six aides came in to use the bathroom. That would change tonight.

The clubhouse had been decorated elaborately in

upper crust "yachting style," according to what the members' wives conceived that to be. It drew profuse, patronizing compliments from visiting members of the New York Yacht Club. They toured the cramped interior with all the feigned adulation of parents at a kindergarten art show. There were at least twenty men worth more than fifty million dollars each stuffed into that room when Aidan walked in wearing a borrowed jacket that was two sizes too big; a pair of topsiders colored abstractly with drips of varnish, bottom paint, and bleach; and the same peeling leather belt he'd owned for fifteen years.

The race registrar greeted him at the door.

"Hello, I'm Aidan Sharpe, captain of the *Cygnet*. I'm here to register for the race."

"Nice to meet you," said the woman. She had perfect teeth, a deep tan, and hair the color of straw that was neatly tucked into a bright red headband. She wore a blindingly white jacket.

"Margaret Egerton of the New York Yacht Club. What's the name of your boat?"

"The *Cygnet*, ma'am."

She looked down a list of boats that had twenty or thirty names on it.

"What class are you racing in?"

"Antiques and Classics."

"Oh yes, here it is. You're all paid up and ready to go." Motioning to the two men who had walked in behind him, she asked, "Are these gentlemen with your crew?"

"No, ma'am. I'm expecting my crew later tonight."

"How many?"

"Eight total, including myself."

"All right then, we'll get their names later. Any changes to the information about the boat?"

This was the time. Aidan looked at Marcus, who

spoke up for him.

"Yes, Ms. Egerton. I'm Father Marcus, one of Mr. Sharpe's sponsors. The name of the boat has been changed since the registration was filed."

"And the new name?"

"*Prodigal.*"

"*Prodigal*—oh, as in 'prodigal son'?"

If the woman wanted approval for paying attention to the readings at mass, she would get none from Marcus that evening. He was off duty and in no mood for church chat with a bunch of uppity New York Episcopalians.

"Yes, I suppose you could say," Marcus answered.

"Very well then, I'll make the change. Here is your packet of racing instructions and rules. All boats are expected on the starting line at the assigned coordinates no later than eight o'clock tomorrow morning. The race gun goes off at nine. You're welcome to walk around and meet your fellow racers. Enjoy yourselves."

Enjoyment was out of the question. Aidan's stomach was a bundle of knots. He and Ibrahim stood close by each other and Marcus like three schoolboys at their first dance. Eventually they found their way to the card table that was serving as a bar in the back of the room.

The liquor was free, and the mood of the crowd showed it. One of them, in particular, was in fine form. He had been watching Aidan ever since he stepped through the door.

"How's that bucket of goose shit you're sailing, Mr. Sharpe?" Rowdy Ponteau had been drinking for hours. He was lit up like a Christmas tree, but the look he gave Aidan now was deadly serious.

"Very well, thank you. How's that gin palace you floated in on?"

Rowdy was fired up and already going straight for the finish line, full bore. He had been waiting all evening for

Aidan to show. Malice churned inside him like a storm.

"And your little strumpet of a girlfriend? You know, the one who parades her ass on deck to drum up business. Let's see, there's a name for women like that—what is it, again?"

Aidan's blood rose like a geyser. He moved closer.

"How's your thigh, Rowdy?" Aidan let his left leg give way, bending his knee into the wound left by Ibrahim's knife.

Rowdy yelled and threw his drink, then threw a fast left jab to Aidan's jaw that caught him by surprise. Aidan rocked backward into Marcus and popped up swinging, but Marcus pulled him away before any punches found their marks. Ibrahim's hand had already found the knife in his pocket, but two giant arms wrapped around his chest before he could move.

"Not tonight, Sambo," Ibrahim heard a man say from behind. Two more men grabbed him from each side and held him steady. Something was just about to ignite in the middle of all of them, when Marcus stepped in.

"There'll be none of this," he said. "Let this man go. Immediately."

No one would challenge the priest. Ibrahim shook himself free. He got a good look at the man who had spoken to him.

Reece Ponteau had been standing across the room, watching, when the scuffle began. Now that a man older than his son was standing around giving orders, he decided he'd better step in.

"Who are you men, and what boat are you sailing on?"

He demanded answers the way a man does who is accustomed to getting them.

"The *Prodigal*," Aidan answered. "You'll want to remember that name because it will be hard for your boy to read it when he's so far back in the race."

Reece Ponteau knew the name *Prodigal*, and his expression fluttered just slightly when he heard it spoken, as though he had just hit an unseen bump in the road.

"Don't lie to my father, you pansy. They're sailing a tub named the *Cygnet*," Rowdy snarled, still massaging his leg.

"And who might you be, sir?" Marcus asked.

Reece Ponteau was not so easily cowed by a priest's collar. "I'm this young man's father and the owner of *Invictus*. I've heard of your boat, the *Cygnet*—sailing in the antique class." Aidan could see his eyes were still anxious. He came back to the question that was now haunting him.

"What's this about a boat named *Prodigal*? There is no boat entered in our class by that name." He looked at his son, then at Aidan, then at Marcus. He seemed worried about something.

"*Prodigal* is the boat's former name. We've given it to the race registrar just this evening, and that will be the name she sails under," Marcus answered.

Reece Ponteau was silent for a long time. He now had questions to which he very much wanted answers, but he wasn't sure it would be wise to ask them. He didn't know how much this priest knew about an old boat named *Prodigal* or whether, in fact, this could possibly be *the* boat of *that* name, but he was tempted to find out.

"How old is your vessel?" The question was asked sincerely and calmly, underscoring the importance of the answer to the questioner.

"It depends on what part of the vessel you're speaking of, Mr. Ponteau. There are some parts of her that were installed only today." Marcus paused then, deciding that because no one would believe what else he had to say, he might as well say it. "And, some might say there is a part of her as old as Calvary."

Reece Ponteau's face darkened. He walked directly to the registrar's table and demanded to see the registration papers for the antique class. Scrolling down the page, he came to the *Cygnet*. That name was crossed out. The name *Prodigal* was written in. There, under "Dimensions," were numbers he knew by heart:

Forty-two feet length overall

Six-foot-three-inch draft

Ten-foot-five-inch beam

Schooner rig

No engine, no wiring, no electric lights

Displacement: 17,000 pounds

Age: undetermined, in excess of 150 years

He held the paper in his hand a long time, before slowly handing it back to the woman at the desk. Then he turned, and with deliberate steps walked to the place in the corner of the room where Marcus, Aidan, and Ibrahim were standing, mulling over all that had just occurred. He came very close to Marcus's face, and for a moment looked like he intended to strike him. Then the elder Ponteau spoke in a soft voice, as if not to be heard by anyone else.

"Is this your idea of joke, Father Marcus?"

"I'm sure I don't know what you mean."

"You mean to tell me that this boat was named *Prodigal* before she was *Cygnet*?"

"That's precisely correct."

Reece paused again for several seconds, saying nothing, before summoning the courage to ask the only question that really mattered.

"In what language was this name written?"

Marcus could see, exactly, the aim of the question. Reece Ponteau obviously knew the legend of *Prodigal*— astounding given the veil of secrecy Marcus assumed surrounded Monsignor McIver's journal and Vatican inquiries—but then the Vatican had its spies as well. Reece Ponteau was also commodore of the New York Yacht Club, whose thunder *Prodigal* had rudely stolen in the defeat of *America* in 1851. Perhaps he knew more of that history and its meaning than any other man alive. If that were so, Marcus reasoned, it would not be wise to give him a reason to try to right old wrongs. So he lied.

"In old Dutch, actually. Took me forever to translate, but apparently *Verloren* is the Dutch word for *Prodigal*." Marcus spoke seven languages, Dutch being one of them.

Reece looked relieved, but only briefly.

Aidan was uneasy with the lie. He respected Marcus and hesitated to contradict him, but he was bursting with an urge to speak that he could not resist.

"I plan on making this man's son pay for the truth in sea miles, so he might as well have it. The name was written in *Arabic*, Mr. Ponteau, in a Moroccan shipyard, more than 150 years ago, and around the same time an old barge from the New York Yacht Club got dusted by a boat less than half its size. Welcome to your worst nightmare."

Reece Ponteau stood motionless and in silence, as if he had been insulted by an impudent child. Then, with malice gathering in his eyes, his words were stirred again.

"I don't know what fairytales you've been reading, Mr. Sharpe, but this is a legitimate race you've entered, and I won't stand for anyone making a mockery of it. Do you mean to suggest that you believe your ship descends from Moroccan royalty almost two centuries old?" He was deadly serious now. The game was on, and it would be played for keeps.

"Who said anything about royalty, Mr. Ponteau? I'm just a simple country boy from Philadelphia. It seems your imagination has been running away with you."

Aidan was now certain, from Ponteau's answer, that the legend was true. Their boat was *the* boat, the lost *Prodigal*, reborn in the sands of Morocco with the heart of a thief.

"I see," said Ponteau, sensing that Aidan was making sport.

He then came close enough to Aidan so that no one else could hear what he had to say. He was less than an inch from his face when he hissed these words: "It takes a thief to know one, Mr. Sharpe." And with that, Reece Ponteau left the room.

CHAPTER 27

Rowdy and his crew were still sulking by the liquor table. Next to them, in a clingy white dress that seemed more to annotate than cover her figure, was a familiar face. Her arms were draped over Rowdy like two wet towels. Bobbi Baker was drinking, which was dangerous for her, and she was drunk, which was dangerous for everyone around her. When she spotted Aidan, her face seemed to light up with excitement. She walked toward him, wobbling so badly in four-inch pumps that she spattered every other step with splashes of rum from an over-filled cocktail glass.

"Well, if it isn't Captain Courageous and his little pirate band!"

Marcus sought to intervene, again.

"You shouldn't be drinking, Bobbi."

"And neither should you, Rabbi." She paused to watch his face. He suspected nothing of what she was about to say, which was how she liked it.

"Oh, yeah, I know your little secret. Did you know his little secret, Aidan? Father pour-me-another, here, trots off down the beach at night with his little wonder dog and hides bottles of communion wine for, well—how shall we describe them, Father?—for *midnight devotionals*."

Marcus felt his face flush with a mixture of anger and shame, not for the opinions of Aidan and Ibrahim, who would gladly have joined him in a drink any day, but for the failure of his own example, the result of which was now staring him in the face with a rum cocktail in her hand. He took no pleasure in watching her drown before his eyes, and he collected his wits quickly for a rescue.

"We all have our challenges, Bobbi, and I certainly have mine. But you're not doing yourself any good here. Why don't you let me take you home?"

Marcus reached for her arm but she pulled it away and, in the process, covered the front of Aidan's jacket with her drink.

"Oo-ohh I'm so sorry!" she said, mockingly. "I spilled that drink all over your pretty jacket." She was laughing now, and falling against Aidan as though she might drop to the floor at any moment.

"I see you're still wearing your clothes two sizes too big. Maybe you could get your little towboat girlfriend to alter it for you. Oh, no—I forgot! She don't wear no clothes. Ha-ha! Y'all can get married and have little naked babies runnin' down the beach—"

"Shut up, Bobbi." Aidan didn't see any point in letting this go on, but he was wrong to think he could stop it. She was a storm that needed to blow itself out.

Bobbi whirled back from him, her face now alive with indignation.

"You don't tell me to shut up, you stuffed-shirt quitter! You wash-out! Fuck you!"

She lurched from anger back to giggling laughter again.

"Oh pardon me, I already tried that, didn't I?" She was laughing so hard she could barely stand. The three men looked at each other. It was obvious something needed to be done for her, but she was still flying high.

"Did you know, Mr. Ibrahim, that your little pal here—he likes to *cuddle*. He's not big on the slam-bam-thank-you-ma'am—even when the ma'am is *beggin'* him for it. No sir, not Honest Aidan, here. He's lookin' for *love*."

Bobbi looked at Aidan.

"Remember darlin'—our little chat about *love*? He told me—"

She was stopped again by her own laughter.

"He told me he needed to feel *love* to be attracted to a woman. It was the sweetest little Boy Scout speech I believe I've ever heard. I mean, it was just a *merit badge* moment. You remember that, baby? Well I sure do. I was listening real close, and then I started making a sweet little speech of my own—right up until the part where you fell asleep.

"Now tell me, Mr. Ibrahim, if you had a fine woman like me sitting on your *ass* without a thing on but what God gave her, do you think you could fall asleep? I'll bet you couldn't, and I'll just bet you'd be thinkin' about something other than *love*, honey."

"Get away from me, you crazy lady," Ibrahim said.

"That's enough, Bobbi." Aidan tried to steady her.

The entire room had fallen to silence and stood in rapt attention at Bobbi's outburst. Two women from the race committee were coming to help her, but she barely noticed them. She went right on shouting at Aidan.

"Enough? Oh no, I don't *think* so. It wasn't enough for me that night in your room, and it's still not enough for me, but I suppose it's just about all your little pixie girlfriend can handle."

"Miss, please let us help you," one of the women said, holding her arm.

"Help me? Lady, I don't need your help, but you see that man over there," she said, pointing to Aidan as she started to leave, "he's a *pirate*, I tell you, a regular Captain Hook! You better watch yourself, 'cause he just might fall in *love* with any one of y'all, and that's the

God's honest truth. Let him try on his little beach dress for you and model it. You'll see what I mean. He's a cutie, all right. He's a pirate of *love*. Ain't you, captain? *Ain't you!*"

Even after Bobbi walked out, her insults could be heard echoing down the stairs and into the parking lot. A low rumble of conversation quickly resumed in the room once she was gone. Rowdy and several of the men were laughing hard to themselves and not bothering to be discreet about it.

"I gotta get outa here," Aidan said to Ibrahim and Marcus. He was exhausted, mentally and physically. He massaged his jaw where Rowdy's fist had connected with it.

"But I need to know where Boyce and his crew have gotten off to. The last ferry should have arrived an hour ago."

Aidan stood outside the clubhouse in the chilled night air, cradling a borrowed cell phone in one hand and straining to read Boyce's number from a scrap of paper. The call went directly to voicemail. The next number he dialed he knew by heart. It was McFadden Brown's night line. Gaylord Dempsey, of course, answered the call.

CHAPTER 28

He hadn't meant to leave the envelope. In fact, it was the one thing he kept reminding himself all day not to forget. Why, exactly, he did forget it and leave it lying on his desk, after so many months of keeping it carefully under lock and key, was now the question he was asking himself as he rode the elevator to the twenty-first floor. He was never careless like that—just the opposite. He must have been badly distracted by something when he left the office that day, which is no wonder, given what he had done and was about to do. Or perhaps for the very reason that he had reminded himself a dozen times that afternoon to place the envelope in his briefcase and had visualized himself doing so, he mistakenly imagined that he actually *had* done so. But he was certain that if she mentioned one more time on the elevator ride back up to the office that she told him to be more careful, he would smack her silly.

The twenty-first floor was dark when they arrived, which was not surprising for ten o'clock on a Friday night—even at McFadden Brown—but the light in his office was on, which *did* surprise him. He hadn't been there since five that afternoon, and the cleaning crew should have turned off his light hours ago. The light in Gay's office was on, of course—the man kept longer hours than God—but Gay's office was at the opposite end of the hall, and there would be no need to disturb him during the few minutes it would take to collect the envelope and leave. Soon he would have the money and the evidence in his hands with plenty of time left to catch the midnight shuttle to Miami and the connection to Grand Cayman.

Gaylord Oliver Dempsey was, in fact, still in the office that night. He earned his money the old-fashioned way—hour by tedious hour—though what he spent it on was anybody's guess. He hadn't added a pound to his tall, lanky frame in forty years, which enabled him to wear the same suits he had bought when he was a law clerk on the Supreme Court in 1962. The VW bug of the same year that he drove was a falling-down disgrace to the memory of VWs everywhere, but it was the first car he had ever owned, and because it hadn't given up on him, he wasn't about to give up on it. He was not just old school. He built the old school and had taught most everyone who had come up through it, which is why the papers on the desk in front him were so hard to comprehend.

After Aidan's telephone call, Gay had walked down to the other end of the dark hall, to the spacious, new corner office where (now senior partner) Boyce Stannard had taken up residence after Aidan's departure. He turned on the light to look for some clue around Boyce's desk as to his whereabouts or the name and cell phone number of one of the associates who had gone with him to crew in the Blue Million. It was then that he saw the envelope. The name written on the outside, *Aidan Sharpe*, in black letters, suggested that its contents might have something to do with the race. But the papers Gay pulled from the envelope and spread out on the desk had to do with something else altogether.

The first thing that caught his eye was a document from the Wake County trial court administrator's office. It was an old calendar notice in the *Adamson* case, addressed to Boyce Stannard at the firm's office address, advising him of the August 29, 2009 trial date. The notice was machine-stamped January 13, 2009. In keeping with standard procedure, the date stamp was initialed by the McFadden Brown employee who opened the envelope in which it arrived: HCB, for Honor Channing Beckett. Attached by a paper clip to the notice was a check made out to Boyce from the trust account of Moriarity & Associates. The figure, two million dollars, was exactly half the amount of the settlement paid to James Moriarity and his client by Dr. Adamson's insurance company.

Behind these papers were several others. There was a series of printed email messages between Boyce and the chief financial officer for a textile company in New York, explaining their agreement to retain Boyce for unspecified "consultative services." It seemed unusual to Gay that a New York textile company would hire a North Carolina defense lawyer until he saw the name "Ponteau." Attached to these papers was a check for $500,000 from Ponteau's company to Boyce, along with application forms required to open a new account at First Caribbean International Bank of the Cayman Islands. Highlighted in yellow on one form was a statement of the bank's policy that required all new offshore accounts owned by foreign nationals to be opened in person. In a separate, smaller envelope were three pages of roundtrip airline reservations for Boyce Stannard and Honor Beckett for a flight leaving in a little over two hours.

When he heard whispering voices and hurried footsteps coming down the hall, Gay moved to the front of the desk and waited. He knew it would be only a matter of time before Boyce remembered the envelope and came back to get it.

"Gay!" Boyce fairly shrieked the name, then pushed a

tortured grin onto his face.

"Mr. Dempsey, what are you doing here so late?" asked Honor, coming up behind. Her plaster-of-Paris smile did nothing to hide the anxiety in her eyes.

Honor and Boyce simultaneously looked at the desk and the contents of the envelope spread out on top of it. All the air left Honor's lungs, and she held herself with both arms as if she were trying to keep her entire body from launching skyward.

"Did you forget something, Boyce?" Gay asked calmly.

"Well, I was—you know, just coming in to—"

"Like your integrity? Or your loyalty to a good friend?"

"Gay, I, am s-s-s-sure . . ."

Boyce had never been very cool under pressure, and right now he was getting ready to blow. He wouldn't get the chance. Lieutenant Commander Gaylord Oliver Dempsey, former All-Navy Middleweight Champion, 1958, unwound eighty-two inches of bad news onto Boyce Stannard's jaw like a pole axe. Boyce's two front teeth went flying into the back of his throat, and a thin spurt of blood shot out onto the front of Honor's white dress. She screamed and ran down the hall toward the elevator in what became her last trip to the lobby from the offices of McFadden Brown.

Boyce's eyes rolled back in his head as he staggered back against the wall and stood there, for a second, before crumpling into an unconscious heap. What he had meant to say and would have said, if he were still awake to say it, was that he had not intended this scheme to cost Aidan his law license or anything of the kind. Aidan had not even been part of the plan. *Adamson* was Boyce's case. He never expected Aidan to take responsibility for the crisis, which was designed merely to convince the insurance company to pay the four-million-dollar policy limit. The appearance of Emily on the jury was a regrettable coincidence, but Aidan's unexpected mistake played perfectly into Moriarity's scheme to jack up the money and split it with Boyce. Of course, none of that explanation would have mattered to Gay, so it was no pity that Boyce never got to give it.

Gay made three phone calls that night. The first was to the rectory, where Nita answered and took a message for Father Marcus that Boyce and his crew would not be arriving. The second call was to the emergency room of Rex Hospital, to send an ambulance for a man who had just suffered a concussion. The third call was to the home of Wilson J. Daughtry III, president of the North Carolina State Bar.

CHAPTER 29

Aidan gave Marcus back his cell phone after hanging up from his call with Gay.

"Gay has gone to look for Boyce or to see if he can find a phone number for one of the guys coming with him. He said he'd call the rectory with any news. I'm headed to the boat for the night. I've still got a few things to get ready before they arrive."

The three men said their goodbyes. Time was now coming down to the wire, and they knew that Aidan would soon be far out to sea and beyond their aid for several days. The feeling at their parting was something like saying goodbye to a soldier before a battle.

"We'll be down at the shipyard at zero-dark-thirty to help you get underway, Aidan," Marcus reassured him.

"You're going to make us proud," Ibrahim added.

"*Prodigal* is going to make us *all* proud, I'm sure of it." Aidan believed this to his very core, but his mind was busy with worry about the reason for Boyce's delay. He could not win a race without a crew. But no matter what, he would bring this ship to face *Invictus* on the Atlantic Ocean in the morning, if he had to row her all the way.

He regularly now heard Sarah's last words to him. Although he did not understand their meaning, they comforted him, and he repeated them like a mantra in his mind: *Follow where it leads. The life it takes, and the life it gives, is everlasting.*

At the shipyard, Aidan stepped gingerly aboard *Prodigal* from her starboard side, amidships. He recalled the same, steady firmness he had felt the first day he set foot on her at sea. She dipped ever so slightly under his weight and cushioned his steps, like a horse nuzzling a beloved rider. Down in the cabin, he lit a brass overhead lamp, now polished to a shining brilliance, and watched the cabin around him awaken in a soft glow. Seeing this reminded him of his last night on the *Sairey Gamp*. It had been only four months since then, but it felt like forty years. Despite his mistakes in life—and there were many—Aidan didn't have many regrets. That night with Molly and Bobbi was one of them.

"Hey, stranger. You in there?"

Aidan heard a familiar voice calling to him from the dock outside. It was the woman who occupied all his thoughts, summoned now as though she were a genie from a bottle.

"Molly, I'm glad you came. I missed you at the party."

"I know—sorry I didn't make it. I'm not much of a party girl, you know."

"And I'm not much of a party guy. But I missed you all the same."

When he said things like that, it made it so much harder for her to hate him. But the truth was, she had stopped hating him a long time ago. Now there was just a callus where the wound used to be. The pain wasn't gone, but neither was the magic of that night. It returned to her whenever she heard his voice around town—on the fuel dock, standing at the ferry office, waiting in line for groceries. Still, to suggest that she missed him, though it was the God's-honest truth, would have been too much for her to bear. If she let that dam crack even slightly, she feared there would come a flood that nothing could hold back.

"So, you ready to do this thing, cowboy?" She gave him a big smile, which came easily and felt so much more natural than the months of self-imposed silence.

Aidan was cheered by her willingness to engage. He smiled back, even though his answer was nothing to be happy about.

"I'd be a whole lot more ready if I had a crew. I've been expecting them all night. They were supposed to arrive on the ferry three hours ago."

"Oh, they'll be a while yet. The ferry office on Cedar Point called the towing dock tonight. They held up the last run due to a pump failure. They got it fixed, but the ferry still hasn't landed. I'll make sure your crew finds you when they do."

Neither Molly nor Aidan knew the truth yet about Boyce, who at that moment was screaming bloody murder in a whistling lisp as a nasogastric tube was passed alongside the fracture in his septum.

"Hey Aidan," she continued, then paused, seeming to struggle for the words.

"You're a good man. And don't let anyone tell you otherwise."

He was so filled with desire, at that moment, that he could have flown from the deck of *Prodigal* to take her in his arms, but it was asking too much for her to remain any longer in that place most dangerous to her heart—close to him. He was like a rip tide—overpowering her will to resist, pulling her out to sea, and threatening to sweep her away, with no hope of return. It still felt safer to remain ashore. She had already turned to head back to the harbor.

"I'll take your word for it," he called after her, "—and keep it!"

The next several hours Aidan spent checking off the

dozens of assorted and miscellaneous to-do lists that multiply like a virus before every voyage. He was just about through the third list when he heard laughter and saw a bright light outside the hatch on the ship's port side. Excited finally to see Boyce and his crew, Aidan came bounding out of the companionway into the scene of a nightmare, instead.

Prodigal's new staysail was beginning to rise with flames. On the dock stood Bobbi Baker, her hand weaving arcs of light in the sky with a torch made of oily rags wrapped around the end of a broomstick. Impossible though it seemed, she was more drunk now than she had been when he last saw her.

"Hey there now, *pye-rate* boy! Looks like you're listing."

She began to stagger and turn in little circles, holding her flaming broomstick like a sparkler fizzling out on the Fourth of July.

"*He's listing to port, evuh-body!* Get a buh-ket! Ha-*haaa*! How're *thangs* aboard yo' little—what are you sailing on?"

"Bobbi—what the *hell* are you doing?" Aidan couldn't believe his eyes. A combination of anger and fear shot through his veins. He ran to the stern to grab a bucket.

Her words made no sense. "You and your ship, and—I'm gonna party now right, carry your ship man, and right about now, fire it up—now, you skinny bastard—what?—what did you say to me? You gonna, you—you—you . . ."

And with that she hit the ground like a brick, where she would remain passed out until the following morning. But Aidan was too busy running forward on deck with a bucket to notice. Johansson's sails might be storm-proof, but they weren't fireproof. A nasty, gaping hole rimmed with black char stared back at him from what had been a gleaming new staysail. He would need that sail in the heavy weather expected between there and the Bahamas, and it was a loss he sorely could afford. But looking out toward the shipyard gate, Aidan saw that she was about to suffer another.

There were four men, maybe five, with tools and brickbats. They didn't seem as drunk as Bobbi, but they were making too much noise to be sober. One of them carried what looked to be a jerry can of something— gasoline. He heard someone shout, "Hey, *luh-vah boy,*" then they all laughed and started to head his way. He would have only a minute, maybe two, to push *Prodigal* away from the dock and head for the safety of open water.

Aidan ran about the decks, rushing from side to side and fore and aft, releasing the docklines that tethered *Prodigal* safely to a world that now seemed only to wish her harm. Taking the long pole that he and Marcus had spent an entire afternoon sanding to a perfect smoothness, he dug one end into the sandy bottom beneath *Prodigal's* keel and pushed with a loud groan. She skittered away from the dock like a leaf and responded so readily to his command that he lost his balance and nearly fell overboard. This was the first moment he had steered her anywhere but toward captivity, and she was ready to run.

For all that had gone wrong so far that evening— which was practically everything—Aidan was blessed in that hour by a flood tide that had just begun to ebb. It was already flowing swiftly past the entrance of the channel to the shipyard and was headed offshore, which was the only place he was sure he would be safe from Rowdy Ponteau and his crew. For the next thirty minutes, and no longer, the water all across the inlet would be deep enough for *Prodigal's* full keel to pass through unscathed, even if she wandered outside the channel proper.

Although *Prodigal's* sails remained furled, when she hit the open water of Pamlico Sound, the current overtook her, and she began to flee swiftly toward the inlet. The old thief had not forgotten how to make a quick exit. Hastily lashing the helm, Aidan ran forward to the first mast and raised the halyard. Under sail again at last, *Prodigal* lurched forward like a wild mare freed from her traces. In a few moments, the shouts of the men on the dock could not be heard over the rush of water running in *Prodigal's* wake.

Despair hung over Aidan like a cloud in the hours he spent hove-to offshore that night, slowly drifting north to windward, just west of the Gulf Stream. He lowered the mainsail and sat on the foredeck that now slowly rose and fell with the ocean swells. He needed to collect his wits and form a plan. The race was lost. If he still had a crew—which he doubted—he had no idea how or where they would find him. He couldn't sail for three days straight with no rest. He feared there would be no requiem for *Prodigal*.

Phosphorescence glittered and swirled in the water passing around the hull, and in the distance a pale moon began to rise. He dared not shine a light. He thought only to shelter his ship in the gentle darkness of a calm sea like a runaway child, fleeing the cruel punishments of her overlords. She sheltered him in return. They were as one flesh, bound together by water, sky, and wood. He would not abandon her to an unseen fate. He was her captain now, and she was his prize.

A faint blush of dawn had already spread across the sea before Aidan realized that he had been rocked asleep by the gentle motion of the ship. He had come into the Gulf Stream, and it was carrying him north by east. In three weeks' time, his current heading would take him to Ireland. He chuckled to himself and shook his head to think of it. Just six hours ago, Ireland was the last place on Earth where he would have thought he might be headed, but now it seemed as good a destination as any other. He had a week's worth of food and provisions for eight. But Ireland wasn't the plan—Nassau was. For Aidan, it was Nassau or nothing. He promised Rowdy Ponteau a fight, and a fight he would get, even if Aidan was the last man standing.

He unfurled the staysail to examine the damage from the fire. The morning light revealed it to be less extensive than he had believed. Johansson had given him several yards of spare sailcloth on a roll, and a one-foot section of it was all he needed to patch the damage.

"Bobbi," he muttered in disgust mixed with feelings of pity. He should have seen that squall coming at the first sign of her in the mini-mart. Just by the way she carried herself, the danger could not have been clearer than if she had been flying storm flags in her hair. But he also knew that he wasn't the first man she had ensnared, and he surely would not be the last.

It was seven in the morning when he put the last stitches in the patch to the staysail. He raised his arms to stretch, then looked out over the sea widening in *Prodigal's* wake. He could see the gray shadows of other boats far in the distance, gathering for the start of the race. He was probably fifteen miles off. It was time he made sail and charted a course for the starting line in order to arrive there when the gun went off at nine. When everything was secure below and all was ready, he stood atop the cabin beside the mast, the main halyard in his gloved hand, and paused again for a moment to wonder at the vast expanse of ocean that surrounded him. He was about to face the sea and this race utterly and completely alone—or so he thought.

What he first assumed was a pod of dolphins breaching in unison, far south of *Prodigal's* position, turned out to be the spray from the bow of a small boat that was riding hard up and over the swells. It would not have been unusual to see a fishing boat this far out, but this one was moving much too fast for any school of shrimp it might have been after. His first thought was that Ponteau and his men had come after him, and he wondered if there were some weapon aboard he could use to defend himself, but within minutes his dread turned to joy. It was the *Sairey Gamp*.

She had been running hard for *Prodigal* all morning. When Molly came back to the shipyard to give Aidan the news that his crew had failed to arrive on the ferry, she found Fielding trying to waken Bobbi where she lay on the dock, still wearing a badly stained party dress, sleeping off the hangover of a lifetime with a charred stick in her hand and ashes everywhere around her. Obviously something dreadful had happened. *Prodigal* was gone. Marcus and Ibrahim arrived minutes after Molly did, each carrying a duffle filled with extra clothes and weathers. They told her that Aidan's crew had bailed out, and they had come to take their place. Molly decided to join them, but they had to find Aidan and *Prodigal* first.

Looking out from the bow of *Prodigal* at sea, Aidan saw an older man at the helm of the *Sairey Gamp* where Molly should have been standing. It was Zoot, and he was smiling broadly, clearly loving being on the open ocean and at the helm of a good boat again. He brought the tug gently alongside the *Prodigal*. Molly, Marcus, and Ibrahim prepared to come aboard.

"Meet your new crew," Molly said.

"Better looking than the old crew," Aidan answered with a ready smile, "but where are *they*?"

Marcus's expression fell. "There's no good news

there, Aidan, and no time to tell it."

Marcus would not ordinarily have returned a call from Gay Dempsey at four o'clock in the morning, but last night Nita had been insistent. Gay made her promise that Father Marcus would call him as soon as he returned. Marcus could scarcely believe the story he had heard, but he knew it meant that he had to find Aidan and get aboard *Prodigal* as soon as possible.

Marcus had stopped on his way to the yard to inform Ibrahim and tell him goodbye. He understood that Ibrahim could never enter Bahamian waters as a wanted man, and no one expected him to. But what happened to Aidan at the pre-race party had affected Ibrahim deeply. When he heard the story of Boyce's betrayal, aided and abetted by money from Ponteau, he began packing his bag without another word. There was nothing and no one who could stop him from getting into that race. With Molly as able-bodied and knowledgeable of boats as any of the men, the four of them made a serviceable crew that would take *Prodigal* headlong into the fight she was born for.

Zoot waved and shouted good luck as he swerved the *Sairey Gamp* to the south to take her back to the harbor, where she would remain until Molly returned. The wind had clocked from the southwest to the northwest with the passing of a front, and it was blowing a steady fifteen knots. The seas were already rising in the Gulf Stream, provoked by the wind. *Prodigal* would have her work cut out for her if she intended to make it to the starting line on time.

CHAPTER 30

The Black Flag was already filling up with customers when Zoot finally got the *Sairey Gamp* tucked into her slip and made his way back to the bar. The race committee and all the sailors were out to sea that morning, but everyone else connected in any way to the Blue Million was growing impatient for breakfast to be served. Eugenio, the Nicaraguan cook who spoke no English, rolled his eyes when Zoot walked by, in a sign that things were not going well in the kitchen. Martha, a waitress who had been covering the bar while Zoot was out looking for Aidan, gladly relinquished the green dishtowel—the scepter of power—and began to make her way toward a table of unhappy customers on the deck. They had been waiting an hour for an order of Oysters Rockefeller and Bloody Marys, and they would be waiting longer still.

Zoot strapped on his apron and felt it squeeze around him like a giant blood pressure cuff. This was going to be one of those days. As Martha passed him on her way to the tables, she nodded her head in the opposite direction and, with raised eyebrows, said, "*There's* one you need to have a look at."

Bobbi Baker, or at least a shattered, disheveled wreck of a woman who vaguely resembled her, was sitting at the end of the bar, alone. Her hair was an urgent mess, with every strand straining to fly in a different path skyward. Running mascara had pooled in the deep, puffy bags beneath her lifeless eyes. The faint shadow of a stain covered the shoulders and back of her dress. In her hand she clenched a wad of bills—three hundred dollars in all. She smelled of sex and whiskey and soot.

Her chin was propped on her right hand, which held a lit and dying cigarette. Her left hand cradled her right elbow on the bar. The distant stare in her eyes was all too familiar to Zoot. It was the look people got when they no longer gave a damn about what they saw.

In front of her were three empty bottles of ginger ale. Martha would have cleared them, but Bobbi insisted that she leave them there. She wanted them visible as a testament to the world—just in case the world was watching—that the lunatic who had nearly lit herself and the *Prodigal* on fire last night, was not now trying to put herself out with gin. She was turning over a new leaf.

"Again?" people would ask. "Yes, again," she would tell them.

But what's another leaf to a woman who lives on a leaf pile? Bobbi had asked herself that question two hours ago, and when Zoot walked up to her at the end of the bar she was still staring straight out into space, searching for a reason to care about the answer.

Women like Martha—who were about Bobbi's age but didn't have her figure—would sometimes say she was a tramp, though never to her face. Most of the older women in the village just felt sorry that she never seemed to have anyone or anything to hang onto for very long. Bobbi felt sorry for herself for the same reason. It was this reason more than any other that had made it so hard for her to accept Aidan's rejection that night in the rectory. She'd thought about it every day since.

The fact that Bobbi could even perceive as "rejection" what happened in the span of those two hours, after she staked out Aidan's room, spoke volumes about the neediness deep in her heart. She wanted nothing more than a chance to be *normal*, and she firmly believed there *was* such a thing, even though she'd never truly seen it. Whatever *normal* meant, she was also certain that Aidan Sharpe offered that to her. But the offer was one made entirely in her own mind. She had gone about "accepting" it in her own way, first by stalking him like a serial killer in the dark, then by trying to seduce him.

Bobbi was incapable of intimacy because intimacy came with the very real danger of injury. She shielded herself with every parry and thrust in the direction of the opposite sex, always staying safely out of reach of any riposte. She *never, ever, ever* told a man what she truly felt. That was Rule One. And she never left herself open. She lacked the otolaryngeal capacity to form the words, "Hi, I'm Bobbi. How about buying me dinner, then I'll say goodnight, and maybe you can call me next week?" That sounded like a dead language to her. She wondered at times whether any woman really *said* such things anymore outside of Disney movies and Amish romance novels.

Now, in her mind, none of that mattered. "New leaf my ass," she mumbled to herself. The game was done. She was a spent force. She was out of options and feeling numb, as if the power cord to her brain had been pulled from the wall. She was a lost soul standing on the banks of the River Styx, hoping only that someone would think to place a coin in her mouth for the boatman.

Pulling up a stool on his side of the bar, Zoot removed the cold cigarette butt from Bobbi's fingers and folded them into his. Her delicate skin looked starkly pale and child-like resting on top of the thick, brown calluses of his enormous hand. His was the touch of a concerned father and a protective older brother, but the gentle sweetness he showed her was more than she could bear. Her face cracked, and giant gobs of tears began rolling down her cheeks, overrunning and breaking the mascara dam under her eyes, and following a trickle of muddy gray water into her mouth.

Zoot handed her a clean napkin and began to push strands of her hair out of her face. There was something like lint tangled in her hair on one side. He tried to pull it out, then realized it looked very much like dried semen. He reached into Martha's handbag where she always hid it, under the bar, and found a hairbrush. Martha watched him do this from across the room and, starting to open her mouth in protest, bit her lip after seeing the hot look he shot her in return. "Don't start," it said.

Bobbi distractedly brushed her hair, still staring out into space and not stopping for a moment to wonder whose brush it was or where it came from. She began to speak. Her lips curled and contorted as she tried to form words through quiet sobs. The voice that Zoot heard was like that of a little child.

"He *hurt* me, Zoot."

"Who hurt you, Honey?"

"Rowdy. He made me feel *so stupid and small.*"

"I know, Darlin, that's what little people do to make themselves look big. If I ever see him in here again, I promise you, he won't feel so tall."

Another minute of tears passed before she could compose herself to speak again.

"It was just the two of us, Rowdy and I, alone in his hotel room. He said I was pretty, and that he liked the way I put Aidan in his place at the party. He said he had money, lots of money, and I was smart—the kind of girl he liked. Then there was scotch. I'd never seen so much liquor. I was drinking so much, Zoot. I got *crazy* drunk. Other men from his crew showed up. I don't really remember everything after that. *God only knows what I did. And then, and then . . .*" Her tears were coming faster, now, falling in big drops from the tip of her chin to the bar like the beginning of a spring shower.

" *. . . then when it was over he handed me two hundred dollars like I was just some kind of whore!* I tried to laugh like he was joking, but I knew he wasn't. He put the money in my hand and made me take it. Then he offered me a hundred more if I would go burn that stupid boat. Well, at that point I was only too glad to get the hell out of there, away from that creep, but Lord knows I needed the money, and I would have burned that damn boat *for free.*"

"Why, Sweetheart? Why would you do a thing like that?"

"Because I *hate that pansy lawyer!*" She started to compose herself. She was talking about Aidan, now, and clearly she had something she wanted to say that she felt was important.

"I hated the way he treated me when that little bitch walked in on us, all high and mighty as if she weren't after him too. When he saw her, he acted like I wasn't even there. I hated what she said to me, then. She made me feel cheap—like she hadn't just walked into his bedroom all dolled up and cute in the middle of the night *herself* with some stupid excuse about a rescue party. *And all he could do was look at her*, like she was something special. He made me feel like dirt—like invisible dirt. *Oh, God, Zoot! Ain't I special too? Ain't I special?*"

"You know darn well you are, Bobbi. What would I do here Friday nights without you to talk to? You're an island girl. You belong here. No one is going to hurt you."

Zoot hadn't followed the meaning of more than a tenth of what Bobbi had just said about Aidan, but he understood enough to know that Aidan was someone whose attention and affection she had come to crave, and that she felt ignored and shamed by him because of Molly. As for the rest of the drama, he guessed that the blame wasn't Aidan's, Molly's or even Bobbi's. The blame didn't matter. The tears did, and once again they overwhelmed her.

Zoot gently rubbed her shoulder. He did his best to reassure her that it would all work out, but he knew she needed time.

Just then, a man wearing a navy blue turtleneck under an expensive-looking, off-white linen jacket, who smelled of too much cologne, swooped up to the bar where Bobbi was sitting. He owned only a small fraction of one of the New York syndicate boats competing in the race, but he swaggered as if he were an Admiral of the Ocean Sea. He had been among the out-of-town guests at the pre-race party the night before, where he had seen Bobbi deliver her command performance. He did a brief double take after recognizing her at the bar, hesitating a moment to look her up and down before speaking loudly to Zoot in a thick, New Jersey accent.

"You know, pal, my group has been waiting for more than an hour for more drinks and a plate of oysters. If you spent more time on your business instead of sitting here making time with this floozy, people might get some service around here."

The word *floozy* hung in the air, like brilliant fireworks that follow the concussion of the blast, then slowly fade as they fall to Earth. Zoot watched the blood drain from Bobbi's face, and he saw her lips begin to quiver. It wasn't the first time some jerk had made a smart remark about her at the Black Flag. She'd slapped more than a few cowboys down to the floor over lesser insults. But that day she looked small and fragile. The cruelty of the man's words had seemed to frighten and cow her, like a beaten dog.

It was just inevitable that there would be blood. The call to defend a woman's honor, by a clarion so clear and near as this, was to Zoot Davis a call to account for his manhood. This insult could not stand. The laws of gravity forbade it.

Zoot may have been old and fat, but if his fight with Rowdy Ponteau had proved anything it was that he was mule strong and still fast with his hands—much faster, in fact, than the loud man standing in front of him had any reason to expect, which is why he never saw coming what came next.

Zoot shot out a giant left hand and, grabbing the man by the hair on the back of his head, slammed his face down onto the bar, instantly breaking his nose. A fountain of blood spurted into the air as the man rebounded backwards and fell to the floor.

"*You sonofabitch!*" The man shouted through the blood filling his throat. He stumbled as he tried to get up and move away from the bartender he had wildly underestimated, just as Rowdy Ponteau once had done.

Zoot's heart rate never ticked up by a single beat through it all, and he didn't move an inch from where he stood behind the bar. Martha's heart, on the other hand, was racing as she circled in front of the injured man, exclaiming "Oh my *God!*" in rapid succession and trying hard not to panic as she dispersed paper napkins everywhere.

A Hyde County sheriff's deputy who had been eating a bowl of grits on his morning break got up from his booth and walked over to the astonished customer. Upon seeing him, the injured man screamed, his speech still barely intelligible, "You need to arrest that *bastard!* Did you see what he did? Did you see what the *bastard* did to me?"

"Not to worry sir," the deputy answered. "I saw everything. You're coming with me."

"What? *What? What the hell for?* He hit *me*—are you *blind?*" The man jerked his arm back suddenly as the deputy took hold of it, which prompted the appearance of a pair of handcuffs.

"Disturbing the peace and resisting arrest is what for," the deputy said.

The handcuffs came together with a cold, metallic crunch, followed by a string of obscenities emanating from the man's still-bleeding face. The young deputy turned to Zoot and, raising his voice just enough to be heard over the man's continued shouting, said, "I'll be by to settle up for the breakfast later, Zoot."

"Not to worry, Gene, it's on the house," Zoot answered. "And tell Sheriff Hudson he needs to let you boys come down here for poker night. The beer doesn't get any cheaper than free."

In all the commotion, Zoot didn't notice that Bobbi had stood up. That dead stare of hers was even more distant now—somewhere far beyond his understanding. She was moving toward the door but seemed unsteady on her feet. He worried she might still be drunk until he saw she was missing the heel from one shoe. He called her name, but she never looked back. Sitting on top of the bar where she'd left them were three wadded-up hundred-dollar bills.

"Your money, Bobbi!" Zoot called out as she disappeared through the door.

"Keep it," was all she said.

As she walked down the street toward the harbor, Zoot watched her through the window. Her back was stiff and straight, and she held her head unnaturally high as she moved slowly, with an air of pride that seemed preposterous given her appearance. Lurching up on her one good shoe, then down on the other and wobbling to the side, she looked as if she were executing the precision march steps of some bizarre funeral rite in a Third World army. She was headed in the direction of the ferry.

The money on the bar stank of scotch and something worse. Zoot had no intention of taking it—not after what Bobbi told him about how she'd earned it, but he couldn't leave it sitting there, either.

In a far corner of the restaurant was a fresh-faced young priest—an assistant rector from St. Michael's, the large church to the north on Hatteras Island. He had driven down that morning to join Father Marcus for breakfast and had waited two hours before deciding to eat without him. He didn't know it yet, but he would be staying on to say mass at St. Anne's and sending for his things to stay indefinitely while the bishop decided what to do about Marcus's unexcused absence. When Marcus returned, there would be another wood-shedding with the bishop, with threats and ultimatums and a great rending of purple robes. Marcus would suffer all of this with scarcely concealed glee, after which everything would return begrudgingly to the status quo.

Zoot walked up to the young priest and introduced himself.

"Zoot Davis, Father. I hope you weren't planning on paying for that fish sandwich, because the Church's money is no good in here." The young priest smiled. He was probably half Zoot's age and used to these sorts of endearments from the old Catholic faithful. From the first sound of Zoot's voice, he guessed that an old altar boy and faithful navigator of the Knights of Columbus was speaking to him.

"Father Tim, pleased to meet you." The priest hurriedly swallowed a mouthful of beer-battered cod and held out his hand. "What a lively place you have here. I don't know how I missed it in my past travels through the village."

"Well, you'll have to come again, Father, when things are less exciting."

Zoot was eager to get to the point and even more eager to get rid of the bills in his pocket.

"Here's something for Peter's Pence, Father. I know the Church will make good use of it." He handed the young priest the money, attempting to smooth and wipe off each of the three bills as best he could before doing so.

Father Tim didn't let on, but he had recognized the troubled woman crying at the bar and had noticed the money she left there. It had been Bobbi's habit to make the hour-long drive to Hatteras Island so she could say her confessions to one of the priests at St. Michael's instead of to Father Marcus at St. Anne's. As dearly as she loved Marcus, she equally doubted whether the absolution knob on his side of the confessional was still connected to anything up in heaven, given his own private transgressions. Had she known more about Father Tim, she might well have decided to make her confession to the fish in the sea instead, but that was another story.

Father Tim had on more than one occasion faithfully discharged his apostolic office to make Bobbi's sins, though as scarlet, white as snow. But forgiven is not forgotten, and that being so he had a pretty good idea where the money she left on the bar had come from. His vaunted sense of piety would not suffer the Lord to spend it.

A regular parishioner of St. Michael's was in the restaurant that morning. He was a Hatteras fisherman who had left for sea early in the morning three days ago, not realizing that he had forgotten to turn off the stove after cooking his breakfast or that the pilot light had blown out. When he returned later that afternoon, he found his wife and their infant daughter dead in their beds where they had lain sleeping. The man was inconsolable with grief and guilt when Father Tim found him weeping in the tabernacle of the chapel the next day. The bodies were now resting together in a simple pine casket on the ferry in the harbor. He was taking them to the mainland. The mainland was the only place to go for cremation.

The man had wanted to bury his wife and child in the cemetery at Ocracoke, but he didn't have the money for a plot or a headstone. Father Tim heard his confession when he came to ask whether cremation would deprive his wife and child of the hope of resurrection. Cremation was no longer considered a sin in the Catholic Church, but the priest could see the suspicion in the man's eyes at his attempts to reassure him of this. Some old-school Catholics wondered whether the relaxation of that rule had been more for earthly convenience than heavenly obedience. Still, the bodies had to be buried.

The weight of uncertainty bore down like a millstone around the man's neck. His great hulking shoulders were stooped. Alone and lost in thought, he huddled in his booth at the Black Flag, brooding over a half-eaten bowl of chowder as if in prayer. He was waiting for the ferry whistle to blow the signal for him to come aboard with the other passengers and accompany his wife and child on their final journey.

"Hello, Frank," the priest said.

The man looked up and smiled broadly to see Father Tim as if he were an angel summoned by the prayer he had just said over his soup.

"I'm sure this is not an easy day for you, and I wanted to know whether you might let me ease your burden."

"My burden, father?"

"What would three hundred dollars mean to you, Frank?"

"*Three hundred dollars?* To me? Right now?" The man's face reddened with determination. "It would mean the difference between taking my wife and little girl to a furnace or laying them to rest in peace in a marked grave on this island." The man seemed incredulous at the question, thinking it would be in the worst taste for a priest to taunt him with such a thing, if it were only supposition, but not yet daring to hope that the money might be real.

"Then take this money, Frank, and bury your wife and child." The priest handed him the three bills.

Tears welled up in the man's eyes. Three hundred dollars, added to the three hundred in his pocket—all the money he had—was enough for the down payment on a gravesite and a small marker in the village cemetery. He opened his mouth to speak but closed it when he heard the ferry whistle blow a long, slow, and mournful note. That sound meant it was time for passengers to embark. The ferry would leave in twenty minutes. With nothing more than a clipped "thank you" but an expression that spoke volumes of gratitude, the man grabbed his coat and ran out of the bar like it was on fire. Father Tim watched him leave, then noticed the unpaid check for the soup still sitting on the table. He added to his investment by placing a twenty-dollar bill next to it. Although Zoot would never know, that day was the first and only day when the Church's money was good in the Black Flag.

Frank McCullough would never remarry, choosing instead to tend his wife's and daughter's single grave with meticulous attention, bringing fresh flowers every day. Two years later, after reading the words on a marker next to theirs and learning of another lost mother and child, he would begin bringing flowers to both graves. The flowers would eventually take root and grow bright yellow blooms each year, and the cemetery would be alive with color for years to come.

While Rowdy Ponteau's money was finding its way to a good cause, Zoot was worried about the woman who had just left his bar. He knew everyone who regularly came and went on Ocracoke Island, so it was hardly unusual that he would have the phone number of the captain of the noon ferry in a book inside the drawer below the cash register. The captain didn't have to ask Zoot why he was calling when he picked up the phone.

"Yeah, I've got her," he said. "She's safe and sound in the coffee room on the bridge deck. Martin is in there with her, now. We won't let anything happen to her. I'll keep an eye on her myself and make sure she gets back tonight."

Martin Alford was the first mate, and Hap Hartman was the captain—a man who had retired to ferry boating after thirty years at the helm of giant freighters all over the world. There was no steadier hand in those waters. Martin ordinarily had other work to do on the noon ferry crossing, but that day captain's orders were that he was to keep up a lively conversation with Bobbi Baker. He and the captain both would eventually insist that she return with them to Ocracoke, protesting that she would break their hearts forever by leaving.

She would come back. If only because she had not a dime to her name and nowhere else to go, she would come home. Martin knew it, the captain knew it, and Zoot was praying for it. They all loved Bobbi for who she was. It was true that she was crazy as a loon most days and touchy as a loaded gun the rest of the time, but she was *their* crazy loon, and they weren't about to give her up.

She would just have to turn over a new leaf, and that was all there was to it.

"Again?" people would ask. "Yes, again," she would tell them.

CHAPTER 31

Rowdy Ponteau was pleased with the weather and the company at the starting line of the Blue Million. It was a crisp spring morning. The winds were rising. *Prodigal* was nowhere in sight.

He thought his father was half out of his mind with stories of ancient crosses and African kings and immortal ships. *Prodigal* seemed to be nothing out of the ordinary. She was a waterlogged, aging bucket of rot. Why his father seemed to dread a race against her, he couldn't imagine. Rowdy welcomed the challenge, but his father insisted on "taking care of it." He was good at taking care of things and always had been. Still, it didn't seem necessary. There wasn't a boat in the competition that could touch *Invictus* for speed off the wind. She had won every race she'd entered since his father had refurbished her from the keel up, five years ago, in a major overhaul. But *Invictus* had astonished even the men who had worked to restore her. How she could be reaching the speeds she had posted on the race to Bermuda in 2006 was beyond anyone, but the results Rowdy was consistently getting out of her had given him an international reputation. Two syndicates were already vying to sign him as their helmsman for the next America's Cup. His father, however, had plans to form a syndicate of his own. He had the money to do it. In fact, he had the money to do just about any damn thing he wanted.

Three skills are essential to winning an ocean race, and Rowdy Ponteau was a master of each. The first is to be first across the starting line. Doing so requires a sense of geometry and timing. A sailboat cannot simply motor up to the line, stand there until the gun goes off, and chug across. Under sail, speed is irregular. It modulates with the wind. Once headed for the starting line, a boat cannot slow down or stop if it arrives too soon without changing direction. A boat that crosses the line *before* the starting gun goes off is required to go back and start again, losing time, which usually means losing the race.

The second key to winning is to maintain the weather gauge, meaning staying between your opponent and the direction from which the wind is blowing. This, Rowdy was notorious for doing with the reckless abandon of a demolition derby driver. Two boats in the last year had their hulls staved in by the bow of *Invictus* while trying to get around him. He jealously guarded his position closest to the wind on any tack, forcing all other boats to struggle to find moving air in the shadow of his sails.

But the third and most important key to winning is more of an intuition than a skill. It is the ability to *read* the wind. Rowdy's father had taught him this skill as a child, forcing him to sail blindfolded for miles, using the angle and speed of the breeze on his face and the motion of the boat beneath his feet to guide his hand on the tiller. As a result, he became a human weathervane. When the wind grew light and its direction difficult for other helmsmen to pinpoint, Rowdy would stand erect in the cockpit, head tilted to one side and eyes closed, his fingers making constant, minutely calibrated adjustments to the helm that kept the *Invictus* moving steadily forward, passing other boats that were sitting dead in the water.

The crew of the *Invictus* was the finest in the sport.

The performance they put on at the start of a race was a wonder to behold. Each man had a job. Each responded instantly to Rowdy's commands, which he spoke calmly and without equivocation at the precise moment when a particular winch was to be turned, a sheet was to be shortened, or a halyard was to be raised or lowered. There was a $50,000 check and a champagne suite at the British Colonial Hilton in Nassau waiting for every member of the crew if *Invictus* came in first. For Arthur Rothschild, Rowdy's race tactician and right-hand man, the prize was $100,000 and a woman of his choosing to go with the room.

Anyone who tried to sum up Rowdy Ponteau would say he was not much of a son to his father and not much of a friend to anyone else, but he had all the allies money could buy. He was not inclined toward business or politics or arts or letters. He never wanted for cash and therefore had no regard for its value. He was not moved by any ambition save one: to drive a sailboat on the open ocean faster than any man alive. That was his singular skill. That's what he did. His father's wealth ensured that he had the time, the training, the crew, the equipment, and the boat to do it well. He'd be damned if anyone challenging him off the coast of Ocracoke that day could do it better.

"Ready for the turn," Rothschild shouted, signaling the moment when they would tack for the final run at the starting line.

"Ready about," Rowdy answered. "Stand by for my count . . . three, two, one, *gybe ho!*"

Invictus whirled about on her spanking-new rudder and pushed a mountain of water to port as she came through the eye of the wind. Five other boats that could hope to do no better than imitate her followed the gybe and fell in behind.

"What's our position in line, Arthur?"

"Lead boat, five boats fifty to seventy-five yards back and falling behind, the rest still coming up on the turn."

"Any sign of that barge?"

"Not a whisper, Captain."

Arthur Rothschild had answered too soon. He hadn't seen *Prodigal* all morning—though not for want of looking. He was certain they had scared Aidan off last night when he gave "that stupid, drunken bitch" a torch, a pack of matches, and another hundred-dollar bill. *What a capital idea that was*, he thought. Bobbi had seemed only too happy to oblige. Arthur had known a few chicks like her in his life—the truly crazy ones—but he'd never seen one quite as wacko as Bobbie Baker. Her performance at the pre-race party was a hoot, but nothing could top the encore she gave later that night at the shipyard. He thought they were all going to wet their pants laughing when she hit the deck. But she served her purpose. Aidan had flown out of there on *Prodigal* with no crew and hadn't been seen since.

Until that moment.

"Belay that, Captain. I think I see something. Well, *by God*—I think it's him. North. Eighteen degrees. Coming fast."

"Glasses," Rowdy called out. He raised the binoculars that were instantly handed to him. Arthur was right. It was *Prodigal*. She was three hundred yards back, close-hauled, and headed for the starting line with a bone in her teeth. Only four crew were visible. Twenty other boats were closer, but Rowdy could tell from how far and fast *Prodigal's* jib dipped below the waves that she was making much faster time than any of them. Whether she crossed the starting line first or last, at this rate, in another two hours, she would be so far ahead they would be lucky if they could see her at all.

"*Fuck!*" Rowdy shouted, throwing the binoculars to the deck. All the crew looked aft in unison. It wasn't a command they were used to hearing from their captain. But Rowdy now knew what his father had meant. In sixty seconds he had watched *Prodigal* erase a little over twelve hundred feet of distance on the rangefinder in his binoculars. Accounting for the fact that *Invictus* was moving away from her at twelve knots, that meant *Prodigal* was moving at twenty knots or more. Something gave speed to that ship that neither his skills nor his boat could match. *Prodigal* was going to be trouble, just as his father had warned him.

The race committee boat was stationed by the starting line, preparing to log in *Invictus* as the first boat across. Scanning the horizon for the remaining boats, the chairman spotted one that seemed to be moving through the backfield as if it were a row of parked cars.

"Holy cow! Who's that?"

His assistant flipped through papers on a clipboard for the names of wooden schooners in the Antique Class.

"Looks like *Cygnet*—no, sorry, the name's been changed to *Prodigal*. It's that priest's boat."

"Tighten leeward sheets," Rowdy called to the men working the winches on the side of the boat farther from the wind. "More . . . more . . . more."

Every inch of rigging on *Invictus* was tight as piano wire now, and she was sailing as close to the wind as was physically possible without stalling. Rowdy did not intend to concede the weather gauge. He had a plan for *Prodigal* that had worked for him before.

Marcus could hardly contain himself. Looking out through the spray flying over *Prodigal's* weather deck, he felt like a sixteen-year-old kid again on Narragansett Bay.

"Run, thief, run!" he shouted with glee, his face

dripping with cool saltwater.

"She runs like a gazelle," Ibrahim added. "I have never seen a ship so eager, so happy to be at sea."

"She is *that*," said Aidan. "There's a power in her that won't be denied. The old gray mare ain't what she used to be, Ibrahim—I do believe she's better."

Aidan looked at his watch. It was almost nine o'clock. The starting gun would soon fire, and they would still be behind the line when it did, but they would make up for lost time fast. He could now read the name *Invictus* on the back of the black shape that was churning above the waves well ahead of them. When he grabbed his glasses for a better look, he saw Rowdy Ponteau standing on the stern rail, staring back at him through his own binoculars.

"Well, hello," Aidan muttered.

"What?" Ibrahim looked up.

"It's our friend, Mr. Ponteau. Get ready to release the leeward jib sheet. When the time comes, I'm going to gybe and leave him to starboard."

Prodigal gained steadily on *Invictus*, to the giddy amazement of *Prodigal's* crew.

"What have you been feeding this girl, Ibrahim?" Molly asked.

"Varnish and sweat—that's all I've got."

"Well, it looks like that's all she needed—and Mr. Johansson's sails. A match made in heaven," Molly answered.

"So it appears," said Marcus.

Within a few minutes, *Prodigal* was staring down the wake of *Invictus*. Rowdy gave no quarter to windward. His leeward rail and a good portion of the leeward deck were awash. To windward, the dagger-shaped, bright-red keel of *Invictus* lifted out of the water with every other wave, looking like a bloody knife stabbing the sea.

Aidan made a sudden move to pass to windward, but

Rowdy threw *Invictus* into *Prodigal's* path, stalling her speed to prevent Aidan's safe passage. Twice more Aidan tested the windward pass, but Rowdy made it clear each time that he would force a collision sooner than let *Prodigal* through. Until Aidan got out of the wind shadow created by Rowdy's sails, *Prodigal's* speed could not exceed that of *Invictus*. Aidan had no intention of watching Rowdy Ponteau's wake for the next one thousand miles.

"Ready to gybe?" Aidan called.

"Ready," answered all three members of the crew.

Aidan was about to pass *Prodigal's* stern through the eye of the northwest wind and leave *Invictus* well to his starboard side. He would fall off the wind just long enough to clear the other boat's shadow, then come up into the wind when he could cross safely ahead of her bow. If all went as planned, this would be the last Rowdy would see of *Prodigal* until the award ceremony in Nassau.

Prodigal was spoiling for a fight. It was as if she could see her enemy before her and was ready to devour him. Aidan gave the command.

"Gybe ho!"

They had exactly enough hands aboard *Prodigal* to execute the maneuver, and they did so flawlessly. Just as the stern passed the median of wind and the ship was about to stall, Marcus released the jib and staysail sheets perfectly, and Ibrahim pulled them in right on cue on the other side. The goal was to sacrifice the propulsion of taut sails for as little time as necessary to complete the transfer of sails from one side of the boat to the other. The mainsheets did not move, but Molly eased them briefly to blunt the force when the giant booms came sweeping across the decks in the turn. *Prodigal* thrilled with excited leaps of speed at this new chance to run for open water.

Rowdy Ponteau had not expected Aidan's maneuver. Every man he'd raced against for the past ten years had stubbornly fought him for the windward advantage. Aidan had chosen a disadvantaged heading, but in doing so had somehow found enough room and speed to get around *Invictus*, and *Prodigal* would soon be in the lead. Rowdy's pride would not bear this.

Every man aboard *Invictus* saw the impending defeat and knew if something did not change in the next sixty seconds, all their work for the next sixty hours would earn them no better than a second-place finish. On Rowdy Ponteau's boat, there was no prize for coming in anything but first.

Aidan never expected what then happened. It made no sense. There was no tactical reason for *Invictus* to turn hard in front of him. It was also a rules violation by Ponteau, because *Prodigal* had turned first, and her intended heading was open and obvious. By turning east in that instant, *Invictus* would suffer at least a penalty or at worst a collision, but she would also give up speed, position, and the windward advantage. There was one reason and one reason only for such a maneuver, and it had nothing to do with the genteel rules of yachting competition. Rowdy Ponteau's sole aim was not to compete with *Prodigal* but to kill her—to do mortal damage by ramming a hole in her vulnerable underbelly, which was now fully exposed and laid out before him on the altar of the sea.

With all his malicious will and no warning to his own crew, Rowdy threw the helm of *Invictus* hard over to port. She responded instantly like a weapon in his hand. Unaware that their captain actually intended this error, some of Rowdy's crew worked to fend off the collision, but their work was in vain. The stiff clipper bow of

Invictus slammed into the hull of her rival, opening a gaping hole a foot wide.

Prodigal shuddered from the impact, then slowed and seemed to stumble—impaled for a moment upon the hilt of *Invictus'* knife-like bow—and was obliged to adjust her pace to her assailant's lesser speed. Aidan raised his eyes from the deck where he had fallen and saw Molly lying next to him unconscious, blood streaming from a gash on her forehead. He screamed her name and lifted her into his arms, forgetting the race and everything else swirling around them.

For a moment the two ships struggled on the sea, leaderless and locked in a deadly embrace. They staggered awkwardly together in a sideways motion, like two exhausted boxers clinging to each other in the last round of a fight. Rowdy ran up onto the bowsprit, which now rose above *Prodigal's* cockpit, to examine the damage. As he'd hoped, *Invictus* was unharmed and *Prodigal* was bleeding badly from the seawater rushing into her bilge. But as he leaned over for a better look, a giant hand gripped his throat like a vise.

He had seen the priest once or twice before, but he had not noticed his size and strength under the pacifying effect of the Roman collar. The collar was gone now, and Marcus's black shirt had come unbuttoned below his neck to reveal the man of flesh and blood beneath. He seemed to tower over Rowdy even from the lower position of *Prodigal's* cockpit, and with an iron grip around his neck that tightened with anger, he pulled Rowdy's face closer to his.

Marcus spoke slowly, with controlled, intense emotion, as he looked directly into the eyes of the now speechless, frightened young man he held by the throat.

"You presume too much, Mr. Ponteau, and you understand too little. If you thought you could stop this ship without a fight, you are about to learn your mistake."

Rowdy's face began to drain of life. Marcus did not let go—he *would not* let go—and he would have taken the life of the man who threatened to take from him all that he held dear: his ship, his friends, and the memory of Sarah that was bound up in them both. But at that moment, when Rowdy Ponteau was about to step from this world into the next, Ibrahim regained the helm. With the aid of a sudden gust of wind, *Prodigal* lurched to the east, removing the blade from her side and escaping the grip of her attacker. Rowdy was pulled from the hand that had all but sealed his doom.

Released from their hold on each other, the two ships veered apart and plunged into the trough of a wave. Rowdy collapsed to the deck. Struggling to get up and holding his burning throat, he was helped by his crew back to the cockpit. There, he eventually regained control of himself and his ship and returned to a southwesterly heading.

Ibrahim had urgent work to do below. He gave the helm to Marcus.

"Keep her on a beam reach with her port side down," Ibrahim shouted above the roar of wind and spray. "That's the only way to keep her from sinking."

With the wind crossing her decks from starboard, *Prodigal* maintained enough angle of heel to keep the hole in the hull on her starboard side high enough out of the water to avoid every other wave, but water was still coming in. Ibrahim went below to inspect the damage. As he raised the large floorboard hatch through which he would gain access to the hull, his eyes widened. Black water had already risen high enough to be seen amidships. There would be no chance of repair from the inside as long as seawater was rushing through. In fifteen minutes, the boat would founder and begin her journey, not to Nassau, but to the bottom. He would have to find another way.

Molly was still unconscious. Aidan had placed her securely in the pilot berth, where she would be best protected from the motion of the boat, surrounded by blankets and pillows to keep her body from rolling in the swells. A cold compress was on her forehead. She was breathing well, and her heart rate was regular. He did not want to leave her, but she was stable, and he knew that Ibrahim would need his help if the ship was to be saved.

A heavy tarp was stretched around the railing on three sides of the cockpit as protection against spray. Aidan eyed it anxiously.

"We can use it to stop the flow of water from the outside long enough to make repairs," Aidan observed, "We just have to spread it tightly over the hole, like a sling."

It was not certain to work—the water pressure might prevent them from getting the tarp in place to form a tight seal. Positioning the canvas correctly over the hole would be difficult, and holding it there very long seemed impossible. But it was the only option they had other than firing a flare and calling for rescue, which meant defeat for *Prodigal* and victory for the man who had put them in this position.

Marcus kept the boat at as high an angle of heel as he could to give them the best visibility of the hole. Once they were ready with a section of canvas secured with lines on all corners, Aidan and Ibrahim walked to the bow of the boat. Standing on opposite sides, they held onto the lines as they eased the canvas under the bow. Aidan controlled the lines on one side, Ibrahim the other. Walking slowly aft, they slacked the lines to allow the tarp to slip underneath and around the keel. When they reached the stern, Ibrahim maneuvered the tarp in place over the hole while Aidan slacked the lines on his side. When the tarp covered the hole, the pressure of the water sucked it into place, and the lines were secured to the railings to keep it there long enough for a repair to be attempted from the inside.

Ibrahim raced below to find his hammer and a scrap of wood he could use to cover the hole well enough that a pump could keep up with the leak. The repairs took two hours to complete. In that time, Marcus kept *Prodigal* on a due south heading while *Invictus* faded out of view to the southwest. *Prodigal* was not sailing the course she needed to win, but it was the course she had to keep to stay alive.

After Ibrahim got the piece of scrap wood in place and it had formed a seal, Aidan pumped the rest of the water from the leak out of the boat. Then, they tested the patch by turning the boat onto a southwesterly heading. All seemed to go well. The ingress of water from around the seams of the patch was slow enough to be managed by constant pumping, but there was another problem.

"We're losing speed," Aidan called from the cockpit. "There's too much interference on the hull."

Where the hull of *Prodigal* had once been smooth and fair, on her starboard quarter there was now an ugly gash in the wood. It was redirecting and slowing the flow of water past the hull on that side, creating suction that robbed her of speed. On a starboard tack, when the boat was heeled over far enough to keep the gash out of the water, she could still sail like a will-o'-the-wisp, but on a port tack she slowed to a speed that was dead even, or a little slower than that of *Invictus*. In any race to the east, that would have posed no problem. But *Prodigal* and her crew did not wish to go east. To reach Nassau, they needed to go southwest, after *Invictus*.

The crew pondered the situation for several minutes while *Prodigal* chuckled along at twenty knots, making wonderful speed in the direction they did not wish to go.

"There's no help for it," Aidan finally said. "We'll have to head east across the Gulf Stream—make as much southing as we can—and hope for a wind shift. We'll never catch *Invictus* on a port tack now. The damage is too great."

Marcus and Ibrahim knew Aidan was right. Their options were limited.

CHAPTER 32

He might have killed him. He would have killed him. Marcus still burned with white-hot rage against Rowdy Ponteau. He shuddered to think what would have happened if the wind had not come to separate the two boats when it did.

Marcus had always been a fighter. He was Gay Dempsey's sparring partner in the navy, and were it not for the fact that Gay was an officer and Marcus an ordinary seaman, the prize for middleweight champion would have belonged to Marcus instead. Those days ended when he went off to the seminary and Gay went off to study law, but that fighting spirit had come rushing back when *Prodigal* took a sucker punch from Rowdy Ponteau.

"We'll take watches, then. I'll take the first," Marcus said. "We'll keep her on this heading until the wind changes."

"And you'd better pray that it does if we're ever to see *Invictus* again," Aidan replied.

Marcus smiled. "On the open ocean, Aidan, there is nothing *but* prayer."

As soon as the boat was secure and steady on her heading, Aidan went below to look in on Molly. She was awake but groggy and in a lot of pain. She had no memory of the collision. Aidan started to ask her questions, but she politely demurred. The last thing she wanted to do was talk. He gave her medicine to help her sleep, and she nodded off. She hadn't asked him to watch over her, but she was glad he was there. With his legs outstretched and his back against the bulkhead of the pilot berth, Aidan cradled her head in his lap. He felt his heart glow when she nuzzled her face into his stomach and stretched an arm around his waist. She was fast asleep, and night was falling on their first day at sea.

All remained quiet in the early evening, until Marcus finally shouted to Ibrahim, "Break out the rum!"

"Pardon me?" Ibrahim knew enough of Marcus's pledge of sobriety to question the command.

"Don't you go pardoning me, you Limey gin-totter."

Ibrahim smiled. Marcus had always teased him for the quaintly formal manner that was the hallmark of his upbringing in a British colony.

"I don't care if I'm not supposed to have it, and I don't give a damn. There's naught but sinners on this boat, and I'm chief among them as sure as the sun rises. It's no use pretending I don't *love* it. We all have our vices. And if I'm going to lose this infernal race to that black-hearted bastard, I damn well don't intend to lose it sober."

Ibrahim brought up a bottle of Brugal 1888, a Dominican rum considered by some—Ibrahim among them—to be the smoothest in the world. It was a Christmas gift from Zoot, but Ibrahim had drunk it very sparingly—not more than two fingers in two years. He had stowed it aboard *Prodigal* with plans for a celebratory toast, but that didn't seem to matter now. He drank it neat (it was heresy to dilute it) and poured two glasses: one for himself and one for Marcus.

Raising his glass into the air, Marcus regaled his shipmate with a toast. "It was a no lesser light than Sir Francis Chichester who once said, 'Any damn fool can circumnavigate the world sober. It takes a really good sailor to do it drunk.' Therefore, I say, let us aim *high*."

With that, twenty dollars worth of Dominican gold disappeared down this throat.

From where Marcus and Ibrahim were sitting, enjoying the night sky and the taste of rum, they could see Aidan holding Molly in the faint glow of the cabin light.

"Do you think she'll be all right?" Ibrahim asked.

"I'm certain of it. The Scots are far too hard-headed to let a little bump like that slow them down. She'll have a whopper of a headache for a day or two, but she'll be our old Molly before you know it. You wait and see."

Marcus smiled at the scene in the cabin below.

"I've never seen two people better suited for each other in my life. If she doesn't forgive that man and give him another chance, I shall have to take her over my knee."

Ibrahim said nothing for a moment. He first looked at Marcus, then below at Molly in the cabin, then again at Marcus. At length he spoke, solemnly.

"She would kick your ass."

Marcus paused before giving his rebuttal, then thought better of his first choice of words.

"Yes—yes, I believe you are exactly right."

After a moment spent imagining the ass-kicking, Marcus resumed the discussion.

"I don't know if I'd have done anything differently myself, if that woman had come into my room and climbed into my bed."

Ibrahim again moderated his impulse to answer immediately, but his raised eyebrows registered disapproval that did not escape Marcus's notice.

Marcus protested. "Well, I *don't* know. Of course, not that she'd ever *try*. Prayer is a good thing, Ibrahim, but we mustn't lay our hopes on miracles."

Ibrahim laughed out loud and, noticing Marcus's glass was empty, refilled it.

"She would bring you to wreck and ruin, Father."

Marcus thought of that for a moment, too, imagining just how wrecked his ruin would be.

"Yes, I am sure you're right about that as well. I suppose, on the issue of priestly celibacy, the Holy Father and I are of one accord, although I fear that may be the extent of our communion."

Ibrahim took the night watch while the rest of the crew slept. The yellow glow of *Prodigal's* stern lantern, suspended above the cockpit, made wide arcs over and around the deck. Were it not for the sound of the wake rushing past and the rhythmic motion of the boat, he could have imagined he were seated by the fireside in his home in Ocracoke, settled in for the night to read a book. It struck him as funny, then, how often he had read books at home of adventures at sea, yet here he was at sea, imaging that place of rest by the fireside.

He knew his life in Ocracoke had come to an end. There would be no work in the shipyard for him now—not after all that had happened. He could not go back. But his life in Nassau had ended years ago. He could not return there—he would not, and let them cage and kill him like an animal—but he knew nowhere else to go, or how to get there. He missed, most of all, the wisdom and counsel of his father. In the years since he had escaped he longed to contact him, to hear his voice, to reassure him and be reassured by him, but the danger that his father might be charged with complicity in his escape was too great. And so his days had been spent in solitude. Perhaps that is why the lonely hours of the night watch passed so easily for Ibrahim, for they were no different than all his other nights on land or sea. There was no light or a signal of any kind in the blackness. *Prodigal* was totally alone and seemingly without hope in this world, just as he was.

Dawn rose on a gray, trackless ocean. The frenzy of

boats that crowded the water at the starting line was gone. Now, for as far as the eye could see in every direction, there was nothing but the sea. As the morning passed and the refraction of sunlight arced higher, the greenish gray tinge of the surface dissolved to neon blue. They were in the Gulf Stream, and though the waves, pushed up by the northwest wind, were running regularly at eight to ten feet, *Prodigal* was undaunted by them. She had kept the same familiar rhythm of motion for the past eighteen hours.

They were running well to the southeast, but the race was still headed southwest. Were it not for the wound in her starboard side, *Prodigal* could easily have gybed and taken the lead running away. The southing she was making now was barely keeping her in the race, but the longer she continued on this tack the wider the angle became that she would have to span, when she changed her heading. Unless the wind shifted soon to allow a turn to the west, all of her speed would be for naught.

A loud noise on deck woke Aidan from a fitful sleep. It was Marcus. He had taken the watch earlier that morning from Ibrahim, who was now snoring in the aft cabin. The ship's clock sounded eight bells. It was Aidan's watch. Instead of simply coming below and telling him to get up, Marcus apparently had decided to wake Aidan and everyone else by brightly singing a chorus of Gilbert and Sullivan:

> *I am the captain of the Pinafore,*
> *And a right good captain too!*
> *I am never known to quail*
> *At the fury of a gale,*
> *And I'm never, never sick at sea.*
> *What never?*

No never!
What never?
Hardly ever!
He's hardly ever sick at sea!
Then give three cheers
And one cheer more,
For the hardy captain of the Pinafore!

Aidan smiled to hear the voice of his dear friend. For all the struggle and strife that had marked the last two days, he was, after all, at sea, and on a good ship with true friends, and distilled to its essence, there was nothing but grace in his life at that moment.

Marcus never had an opportunity—not with Nita's constant attention to the needs of the rectory—to show his skill in keeping a proper house, but he was doing a fine job of keeping ship. When Aidan awoke, a warm fire was glowing in the coal stove, and a pot of coffee was already steaming. He found Marcus in a very contented mood, sitting in the cockpit that was neatly swept and squared away, with one hand on the wheel, one hand on a mug of coffee, and both legs propped up over the rail.

Marcus asked him how he slept, and how Molly was getting along, and what he thought of all this business of rapacious sailors and ghost ships and such. They were losing the race and sailing a badly wounded vessel that might yet sink, but Marcus was as chipper as a spring morning. He was a study of great interest to Aidan, who had made a career of reading people to determine what they wanted and how to give it to them. What motivated Marcus he could not say. He remained to Aidan an enigma. He was the most lighthearted and playful and erudite of men, but when challenged he was immovable—a fierce, even terrible defender of what he cherished. That trait of character had been in full flower the day before, when he held Rowdy Ponteau by the throat, and for an instant the healer became the reaper.

"How did you know that *Prodigal* was worth it, Father?" Aidan finally asked.

"What do you mean?"

"I mean, when did you decide—or figure out—that she held the heart of the penitent thief? There were two thieves and two crosses. How did you know that *Prodigal* carried the cross of the one who was promised paradise?"

Marcus laughed and looked out over the ocean for a long time—so long, in fact, that Aidan thought he had forgotten or perhaps not heard the question. Eventually, Marcus turned to Aidan and smiled.

"Look at you, boy! Twenty years and you didn't darken the door of a church, and after six months with me, you're ready to face the devil and all his angels." He laughed again. "Faith is a marvelous thing. It's like yeast that never fails. It leavens some lives steadily to great heights, where in others it may lie dormant for decades until it is needed. I'll never understand it."

Marcus could see that Aidan was unsatisfied with this attempt to evade the question, so he began to speak in earnest.

"History is full of fables, Aidan. No one can be certain he knows the absolute truth about something that happened twenty centuries or twenty minutes ago—not I, not you, not Monsignor McIver, not the bloody pope. In the end, all you can really see or know is what your heart tells you to be true. That's where God speaks to each of us.

"And as for good thieves or bad thieves, I challenge any man to tell me the difference. Penitence is a temporary thing. We're all thieves by nature and saints only by grace. I don't know about you, but I'm hoping that God will save me in spite of my nature—just as I believe he saved *both* thieves at Calvary. But I can tell you that's not the Gospel according to Jimmy McIver, and I believe that's the very reason why he wanted so badly to know whether I had found the *Prodigal*."

"I don't follow you—you'll have to connect the dots for me," Aidan insisted, feeling the same unease he had felt the last time he tried to engage Marcus in matters of faith. But Marcus knew he had already said too much. This ragtag crew had kept *Prodigal* in the race because they *believed* in their ship, and he saw no profit in sowing doubts. Their faith was a power far stronger than the malice that drove *Invictus,* and in the end the heart of a ship, like the heart of the one who sails her, is known only to God.

Marcus looked into the cabin, where Molly had gotten up to pour herself a cup of coffee, and changed the subject.

"Hello, gorgeous!"

"That's Captain Gorgeous to you," Molly answered, in a hoarse, sleep-filled voice. "By the way, anyone see the white whale that landed on my head, anywhere?"

"What hurts this morning?" Aidan asked

"My pride, mostly, but I'll get over it. Can I make anyone breakfast? I'm a genius with buttered toast and jam."

"That would be lovely," Marcus answered. "Let me help you."

A half hour later, Molly stepped out into the cockpit, bearing a plate of fresh fruit and bread and a pot of hot coffee. Aidan could hear Ibrahim begin to stir in the aft cabin below. The smells of home wafting through the ship had awakened him. After setting the breakfast service on a table in the cockpit, Molly took a seat next to Aidan. They sat there a long time together in silence, just looking out over the sea and admiring how well *Prodigal* was sailing. Then Molly moved closer.

"Do I have to be bleeding and unconscious in order to rest my head on your shoulder?" she asked Aidan.

"I was hoping I wouldn't have to club you again," he answered.

He put his arm around her and drew her closer. She laid her head back on his chest and closed her eyes, letting the gentle rhythm of the ship overtake her. Time slipped away. The air was warmer now than the day before, and it felt warmer still with each mile of latitude stolen in *Prodigal's* wake. Surrounded by the sea like a blanket, she felt hope return. A feeling of trust in Aidan was coming back to her, too, like the green shoots of a spring re-emerging from a May snow. Soon she was fast asleep again. Aidan kept her secure by his side at the helm. He could not imagine any place in the world he would rather be than where he was at that moment.

Fifty miles to the east of the place where *Prodigal* was cleaving a southern path through the Atlantic, Rowdy Ponteau stood on the deck of *Invictus,* his head held high. His senses were straining to confirm what his mind suspected from the looks of the horizon to the west. The wind was clocking to the north, at first slowly, but now unmistakably. A storm was coming, but that was not what he feared most. The change in the wind threatened the return of *Prodigal* and the crazed priest aboard her who had nearly strangled him to death.

He knew that the damage *Invictus* had done to *Prodigal* was not a fatal blow. With a north wind, *Prodigal* could sail east with her port shoulder into the waves and her starboard quarter high enough for the damaged section of the hull to clear the surface. She would be hobbled in her ability to maneuver, but on that one point of sail she would be unbeatable. He had seen that with his own eyes.

Rowdy gave the command to gybe. If *Prodigal* was now sailing southeast, they would sail southwest to intercept her. Once past Memory Rock on the Bahama Banks, *Prodigal* would have a clear path to Nassau, and nothing would stop her. Rowdy had no intention of letting that happen. He meant to finish the job he had started.

Invictus's long, blunt spear of a bowsprit had escaped the collision undamaged. It was made of Egyptian bull oak—the hardest wood on Earth. It cost his father as much as the rest of the boat combined, which seemed to Rowdy at the time a needless extravagance for a piece of wood. Teak or mahogany would have been more than ample and far less expensive and heavy, but it was his father's money, and Reece Ponteau could not be persuaded otherwise. After hearing that a large piece of bull oak was for sale by a rare-woods merchant in Mogadishu, his father had gone there personally to purchase it and bring it back in a container ship. He was gone for three weeks, and he spent another two personally overseeing the work in the shipyard to replace the existing bowsprit. Rowdy had not expected what an effective tool for winning races this part of his ship would become. If need be, it would be ready when called into deadly service again.

CHAPTER 33

When Aidan felt the wind shift, Molly was still sleeping on his chest. He gently rubbed her shoulders until she awoke.

"I'm sorry to cut short your nap," he said, "but the wind has changed. We may have an opening to head east, but it won't be easy. A storm will hit soon. We need to shorten sail."

It was nine in the morning. He called below for Ibrahim, who woke Marcus. While Molly steered, together the three men put one reef in each of *Prodigal's* sails and bent the storm jib onto the inner forestay. In a few minutes, *Prodigal* had her rough knickers on and was properly dressed for a big blow. Although the wind was still moderate, once it piped up to gale force, it would be no time to be on deck wrangling sails.

They had been sailing for twenty-four hours. Looking at their position on the chart, Aidan estimated they had come 427 nautical miles since the start. By the rules of the race, they were required to round Memory Rock—a waypoint on the Bahama Banks, fifty-three nautical miles east of Palm Beach, Florida—continue south around the island of Grand Bahama, then head east for the Berry Islands and the final run south to the finish line, just outside the harbor at Nassau. The shift of the wind from the northwest to the northeast had made it possible for them to alter course and, perhaps, regain the lead in the race. But Memory Rock was still

275 miles away. Their heading would be improved, but their comfort would be greatly diminished once the high winds of the nor'easter set in. And once they got there and a tack back to the west became necessary, what would happen was anyone's guess.

"What's your best estimate of the speed of winds in the storm, Ibrahim?" Marcus asked.

"From the looks of those low clouds to the west, thirty knots with gusts to forty, maybe more."

That sobered everyone. Forty knots of wind meant they were sailing into the teeth of a survival storm, where the primary concern would not be navigation or speed, but the hope of coming through it alive. Aidan was the first to offer the group an out.

"We don't have to do this. On our current heading we'll be in the Abacos in less than a day, and in the Eleutheras in two. Who gives a damn about this race anymore, anyway?"

"I do," said Molly.

"Me, too," Marcus answered.

Ibrahim would have preferred the Abacos or the Eleutheras, where he was less likely to be apprehended right away, but he wasn't about to let his problems interfere. "We have to try, Aidan," he said.

In two hours, the nor'easter hit, and the wind speed rose to twenty-six knots. *Prodigal* again gave no sign of yielding to wave or weather. The worse conditions got, the more resolutely she plowed through them. Aidan clocked her top speeds at close to twenty-five knots. She felt like a runaway freight train beneath his feet. She was unstoppable.

By the time *Prodigal* was in sight of Memory Rock, the wind had risen to a steady thirty knots, with higher gusts. It was seven o'clock in the evening. Clouds covered the moon, and wind and the spray covered everything else. But in the distant blackness they could see a collection of lights.

Their one connection with the outside world was a handheld VHF radio that they had not yet used. They decided to turn it on to listen for news from the ships whose lights were moving away from them, toward the mainland. As the radio crackled to life, they heard a desperate, frantic call for help.

"Mayday! Mayday! Mayday! *Ceci est le* Paschale*! Le* Paschale*! Nous sommes chaviré! Nous aider! Nous aider!*"

"The Mayday was clear," Aidan said, "but the rest—"

"I speak a little French," Molly began, cautiously. She moved closer to listen to the radio in Aidan's hand, then took it in her own. "If I heard right, it was a call from a boat named *Paschale*. But that's all I got. Let me try to get them to repeat."

Molly pressed the button and began to speak in halting but passable French.

"*Bonjour* Paschale. *Ceci est* Prodigal. *Repeter, s'il vous plaît.*"

A moment passed before another badly broken signal came across the radio.

"*Nous sommes chaviré! Nous sommes deux hommes. Nous ne pouvons pas nager.*"

"There are two men in the water," Molly explained. "Their boat is capsized. They can't swim."

Marcus was at the helm, listening to the call. "I can't see a bloody thing out here! You've got to get their position somehow!"

"Paschale, Paschale," Molly continued. "*Nous sommes* Prodigal. *Pouvez vous déclancher une fusée de détresse?*"

"If they can find a flare and fire it off, we can find them," she said.

Only a partial answer was returned.

"*Nous ne pouvons pas nager, nous ne pouvons pas—*"

The radio went silent.

Ibrahim looked frantic. "What did they say?"

Molly shook her head. "They repeated what they said before—that they can't swim."

All of them climbed out on deck to look for the men. *Prodigal* was rising up and over ten-foot waves and falling down into the troughs, again and again, like a wild carousel pony. Aidan stood at the port rail, holding tight to the rigging with both hands to keep from being thrown overboard by the motion of the boat. He scanned the foam-streaked darkness beyond the sanctuary of *Prodigal's* decks. Molly stood beside him. Ibrahim was at the bow. For the next five minutes, Molly slowly and methodically repeated her plea for *Paschale* to answer on the radio.

"Paschale, Paschale, *ceci est* Prodigal. *Parler s'il vous plaît!*"

No answer came. They continued to search the darkness in vain, with no idea whether they were anywhere near the stranded boat. They knew a radio call could have come from as far as twenty-five miles away.

Hidden from their sight were two young brothers—fishermen from the island of Guadeloupe, who had been surprised by the storm and decided to run for Indian Pass, a narrow channel just off of the west end of Grand Bahama Island. The pass led to the shallows of Bahama Banks, where a boat could safely anchor in a storm. They had planned to cross onto the banks for shelter, but they allowed their boat to drift too close to one side of the narrow opening. A breaking wave caught and capsized them. They were now in the water, holding onto the wreckage of their boat, which was being pulled onto the reef and pounded to splinters by the storm. In a short while, they would either be swept out through the pass into the chaos of the open sea, where they would surely drown, or their bodies would be dashed onto the reef and broken.

The brothers' radio—the one on which they had

heard the blessed voice of a woman in the night—had fallen out of one brother's hand in the violence of a breaking wave. Now their only hope of rescue was a box of shotgun flares inside the boat to alert the woman to their location. But their boat was underwater, and the box of flares was somewhere inside. The blackness of the night and the howl of the wind dulled their faculties to every sensation but the solid grip of two hands that preserved the bond between them. Then, with a final squeeze of his brother's hand as his only prayer, one fisherman took a deep breath and submerged beneath the wreckage.

Despair settled over the crew of *Prodigal* as the minutes passed with no word or sign from the *Paschale*. They still had no idea how close or far away they might be, but in the hope that they were close enough to do some good, *Prodigal* was hove-to, nodding slowly to windward and maintaining her current position in a silent vigil, waiting for an answer.

The storm seemed only to gather strength. The others looked to Marcus for benediction, but he refused to give any. Instead, he felt a torrent of frustration and anger rise within him that would not be quelled. He could be silent no longer. He would not suffer this outrage meekly.

Aidan watched as the old man climbed up the mast step, his face alive with fury. He clung to the mast with one arm and shook the other menacingly toward the sky. Aidan again saw in Marcus's face the abject rage that had nearly squeezed the life out of Rowdy Ponteau.

"Why do you *abandon them?!*" Marcus shouted into the wind and the darkness. He was screaming at God as though God were an indolent umpire making the wrong calls in the last inning of a losing season. Marcus's voice sounded wild and frenzied—nothing like his calm, measured invocations at mass. Perhaps, Aidan thought, it was because God was nearer now than then.

Ibrahim felt his blood run cold to hear in Marcus's screams the dying reproach that Jesus had uttered from the cross. Ibrahim knew they did not have such standing to despair of God's indifference, nor was the cross upon which they sailed so worthy.

The screams and accusations continued. Marcus was just warming up.

"Why do you let them *die,* and ask me to bury them? Where is your great *mercy?* Where is your *Gospel?* Where is your *heaven?* You *coward!* Show yourself! Come and *fight* for your children, just as surely as the Devil fights against them!"

Marcus was not beseeching God for mercy, as Aidan and the others had already done in mumbled prayers of their own. He was indicting him, like a fugitive. They were not witnessing a crisis of faith but the indignation of true faith. Marcus felt that he was being robbed of the harvest, and he was now demanding, as from a dishonest broker, that his rightful share be returned to him. He didn't beg for a miracle; he sued for justice. He was accusing God of a breach of promise, and demanding that the promise be honored. Hearing this closing argument inveighed against the heavens, Aidan was certain the jury was with Marcus.

The old priest finally collapsed in exhaustion where he stood at the mast. His eyes were closed and clouded from wind and tears. It was for that reason he did not see, in the night sky to the east, the faint, rising star. It glimmered only for a moment, then fell into the sea. It was a flare from the crew of *Paschale*—the first and last sign of their hope.

Ibrahim had seen it.

"Come about east!" he shouted like a madman. "East! East! East! They lie to the east! Make way, dammit! Make way!"

Ibrahim remained at the rail, his eyes fixed on the place in the darkness where he had last seen the light. He would not look away from that position, no matter what happened around or underneath him. His outstretched hands directed Aidan at the helm, first to one side, then to the other, until they were on a straight course for the location of the flare.

"We're headed straight for Indian Pass," shouted Aidan. "That must be where they are. But we can't get through. The pass is too narrow."

"Get me as close as you can," answered Marcus. "I'll get us the rest of the way."

Carefully, Aidan maneuvered *Prodigal* into place by a series of tacks and gybes until she was no more than fifty yards off. Whichever way the ship turned, Ibrahim remained fixed like a flagpole on deck, pointing the way to the last memory of the flare. Where *Prodigal* now stood was deep water, but in the pass the depth shoaled to just a few feet—even less where stony coral heads jutted skyward beneath the surface.

Marcus and Ibrahim hurriedly untied a ten-foot wooden tender loaned to *Prodigal* for use as a lifeboat—the same one that Marcus had spent the past twenty years puttering around in on Ocracoke Island, when the fever to go sailing overtook him, which was fairly often. With a spare halyard and a bridle, they hoisted it up and over the rail into the water.

"Here, take the helm, Marcus, while I get in," Aidan said.

"Not on your life," Marcus answered. "You stay aboard and hold your position. I want this ship to be here when I get back." Marcus was the *de facto* leader of their expedition, and Aidan felt an impulse to obey. Before Aidan could protest the decision, Marcus had jumped onto the sole of the lifeboat in the water and was calling for equipment to be handed down to him.

It was a foolish move. There were two men aboard nearly half Marcus's age, with stronger backs and deeper lungs, who should have gone in his stead. But Marcus wouldn't hear of it. By his own lights, the flare had been a sign. If he were going to take umbrage at the Almighty for the insufficiency of his mercy, he damn well better be the one to accept when heaven made a counter-offer.

The three crew members remaining aboard *Prodigal* watched as their beloved shepherd and guide rowed off into the darkness toward the roar of the unseen surf crashing on the banks. A lantern, hung on a boathook lodged in the bow, swung violently from side to side as Marcus struggled to keep an even keel. From his seat in the dory, his feet braced against the transom, Marcus watched the light of *Prodigal* dip astern, then disappear altogether. He fixed its last location by the stars as a guide for his return. Closing his eyes to concentrate on what he could hear, he rowed in the direction of the greatest noise—a clue to the location of the surf crashing on either side of Indian Pass.

As he neared the opening, he began to distinguish from the sound of the waves the higher-pitched sound of the frantic shouts of the men in the water. They had no more flares to guide their rescuer.

With one oar, he brought the lifeboat alongside the opening to the pass, beam-to, still several yards off. He had difficulty steadying the boat in place. On either side of the opening, breakers were crashing with enormous fury. He could see that the pass was clear, but it was too narrow. A width of only ten feet was safe for navigation, and within that channel the current was fierce. An error of just a few feet to either side would put the lifeboat in the path of the breakers that would carry it onto the reef.

To the south, Marcus could see a wide, open section of water that seemed to allow safe passage around the reef to the place where the men lay waiting. It seemed the perfect solution. He decided to take it. He dug his starboard oar deep into the sea and whirled the bow of the lifeboat around in the direction of the smooth water. Less than fifty yards separated him from the men.

What Marcus could not see were the sharp forks of coral hiding just beneath the surface. They barred safe passage. The water running through them moved swiftly and falsely appeared to be deep and safe. In fact, where the swift water rose and fell over the coral, thorny fingers waited to impale anyone who attempted to pass. Marcus was headed for them with all deliberate speed, ignorant of the danger, when the lifeboat rode high on the crest of one wave and crashed onto the reef in the trough of another.

The dory made a sickening sound as the coral dug into the wood. The force of the impact, just off center of the keel, flipped the boat over like a cockleshell and sent Marcus flailing into the sea. He struck the coral head-first, opening a wide gash above his eyes. His shouts of pain were unheard by anyone aboard the *Prodigal*, and the men from the *Paschale*, who watched in horror, could offer him no aid.

The next swell threw Marcus onto a horn of coral that pierced his abdomen. Blood flowed into the sea around him, indistinguishable from the inky water in the darkness. Thoughts of death crept into his mind, and a feeling of peace overcame his fear, but his work was not done. When he had recovered what he could of his breath, with all his remaining strength he righted the lifeboat and climbed inside.

The boat was awash and unstable. With one arm he held on and braced for another capsize, and with the other he sculled water over the gunwales. Soon he could steady the boat enough to position himself, but by then he had drifted another fifty yards south, and the pass was out of sight. The only hope for the men was for him to return to *Prodigal*.

Ibrahim, Aidan, and Molly saw nothing in the night sea, but still they called Marcus's name, hoping for some report. The time seemed interminable, but at last they heard a noise. It sounded nothing like their dear friend. Impeded by the blood now flowing into his left lung, Marcus could manage only a guttural moan to alert the figures standing on deck that he was near. Molly spotted him first.

"There he is! Come about! He's drifting twenty yards off the stern! He looks hurt!"

Aidan was careful not to move the helm too quickly and risk dropping all of *Prodigal's* great weight onto the lifeboat. He steered only close enough for Ibrahim to throw a claw anchor that caught one gunwale. They brought the lifeboat back aboard. Stowing it hastily on deck, Ibrahim carried the wounded passenger below.

Death was near. Marcus knew this even as his friends banished all thought of it. No fear was in his heart, but desperation for his mission remained. He struggled to force air through his lips against the pressure of the blood now swelling his chest. Molly bent close to his lips to speak to him while Aidan and Ibrahim packed the wound below his ribs.

"We love you, Marcus," she whispered through a steady stream of tears. "Please don't leave us. Please hang on." She kissed and caressed his face repeatedly. She thought she heard him trying to say something.

"Aidan . . ." was the name spoken in a thin, small voice.

"Aidan, he's calling for you," Molly said.

Aidan looked up from the bandages and tape he was winding around Marcus's chest and leaned his head closer.

The thin voice spoke again. "Remember the garden."

Blood oozed from Marcus's lips, stifling his speech.

Aidan was not sure what he had just heard. The words seemed disconnected from any meaning. He thought Marcus must have been delirious, though he could rightly understand why his mind would drift to the loveliness of his garden at St. Anne's in that moment. He looked into Marcus's eyes and realized that their shepherd and friend was gone.

Faith was far from all of them in that hour. They wept, and for a time the tumult of the wind and waves swirling around them seemed so very mean and small, compared to the devastation before their eyes.

Molly fumbled to find the dials on the radio.

"Mayday, Mayday, Mayday," she called, in a voice garbled by her sobs. "This is the sailing vessel *Prodigal*. We have a man aboard who needs a doctor right away. He is bleeding, and I'm afraid he is dying." She refused to say—she could not bear to say—what her heart told her was true: Marcus was already gone.

"Mayday, Mayday . . ."

Aidan did not wait for an answer. Marcus was now beyond their aid, but some hope remained for the men capsized in the pass. He would not suffer Marcus's brave but failed attempt to go unrequited. He resolved to find the men himself and bring them back to the ship.

Ibrahim fought against the idea. The storm was now at its peak, and *Prodigal* had drifted well north of the last sighted position of the men aboard *Paschale*. But Aidan believed that with the aid of the wind and the waves, he could make it back there. He had to believe it. It was all he had left of what Marcus had given him.

Soon the dory was back in the water, and Aidan was rowing hard for the sound of the surf. He arrived swiftly, carried by the wind, at the entrance to the pass. White foam cresting on top of the enormous waves breaking on both sides of the bar shone dimly in the glow of the night sky. The pass was clear but unnavigable. It was too narrow. Only a fool would attempt it in these seas, and he did not doubt that such an attempt had led to the loss of the *Paschale*. He saw the wide, calm water to the south and decided, as Marcus had, to head for what seemed a safer way around. Before he reached it, light from stars reflected on the water revealed to him, only for an instant, the coral heads as they were exposed in the falling swells. Aidan pulled back hard with both oars, bracing against the powerful current that threatened to take him there. With all his might he came astern and drove the lifeboat back in the direction of the pass.

The pass was guarded on both sides by a furious surf that seemed certain to devour him. Getting through would be impossible—like a blind man threading a needle—but he had no choice other than to try. When he resolved to do so, realizing that the attempt might be his last moment on Earth, Marcus's last words suddenly made sense. "Remember the garden," he had said, with what little breath was left to him. He was directing Aidan to the verse written on the garden fence at St. Anne's: "Enter through the narrow gate." Marcus's intended meaning had nothing to do with gardens and everything to do with faith.

There was no knowledge or skill or power of sight that could take Aidan safely where he needed to go. Only faith would sustain him. He had to summon the faith to attempt what seemed to be impossible, and he was equally certain that Marcus would be with him when he did. He had to pull directly into the swift, deadly current of Indian Pass.

Aidan looked to the west for some sign of *Prodigal's* position. He saw nothing but the blackness of the open sea. Stabbing the water furiously with both oars, he drove the lifeboat toward the waiting maw of the pass. As he entered it, the sea descended all around him and upon him, as if he were suddenly within a waterfall. He immediately lost his bearings and the confidence to steer in any one direction. The boarding waves quickly filled the lifeboat halfway to the gunwales. The decrease in buoyancy made the boat unstable, and Aidan's instinct to steady himself only made matters worse. In an instant the lifeboat flipped and capsized. He suddenly found himself trapped underwater in a dark world, beneath the overturned hull. He immediately felt the impulse to surface, but when he did he hit his head hard against the cockpit sole. There was no pocket of air he could reach, and the waves still descending on the outside of the hull created a suction he could not break. When he then tried to dive out from underneath the lifeboat, he felt something tug at his chest harness and pull him back. The towrope had gotten fouled in his safety gear during the capsize. He was tethered beneath the water, unable to breathe and unable to reach the surface.

Growing desperate for oxygen, he felt a furious surge of energy shoot through his body. He was battling for the seconds he had left before he would lose consciousness. Anything, everything within his power to do he would do to gain his next breath. His muscles were electrified with resolve for the challenge, but the strength of ten men could not have parted that rope. Instead, his fight was against a growing sense of panic and hopelessness while he worked feverishly to find the place where the rope was snagged in the safety clasp of the harness on his chest. As precious seconds of life slipped away, the fog of oblivion was already beginning to cloud his mind when, suddenly, he felt himself floating free. With one last, thrusting force, he dove out from underneath his tomb and found a path to the surface.

When his body finally shot up into the night air above the sea, his chest was ready to explode. He felt as if his lungs would inhale all of heaven before the rest of his body would be sated. It was then, in the throes of some strange psychosis known only in the nearness of death, that his mind wandered to the oddest of places. He found himself suddenly thinking about Dr. Adamson's patient and the trial that had ended his legal career. That patient—or so Boyce believed the evidence showed—had experienced the same deprivation of oxygen and the resulting, involuntary impulse for survival that Aidan had just experienced, but for him the next breath never came. Something about that story didn't fit. It had bothered Aidan ever since Boyce first explained it to him, and he hadn't understood why until that very moment.

But it was hardly the place or the time for legal theories. Aidan had again found air to breathe, but he could breathe only as long as he could float, and without a boat in those seas, that didn't promise to be much longer. The two Guadeloupian fishermen still waiting for rescue knew that better than anyone.

Just as Marcus had done only minutes before him, Aidan struggled to right the swamped lifeboat, eventually turning it over and steadying it, still half-submerged, in an upright position. He slowly bailed water over the sides using his hand. When the lifeboat was floating high enough, he eased his body over one side and slid onto the floorboards, where he continued bailing until only two inches of water remained. By then he had drifted nearly half a mile downwind from the pass, and eight-foot seas were pushing him farther still.

Aidan knew his second attempt to enter through the narrow opening in the reef would be his last. He did not have the strength to do again what he had just done. His arms already felt like lead weights, but when summoned, the muscles in his body again responded to the call. He pulled with such force he feared the oars might snap in their locks. He was making slow progress but was still a good distance away when he detected something in the sound of the surf that he hadn't heard before. There was an unevenness to it—a break in the rhythm that his mind was already conditioned to expect. It was the seventh wave.

As he counted the intervals in the sound of the breaking surf, there was a period of roughly thirty seconds of calm and quiet after every seventh wave, when the water within the pass was navigable. Hearing this filled him with renewed resolve to make it back, in hopes that he might yet reach the men of the *Paschale* in time.

Once he was finally again in position at the entrance to the pass, Aidan listened and counted the waves to find the interval in which he would make his final attempt. *"Four, five, six . . ."* When the moment finally came, he dug the oars down deep and ignored the burning fire of fatigue in his shoulders. The lifeboat—pulled as if by ropes on the tide rushing back through the pass toward the banks—kept a straight heading. After clearing the first swell, he waited for the trough of the next wave to make his final push for the other side. Then, with a heave and a groan that welled up from his gut, he ran for the protection of the banks that he could not see and prayed that his tiny vessel would find the way.

As if a curtain had been drawn around him in that moment, Aidan felt the backwash of a wave grab the lifeboat like a bath toy and throw it eastward into shallow water. He had scarcely realized that he had made it when he heard the scream of one man.

His brother Emile was unconscious, but Henri refused to let go of him. With only one arm to swim by, when he let go of the doomed vessel, Henri's strength failed him. He began to sink, but his right hand remained locked in his brother's. Aidan raced to their side. He threw a line in the water, but Henri was too slow to grab it. He drifted out of Aidan's reach and westward into the teeth of the pass. Again Aidan drove the lifeboat toward him, and on the second attempt Henri managed to grab the line. Minutes later, both fishermen were coughing up water on the floor of the lifeboat while Aidan braced the oars to keep the boat on a straight course in the channel back through the pass. The going was much easier and faster than the coming. "A man passes for what he is worth," Aidan thought.

Like a log shooting through a flume in an amusement park ride, the lifeboat shot out through the narrow gate out of Indian Pass into the dark world of the sea beyond.

Ibrahim's heart soared when he saw Aidan, then sank when he saw the lifeless appearance of the two men in the boat. He fitted two halyards to one of Johansson's sails to use it as a sling. Lowering the sail to the lifeboat below, he waited until Aiden had rolled both men into position, then used a winch to bring the sail back up and hoist them over the rail. They were badly hurt. One was barely breathing, but both were alive.

CHAPTER 34

The Coast Guard cutter *Mohawk* out of Key West had picked up Molly's Mayday call and immediately started steaming for *Prodigal's* position. The ship arrived just before dawn and stood a hundred yards off, dispatching a search-and-rescue team in a patrol boat to retrieve the body of Father Marcus. A second boat brought Henri and his brother Emile back to the *Mohawk* for medical treatment. Aidan, Molly, and Ibrahim spent the morning in the silence of shock, interrupted by questions from the officers about the events of Marcus's death.

When the officer filling out the report learned that *Prodigal* was one of the boats racing in the Blue Million, he informed them that the race had been called the previous afternoon because of the sudden storm, to encourage the participants to seek shelter. The lights in the Gulf Stream that they had seen early the night before were from several boats in the race that were headed back to Miami.

The hole in Marcus's ribcage made by the horn of coral looked very much like a knife wound. That could have explained why the Coast Guard was very careful in its questioning of *Prodigal's* remaining crew. Because Marcus had died of an unwitnessed, accidental cause in Bahamian territorial waters, Bahamian law required that he be transported to Nassau for autopsy. The *Mohawk* would steam ahead, with the understanding that *Prodigal* and all its crew would follow and remain in Nassau for questioning until the inquest concluded. A funeral would be held on the island. It was Marcus's wish that his ashes be spread at sea, and there seemed no more fitting place than the sea on which he had died. Aidan gave the Coast Guard Gay's and Nita's contact information to make the arrangements.

The officer's first question, as he completed the report, was for their full names, countries of origin, and photo identification. Molly and Aidan produced their passports. Ibrahim produced a Bahamian driver's license that still showed his father's address. The officer told them that he would file the report with authorities in Nassau. Ibrahim felt his throat swell. A routine check of his date of birth would reveal the warrant outstanding for his arrest. He was headed to prison now, it was certain. But he said nothing to the others of his fear. All of their thoughts, that day, were with Marcus.

By noon, the wind had clocked to the east. It was time to head for Nassau. Trade winds were now starting to fill in around the southern end of the Abacos. *Prodigal* labored on a port tack, with the wounded, starboard side of her hull beneath the waves, creating suction and drag. Even with this impediment, she was sprinting along at a steady twelve knots—championship speed for many boats of her size. But thoughts of the race and Rowdy Ponteau were far from everyone's mind. The crew of the *Prodigal* sat in studied silence beneath a beautiful, blue March sky as they rounded the tip of Great Harbour Cay, in the northernmost reaches of the Berry Islands.

There, they saw the black ship again. *Invictus* and her crew were waiting for them. Rowdy, who had monitored the Mayday calls of *Paschale* and *Prodigal* and not bothered to slow down for either, had hove to and stopped altogether when he heard the Coast Guard radio report the death of one Marcus O'Reilly to the Nassau Harbor police. A swell of perverse satisfaction filled his heart. With a steady trade wind now blowing from the east, Rowdy knew that *Prodigal* would be close hauled on a port tack coming into Nassau, slowed by the gash in her hull and its makeshift repair. Now was his chance to beat her. Now was his chance to show his father that his stories about that bucket of rot were just old wives' tales. Now was his chance to show the world that he, and his boat, were invincible.

Aidan could not believe his eyes. He had been staring out to sea for hours without really seeing anything but the images in his memory. It had not registered with him that the black-hulled schooner standing off their port bow was *Invictus* until they were less than three miles apart. He could now see that *Invictus* was waiting for them—waiting for a race to the finish. Rowdy Ponteau meant to challenge him, and Aidan was only too eager to accept.

He turned to Molly and Ibrahim beside her in the cockpit. They had already seen *Invictus,* and it was apparent to Aidan that they were all of the same mind.

"Let's do it," Ibrahim said.

"For Marcus," Molly answered.

Aidan remained on the tiller while Molly and Ibrahim sprang to life on deck. They tore down the storm sails that, in the lethargy of their grief, they had not bothered to change since the storm ended six hours ago. Every inch of Johansson's canvas that would fly was now sent aloft. Aidan felt the great ship respond with glee. This was what she was born for. This is what she had waited more than a century for. Although her speed was undeniably diminished by her wound, she was not defeated by it. In the length of one hour and a distance of fifteen miles, she had pulled even with *Invictus*.

Two hours passed. Both boats were sailing hard on the wind. But for the wound in *Prodigal's* side, *Invictus* would have been a distant blemish on the northern horizon by now. As if she somehow knew this, *Prodigal* was straining with effort.

Molly heard someone on the radio from the committee boat acknowledge that two teams were finishing the race provisionally. The prize money was no longer at stake with the race having officially been called the day before, but a trophy and the bragging rights that went with it remained to be won. The committee boat would stand by on the finish about five miles outside the entrance to Nassau Harbor, marking the line formed between the boat and a large, floating marker.

By the fourth hour, *Prodigal* had opened up and was holding onto a lead of four boat-lengths. Victory was in sight. The crew of *Invictus* worked feverishly to move ballast and adjust trim for every extra tenth of a knot of speed they could earn, but nothing seemed to be enough. The sky was growing dark from clouds that had moved in from the east. Rain was coming, with more wind. They were nearing the end, yet still there was neither despair on *Invictus* nor rejoicing on *Prodigal*.

Unseen below, in the flexing timbers of *Prodigal's* hull, Ibrahim's makeshift repair had been steadily working itself loose for hours. Now, with the finish line just eight miles away, it suddenly broke loose entirely.

Water gushed through the hull, and Aidan felt the ship shudder and stall, as if she had again been speared in the side. Ibrahim heard the water moving in the wood and ran below to inspect. *Prodigal* was losing speed. *Invictus* had made up a full boat length before Ibrahim, covered in seawater and tar, stuffed enough debris into the hold to permit him to reattempt the repair. With his fingers beneath the rising water, he felt around first for the dislodged panel, then for the hammer he would need to fix it in place. With a mighty blow, he sunk the first nail, then the second, then a third and fourth. The flow of water slowed, but by then it was up to his waist. *Prodigal* agonized under the leaden weight of so much water in her hold. *Invictus* had now cut their lead in half. Just two boat lengths separated them.

"Ibrahim, the pump!" shouted Aidan.

Molly found the long, steel handle that operated the manual bilge pump and handed it to Ibrahim as he ran out of the cabin on deck. Like a madman, he worked the handle up and down until a steady gush of water was exiting *Prodigal's* hull. But still *Invictus* came on, gaining speed and distance.

Aidan gave the order, and Molly used a winch and both feet to brace her weight as she leaned back hard on the lines trailing from the main and auxiliary winches to shorten both the mainsail and the jib. *Prodigal* was as tight and sharp as she could be. She surged with renewed effort as the water level below gradually descended, but *Invictus* had pulled dead even, and the finish line was only three miles away.

Rowdy could taste the sweetness of revenge, and judging from the smile on Rothschild's face, so could he.

"Max out the winch on the mainsail," shouted Rowdy.

"She's maxed out already. Let her ride," answered Rothschild.

"Max it out," Rowdy shot back. "I don't want merely to beat them. I want to bury them."

The winch that controlled *Invictus's* mainsail made a

shrill clacking sound as two men put all their weight into getting one more notch on the gears.

It was a mistake.

Below decks, hidden deep in *Invictus's* framing, was a flaw. A ship's masts and rigging can be repaired, but the hull never grows stronger than the day her timbers are laid. On that day more than a century ago, a length of wood used to form the hull of *Invictus*, in a place strained by punishing loads from the ship's rigging, was hollow. How it came to be so was a small matter, long forgotten.

High in the mountain forests of Ethiopia, a careless and disobedient child, climbing on the low branch of a tree, broke first the branch and then his arm. Years passed, and the child grew in knowledge but not in wisdom. As the child grew, so did the tree. A callus formed in the bone of the child, and a knot formed around the broken branch in the tree. The child became a builder of ships. The knot of the broken branch became the timber that became the board that became part of the hull of the ship that was *Invictus*.

It was a board that should have been rejected by the builder, but in his carelessness he kept it, hiding it where he was certain the impetuous young prince would not notice it. In this much he was right. The prince had searched long and far for the ship that had been stolen from him. Despairing that he might never find it, he turned from the sea to search instead for old relics among fables of lost caravans and ancient crosses. His search took him to a monastery on the island of Syros, where he persuaded the monks to accept a great price for an old shard of wood that fascinated him.

The prince commissioned the building of a new vessel that was larger, faster, and stronger than the one stolen from him, and he pledged to pursue the thieves over the far oceans of the world. In the keel of this ship he interred the relic that he believed would endear the angels to his cause, but he died in his old age before the vessel ever sailed. It was eventually completed and passed on to other owners. In all the ship's many years of life since then, the flaw had remained hidden until this hour.

At first the crew of *Invictus* heard nothing more than a pop. It sounded almost as if it had come from a distance—the race committee, they thought perhaps, had prematurely fired the gun to announce their victory. But then the pop was followed by a sickening, unmistakable wail in the rigging. Two stays supporting the mast ripped from the side of the hull. Sharp splinters of wood went flying. One of them pierced Rowdy's hand. He screamed in pain and released the wheel. In an instant, triumph was snatched from his grasp. The ship that only a moment before had seemed possessed of power invincible was revealed in weakness irredeemable. Now leaderless, she rounded up sharply into the wind. Her tall main mast wavered and began to descend from above. Her proud crew, once confident of victory, abandoned their posts and leapt into the sea, fleeing from the debris and rigging that whipped the air above their heads. In one deafening crash, all that once was high and proud was brought to scandal and shame. *Invictus's* rigging fell into the sea. Cables and sails were dragged alongside her like dead and drowning men. Three hundred yards from her goal, she stumbled, listing and broken, to a final stop. She had neither the will nor the strength nor the crew to sail a yard farther.

Aidan let out a gasp, then a guilty cheer as *Prodigal* went soaring past the finish line to the sound of the gun on the committee boat. He ran to Molly, and she saw in his eyes a fire she had not seen since their night together on the *Sairey Gamp*. He held her face in his hands and kissed her, passionately, without thought of the ship, the shore, the race, or anything or anyone else. It was a kiss that revealed what had been hidden between them—a kiss that pledged all he was and all he had to her, that said *I love you, I will never leave you, I will always cherish you, and I beg you to take me as your own.*

Molly and Aidan stood on the foredeck, in the warmth of that embrace, as time seemed to stop. They could not have said how many minutes passed before they turned to their friend to share with him their wonder and their joy and realized he was not there.

Molly shouted as she ran the length of the deck to find him. She and Aidan ran below, calling Ibrahim's name, then came back on deck to look more closely around every corner of the ship that had carried them all across a thousand miles of ocean. Their shouts brought no answer. He was gone. Their dear friend, champion, and defender was gone.

"Man overboard!" Aidan shouted desperately to anyone who might hear. The race committee boat was at least a mile away and busy coming to the aid of *Invictus* and her crew. Molly steeled herself, insisting in her mind that this was an emergency, not a tragedy. Ibrahim must have fallen overboard in all the commotion and the excitement of the finish, she thought. She scanned the horizon, seeing nothing but the vision of destruction that once had been *Invictus*. If Ibrahim had made any cry for help in this chaos, no one would have heard him.

Aidan knew exactly what to do. His sense of duty banished any thought of panic. He seized the helm and began to turn *Prodigal* around to retrace her course in a long figure eight—the man overboard maneuver that had been drilled into him as a boy—while watching along his route for the waving arms of a man in the water. Molly stood in the cockpit to handle the lines. If Ibrahim had gone overboard, they would encounter him at some point on this route and bring him to safety.

After the first pass revealed no sign, Molly ran below to retrieve the radio, and for the second time in two days she sent out the Mayday call. But the race committee was by then deeply engaged in the rescue of *Invictus*. The hailing channel was full of chatter between the committee boat and the harbor police. Her calls couldn't break through. Ten minutes had passed before anyone heard her pleas and responded. In that time, Aidan continued his widening arcs, calling out for Ibrahim to answer. They heard no sound but the sea.

The harbor police along with three other boats spent all of that afternoon and evening sweeping the waters where it was presumed Ibrahim had fallen, five miles from the harbor entrance. It seemed futile. In the rough seas, it would have been nearly impossible for anyone to swim ashore from that far out. They should have seen the body, floating, but left unspoken was the well-known fact that the warm waters off Nassau were infested with sharks. After eight fruitless hours of searching, the chief of police put a finer point on the matter than Molly was prepared to accept. Ibrahim was dead.

CHAPTER 35

Molly had not eaten anything for two days. She barely drank. The tragedies of the past week seemed surreal, and the people now arriving in Nassau from around the Bahamas and the world for the funerals of Ibrahim and Father Marcus added to the feeling of unreality. She could not bear to speak to any of them except Nita and Gay, and to David, the man she had just met under the worst of all circumstances.

David Joseph was Ibrahim's father, a dignified, proud, little sprout of a man, so unlike Ibrahim in size and strength, yet so very much like him in gentleness of spirit. After learning the news, he ran to the docks, and when he saw Molly and Aidan, he fell to his knees and wept. Molly hadn't been able to hold back her own tears for more than an hour at a time since then. Through it all, Aidan had been her rock and refuge. He never left her side. She was certain she would not have survived in her right mind without him.

David insisted on seeing the boat that had brought his son back to him. When he learned that Ibrahim had saved them from disaster through the patch he made in the hull, he quietly left, returning in one hour with an array of tools—saws; planes; sanding blocks; vises; brushes; and buckets of glue, varnish, and tar. Without a word, he set straight to work inside *Prodigal.* If he could not heal his son, he would heal his son's ship and finish the labor he had begun.

The autopsy produced a shard of coral from deep within Father Marcus's abdomen, and the report of death was approved as conforming to the story given aboard ship at the time he was found. His body was cremated, and his ashes were prepared. On the morning of the third day, Marcus was to be buried and Ibrahim was to be memorialized at sea. Molly and Aidan went with Gay and Nita out on a harbor launch for the ceremony.

While cremation was allowed by the Catholic Church, ashes were required to be interred or buried in a gravesite with all the formality accorded a traditional burial. Scattering ashes was a violation of Catholic teaching on the handling of mortal remains. The bishop had sternly warned Gay about this, in one final, failed attempt to exercise some modicum of control over Father Marcus O'Reilly. Gay had politely ignored him in deference to Marcus's wishes. Molly and Aidan decided it was fitting that Marcus should end that way, a renegade to the last.

Nita wept inconsolably when Marcus's ashes flew to the winds. It occurred to Molly only then that Nita might not find a place anywhere else in this world, without Marcus. She knew, if it came to that, that she and Aidan would not abandon her to a life of loneliness.

Gay eulogized Marcus as nothing less than the finest man he had ever known. Gay never said anything he didn't mean, and so those words struck Aidan with special poignancy. Until he had met Marcus, Aidan would have said that Gay was the finest man *he* knew. He counted himself blessed to have spent time with both of them.

Ibrahim too, was celebrated and remembered, and his soul was commended to the deep in Father Marcus's and the Lord's safekeeping. Molly imagined the three beloved friends she had so recently and quickly lost—

Sarah, Marcus, and Ibrahim—together forever. She was certain that heaven waited for all of them, a sunny shore somewhere across the sea.

They returned to *Prodigal* for a quiet reception that Molly and Aidan had prepared for Nita, Gay, and David. In a few hours, Gay and Nita would board a return flight to the states, and David would return home to begin the long twilight of mourning for a lost only son.

Molly and Aidan, the surviving salvors of *Prodigal*, were uncertain as to the ship's future. Selling her seemed the only practical thing to do, but they were loath even to consider it. Selling *Prodigal* would be an affront to everything they had endured together. It was a subject they both had avoided since their arrival in Nassau, and it was a conversation, that afternoon, they were not eager to begin.

Gay began his long-dreaded goodbyes. As he stood to go, he presented an envelope to Aidan. It was addressed to him from the State Bar of North Carolina.

"What's this?"

"It's your law license."

"How is that? Are you a miracle worker as well as a lawyer, Gay?"

"Only minor miracles, I'm afraid. Your license was suspended for one year. This order leaves the suspension on your record but shortens the duration to six months. I explained what happened with Boyce to the president of the bar over a glass of some very old Scotch the other night. We ended the evening certain of one thing, and that was that you shouldn't suffer unduly because you fell into a trap that was laid for you by your own partner and Moriarity. Welcome back, counselor."

Aidan didn't know what to say. Redemption and forgiveness seemed too much to hope for, even after all that he had learned about the events leading up to the trial. He thanked Gay for this gift.

"It's not a gift of my giving, Aidan. I know who you are, and I know what you're capable of. You're a good man."

Aidan smiled and looked at Molly.

"Yes, well—so I've been told."

Gay offered to return him to his position as a full partner at McFadden Brown. The offer was more than generous. It was the kind of second chance that most lawyers who had made the kind of mistake he made never got. But it was a chance he was not willing to take.

Molly had tried to look anywhere but at Aidan ever since Gay had brought up the subject of returning to the firm, but now she could look nowhere but into Aidan's eyes. She was pleading with him to stay. She dared not speak those words, but Aidan understood all the same.

"I'm sorry, Gay. I'll have to pass on the offer. I think I've finally found my place in the world, and if I'm a very lucky man, I'll get to stay there."

Gay looked at Molly. She was young and beautiful in a way that reminded him of the girl he had married, and Aidan was a man of his word who very much reminded him of the navy seaman and lifelong friend he had just laid to rest.

"But there *is* something I need to tell you," Aidan continued. "Now that we know the *Adamson* settlement was a sham—that Moriarity and Boyce fixed the whole thing up—I imagine Dr. Adamson will get a new trial."

"You're right about that. His insurance company just rehired us to make the motion. We're not charging them a dime, of course, given that it was one of our own who got them into this mess."

"I need to tell you something that the lawyer who takes the defense will want to hear," Aidan said. "Adamson's patient didn't have a heart attack because he vomited and stopped breathing. He vomited and stopped breathing because he had a heart attack."

"What, you're a doctor now too?" Gay laughed. "You know, the medical examiner . . ."

"I don't care what the medical examiner said. The medical examiner was wrong. The heart attack came first, and that's what killed him. The vomiting was just—well, pardon the expression—*icing on the cake.*"

Gay was listening, now. He had known Aidan long enough to know not to underestimate his intellect on *any* subject, as more than a few lawyers had learned to their sorrow through the years.

"Think about it, Gay. The wife walks in to visit her husband and discovers him lying peacefully in bed, under the covers, dead, with a mouth full of vomit."

"Right," Gaylord answered, "which is exactly why—"

Aidan interrupted him again. "Think about that scene for a moment. If the medical examiner is right, that means that the man was lying in bed as alive as you or I, one moment, and the next thing that happens—the only thing—is that he is suddenly unable to breathe through a mouth full of vomit. Yet he just lies there and walks into eternity calmly, not even ruffling the covers on the bed. The man wasn't paralyzed, Gay. He had an ileus. He could get up out of bed if he needed to, and if he's still alive with a mouth full of vomit that's keeping him from breathing, he's gonna *really, really* want to get up."

The light of understanding began to dawn in Gay's eyes. "The covers were neatly in place," he said, staring distantly and speaking softly, almost as if to himself.

"Drowning men don't go peaceably down to death, no matter how ready they might be to meet their maker. I know, because I *was* one—out there on the banks, during the rescue of the fishermen, when my lifeboat capsized. I came closer to death than you know, and I can tell you I was fighting with everything I had to stay alive. Adamson's patient would have done the same, if he had drowned in his own vomit. He didn't. He was already dead of a heart attack when he threw up. Look it up in the literature. One of the classic responses to a primary cardiac arrest—"

"—is vomiting." Gay was filling in the blanks quickly, now. "You're right. I don't know why anyone didn't see it sooner. The vomiting was a symptom—an aftereffect, really, not a cause."

"Whether Dr. Adamson was negligent or not for giving the man solid food," Aidan continued, "he can't be held liable if his negligence wasn't the cause of the man's death. In other words, you can't kill a man who's already dead, no matter how many times you flunked your medical boards."

Gay smiled at the macabre humor in this, remembering that Dr. Adamson was no one's idea of a dream client. But the doctor would be happy to learn what Aidan's sharp legal mind had revealed, and that a great number of well-paid experts had failed to see. It was a heart attack, plain as day.

Gay knew that a winning jury argument was only as brilliant as it was simple, and this one was dazzling. It was really no surprise. After all, that's what everyone had always said about Aidan, from the time he was a spanking-new lawyer at McFadden Brown. Aidan had always won, in spite of everything and everyone against him.

"They're going to want you back on the front lines, at Rampart, when I tell them you came up with this defense while drowning on the ocean," Gay said. He was still angling to get Aidan back. "We'll miss you, son. The bar is losing its brightest star, and McFadden Brown is losing its best lawyer. You know I've always believed that—even through all this mess. You're special, Aidan. I know it, your clients know it, and—"

"—and you can bet I know it," Molly interrupted. It was about time she made her feelings clear in the matter. Gay smiled, realizing that he had, again, hugely missed the point.

"Don't let an old man like me get in your way, Molly. You and Aidan are making the right decision."

Gay gave Molly and Aidan each a giant hug, and Nita kissed them both. As she was gathering her purse, Nita remembered something she had brought with her that she had meant to give Aidan and Molly earlier.

"These came for Father Marcus at the rectory after you left. I didn't want to open them, but I think they have something to do with Sarah and the boat."

Nita handed them two envelopes. One was from the commander of the United States Coast Guard Group at Elizabeth City, North Carolina. It explained that a derelict ketch, the *Bel Sogno,* was found drifting at sea off the coast of Nova Scotia, submerged just below the surface. An investigation revealed that a hose on a thru-hull valve had cracked and parted, causing the vessel to take on water and founder. The body of a woman was recovered from the wreckage. Her DNA matched that of a patient named Alina Andreescu, reported to have escaped three years earlier from a psychiatric facility in Norfolk, Virginia. The *Bel Sogno* was destroyed and sunk by the Coast Guard as a hazard to navigation. The body of the woman was badly decomposed. Her cremated remains were accepted for burial by the First Romanian Orthodox Church of North Boston. The report was sent to Father Marcus in conclusion of the Coast Guard investigation he had begun when Sarah went missing.

The other envelope was from a law firm in New York City.

"As Marcus's personal lawyer for the last thirty years, I took the liberty of reading this one, Aidan," Gay said.

"It was sent on behalf of the owner of the *Cygnet*. He claims the boat was being towed from New York to a shipyard in Norfolk to be refurbished after spending quite a few years in storage. A storm came up, and the towing cable parted in rough seas. The towboat captain was unable to recover the vessel, due to the conditions, and had to return to port. The owner went to the New England Registry, searching for any information that might have been reported about recovery of the vessel. The people there remembered Marcus's inquiries about a boat of the same name. He's offering a handsome salvor's fee: one million dollars."

Aidan and Molly were shocked by the news of the woman they had known as Sarah and horrified to think of what her last hours had been like. No wonder *Bel Sogno* had disappeared from their radar. That must have been the moment when she capsized, Aidan thought. But Molly wasn't so sure. They had seen *nothing*, that morning, when only seconds earlier the *Bel Sogno* had been visible on radar. She doubted that a vessel the size of the *Bel Sogno* could have foundered so quickly as to disappear entirely beneath the surface. And as for Sarah, Molly had seen nothing in her in all the time they had been together that suggested she needed to be in a psychiatric ward. In fact, the entire world around her seemed to be going mad compared to the quiet sanity with which she lived her life. Still, her midnight flight to sea remained a mystery. Perhaps now they had the answer.

They both should have been excited at the offer for *Prodigal*, but Aidan and Molly were crestfallen. Aidan read the letter for himself. The attorney enclosed papers showing that *Cygnet* was built in 1916 at a shipyard in Mamaroneck, New York.

"You know, I think I liked things better when I believed that *Prodigal* was some ancient legend, and that we were a part of that story," Aidan said. Molly nodded in agreement.

"Oh, I don't know," Gay answered. "I certainly think destiny brought the two of you together, and I believe *Prodigal* was meant to play the role she did."

Gay shook Aidan's hand, kissed Molly, and offered Nita his arm. Then, just after he turned to leave, he stopped and looked back.

"Say—if you don't mind, Aidan, may I have another look at those two letters?"

Aidan handed the envelopes back to him, but Gay didn't open either one. He studied the outside of each carefully, then returned them, shaking his head. There was the hint of a smile on his face.

"I thought I noticed something strange."

"What is it?" Aidan asked.

"They both have the same postmark from the same city and zip code, and they were both mailed on the same date."

"How could New York City and Elizabeth City, North Carolina have the same zip code?"

"They don't. Both of these letters were mailed from Boston College, zip code, 02467."

"How on Earth do you know the zip code for Boston College from memory?" Molly asked.

"The girl I married went to Boston College. I must have addressed a thousand letters to that zip code from naval stations all over the South Pacific."

Aidan looked at the postmarks more closely. They were machine stamped and identical. This would have been a remarkable coincidence if the letters were both not so clearly the work of Jimmy McIver. Aidan knew then that Father Marcus had been right. The Gospel according to Monsignor McIver could not abide a paradise filled with disobedient thieves.

Molly pulled them from his hands to see them for

herself. "You don't miss much, do you, Gay?"

"I don't know, Molly. I missed a lot where Boyce Stannard was concerned. I never saw that coming."

Aidan sighed. "Yeah, me neither."

"So, these letters, then," Molly asked. "Are they fakes? What's the truth about *Prodigal,* and Sarah, and all of it? How do you explain it?"

Gay paused for a moment, seemingly lost in thought, then smiled.

"You'll have to forgive a sentimental old man, but somehow, just now, I can hear the voice of Marcus O'Reilly telling me not to try—to just accept it on faith, along with everything else we don't know or can't understand. I advise you and Aidan to do the same."

That was good enough for Molly and Aidan too.

"And one more thing," Gay said, as he turned to go. "I wouldn't sell that boat to anyone, if I were you. Not for all the money in the world."

CHAPTER 36

After Gay and Nita left, Molly and Aidan looked at each other in seriousness for a moment, then burst out laughing. They weren't laughing at anything in particular or anyone—only at the fact that it felt so good to be together, and to share that feeling of complete trust and total acceptance of the destiny that had brought them to where they were now. He took her hand in his and walked with her down *Prodigal's* wide decks into the cabin, where David Joseph was finishing his repairs to *Prodigal's* hull.

Aidan peeked into the hold with a flashlight, and what he saw astonished him. He had heard that David was a master carpenter, but what he done to heal *Prodigal's* wound was a work of artistry, not carpentry. The ship was perfect again.

David wanted to sit awhile inside the hull. It made him feel closer to his son, somehow. Molly and Aidan crawled in with him to admire his work by lantern light. Aidan passed his hand over the smooth wood where the hole had been.

"It's amazing. Like it was never there. She's as good as new."

David smiled a cheerful smile—lost in his work and devotion to Ibrahim's vessel, he had forgotten his grief for a moment.

"She's as hard as a New York sidewalk," he said, "and she'll stay that way for as long as any man has the

339

heart to sail her." He rapped the wood three times with his knuckles to accentuate the point.

From the other side of the hull, three raps came back.

They all looked puzzled to hear an echo. David rapped three times again. This time, four taps came back. He looked at Aidan and Molly. Their faces formed a picture of bewilderment in the lamplight. Then, a wave of understanding came over them.

Aidan leapt up. He hit his head hard on a beam overhead in the cramped quarters and cursed the pain.

"Out of my way!" David shouted. His stubby legs streaked past Aidan in a flash toward the companionway. A moment later, all three of them were standing in the cockpit in the darkness, waving a lantern over the side of the boat as if they were fishing for flounder. In the glow of the light, a man's head emerged from the black water.

It was Ibrahim.

David Joseph screamed his son's name in a shout of joy, then covered his mouth with his hand in mimicry of the same motion made by Ibrahim in the water below him. Slowly, and looking all about the harbor carefully to make sure no one saw, Ibrahim climbed over the side of the boat. He was soaking wet, but that made no difference to his father or to Molly. Both threw themselves upon him and pinned him to the floor of the cockpit, the only motion of their bodies formed by the heaving sobs coming from all three of them.

When he finally found a way in between them, Aidan grabbed Ibrahim's broad, smiling face in his hands and kissed his cheek. He could hardly contain himself. When the tears subsided, Molly and Aidan demanded a full accounting of the Houdini act Ibrahim had pulled at sea, and Ibrahim insisted on hearing all the details of the funeral he had just missed.

As they were talking, a Nassau police van rolled slowly through the parking lot of the shipyard where the *Prodigal* had been given a temporary berth on the outer dock. It was a routine security check, but the searchlight the officer shined into the cockpit nearly caught Ibrahim off guard. He dropped to the deck. The officer came to investigate, but Aidan and Molly were able to wave him off with an all-clear.

It was obvious they could not stay much longer. It was also obvious that Ibrahim, now more than ever, was a man without a country. As far as the Bahamian government was concerned, he was no longer even alive. Aidan quickly formed a plan, and Molly was right behind him. They would put to sea—immediately, the four of them, together.

There was little time for preparation. David Joseph refused to leave his son, and his son could not leave the boat and risk being seen. So, the four of them hauled up the anchor and prepared to make sail.

Aidan, despite having lived and breathed in the very soul of *Prodigal* for the past three days, was hardly prepared for the transformation he was about to witness. The ship's speed and agility in her escape from the harbor was a sight to behold. She fled as though two hundred men were after her, threatening her very life. She fled as though she had all eternity and nothing but the endless sea before her. Her sails snapped crisply to the tension of the lines in Ibrahim's hand. The thoroughbred had found her master once more.

In a matter of a few hours, they were again approaching the Gulf Stream close to West End and Indian Pass. These places that had only recently brought such torment were now occasions for such joy. In the hours that he and Molly and Ibrahim and his father spent laughing and talking with one another—telling stories, breaking bread, and sharing wine—Aidan's thoughts had been occupied with the future and the decision that lay ahead for all of them. He finally found the courage to speak of it.

"I want you to take the boat, Ibrahim."

"I feel the same," Molly piped up. She seemed so close to Aidan's thoughts, now, as if they were already of one mind.

Ibrahim at first did not understand, but then he understood completely. He could not return to Ocracoke or to any place of hiding and secrecy. It was time for him to come into the fullness of his manhood and his life. It was time, too, for him to be a son to his father, and for his father to banish his grief, forever.

"We can put ashore in Miami—" Ibrahim began.

"No, Ibrahim, we cannot. You can't go to Miami any more than you can return to Ocracoke. There's a stout dory on the foredeck, and it's a beautiful, calm, starlit night in the Gulf Stream. Molly and I will cross to the mainland and find a way home. You can't come with us. You can't give your enemies that chance at you. I don't know where your life will unfold—some distant and lovely place, I believe—but I know it cannot be among those who would question and doubt you and persecute you. Go and find your paradise, Ibrahim, and peace be with you—with both of you."

Ibrahim and David Joseph thought for a long time about the words that Aidan and Molly had spoken. Father and son rose and walked to the foredeck, where they sat together and talked for more than an hour, looking out over the shimmering night sea. When *Prodigal* was close to the Gulf Stream, not far from Memory Rock, they returned to the cockpit and embraced Aidan and Molly. Then Ibrahim sat down in front of both of them and spoke.

"I will do this thing. I will accept this great gift that you give to me and my father. But you must accept my gift in return."

"Anything, Ibrahim," Aidan said.

"One day I will return in this ship and ask you and your wife to come away with me. You must promise that you will accept—that we will sail together again, someday. I could not bear to watch you go, otherwise."

Your wife. The words had not escaped Molly's notice and brought an immediate and embarrassed smile to her face. She wondered if Aidan had any idea that, in truth, it was what she wanted more than anything in the world. But she had to say something quickly to make light of the matter or risk a mortifying silence that she could not endure.

"A sailing honeymoon on *Prodigal*? Storms? Head injuries? Marauding pirates? What could be better? You don't have to ask me twice," Molly said with a wide grin.

"We're all in," Aidan answered, not yet fully aware of the maelstrom swirling in Molly's mind over Ibrahim's innocent assumption about their intentions.

When the dory had been prepared and loaded nearly to the gunwales by David Joseph with an overabundance of fruits, breads, coconuts, rum, water, and thick blankets, Johansson's unsinkable sail was bent onto the mast and all lines were made ready. It was only a day's journey to the mainland from there, but Molly and Aidan were fitted out for a month, if it came to that. They said their final goodbyes to Ibrahim and his father. They wept and they laughed. They wished each other fair winds, and they promised that their prayers would follow them wherever they might go. Then the *Prodigal* swept away like a magic carpet on the sea, unbound by any natural law of this Earth. Molly and Aidan were unable to look away until the last flicker of her golden lantern lights had dimmed beneath the waves.

In the dory, Aidan took the mainsheet in one hand and the tiller in the other as he searched the sea for his heading. They had no particular destination in mind, although they knew that after they came ashore they would somehow find their way home again to Ocracoke. The breeze that night blew soft and warm from the southwest—the prevailing wind of those latitudes. It would push them on a gentle, broad reach to St. Augustine by the following morning.

"You know, Molly, there's a beautiful old church in St. Augustine."

"Oh, *is* there now? Why, you have something to confess?"

"Yes, indeed I do. But a wise priest once told me that there is forgiveness for a penitent man—even if he is a thief."

"A thief of hearts, you mean. But for a truly penitent thief, yes, I'm certain there is forgiveness."

She was quiet for a moment while she studied Aidan's face, but he made it impossible for her to resist. She adored him—she always had. She now even dared to believe that he adored her. But she could no longer put off saying to him the thing that, however silly and small, had been bothering her for months. So, she just blurted it out.

"You know I'll never get a boob job."

"Wouldn't ask," he said.

"Wouldn't do you any good to ask."

"Won't do it," he said again.

"Better not—ever!"

"Not a chance," he said a third time.

Satisfied that she had won the first volley, Molly prepared for another.

"I hear there's an opening for a deck hand on a towboat in Ocracoke."

"So, am I going to be taking orders for the rest of my

life?"

"You know, as a lawyer who has just been reinstated to the bar, you should be aware that by the law of the sea, the captain of the *Sairey Gamp* is lord high master of all that she surveys, second in authority only to God."

Aidan thought it important that he appear at least to consider the point before answering, but she was, of course, absolutely correct on the law.

"Well, I'm glad at least there will be some limit to your jurisdiction—my lady."

Molly's face brightened into a smile that, in Aidan's eyes, seemed to rival the stars above. And in that moment he believed, as fools and sages ever have, that he would love her forever.

Perhaps.

Or, perhaps in time this dream of love, like so many others, would come to grief and bitterness. But there is no harvest except by planting, and what may be wheat or weeds can be known only by the sprout, not the seed.

Molly looked at the boyish man beside her and felt herself lifted by waves of womanly tenderness. It was clear that his wild riot of hair would never fully surrender to the tyranny of a comb, nor would his restless heart ever be entirely still. She knew that the way ahead for both of them would not be without its storms and perils. Her resolve to face that future with Aidan was born not of ignorance but of faith—faith that there was something fine and high in him, and that the voyage they would make together, whatever its destiny, was worthy of the attempt. Safe harbors were for old men and little children. Life was lived on the open sea.

Although by the laws that govern affairs of the heart she scarcely knew him, it seemed to her as if they had already lived a hundred lifetimes together. She trusted him—instinctively, completely, with her life and with her soul. And if it may rightly be said that trust is the leaven of true love, their love was already a feast.

ABOUT THE AUTHOR

Michael Hurley and his wife Susan live in Raleigh, North Carolina. Born in Baltimore in 1958, he holds a degree in English education from the University of Maryland, a law degree from St. Louis University, and a captain's license—albeit long-since expired—from the United States Coast Guard. He entered the private practice of law in 1984 and has tried numerous jury cases involving allegations of medical malpractice. He enjoys keeping up with readers and life in general at mchurley.com.

Michael's first book, *Letters from the Woods*, was a collection of essays, self-published in 2005, based on wilderness canoeing expeditions with his children. It was selected as a finalist in the Nature category for *ForeWord* magazine's Book of the Year award. In 2013 Hachette Book Group published his memoir, *Once Upon A Gypsy Moon*. *The Prodigal* is his first novel.